CONVERGING PARALLELS

CONVERGING PARALLELS
TIMOTHY WILLIAMS

SOHO
CRIME

Copyright © 1982, 2014 by Timothy Williams

Published by
Soho Press, Inc.
853 Broadway
New York, NY 10003

Library of Congress Cataloging-in-Publication Data

Williams, Timothy.
Converging parallels : a Commissario Trotti mystery /
Timothy Williams.

ISBN 978-1-61695-460-4
eISBN 978-1-61695-461-1

1. Police—Italy—Fiction. 2. Murder victims—Fiction.
3. Kidnappingvictims—Fiction.
4. Murder—Investigation—Fiction. I. Title.
PR6073.I43295C77 2014
823'.914—dc23
2014014476

Printed in the United States of America

10 9 8 7 6 5 4 3

Glossary

ALBERGO: hotel

ALFETTA: nickname for the Alfa Romeo model 158/159

ALPINI: an elite mountain military corps of the Italian Army

ALTO ADIGE: a region in Northern Italy bordering Austria and Switzerland

ANALCOLICO: non-alcoholic

ANONIMA SEQUESTRI: the Mafia branch notorious for criminal activity from the 1960s to 1990s, especially kidnappings in Sardinia

APERITIVO: apéritif

APPUNTATO: constable

ARCHITETTO: architect

ARRIVEDERLA: goodbye

AUTOSTRADA: highway

AVVOCATO: lawyer

AZZURRI: "the Blues," the Italian national soccer team

BENINTESO: of course

BOTTEGHE OSCURE: via della Botteghe Oscure, literally meaning "the street of dark shops"

BRIGATISTA: member of the Red Brigades

BUON APPETITO: bon appétit

BUONA SERA: good evening

BUONDÌ: hello, good morning

BUONGIORNO: hello, good morning

CAPITANO: captain

CARABINIERI: Italian national police force

CASA DELLO STUDENTE: student union

CIAO: hello/goodbye

CIVETTA: police car

COMMISSARIO: commissioner

COMPROMESSO STORICO: historic compromise

CORRIERE DELLA SERA: *The Evening Courier,* an Italian daily newspaper published in Milan

CRONACA NERA: crime

DIGESTIVI: digestif

DIRETTRICE: headmistress

DOTTORE: doctor

ESPORTAZIONI: an Italian cigarette brand

FAMIGLIA CRISTIANA: *Christian Family,* an Italian magazine

To Tonì, Nino, Pi, Rosanna,
Valerio, Roberta and Antonio, Piero,
with love.

FINANZA: autonomous police force concerned with customs and excise

GELATERIA: gelato parlor

GELATI MOTTA: a type of ice cream made by Nestle™

GIOLITTIANO: supporter of Giovanni Giolitti, Prime Minister of Italy for five terms between 1892 and 1921

JUVENTUS: a professional Italian soccer club based in Turin

LAVERDA: an Italian brand of motorbike

L'INTREPIDO: an Italian children's magazine

LOTTA CONTINUA: a newspaper of the far left

LOTTA CONTINUA: a non-terrorist extreme leftist group

LUNGOFIUME: waterfront

MARCHE: a region in Central Italy

MEDICINA LEGALE: forensic medicine

MEZZOGIORNO: Southern Italy

MONTALE: a Genoan poet who won the 1975 Nobel Prize in Literature

NASTRO AZZURRO: an Italian beer produced by Peroni Brewery

NAZIONALI: an Italian cigarette brand

NONNA: grandmother

NUCLEO INVESTIGATIVO: investigations unit

NUCLEO POLITICO: political segment of the Carabinieri

O, DIO MIO: Oh, my God

ONOREVOLE: Honorable (as in a mode of address)

PIAZZA: plaza

PIZZA PUGLIESE: an onion pizza with no tomato sauce

POLICLINICO: hospital

PREFETTO: magistrate

PRIMA LINEA: Italian Marxist-Leninist terrorist group

PROCURATORE DELLA REPUBBLICA: state prosecutor

PRONTO: hello (as when answering the phone); right away

PRONTO INTERVENTO: the police department of the Carabinieri in urban centers

PROVINCIA PADANA: an Italian newspaper, also known as *La Padana*

PUBBLICA SICUREZZA: Italian police force

QUATTRO STAGIONI: literally "four seasons," a pizza divided into four sections with different ingredients, traditionally artichokes, mozzarella, ham and olives

QUESTORE: chief inspector

QUESTURA: police headquarters

QUESTURINO: policeman

REPUBBLICHINI: Republicans

ROTA: rotation, shift

SALUTE: cheers, to good health

SBIRRO: policeman

SCOPONE: an Italian card game

SCUOLA ELEMENTARE: elementary school

SEI POLITICO: six out of ten, the lowest passing academic grade

SEZIONE LAUREATE: postgraduate annex

SIGNOR: mister

SIGNORE: sir

SINDACO: mayor

SQUADRA MOBILE: first response team

TELEFONI BIANCHI: a type of film made in Italy in the 1930s in imitation of American comedies of the time, often featuring Art Deco sets with white telephones (symbol of bourgeois wealth)

TOPOLINO: the Italian name for Mickey Mouse, as well as an Italian digest-sized comic series featuring the Disney characters

TOTOCALCIO: Italian soccer betting pools Ufficio Provinciale del Turismo the regional department of tourism

UPIM: an Italian department store chain

VIA: street

VIALE: boulevard

VICOLO: alley

VIGILE URBANO: municipal policeman

1

TROTTI SAT AT his desk and for a moment stared out of the window.

The sky was dark with future rain and the tiles of the neighboring rooftops had lost their terracotta glow. A swallow dropped through the air. The cooing of the pigeons had ceased.

He felt depressed, slightly sick. After a week of hot summer days—and this at the end of April—dark cloudbanks had formed to the north and had come up over the Alps, bringing a chill air. His ankles were cold in the short white socks. At the same time, he felt sticky and uncomfortable.

"Magagna!"

Brigadiere Magagna stuck his head through the door. "Dottore?"

"Bring me a coffee. And one for yourself."

The door closed.

He looked again at the photographs on his desk: a dead piece of flesh. Without meaning, without purpose, photographed in a glossy black and white.

Trotti had seen his first corpse when he was seventeen years old. A couple of partisans, not much older than himself, in shabby clothes, the red scarf still around their necks, had been strung up by the repubblichini and left to bleed to death. At the time he had wondered what had become of the amputated hands.

The smell, the dark blood on the cobblestones and the flies—they had been part of his nightmares ever since.

Magagna knocked and entered carrying a small tray; the air of the dingy office filled with the reassuring aroma of coffee.

"Grappa?" Trotti took the bottle from the cupboard of the desk and without waiting for a reply, poured a shot into each cup. Small, plastic cups with vacuum filled walls and screw-on caps.

They drank.

A Vespa went past in the narrow street below; the engine sounded hollow and angry beneath the old brick walls of the Questura. Several birds darted upwards, touched at the gutter of the roof opposite and then flew away.

Magagna drank noisily, the froth of the coffee tinting the ends of his mustache. "Good." He always said that. He placed the cup back on the tray. "Thank you, Commissario." He wiped his mustache with the back of his hand.

"Sit down, Magagna. I want to speak to you."

Magagna took the green canvas armchair; the cloth was worn and in need of sewing. He was a good-looking man, with a broad forehead and dark black hair. From Pescara. He had the healthy complexion of a peasant. Wide shoulders filled the uniform shirt, neatly washed and creased. A pair of American sunglasses; the thin arms ran parallel to the line demarking his hair and his well shaven cheeks. He smiled readily, showing even teeth.

"I'd be grateful if you dealt with this matter." He pushed the photograph across the desk. "I'm busy at the moment. It's nearly seven weeks since they kidnapped the most important man in Italian politics and nobody is any closer to catching the criminals. Or saving Moro's life. It's nothing to do with us here but Leonardelli seems to think differently. And in ten days' time, we've got the municipal elections."

Trotti laughed without humor. "Leonardelli could put us all on traffic duty and say it was a national emergency. 'In this moment of crisis and political tension, the state knows that it can count upon the loyalty of all the forces of order and in particular upon the Pubblica Sicurezza, who acting upon the instructions of a democratically elected government . . .'" Trotti had raised his hands; he now let them drop back on the desk. There was a packet of sweets by the telephone. He unwrapped one—rhubarb flavor—and placed it in his mouth. "He's a politician."

"What do you want me to do, Dottore?"

"Everything. Get a report from Medicina Legale. It looks like a woman. Put out a check on lost persons. Try the Carabinieri and the Pubblica Sicurezza of the up-river urban centers. And try Milan. See if you can . . ."

"Commissario!"

There was a hatch door in the wall; from the other side Gino was banging against the thin panels. "Line three, Commissario, for you. It's a private call."

"Excuse me." Trotti leaned forward and picked up the phone. "Pronto."

It was not Agnese. The voice was male and hoarse. "Commissario Trotti?"

"Speaking."

There was a pause. The faint bell of a cash register tinkled; muted voices speaking in the background.

Silence.

"This is Commissario Trotti speaking."

"I must speak with you."

"You are speaking with me."

"In private."

"Who is that, please?"

The deadened scraping of fingers against the plastic mouthpiece. "I am a friend, Commissario. You know me."

"I am here in my office. The Questura, third floor. I shall be here for another couple of hours. You can speak with me here."

A click of exasperation; air being sucked in. The voice was now louder, a hint of anger. "That is not possible. I must see you alone. You understand—away from your office."

"I am a busy man."

"You have a daughter, Commissario."

The first fat drops of rain fell with sudden ease onto the sill of the window; dark blotches multiplied like the plague on the concrete ledge. Magagna stood up to close the windows; he stepped over a pile of beige dossiers.

"I imagine you care for your daughter."

"Pioppi?" Trotti's knuckles had whitened. "Where is she?"

"I must see you. Now."

"Where is Pioppi?"

"In fifteen minutes; by the old stables near the river."

"Where is she?"

"Come alone." The man hesitated. "Please."

Then with a click, the line went dead.

2

THEY TOOK THE Alfetta and raced through the city center. The streets were empty of traffic. A few pedestrians hidden beneath dark umbrellas hurried along the pavements.

At the edge of the town they joined up with the flow of traffic, cut across Viale Gorizia—Magagna had turned on the siren—went across the iron bridge and followed the dark line of the canal to where the water gushed over the lock into the river.

They came to a halt by the rusting dredgers. "Wait here and turn that damn thing off."

Trotti got out, opened his umbrella and buttoned his jacket. The pistol weighed at his pocket. He walked fast, shoes splashing on the wet road. The wail of the siren slowly died in the damp air.

This was the edge of the city where the old houses gradually fell away and where the road became a cart track, running parallel to the river—a no-man's land inhabited by a thin phalanx of plane trees. To Trotti's left, one or two flat farmhouses, red brick with sloping, tiled roofs—a few uninhabited. Beyond them, the low-lying allotments, then the textile factory, its chimneys and its satellite apartment blocks, tawdry beneath the grey rain.

On his right, the Po.

The rain was coming down hard, thundering against the taut black nylon of the umbrella. He slipped on the wet mud and swore. An ugly place, part of the city and disowned by it. The rain could not hide the sharp, unpleasant smell of acid that came from the factory chimneys. People had been complaining about it for years. Nothing had been done; the company could not afford the cost of a filter. When the complaints grew too strident, the director threatened closure and the loss of jobs. For a time, the complaints ceased.

An ugly place; twice a year the river broke its banks and swamped the saplings. Then in its retreat, the Po left dead wood and industrial detritus, plastic shopping bags and bleached ciga-rette packets. And a patina of mud that turned to powdery dust in the summer months.

He followed the track along the river; it curved and at the bend there was a wooden shack and two rusting caravans. Smoke poured from a perforated oil drum, billowing fumes of rubber. A dozen cars, piled up, stood like gaunt carcasses against the grey water of the river. Gypsies, vagrants, rag-and-bone men—they lived here, earning a living from the scrap metal. Two mongrels bounded towards Trotti and yapped at his ankles.

He stepped round an old jukebox, lying on its tarnished chrome in the mud. The dogs barked louder.

A fat, blonde woman quickly disappeared through the door of one of the caravans. She was smoking.

The road curved away and the dogs lost interest in him and scampered off. Trotti was now hidden from the caravans by a row of bushes. He went up a slight slope where the ground was drier and he broke into a run. He tried not to think of Pioppi. He placed his hand against his pocket to stop the gun from slapping against his thigh.

Rain pattered overhead onto the leaves of the trees. Trotti stopped when he saw the man; he was leaning against the cor-rugated wall of the stables.

Thirty meters between them. Trotti walked.

Two horses stood in an open field, staring at the rain with mournful eyes; they nuzzled at each other, as though looking for warmth. Painted wooden hurdles and white barriers lay scattered across the grass.

Ten, twelve years ago, it was here that Trotti used to bring Pioppi in her horse riding days; sometimes Agnese came too.

He gripped the Beretta in his pocket.

Bales of hay had been piled beneath the sloping iron roof. The man moved away from the wall and came towards Trotti.

"I'm glad you could come."

Although the face was hidden by a woman's umbrella, there was something familiar in the way the man walked. The body leaned backwards and he set his weight heavily upon each leg in turn.

"Trotti." The red umbrella went back, revealing the tired, pale face.

"Ermagni."

He tried to smile. White, unhealthy skin, dark eyebrows and bleary, bloodshot eyes.

"What are you doing here? Where's Pioppi?"

"I'm sorry. It was a silly idea."

"Where is she?"

Ermagni shrugged. "I don't know. School, perhaps."

"She's not with you?"

"Of course not—but on the spur of the moment, I couldn't think of any other way to persuade . . ."

Trotti heaved a sigh of relief; the shirt on his back felt hot with sweat. He released the grip on the pistol and he noticed that the palm of his hand hurt.

"I'm sorry, it's my fault." Ermagni came towards Trotti, the umbrella over his shoulder and holding out his large hand. Trotti struck him; the back of his hand against the stubble of the jaw. Ermagni stumbled backwards and fell into the mud. The red umbrella rolled away.

"I didn't know what else to do."

"I almost killed you."

Rain splattered the large face, forming more tears that ran over the fat cheeks and fell to the mud. "I was beside myself. I didn't know what to do."

He rolled heavily over onto his hands and clambered upright. Trotti picked up the red umbrella. "I had to talk to you. You've always been good to me." He smelt of stale perspiration. He was wearing a jacket that was crumpled and now smeared with fresh mud. "You're her godfather."

"Let's get out of the rain."

They stepped beneath the curving roof of the stable as one of the horses neighed.

"I wanted to go directly to the police but he wouldn't let me. He said that he wanted to keep things quiet—for the time being at least—in case they contacted us. In case there is a ransom to pay."

"Who said this?"

"Said what?"

"Not to come to the police?"

Ermagni smiled vaguely. "Rossi—my father-in-law. If he knows that I'm seeing you, he'll be furious. He hates the police—and he doesn't want the bank account to be blocked. You see, that's why I had to speak to you in private."

Trotti pulled the pistol from his pocket. "You nearly got yourself killed."

With dull eyes, Ermagni glanced at the pistol, heedless—or perhaps unaware—of its menace.

"Five minutes." He held up five stubby fingers. "Five minutes of your time, that's all I ask. Please, Commissario. You're her godfather. I wouldn't ask you unless . . ."

Another tear swelled at the corner of his red eyelids. Ermagni turned away and gulped like a man in need of breath. Above them, the rain battered against the iron roof. A puddle had formed in an old tire track. The two horses stood motionless in the open field.

3

ANNA ERMAGNI WAS a timid child, six years old, with black, bobbed hair and a serious expression. She had her mother's grey eyes. On the afternoon of 3 May 1978 she disappeared.

Ermagni had accompanied her to the public gardens in via Darsena at three o'clock. There she played with her friends. At 4:20, hearing the sound of screeching brakes, of broken glass and of people shouting, Ermagni went out of the gardens and round the block into Corso Garibaldi. A motorbike had run into the back of a car. Nobody was hurt. When he returned to the gardens fifteen minutes later, Anna was not there. The other children did not know where she had gone. They shook their heads at the father's worried questions. They had seen her, they had been playing with her. Then she had gone away.

The father ran back to the bar in Corso Garibaldi. His father-in-law was behind the bar, wiping glasses. He threw the dishcloth over his shoulders and bent forward across the counter as Ermagni whispered hoarsely. The old man turned pale.

They closed the bar, pushing the grumbling clients out onto the dusty street. Signor Rossi sent the two waiters home and pulled down the iron blinds. His wife came clambering down the stairs, her freckled hands trembling as she repeatedly crossed herself. When she heard that her granddaughter had been kidnapped she fainted.

The two men took the small Fiat and drove through the town,

stopping in the parks, going into private courtyards and driving along the cobbled streets. They went out into the suburbs; they went back to the fairground several times. They drove along the river and questioned the dark-skinned gypsies in their camp. They went to the far side of the river where children were still swimming in water tinted red by the setting sun. They spoke to the children. Nobody had seen a little girl with black, bobbed hair and grey eyes.

"You should have contacted the police immediately."

Ermagni looked at him, squinting, "No."

"We know where to look."

"My father-in-law wants to have nothing to do with the police."

"We've got the experience—and the manpower."

"You haven't found Moro."

Trotti was about to reply, but Ermagni interrupted, "Commissario, my daughter has been kidnapped. And we will pay the ransom."

"You've got the money?"

"I'm a taxi driver. Money . . ." He raised his shoulders. "I've been able to put some aside." He counted his fingers. "Two million, three million perhaps. Things are going well—they've been going well since the mayor closed the city center to traffic."

"Three million is no fortune. Has your wife got something?"

"My wife is dead, Dottore."

Trotti frowned. "Flavia?" He could remember a small, narrow-shouldered girl. Young, with beautiful grey eyes.

"Her name was Fulvia." The shoulders of the muddied jacket—coarse weave and badly cut—fell dejectedly. "Anna's all I've got left—that's why I had to talk with you, I knew you'd help me. Without her . . ." His voice trailed away.

"You never told me your wife was dead."

"There was nothing the doctors could do. It was a kind of cancer. She died last February." He paused. "It was in the paper."

"You should have told me."

"I didn't know you were back; you never informed me. I thought you were still in Bari—until I caught sight of you a couple of months ago in the street." He added, hope in his voice, "You will help me, won't you?"

"I don't work for a private detective agency."

"Commissario Trotti, my father-in-law owns the San Siro bar. He will sell. If it is necessary, he will sell everything. Ninety, a hundred million, perhaps more. But if the police are involved, they will block his account. That's the official procedure, you know that. Things have got worse since Moro was taken." He lowered his voice. "I could never allow that, Dottore. Never."

He started to sob again.

"Has there been any contact?"

Ermagni brushed aside the tears with a large, clumsy hand. "My mother-in-law has not left the phone—not even to sleep. She just waits for it to ring."

"She's taking it badly?"

"She feels guilty. We all feel guilty. I should never have left Anna alone in the park. But it's a small place and not many people know it. Local children go there. And lately, I've been trying to get my afternoons free—to be with my daughter. Normally I work nights but lately I've been able to make arrangements with my colleagues. I want to be with her—now that her mother . . ."

Trotti turned away.

"The gardens have always been safe."

"Until yesterday."

"Until yesterday," he repeated lamely. He took the woman's umbrella from Trotti.

"It doesn't sound like a kidnapping—not without a contact."

"A game, a psychological game." Ermagni had difficulty with the word. "The uncertainty, the waiting. It's done to soften us up."

"You have enemies?"

"I don't think so."

"There is another possibility."

Ermagni raised his large head. "What's that?"

"It could be a maniac."

4

THE SCUOLA ELEMENTARE Gerolamo Cardano was on
the west side of the city, beyond the railway station, in one of the
newly built suburban roads. It was wedged between two blocks
of flats. The pavement was littered with parked cars that suffo-
cated the sparse young trees. Trotti entered the school gates and
walked along a modern portico—square columns with marble
tiling that was beginning to fall away, leaving irregular checkers
of rough plaster.

He went through a door and found himself in a long corridor;
it was somber and the air was heavy with the smell of chalk and
floor wax.

"Signore?"

The porter came out of his glass cubicle, buttoning a blue
jacket and looking with disapproval at Trotti's wet shoes. He
was smoking. He had a round face with a protuberant, aggressive jaw beneath the peaked cap. The enamel arms of the city
gleamed importantly from the rim of the cap.

"Pubblica Sicurezza."

The man stiffened and made an awkward bow as he threw
away the cigarette.

"I should like to speak to the headmistress."

"Of course." Another slight bow. "This way please." He produced an umbrella and opened it. They went along the corridor
and entered a colonnaded courtyard. A low fountain flowed into

a fishpond. The lethargic shadows of fish. The steel tips on the porter's shoes echoed along the cloisters. From somewhere there came the sound of children singing and Trotti was reminded of his own school years—the patriotic songs, the uniform, the wooden guns.

They climbed a wide stairway, the deep red slabs pocked like bad skin. The porter wheezed unhealthily. "I retire at the end of the year." He laughed uncertainly.

The headmistress was in her office.

On the door, there was a nameplate of transparent plastic with red lettering: DIRETTRICE, SIG.RA BELLONI.

The porter knocked and they entered a small, bright room with Piranesi prints on the wall and high-backed chairs encircling a walnut table. Several flowerpots lined the window sill; the air was fragrant with camellia blossom. Like a stuck insect, an immobile fan blade was fixed to the ceiling. The headmistress came forward. She held out her right hand while with her left she tapped at the hair of her bun.

"Commissario Trotti of the Pubblica Sicurezza." He bowed and they shook hands. She smiled, and stepping back, folded her arms.

"How can I help you?"

Trotti turned slightly towards the door where the porter stood, one hand holding his cap, the other on the doorknob and a look of unconcealed curiosity on his peasant face. "If we could . . ."

"Of course." Her hair was light grey, almost white. "That will be all for the time being, Nino. Grazie."

The porter left reluctantly.

A smile flitted across her face. "A good man." She glanced at her desk where several books lay open. "Without being discourteous, Dottore, I shall ask you to be brief." A hand went to the small pearl placed in the lobe of her ear. "Next week we are closing down for the municipal elections. I have to organize the complete disinfection of the establishment—both before and afterwards."

"I have to speak with you. In confidence." He placed a hand

on her arm and noted the fleck of worry in her eyes. "About one of your pupils."

She looked at his hand on the blue wool of her cardigan. "I am busy."

"So am I." He nodded to the desk. "I wouldn't take up your precious time . . ." He let the sentence hang. He himself sat down on one of the high-backed chairs, turning it to face the headmistress. "Please understand."

Behind the headmistress, a crucifix had been attached to the wall; the plastic head of the Christ lolled in pain.

She tapped at the neatness of her bun as she lowered herself into the chair. She crossed her legs and brushed at imaginary dust on the folds of her blue serge dress.

Trotti waited a few seconds. "This is in confidence and I trust that nothing will be repeated outside this room."

"You talk like a priest."

"I am a policeman."

She smiled; she wore no lipstick.

"A child has been kidnapped, signorina."

A sudden movement of her hand and he had noticed the absence of a ring. The long delicate fingers and the clean nails—no varnish—belonged to the hands of a girl. The skin was white. He wondered how old she was; in her mid-forties, he decided. The grey hair made her appear older; but she still had the living softness that disappears as a woman goes through the change. A few years older, perhaps, than Agnese.

"You are not joking, Commissario?"

"A child's life may be in danger."

"One of my children?"

"Anna Ermagni. The daughter of a friend. He used to work with me in the Mezzogiorno. He left the force to become a taxi driver."

"Kidnapped?"

"She disappeared yesterday afternoon—from the gardens in via Darsena. Her father believes she's been kidnapped."

She looked at him, catching his eye and holding it. Her own eyes were hazel. "What do you think?"

"It's early yet. But Ermagni is not particularly rich—not the sort of person who has enough money to pay a ransom."

"The mother's dead."

"You know Ermagni?"

"A taxi driver?" She nodded. "He came to see me. He was very upset because his wife had just died. I remember it clearly because it was the day they took Moro—a Thursday. School closed down and I was alone here. He phoned, insisting that he saw me. A strange man. From the hills; he'd married a local girl. The parents have a bar in Corso Garibaldi."

"The San Siro."

"She died in the hospital. The doctors diagnosed cancer but it wasn't certain."

"You knew her?"

"The mother? No, I never met her."

"Why did Ermagni come to visit you?"

"He was upset—there was no precise reason for him to see me." She lifted her shoulders. "He said he was concerned about Anna. I don't think he really wanted anything; he just wanted to come to the school and speak with me. It was all rather strange. That morning Moro had been kidnapped in Rome—his bodyguards killed in cold blood—and I couldn't help feeling that something terrible was going to happen. I don't know, the atmosphere, the complete shock. Nino had heard the news on the radio and had come running in, quite white." She shook her head. "I was sure there was going to be a coup. Now it sounds rather silly; we've grown used to the Red Brigades and their threats, their communiqués. But at the time—just seven weeks ago—it was weird. The horror; those poor men assassinated in daylight." She gave him another glance of her hazel eyes. "We are both of the same generation, you and I. We've been through the war—which for us Italians was a civil war. I felt when Nino came rushing through the door . . . I felt it was as though everything that Italy's built up over these last thirty years was just crumbling apart. The end to everything."

"A lot of us felt that way."

"Ermagni didn't seem to care. He insisted all he wanted to talk about was his daughter."

She stopped and looked out of the window. In the distance, the dome of the cathedral glinted greyly through the rain.

"He said that he was worried about his daughter. Too timid, he said; too timid towards her own father and too reserved. Reserved—that was the word he used. I tried to tell him he had nothing to worry about, that shyness was quite normal in a girl of her age. He wanted to be reassured but he wouldn't let himself. Perhaps he felt guilty—I don't know. He said that she had always been very close to her mother—the marriage was not very successful, I gather. He felt that Anna had become a stranger now that she was living with her grandmother. He said that he couldn't talk to his own daughter—that she was drawing further and further away from him. And he said that the grandparents were making things worse."

"He doesn't get on well with them."

"They had always hoped their daughter would marry a professional person. Apparently she had been to university. Ermagni is not particularly well-educated. It doesn't require much—excuse me—to be appuntato with the PS."

"He is not stupid, either." A pause. "What did you tell him?"

"About his daughter?"

"Yes."

"Commissario, I never had children of my own." The hint of a sigh as the cardigan lifted slightly. "I did not marry not because I didn't want to." She looked at the fingers of her left hand. "There are other reasons that I need not bore you with. However, I have been in this school for twenty years and I have been teaching for twenty-seven. In twenty-seven years, you learn a lot about children—and adults, too. And one of the most important lessons that I have learned is that you cannot change people. You can help them, you can advise them—but you cannot change them if they themselves do not want to change. Change people, force them to be different, to be not what they are but what we want them to be—that is Fascist philosophy, Fascist thinking. And I hope that you and I have had enough of that."

"You told Ermagni that?"

She smiled, showing brilliant, even teeth. The corners of the hazel eyes wrinkled. "I didn't talk about Fascism, if that's what you think. A man who has just lost his wife and who feels that his daughter is drawing away from him—or being drawn away—is not the sort of person who cares about politics. Who comes to visit me on perhaps the blackest day in this country's history. Fascism was uppermost in my mind. I was convinced that we were about to see the end of the Republic that day, and that the Fascist elements—they call themselves Red Brigades, but of course, they are Fascists, they think and act like Fascists—were bringing about the end of this fragile, lopsided freedom. But what would Ermagni care?"

"What did you say?"

"That there were two possibilities. Either Anna would grow out of her shyness in time. That he had to show her affection, show her that he was her father and that he loved her."

"He is affectionate by nature."

"And that if that didn't work, quite simply she must be naturally shy and that there was nothing he nor I nor anybody else could do about that. Children are like flowers, Commissario— yes, I would have liked to have children of my own—and you can water them or you can starve them." She glanced briefly at the potted plants along the sill; rain fell on the large green leaves. "There was no question of Anna being starved. I don't know her particularly well—unfortunately I get less and less time to teach because of all the administrative work—but I know that she is happy in a happy school. We've got our problems, but we are happy here. And I know that she has a father who loves her, grandparents who care for her."

"She lives with the grandparents?"

"Even before the mother's death she spent a lot of time with her grandmother. The father works long hours—he's on night work—and he comes home at irregular hours. Towards the end, the mother was in the hospital a lot of the time. She was very ill." Signorina Belloni looked again at her long hands. "Believe me, there are a lot of children who have both a mother and father and who are

not as lucky as Anna. I sometimes catch sight of her in the courtyard. She doesn't smile a lot but she plays normally with the
other children. She is a serious child. And particularly pretty."

"Perhaps that's why she's disappeared."

The headmistress looked at Trotti. "I don't think so. It is very
unlikely that she would go off with a stranger. You think she
was picked up by a man, don't you? A child molester? Unlikely.
She is a shy girl—at that age a lot of children are. I think it is
much more likely that there is a misunderstanding. Perhaps she
has gone with some friends—or an aunt. It happens. You know,
people often think that children are innocent and that they don't
understand the dangers that surround them." She smiled faintly.
"At that age, the world can be a very frightening place."

"Ermagni tells me that apart from the grandparents, there
are no very close relatives."

"Friends?"

"He works too hard to have many friends. At one time, perhaps, I was his closest friend. I'm the child's godfather."

"If Anna really has disappeared, Commissario, I think you
must assume she's been taken under duress." Again the hazel
eyes turned away to stare across the roofs. "I believe she's with
somebody she knows well."

"You have known cases of kidnapping, signorina?"

Irony plucked at the thin eyebrows. "This is a quiet, law-
abiding city—with no crimes more heinous than tax evasion.
And a lot of adultery."

"You don't live here?"

She blushed. "I'm not quite sure what you mean by that." A
light, almost girlish laugh. Trotti wondered why she had never
married, and why she should talk about adultery. "I live here and
have lived here for the last twenty years. But I am from Milan—
from the big city up the road—and I still remain an outsider. This
is a very provincial place, as I am sure you know." Her fingers
touched the *Provincia Padana* that lay folded on her desk. "The
violence, the kidnapping, the senseless murder which has become
the trademark of Italy over these last nine years—our only growth
industry—has somehow bypassed this provincial backwater. A

provincial city, with all the faults of provincial complacency and petty-mindedness. But with the great virtue of peace."

"There are riots."

"We have a large university, Commissario. Sometimes the students get excited, they spray the walls with their philosophy, they even throw stones through the windows. But it's nothing very serious. They are unhappy about their rents or the quality of the spaghetti in their colleges. It's the fashion and they are young. But this is a human city, where people are people and not merely statistics."

"We have our problems."

"There are problems everywhere. That is why I feel Paradise must be a very dull place—not that Paradise concerns me. Here there are not the immigrants that you have in Milan or Genoa or Turin. There's no heavy industry—just the textile factory and another that produces sewing machines. We have been fortunate. The Italian miracle that has changed so many cities into industrial ghettos has bypassed us. Perhaps we should thank our mayor."

"He is a Communist."

"You don't approve, Dottore?"

"I try not to get involved in politics."

"You must have your opinions."

"I keep them to myself."

"Yet you want mine?" The smile had hardened.

Trotti lowered his head in apology. "I am being rude. I beg your pardon."

"Not rude, Commissario. You are being cold."

"A professional risk, signorina."

"As a policeman, can't you admit that our mayor Mariani has done a lot for the city?"

"Perhaps."

"He has kept it small. He has prevented the big industries from stepping in, taking over the small factories and transforming them into industrial complexes. We have no sprawling suburbs, row upon row of box-like tenements that you will find everywhere else. No colonies of Sicilians and Calabrians brought north to work like animals on the production lines. The mayor has done a lot to keep the artisans and the small shopkeepers in work. And in doing so, he has managed to preserve this city as it was twenty years ago. Our river is not polluted. Where else in Italy can children swim in a river without poisoning themselves? You're a policeman, you must know the statistics better than I do. Where else can a woman go down the streets at night without fear of attack? Where else can she do her shopping without being afraid that teenage gangsters on motorbikes will snatch her purse?"

"You don't think it is a maniac that has taken Anna?"

She frowned. "I don't understand."

"A maniac, a child molester. You don't think that Anna has been kidnapped—not in this old-fashioned, crime-free city?"

"I know of only one case of child rape," she said rather coldly. "And that was a couple of years ago." She spoke in a flat, dull tone. Trotti felt that he had annoyed her.

"In this school?"

"On the other side of the river, in Borgo Genovese. A twelve-year-old girl was made pregnant. She was mentally deficient."

"Raped?"

"Every evening. By her two brothers."

The phone suddenly rang and for the next two minutes, the headmistress spoke into the mouthpiece. From time to time, her thin fingers pushed at the grey hair of the bun. Trotti stood up and went to the window. He looked out on the damp concrete courtyard. The fountain still spurted mournfully. Children in uniform were streaming out of a classroom, their cheerful shouting dulled by the windowpane. They wore black overalls and white cardboard cravats.

One little boy—he had blond hair and socks down over his ankle boots—was waving the Italian flag on the end of a stick; rain had caused the red and green to run. The colors had dribbled onto his fist.

There was a teacher; from where Trotti stood, she did not look much older than her pupils. She scolded them for making too much noise.

Trotti's feet were cold and damp. He wondered if Agnese would be back.

"Can I offer you something to drink before you go, Commissario?"

The headmistress had hung up; Trotti turned slowly away from the window. "That was the health inspector," she said with apology. "He wants to know when he can send in his team to disinfect. He's been phoning me every week now for the last two months; yet he still phones up to ask the same stupid questions. If his men are anything like the ones I had last time—the general elections in '76, I think—I'll have to spend two weeks cleaning up and disinfecting after them."

"Perhaps I could speak to Anna's teacher?"

Signorina Belloni's face hardened. "I cannot stop you; but I should be most surprised if she could tell you anything about Anna that I do not know."

"You don't want me to talk with her?"

"Signora Perbene is a good teacher—a bit modern perhaps, she has some rather unconventional ideas. But I am concerned for Anna's welfare."

"I don't understand."

"Your enquiry must be discreet. I suggest you wait before talking with Signora Perbene."

"I'd rather talk to her now." Trotti smiled. "I can ask her certain questions without raising any suspicions."

"As you wish, Commissario." She pressed the button on her desk; a distant bell rang. "Nino will accompany you; in a few minutes, she will be coming out of class." She tapped again at her bun. "While you wait, can I offer you a cup of coffee? The best arabica, toasted and ground by me." She smiled, almost childishly, showing her teeth and pointed to a small espresso pot standing on an electric ring in the far corner of the room. "An old spinster's vice."

5

"THE AZZURRI WILL make the final. Believe me, Dottore. Probably with Scotland or Germany. I shouldn't be surprised if we win."

Nino held up the umbrella to protect Trotti from the light rain as they crossed the courtyard. The sleeve of his jacket fell back, revealing a worn shirt cuff.

"You're an optimist."

The small man smiled knowingly and the red face creased with wrinkles. "We've got a good team. We deserve to win. And don't forget"—he placed the other hand confidentially on Trotti's sleeve—"Dino Zoff's one of the best goalkeepers of the century."

"Goalkeepers don't score."

"Who can beat us?" He offered a packet of Esportazioni. Trotti shook his head. "Bearzot has got the cream of the clubs to choose eleven men from," Nino said, placing a cigarette in the corner of his mouth.

"And England?"

The porter stopped suddenly; Trotti almost lost an eye as he stepped into the iron rib of the umbrella. "You don't know?"

"Know what?"

He whispered softly, almost in awe, "England's eliminated. They're out of the cup. Here." He handed Trotti the handle of the umbrella while from his pocket he took a packet of household matches. "Germany, Scotland or Brazil; that's who we've got to be scared of. But believe me, Dottore, Italy's going to win." He tapped his chest. "I can feel it in my bones." He lit the cigarette and flicked the burning match into the fountain.

Children were playing in the porticoes, under the watchful eye of their young teacher. The small blond boy was still waving the faded tricolor. Nino patted him on the head.

They came to a corridor.

A green, chipped door was slightly ajar. Nino lowered the umbrella and opened the door for Trotti to step through. "Signora Perbene."

She was younger than Trotti imagined. A lot younger. The classroom was empty and she was sitting cross-legged on the teacher's desk. She wore jeans and a white shirt. A woolen sweater of soft beige was loosely placed about her neck. She was reading *Lotta Continua*.

Looking up, she turned towards the door.

"This is Dottor Trotti, signora." Nino held his cigarette between finger and thumb.

The girl lowered herself lithely from the table. She had black eyes and black hair, parted in the middle and pulled back austerely into a short tail. Her complexion was soft, Mediterranean, yet the absence of makeup—apart from pencil along the eyebrows—gave her face a certain hardness. It was as if she refused her own prettiness. She did not smile. The black eyes stared calmly at Trotti. She held a lighted cigarette.

"Can I help you?"

Trotti turned to the porter. "Thank you."

Nino backed out of the room, closing the door slowly. To the girl, Trotti said, "I won't waste your time." They shook hands.

"In five minutes the children will be coming back." She had the accent of the city, a slightly rasping—but not unpleasant—voice. She placed the cigarette in her mouth. Her fingers remained against her lips as she inhaled. Her chest rose and Trotti could see that she was not wearing a brassiere. High, unaccentuated breasts. Her other hand remained on her hip. Her body was narrow, boyish.

"I could do with your help. In complete confidence, of course. I will only take a few minutes of your time."

She inhaled again before answering; the fingers about the yellow filter were slightly stained. "What do you want to know?" Wisps of smoke were released with each syllable.

"I work for the city Welfare Department and it has come to our attention that"—he took a notebook from his jacket pocket and consulted the first few pages—"that Signora Fulvia Ermagni died a few months ago. The husband is a taxi driver. He works nights. We would like to know whether any action should be taken to guarantee the welfare of the child of the union . . ." Again Trotti looked at his notebook. " . . . Anna Ermagni, a girl."

"The child lives with her grandparents."

"That is correct. Now, is there anything you can tell me about Anna? Is she clean? In your opinion, does she come to school properly dressed? Does she have lice? Does she soil herself in class? Is she prone to disease? In your opinion should I ask the welfare officer to intervene? Of course, your answers are in total confidence—and I must ask you, for the child's sake, to repeat nothing outside this room."

"Anna is always very neat. Her grandparents are well-off and I have the impression the grandmother likes to spend money on Anna. She always has lovely clothes."

"She is properly nourished?"

"Of course."

Trotti looked around the classroom. The blackboard was of a deep green, smeared with chalk dust. One word, written in neatly printed characters, AMORE. The room was filled with rows of empty desks; on the bright walls, several children's paintings had been pinned up. There was also a poster on the far wall. With an unexpected jab of recognition, he identified the white facade of the cathedral in Bari.

"Does she see her father? What do you know about him?"

"Ermagni?" She shrugged. "A typical Italian male. He is possessive. He doesn't consider his daughter as an autonomous human being. He considers her as an object, as an extension of himself to be dressed up and to be shown to the world. Even before the mother's death he was like that. Recently things have got worse. He is neurotic about his child."

"You speak to him often?"

"I used to. I didn't have much choice." She breathed at the cigarette and stubbed the filter on the ground. She was wearing navy blue moccasins; a minute American flag had been stitched onto the leather at the heel.

"He pestered me."

"In what way?"

"I thought at first he was merely concerned with his daughter's education. I liked him and I was helpful. It is my duty to be in a permanent and constructive dialogue with the parents. This was at the beginning of the year; however, it soon became apparent that he had other intentions."

"Of what nature?"

She caught her breath. "Marriage as we know it is a bourgeois concept. I reject marriage if it means unhappiness and constraint. Personally I am married—but I do not consider that I have lost my freedom. I have the freedom to choose other partners if I so wish. My body is my own, it belongs to me and I can share it with whom I wish." Her eyes did not leave Trotti. "My husband has the same freedom. However, I refuse to have any choice imposed upon me. I am a woman; I am a free woman and I am not an object. I refuse to be the plaything of any self-styled Latin lover."

"Ermagni tried to seduce you?"

"Yes." There was a short silence while the girl continued to stare at Trotti.

"I would have thought," he said, "that in the course of his work—he must come into contact with a lot of women—he has ample opportunity to play the role of a Latin lover."

"He said that he was in love with me."

Trotti frowned. "When was this?"

"On several occasions—before the death of his wife. He kept coming here. He said it was to pick up his daughter but in fact it was to talk to me. Sometimes he came to see me instead of going to visit his wife in the hospital. He invited me out even."

"You didn't accept?"

"I accepted once—and that was enough. He took me to a dirty trattoria in Borgo Genovese—a place where truck drivers go—and then he tried to grope me. I told him to stop but he wouldn't. I hit him. We were inside his taxi."

"When was this? What time of day?"

"About nine o'clock in the evening."

"I thought he worked nights."

"He mentioned something about having made an arrangement with a friend of his."

"What did you do?"

"When?"

"When he started touching you?"

"It was unpleasant. His hands were so large and they were all over me. I slapped him very hard."

"And what did he do?"

"He went quiet. He let me go and he said nothing. He just took me home."

"After that you saw him again?"

"He still comes to school to pick up his daughter. But I don't speak to him." Her face softened slightly. "Perhaps I should. I was sorry for him when I heard his wife died. They weren't happy together—he told me that—but he loved her. He looked up to her; and she despised him." Her hand went to her forehead. "I realize now that perhaps all he wanted was my company. Trying to fondle me—his hand between my legs—perhaps that's just social conditioning. He was with a different woman and he didn't know what to do, so he did what he's always been taught to do. The conditioning of a phallocratic society." She stopped. "I'd like to speak to him, but I don't dare. Not now. I offended him, I offended his male pride."

The door was flung open and a ragged file of shrieking children entered the classroom. Trotti noticed a little boy with a sad expression and a pudding-bowl haircut. The children stared at him inquisitively; a couple of girls giggled behind their upheld hands.

"Which one is Anna?" He shouted to make himself heard.

"She's not here today."

"Ah." Trotti made a note on his pad. Without looking up, he asked, "Why not?"

"I don't know."

"Is she often absent? Or late?"

She looked at him sharply while small heads filed between them, heading towards the desks. "Never," she said, then turning abruptly away, she clapped her hands. "To your desks, please children, and sit down. Without talking, Gianmaria. You have work to do; get on with it. Show our visitor that you are well-mannered, responsible people." The vein in the side of her neck vibrated as she spoke. The children fell silent.

"I'm sorry to have taken up your time, signora." They shook hands again and Trotti moved towards the door. "Arrivederla."

He was already several steps along the portico when he heard her behind him.

"Dottor Trotti."

He stopped.

"There was no need to lie."

"Lie?"

"You are not a welfare officer. You are a policeman." She stood with a hand upon her hip. "You talk like a policeman."

"You are very shrewd." He smiled, genuinely amused. "I know I can count on your complete discretion."

"Has something happened to Ermagni?" Her forehead was wrinkled with concern. "Has he done something wrong—or stupid?"

"He is all right."

"And Anna? Where is she? Why is she not at school today?"

"Anna is quite safe and well, signora."

He could see that she did not believe him.

6

MAGAGNA HAD GONE, taking the Alfetta and the umbrella. It was still raining and Trotti's feet were cold. There were puddles on the pavement. He walked back to the station and in the small bar next to the second-class waiting room, he bought a packet of sweets. Barley sugar. He undid the cellophane wrapping and placed one in his mouth.

Sitting in the far corner of the bar, beside the window that looked out onto the wet platform and the railway tracks, a man was looking at the dregs of a glass of wine. The face was familiar. Trotti left without the man looking up.

He hailed one of the waiting taxis and sat in the back, his eyes half closed.

"Where to?"

"Via Milano."

"Mind if I smoke?" the driver asked.

Trotti lived in the suburbs and as the taxi reached the edge of the old part of the city, the car stopped at traffic lights. The driver waited, the meter quietly clicking, while articulated trucks trundled south towards Piacenza and Bologna, blocking the exit roads and filling the air with damp spray and billowing diesel fumes.

"Of course not."

The driver had a narrow head and sloping shoulders. There was a comic book on the dashboard and beside it an overflowing ashtray.

The man half turned in his seat to offer a packet of Nazionali. "Care for one?"

"I gave up smoking ten years ago."

"Wish I could—a packet a day, sometimes more. My wife is worse, mind you—only she smokes the expensive ones." He snorted his disapproval. "With the charcoal filter. Eight hundred lire."

The windows of the taxi had misted up and the air smelled of smoke and new plastic seat covers. The windscreen wipers beat rhythmically. Beside Trotti, on the back window, a puppy dog with a spring for a neck stared with mournful eyes while his head wagged faithfully.

The driver was lighting his cigarette as a traffic policeman beckoned them on. The taxi moved forward and the driver raised his hand in a salute. Once out of sight, the driver spat. "Police," the driver said over his shoulder. "I need them like I need brain surgery. Always there when you don't want them. And when you need them . . ." He made a faintly obscene gesture. "They should be looking for those murdering bastard terrorists—the sons of whores—and not competing with perfectly good traffic lights."

"Not many terrorists in this town."

The driver gave a cynical cough; smoke spurted through his nose. Small eyes looked at Trotti in the mirror. "There's crime, isn't there?"

"Is there?"

"I was robbed a couple of weeks ago. At four o'clock on a Saturday afternoon. They stole my takings."

"You reported it?"

"You're joking. Go to the Questura to complain and they arrest you. Tax evasion, no license, worn-out tires—they can always find something to stick on you. It's a mug's game." He raised his shoulders. "It was just a couple of kids. They took twenty thousand lire. On a good day I can make that in an hour."

"It's still money."

"Peanuts."

They took the bridge over the railway sidings. The driver fell silent. He kept his two hands on the steering wheel while the cigarette smoldered between his lips. "Peanuts," he muttered to himself.

"You can afford to lose twenty thousand? Business must be good."

"You hear me complaining?" He turned to give Trotti a hurried glance. "I'm voting Communist, if that's what you mean."

"For the dictatorship of the proletariat?"

"I'm voting for Mariani. He's a good mayor."

"You want to drive tractors on the collective farms?"

"This isn't Cambodia. Free enterprise. I'm voting for free enterprise and the mayor closed the city center to traffic. What's good for business is good for me, Communist or not. At least he's done something for this town. The shopkeepers and the small businessmen were all against it—the biggest pedestrian zone in Europe. They said they'd lose their customers, they said it was the death toll for business in the city. And now look."

"Yes?"

Again the driver caught Trotti's eye in the mirror. "It's obvious, isn't it? No cars and no motorbikes in the old Roman center. Now it's a nice place to be in. Piazza della Vittoria used to be a parking lot; now you can go there for a stroll—without choking to death on carbon monoxide—and without some flash lunatic running you over. It's clean. No petrol fumes. More shoppers and more people. Tell me, when did you last see women pushing prams in an Italian city? And all the cars—such piss-awful drivers—he's chased them away into the suburbs."

"It's good for business."

"Sure—and what's wrong with that?" The tone was slightly querulous. "Only buses and taxis have access. Sure it's good for business, but not only mine. The shopkeepers have never had it so good. Believe me: inside the polling booth, where nobody can see them, they're going to be voting Communist."

"Against their principles."

The driver laughed. "Principles—that's a word for politicians—or schoolteachers. The rest of us, we're just pragmatists. Like you and me. That's the way it is today. Principles—try clothing and feeding your wife and family on principles." He laughed again.

The road curved, past the sprawling Fiat showrooms; the driver had to swerve to avoid an old woman—dressed entirely in black—on a bicycle. "The old bitch." He turned his head towards Trotti. "We're pragmatists because in this world, you've got to look out for yourself. Nobody owes you a living—and enough parasites are trying to live off what you earn." He snorted. "Pragmatist, my friend."

Trotti leaned forward and pointed through the windscreen. "Over there, next to the new pizzeria."

The taxi stopped and Trotti got out.

"Two thousand and fifty lire."

"As a Communist, you won't be wanting a tip." Trotti held out the money but did not release his hold. "One other thing."

The shadow of worry in the driver's eye.

"Ermagni—Luigi Ermagni. Does that mean anything to you?"

"He plays with Juventus."

"A taxi driver. He's not a football player."

The man thought for a second. "A large man, a bit over-weight? With a face that always needs shaving?"

"That's right."

"Yes," the driver said cautiously, "I know him. What of it?"

"He's a friend of yours?"

"Friends? I'll have time for friends when I retire."

"But you know him?"

"We're in the same business, aren't we?" He paused. "What do you want to know for?"

"I was his friend once." He released the three thousand lire. "I haven't seen him for a long time."

"His wife died," the man remarked without sympathy. "He's got a kid—that's why he prefers to do night work. And why I don't often see him."

"Why night work?"

"To be with the kid, I suppose." He leaned forward and tucked the notes into a grey metal box attached to the dashboard and closed with a padlock. "Not the sort of person I get on with. I like to earn a day's wage and he's unreliable. He's got a nasty temper. He can get angry like a child in a tantrum. The sort of person I can do without." Disparagingly, he added, "He used to be a policeman."

Trotti thanked him and the yellow taxi surged away; there was a gap in the traffic and the driver executed a neat U-turn. The car stopped.

"You should ask his friend," the driver called from the other side of via Milano. "Ask Pistone." He threw the cigarette onto the wet tarmac. The exhaust pipe vibrated as the car headed back to the city.

Trotti went into the house.

He lived on the first floor of a detached building above the garage. There was an outside staircase, an iron banister and plot plants, geraniums and cyclamen, to each concrete step. On fine days, the flowers caught the afternoon sun; now they looked bedraggled, battered by the rain.

He did not ring. The door was locked; he turned the key three times and the bolt moved heavily and as the door came open, he was greeted by the familiar smell of wax and fresh linen. The hallway was dark; the blinds were drawn and from beyond the window came the soft murmur of traffic along via Milano.

Two eyes gleamed; Pioppi's ancient teddy bear stared down from the top of the bookcase. In the kitchen, the breakfast plates lay unwashed in the sink.

The house was empty.

He changed his socks, first rubbing his pale, cold feet. He then put on a heavier pair of shoes. He made a pot of strong coffee; the kitchen filled with the pleasant smell and he added a thimbleful of grappa. He felt better and was about to pour a second cup when the phone rang. He reached the receiver on the third ring.

"Pronto."

Silence.

"This is Trotti here."

A click; the line died.

7

LIKE OLD LOVERS, Gino and the Principessa had grown to look alike: the same watery eyes and the same loose flesh to the jaws. The Principessa was now half asleep, her white paws sprawled out before her on the marble floor.

"A couple of phone calls for you, Commissario," Gino said as Trotti stepped out of the lift. Trotti had often wondered how the old man could recognize him; a highly developed sense of hearing perhaps. Trotti approached the desk. He now felt warmer and he had put on another sweater. The rubber soles of his shoes creaked on the floor.

"Important?"

Gino smiled. "They always are." He lifted his head to give Trotti a wan smile. The eyes were large behind the thick lenses. "A man called Ermagni."

"And the other?"

"Avvocato Romano." The fingers ran across the Braille typing. "He said it was urgent. He wanted to speak to you personally and he would ring back."

"Thanks."

"One other thing." The old man put out his hand and found Trotti's elbow. He pulled the younger man towards him. "Leonardelli," he whispered. "He's looking for you. Very polite, of course; but he's been out of his office four times."

Under the table the Principessa stirred.

"What does he want?"

"No idea." There was spittle at the corner of Gino's cracked lips; there was a distinct smell of wine on his breath. "No idea," he repeated, shaking his head.

"Is there any news from Magagna?"

"He's still waiting for the medical results."

Trotti thanked the old man and patted his shoulder.

"Commissario," Gino said softly, still holding Trotti by the elbow. "Be careful. Leonardelli is an ambitious man."

"I know."

The blind man released his hold and slumped back into his chair. Trotti went into his office. It needed dusting. He opened the window and called through the open hatch to Gino to give him an outside line; just as he picked up the phone, there was a knock on the door.

"Ah, there you are." Leonardelli smiled.

"Good afternoon."

"If you are not too busy, Commissario, could you come along to my office? I'm afraid something—something important—has come up and . . ." He paused and smiled again. "Unless of course you are on a particular enquiry . . ."

Leonardelli waited and then slipped his arm through Trotti's.

Together they walked along the corridors of the third floor. "You're still coming to work on your bicycle?"

"It's my wife's idea," Trotti said. "She says it'll keep me fit."

"I must say you're looking well."

"Unfortunately, when I'm in a hurry to get home—or when it rains—I have to take a taxi."

"But a bicycle is healthy. I think I'll have to follow your example. There's no excuse now that the center of the city is free of cars."

They came to the office; the Questore pushed the door open and, standing back with his arm outstretched, he beckoned Trotti to enter.

"Please sit down."

The room was large and bright, like something out of a magazine. A large desk stood on the white carpet, almost empty except for an ashtray and a couple of white telephones with push-button dials. Two low armchairs of white, plump leather. Leonardelli pushed one towards the desk. "Please," he said softly and took his own seat on the other side.

Trotti sat down; the chair was lower than Leonardelli's.

"I'm sorry to have to call you away from your work." As he spoke, Leonardelli took a cigarette case from the breast pocket of his jacket. Trotti shook his head at the offered cigarette. "A drink perhaps, Dottore?"

Leonardelli was a couple of years younger than Trotti but already he was going bald; at the temples, the grey hair had been allowed to grow and was neatly brushed back. Black, thin-framed glasses. Well dressed in a double-breasted suit, a white shirt and a dark tie, Leonardelli looked like a middle-aged athlete; broad shoulders and a trim waist. Bench-grade shoes imported from England.

"A cup of coffee."

Leonardelli pressed a bell somewhere beneath the desk. Then, smiling—his lips were thin and rather bloodless—he said, "This is a hectic time for us all."

Trotti nodded.

"I don't wish to pry. You have—indeed since your arrival you have always had—my complete confidence. I admire the Squadra Mobile and the way you run it. I know that despite considerable difficulty, you manage to run a highly organized and efficient team. Financial difficulties, logistic ones, human ones—difficulties that we all have to live with but which must be a particular burden for you." He paused for an instant. "I have always been aware of your competence, Commissario, and I needn't remind you that I was instrumental in getting your transfer here."

"Thank you."

Leonardelli folded his hands on the desk, the cigarette held between two fingers. "I must ask you for a briefing."

He used the English word. Trotti frowned.

"A briefing on the present state of progress in the Squadra Mobile."

Trotti answered in a neutral voice, "Of course." A short, awkward silence.

"You must understand that there have been developments— political developments that can affect us all. You understand."

The door was opened by an officer in uniform who entered carrying a tray. He placed the tray on the desk—cups and tray, Trotti observed, of matching porcelain—saluted and left.

"Sugar, Commissario?"

"No thank you."

"You don't smoke, you don't even take sugar. You are a man without vices, I see."

"Sometimes I take grappa in my coffee—but not on duty."

Leonardelli laughed without taking his eyes off Trotti. He placed his cigarette in the ashtray—the same, delicate porcelain—and handed Trotti a cup. The dark eyes continued to watch Trotti with interest.

Leonardelli propped his chin against two fingers and a thumb. In the other hand, he held his cup of coffee. Slight wisps of smoke danced and writhed towards the ceiling. He made a few discreet sips.

They drank in silence. The coffee was foul—hot water and powder out of the vending machine at the end of the corridor.

"We're involved with what looks like a murder," Trotti said, placing the cup back on its saucer.

"Murder?"

"A couple of children were swimming in the river yesterday. Just beyond the lido. There is a natural beach there with a few bushes at the edge. Sometimes, when the river is full, it covers the bushes completely. The two children saw a dark object stuck among the branches and as one of the boys was swimming past he noticed what looked like a hand. In fact it wasn't a hand; it was a human foot."

Leonardelli grimaced.

"It had been stuck in a plastic bag—one of those plastic bags that people put their rubbish in."

"Can it be identified?"

"The bag? They've got it up at forensic now. As for the

leg—there was nothing else, it had been severed off at the thigh—it's been taken up to the hospital. Magagna's at Medicina Legale now, waiting for the report. There's not much we can do until we've got more information." Trotti added, "It looks like a woman's leg, but it's too early yet to be certain."

Leonardelli had not moved. "Murder, in your opinion?"

"It is just possible that rather than be buried or cremated, it was the victim's last wish to be cut up and put in refuse bags."

Leonardelli raised an eyebrow.

"We've put out a general ID, but until we get the medical report, there's not much that we can do."

"I understand."

The rain clouds were scudding away towards the east and the sky presented large patches of blue; an unexpected shaft of light came through the window, casting a square of warm, afternoon sunlight on to the white carpet. At the same time Trotti noticed the portrait on the wall. The president of the Republic, rotund and Neapolitan, smiled with avuncular goodwill from behind a dull, steel frame. Apart from the portrait, the wall was white and quite bare.

Leonardelli sipped again at his cup; by now the coffee was cold. "And the others?"

"What others?"

"There are ten men attached to the Mobile. Normally I wouldn't request . . ." His voice died; he nudged at the black frame of his glasses.

"Eight men," Trotti corrected. "Since the Moro kidnapping, I have lost two men to general duties."

"And what are they doing, these eight men?"

"Routine matters."

"Such as?"

Trotti hesitated, glanced sharply at Leonardelli. "Benedetto and Galli are involved with stolen cars—probably a gang, probably based in Milan and working out in the surrounding provincial cities. There's been a forty percent increase in car theft since March. And a sixty percent increase in the number of cars broken into—radios, cassette recorders. It's possible that we're dealing with an organization that uses children—but as yet we have no definite lead. Several other cities—Vercelli, Novara, Brescia, Alessandria and up on the lakes as well—seem to be having a similar increase. That's in fact what I should be working on but these last few days I've been involved with the gypsy camp."

"On the far side of the river?"

"They arrived there a couple of weeks ago. Yugoslavs. There's been a series of complaints about shoplifting in the Rione San Carlo and in Borgo Genovese. Magagna was helping me until the leg turned up."

"I'd be grateful if you could put somebody else on it. Pisanelli, perhaps."

"It's sensitive. Very sensitive."

"Something has come up and I'll be needing you and Magagna."

Trotti hesitated. Then he said, "Dealing with the gypsies is not easy. Everybody knows that they steal, everybody knows that they send their children into the shops to take anything they can lay their hands on. But particularly at election times we have to be careful. This town is not made up of shopkeepers alone. Nobody wants to be accused of racism."

"I understand, I understand, Trotti, but I need your talents elsewhere. In the normal run of things, I'm only too happy to let you get on with it."

"Yes."

Leonardelli stood up and went to the window; from where he was sitting, Trotti could not see what Leonardelli was looking at. The window gave on to Strada Nuova and all Trotti could see was the top of the war memorial; and on the other side of the street, the roof of the university.

"As though Moro wasn't enough. I've got my men stretched to breaking point and all I can do is keep on stretching them. We're undermanned, undertrained and underpaid." Leonardelli spoke with unexpected vehemence. "I'm supposed to scratch up men from nowhere and to send them on thankless tasks—an entire army of men to do soulless policing duties. At the railway station, at the bus garages and outside all the public offices. Walk down the streets, Trotti, and you'd think Italy was under a state of siege. An explosion of terrorism and of course we're the first to be accused of incompetence—or worse still, of connivance. The fact that we've never had the first hint of terrorism in this town is without importance. People need to be reassured; they want to see uniforms. Thank God the Carabinieri do most of the bodyguard work—we've got one minister and three onoro-veli living here. But I still have to find men to do the other jobs. We've now got three men on permanent duty outside; and all the doors and windows have been barricaded with anti-bomb grilles." He sighed. "As if that wasn't enough, we've now got the wretched municipal elections. Believe me, Trotti, they couldn't have come at a worse time." He opened a low drawer in the desk and, taking from it a white envelope, said, "Have a look at these, Commissario."

The envelope bore the seal of the Carabinieri.

"If they can't find subversives," Leonardelli said as Trotti removed half a dozen photographs from the envelope, "the Carabinieri have to invent them."

"Subversives?"

The photographs were not from any judicial file; they were professional pictures that had been taken at street demonstrations; some of the prints had been blown up considerably until the grain had become almost blurred.

"Anybody you recognize?"

The six photos were postcard size, in black and white with a high gloss finish. Five were of men; one showed the boyish form of a young woman, a scarf about her neck and in a loose shirt. She was shouting and her arm was pulled back as though she were about to hurl an object.

"Some faces seem familiar."

"Who?"

"They are students." Trotti tapped a photograph. "I think I know this one."

"Antonio Schipisi."

"That's right—he's a nephew of the commercial lawyer."

Leonardelli corrected, "His son."

Trotti placed the photographs and the envelope on the desk.
Leonardelli lit another cigarette and returned to the window.
He did not look at Trotti. "Students, left-wing ideas and flirting
with Marx. Middle-class kids, as much as anything, they do it
to shock their parents. Not subversives."

"Who calls them subversives?"

"The Carabinieri, Commissario."

"It seems rather unlikely."

"It's patently absurd. We've never had any real political mili-
tancy from the university. This is a quiet, middle-class town with
a quiet, efficient university. And a wealthy one. Have you ever
been through the university courtyards in winter, Commissario?
Most of the girls wear fur coats and pearl necklaces. Of course
there are a few hot-heads, a few young people going through
a difficult age. They reject traditional values—which is quite
normal when you're twenty. Long hair, shouting in the street,
dirty fingernails and writing on the walls. But it's something
they grow out of. Their revolt is a fashion, a lip service to short-
lived ideals. These young people know where their real interests
lie and they know about the unemployment that awaits them if
they don't get their diplomas. This is not Naples, Trotti, where
you get doctors sweeping the streets because they can't get jobs
in the hospitals. There's work for those who want to work. And
our students work." He nodded towards the photographs. "You
know the others?"

"I don't know their names."

"Trentini, Alvarez, Guerra, Gracchi, Petterle—do those
names mean anything?"

Trotti laughed.

"You see the problem now. This could be very embarrassing."

"Leave it to the Carabinieri."

"You are joking, Trotti." He gave Trotti an uncertain glance.
"You know as well as I do what the Carabinieri are like. Hardworking, reliable and honest. But also unimaginative and stupid.
And worst of all, outsiders. They are probably a bit more intelligent than the appuntato in the street—who knows, perhaps
they can even read and write—but they are still Carabinieri with

all the limitations of Carabinieri. With the kidnapping of Moro, virtually all political work has been taken out of my hands and given over to the Nucleo Politico. Fortunately, I've got a couple of contacts." Leonardelli moved away from the window; his face was taut behind the glasses. "This is a sensitive matter, it has to be handled with care. It's not hard to dig up scandal and perhaps one or two of these young people have broken the law—in theory. But they are not subversives, they don't plant bombs, they are not a cell of the Red Brigades."

He moved round the desk and stood behind Trotti; he spoke in a softer voice, one hand on the back of Trotti's chair. "The actual political situation—who is in power and who is in opposition—concerns neither you nor me professionally. As citizens we vote; but as functionaries of the state—unthinking, flatfooted questurini—we carry out our orders. Perhaps at a human level our sympathies are towards the right—but our sympathies cannot and must not interfere in our work. What must concern us, however, is irrational, unthinking change. We have a quiet city, a law-abiding city. The mayor is a Communist and whether he stays or goes is no business of mine. But I do know that we can work with him—that the entire Questura can work with him. There is an understanding. He is a Communist, sure, but he works within a framework that we're used to. Let those photographs get into the wrong hands and the whole damn boat is going to go down. Alvarez and Guerra are well-placed lawyers. Gracchi is the chief city architect and his brother is one of the town planners responsible for the new city bypass. Let the press see these photographs, let them know the sons of powerful local notables are being investigated for sedition and the overthrow of the Republic." He shook his head. "And the shit hits the fan."

Trotti smiled.

"It's not funny—it's frightening. Since I've been Questore, I've succeeded in placing men like you in positions of authority. You are from the area, you understand the people of this province, the people of this city. That's why I was happy to get you back from Bari. You were wasted in the South. You are a Northerner; you behave and think like a Northerner. You can understand that this is a very delicate matter. A scandal here would be playing into the hands of the extremists, the real revolutionaries—not here but in Rome—the same people who would be only too happy for this city—a model of Communist administration—to flounder and sink. It happened last year in Bologna. I don't want it to happen here, I don't want the same anti-Communist fanatics to cause trouble here." He paused. "The same people, Commissario, you can believe me, who were frightened by Moro's overtures to the Communists, by his 'converging parallels,' and who had to have him destroyed at any cost. Politically destroyed."

Leonardelli had returned to his seat and he now stared at Trotti. He lowered his voice. "I'm not making any apology for the status quo—but at least this town works. No violence, no kidnapping, jobs for those who want to work. It's not a question of left or right, of Communists and Christian Democrats. It's a question of whether we want this city to stay as it is, to develop properly, to evolve. Or whether everything we have built up—all of it, our provincial peace—we want to throw to the dogs. Because believe me, that's what'll happen once the Carabinieri poke their noses into our affairs."

"The Nucleo Politico must do its duty."

"Duty!" Leonardelli slammed his fist hard against the desk; the coffee cups rattled. "The Carabinieri and their damned NP don't understand anything. Somebody in Rome tells them that there's a Red Brigade cell here—what do they know? Outsiders, Calabrians and Sicilians? They're dull, honest men. Not even clever enough to get a decent job with their local Mafia. What the hell do they know about us, about the North? What do they understand about our careful balancing act of provincial freedom?" He snorted. "Pig-ignorant peasants."

Somewhere in the street below there was the screech of brakes.

"What do you want me to do?"

"I've made a few phone calls, Trotti." With an outstretched arm he turned four photographs over. "We needn't bother about these. The family will take charge; they will get their revolutionary sons out of the way for a couple of weeks—until after the elections." He pushed aside the four white rectangles.

Only the girl and a man remained. The man had long hair and a narrow, beak nose, an unshaven, dark skin and a strange glint in his small eyes.

"That just leaves us these two." The Questore tapped the remaining photographs. "Valerio Gracchi and his girlfriend, Lia Guerra."

8

CORSO GARIBALDI HAD not been closed to traffic; the wide tarmac was now busy with cars returning to afternoon work. The surface was still wet from the morning's rain. Trotti pedaled carefully; stationary cars littered the pavement, their noses touching the shop fronts and the damp electoral posters. As they overtook him, cars and vans edged his bicycle into the parked vehicles. Small, noisy motorcycles roared past.

It was nearly four o'clock; the town was coming alive again after the midday break.

He turned right into vicolo Lotario. The bumpy, cobbled surface shook the wheels of his bicycle and as his wrists, absorbing the vibration, began to ache, he dismounted. Trotti was proud of his bicycle—a pre-war Ganna with wooden wheels. It was a present to himself for his forty-fifth birthday.

This was a part of the town where he rarely came, off the main thoroughfares, and it now seemed unnaturally quiet after the noise and energy of Corso Garibaldi.

In the Middle Ages, via Darsena was where the docks used to be. In time, the docks had silted up, the river had drawn back and the city had ceased to be an inland port. This stretch of arable land had become private orchards and then, when the Fascists had built the new Lungofiume in the early thirties, the entire zone had become an encircled oasis of trees and meadows.

In via Darsena, the air was heavy with the scent of honeysuckle and wet bricks.

The public gardens backed onto a large, whitewashed edifice, reluctantly Liberty in style, with sloping terracotta tiles and bas-relief ornamentation that had been flattened by many coats of white paint. 1891—the date stood out against the wall; and from behind the ground glass windows, there came the muted sound of children singing. The Mother of Mercy Institute for Deaf and Dumb Children. All the windows were closed. The sun was warming the puddles between the cobblestones as Trotti propped his bicycle against the wall of the gardens. A sign, neatly hammered into the dusty brickwork, exhorted the citizens to respect the public gardens and not to harm the plants and trees. Similarly they were asked not to introduce perambulators or bicycles into the gardens and not to leave litter. The city arms, a white cross on a red escutcheon, gave civic authority to the enamel sign.

Trotti pushed open the gates and entered the gardens. The grass had been allowed to grow and needed cutting except near the swings—painted an unexpected green and yellow—where the earth was worn bare. There was a water pump—again with the city arms in rusting bas-relief and the accompanying lictor's fasces, emblem of the Fascist regime. A few empty benches and here and there scattered litter, wet sweet papers and cigarette packets slowly disintegrating. Playing desultorily near the wall of the Institute were three boys.

There was no one else in the gardens.

Trotti approached the boys. "Ciao," he said and smiled. They were about eight years old, perhaps slightly older. They moved away. One held a branch; it was wet with fresh sap and had clearly just been pulled from a tree.

"We've done nothing wrong."

"I want to talk with you."

They edged further away, their dark eyes looking at him. Only the smallest hesitated; his body wanted to follow his companions while his feet remained motionless on the ground.

"Ciao," Trotti said, looking directly at him. He was blond

and had large, brown eyes the color of chocolate. His clear skin was smeared with dirt and his fingers were grubby.

The child replied, "Ciao," unsurely.

"I'm a friend and I need some help. Perhaps you can help me."

The others had stopped and the tallest now looked distrustfully at Trotti. "What do you want?" His hair was cut in a mop that fell across his eyes; across his T-shirt, an advertisement for San Pellegrino mineral water. He held the stick in both hands. "You can't do anything to us."

Trotti kept his eyes on the small boy. "We can play a game and you can earn some money. I want to ask you a few questions."

The child spoke with a lisp, "We're not supposed to speak to strangers."

The third boy had a black eye, mud in his hair and his lips were bruised; his jeans were ripped at the knee. "We don't know you." He had cunning eyes.

"I am a detective, a police detective." He held out his identification and let them touch the wallet, their dirty small fingers touching inquisitively at the perspex. "I work for the government."

The small boy spoke solemnly, "Papa says there is no government in Italy."

"I know you all have a good memory—and here." He took a thousand lire from his pocket. "You can share this if you help me. I'm looking for a girl."

"We don't like girls," one said and the others nodded.

"I know how you feel. But she is very nice—I think she is a bit younger than you. Anna—her name is Anna."

They shook their heads; the boy with the bruised lips stared at the note in Trotti's hand.

Trotti waited without speaking; he watched the youngest boy and saw the doubt clouding his brown eyes.

"Has something happened to her?" He lisped slowly; his smooth forehead was puckered. "Something bad?"

"I don't know—that's why I need your help."

"Is she safe?"

"She may be. I hope so. You see, I don't know what's happened to her. I want to know where she could have gotten to. Did any of you see her?"

The tall boy folded his arms. "We don't play with girls."

"Has she got black hair?" the youngest asked hesitantly. "And bangs, like this?" He put his hand to his forehead.

Trotti felt a surge of excitement. "You saw her?"

"She was playing over there. By the pump on the bench. She always plays there with her friends." With false scorn, he added, "They think they are nurses."

"She was playing with them yesterday?"

The two other boys nodded.

"We were playing commandos. Then there was a big noise outside." His outstretched arm indicated Corso Garibaldi, beyond the Institute. "And the others went off. I'm not allowed to leave. Mama says I must not. Then I saw her go off."

"Who?"

"The little girl. I saw her go away. Normally there's an old lady who comes to fetch her. She sits over there knitting. She gets angry if we throw stones and she tells us off."

The other boys giggled.

"I don't like the old woman."

"What happened yesterday?" Trotti was confused.

"There was the man. He's very big and he's got funny eyes that look at you. I think he's her father because he comes when the old woman is not here. Often he just sits there staring. But when he heard the noise, he went outside. When he came back, she was gone."

"Gone?"

"We didn't see anything," the tallest interrupted.

"I did." The youngest turned on him. "I didn't go out and I saw. I saw what happened." He had lost his lisp.

"What did you see?"

"There was a man," he said defiantly.

"What sort of man?"

"A man." He shrugged his shoulders. "I heard him calling. Her name is Anna, isn't it?" The small child blushed slightly.

"How old was he, this man? What did he look like?"

He hesitated. "He was really old, I think. Like you."

"And Anna went with him?"

"I think so." He bowed his head.

"Did you tell the father this? He was worried. You should have told him."

"Mama came and I had to leave." He shrugged. "I didn't know."

Trotti handed the boy the banknote but he clenched his fist and would not take it. He shook his head.

Trotti spoke softly, "This man who was calling Anna—where was he standing?"

The child stared at his shoes. "By the gate," he mumbled.

"And what's your name? You're being very helpful, you know. Take the money."

He shook his head.

The boy with the bruised lips answered, his voice jeering. "His name is Antonio Bennetti and he lives in via Varese, thirty-two, and he is in love with a stupid girl."

A deep crimson blush crept over Antonio's face, tinting even the small ears. "I'm not in love, I'm not in love! So shut up!"

"Don't worry, Toni," Trotti said quietly and placed a hand on the blond head. "Don't worry, Anna will be all right." The narrow shoulders had begun to heave beneath the T-shirt. Two tears, one after the other, fell onto the grass.

"She's safe, isn't she?"

"Of course," Trotti said, "of course," trying to convince the little boy.

And himself.

q

LEAVING THE GARDENS, Trotti looked up. Open blinds, like eyes, peered down from the high wall opposite. The plaster surface had been recently painted a dark brown and the woodwork of the windows was newly restored. As he came out of the gates, Trotti was surprised to see that the lower parts of the wall had not yet been defaced with the habitual slogans in scrawling paint. Clearly this was a quiet part of the town.

The sky had darkened again and the old man who pedaled past held an opened umbrella in one hand while he steered his bicycle carefully over the irregular cobbles. A pessimist, Trotti thought, until a cold drop of rain fell onto his neck.

At some of the windows above, lace curtains billowed in the breeze.

A heavy marble stone freshly engraved and polished had been embedded into the wall at eye-level. *Collegio Sant'Antonio di Padova* in flowing italic letters and a coat of arms. In smaller letters: SEZIONE LAUREATI.

Trotti was standing before a large wooden gateway; the dark varnish looked so new and its smell was so fresh that Trotti was afraid to smear his fingers. The doorbell was to one side, a row of individual buttons and neat iron slats hiding a mouthpiece. He rang one of the bells at random; a scratching voice called angrily through the mouthpiece, a click and a door—part of the larger doorway and cut into it—swung open. Trotti had to bend to step through.

He found himself in a large hall. The floor was of gleaming marble with deep veins running through it like gorgonzola. The surface reflected the grey afternoon light. The far wall was a series of parallel jute blinds partially hiding a vast floor-to-ceiling window. Beyond the window, Trotti could make out an enclosed courtyard.

"A nice place."

"Can I help you?" A woman approached him. She was short and large and as she waddled across the brilliant floor, her legs seemed to be pulled by her flat cloth slippers.

"Dottor Trotti."

He held out his hand. The woman hesitated, glancing distrustfully at his face. She put her hand to the back of her squat neck and then rubbed the same hand on the floral pattern of her apron. Then they shook hands—hers was hot and damp—and she nodded, her eyes not leaving his. She had a large face, rather pale. Two parallel lines, old white scars, ran down either side of her chin; the bulging skin graft gave her the appearance of an ageing ventriloquist's dummy. Her hair formed an unkempt halo about her head.

"You are looking for someone, Dottore?"

"Perhaps. I have never been here before."

"It used to be a convent." She had a rasping voice. "But it has been converted—to the tune of three hundred million lire." She pointed upwards and Trotti looked at the ceiling. Ancient wooden rafters, newly conditioned and varnished, held up the criss-crossing timbers. "This is the annex to the Sant'Antonio." Her eyes returned to his. "Nothing but the best for the young gentlemen."

"Which young gentlemen?"

"The doctors and the lawyers—the young graduates."

"I don't understand."

"Nowadays everybody is in a hurry." She crossed her arms. "Give me time to explain."

Trotti smiled. "Please explain, signora."

"This is where they come, the young men. After they have

finished their studies at the university and they are embarking upon their new careers. Young doctors doing their internship—or lawyers looking for their first job. For the most part they are old students of Sant'Antonio—the main college is across the fields," and with a wave of her hand, she indicated vaguely beyond the quiet courtyard.

"It's a Catholic college, isn't it? With scholarships for gifted boys?"

"That's right."

"There was an inauguration in March? I remember reading about it in the paper."

"By the Bishop of Milan—he's an old boy of the college." When she smiled, she revealed a straight line of false teeth. Her face was softly wrinkled with the lines of a lifetime's work. "And my son, too."

"He's a bishop?"

She put a hand to her mouth to hide the silent laughter. "Of course not, Dottore. My son is a student at the Sant'Antonio and he's only got three more exams to sit and his thesis before he graduates. He's on a scholarship, of course—for we are poor people. But he's a clever boy—though I say it myself—and I think the dean of the college has taken a shine to him." She lowered her voice. "That's how I got the job."

"What job?"

"For seventeen years I was in a school canteen." She gestured towards the marble floor, the dark wooden fittings and the jute blinds. "It's a lot nicer here and I'm my own boss. My husband is already beyond retirement age." She tapped her ample chest. "I'm the concierge."

Trotti tried not to smile; she pronounced the word according to Italian orthography, con-cherdge.

"Of course he has to help me with the housework—making the young gentlemen's beds and the sweeping. I'm not as young as I once used to be and I've got my troubles. I have to go to the hospital, you know. Dr. Gallese—he's very good." She added, somewhat ominously, "Women's troubles."

Trotti nodded sympathetically.

"You'd care to sit down?" She nodded towards a couple of low armchairs isolated in the empty hall; their reflection was caught by the polished marble. "You lecture at the university, Dottore?"

"No."

There was an awkward silence. The woman looked at him expectantly but her smile, deformed by the double scar on her chin, was nervous. She was slightly ill at ease, Trotti thought, as though she expected him to break bad news—as though she expected all strangers to break bad news.

"Where's your husband?"

"He's in the garden—Giovanni's in the garden with the lettuces. We have a little patch for ourselves, radishes and salad and runner beans. Sometimes I think Giovanni would be happier married to a lettuce patch and then"—the pale skin blushed—"I don't think he would." She smiled. "We had four children but only one is still alive. Giovanni is a good husband." She stopped short and gave Trotti a searching look. "Has Giovanni done . . . Has he . . . ?"

Trotti laughed. "Nothing, signora, nothing."

"Sometimes he likes the ladies too much—even at his age."

Trotti placed a reassuring hand on her shoulder. He spoke in the dialect: "You are from the hills?"

"O, dio mio!" The false teeth slipped out of place. "How can you tell?"

"An accent you can cut with a knife, signora. San Michele in Collina?"

"Santa Maria," she said and gave him a proud smile.

Trotti laughed.

"You know it?" Her eyebrows were raised in astonishment.

"Do you know my Aunt Anastasia? And Uncle Vincenzo?"

"Vincenzo Trotti—Tino—who worked in the post office until he won the football pools?"

"He now lives in a large villa on the edge of the town and plays dominoes with all the old men while he waits for his own contemporaries to retire."

"And a wife, Anastasia, who spends all her time in church

lighting candles and then spreads scandal behind your back—a pious old hypocrite." The mouth snapped shut. "Oh, forgive me."

"Nothing to forgive. It's quite true."

They both laughed; then, brusquely, she took him by the arm and saying, "Come, come," she pulled him into her little apartment.

It was a couple of small rooms off the luxurious hall; by comparison, everything was tawdry. Something was cooking on the gas stove and the windows were steamed up. The floor was of bare concrete and the furnishings were old and inelegant.

She pushed him into the kitchen and set him down on a stool before a plastic-topped table. "Here." From under the table, she hauled up a demijohn in a wicker flask. "Pinot—from the hills." She poured red wine into two glasses and they drank—she noisily.

"Do you go home?" she asked, wiping her lips.

"I'm originally from Acquanera—five kilometers down the road from Santa Maria." He shrugged. "Sometimes."

"You have a family?"

"I married a girl from the city."

"Pretty?"

"Very." He lifted his glass. "Salute." He finished the wine and placed the glass on the table.

"And what," the woman asked, about to pour more wine into his glass, "brings you here?" She was not looking at him.

"A thousand thanks." He placed a hand across the top. "I am on duty."

"Duty?"

"I am Commissario Trotti of the Pubblica Sicurezza."

A few drops of wine fell from the neck of the demijohn on to the table.

"Pubblica Sicurezza?"

Trotti recognized the weary look of resignation.

"Squadra Mobile."

"If it's about Giovanni—well, there are explanations." She lowered the large flask to the floor.

"Enough." He held up his hand. "Signora, I have not come

to spy on you. We are friends, we are from the same part of the world." He smiled. "I need your help."

She visibly relaxed. "What help?"

"I am looking for a child."

"Your own child?"

"The daughter of a friend. She may have been kidnapped." He took a photograph from his wallet. Ermagni had given it to him; the white edges were dog-eared. Anna—it had been taken the year before at San Remo—sat cross-legged on the beach. One hand was placed on an inflatable plastic beach ball, red, white and green. She stared unsmiling into the camera; in the background, on the deep blue of the Mediterranean, a couple of pedalo boats approached the beach. Anna stared seriously. She wore a minute green bikini.

"When, Commissario?"

"Yesterday afternoon, at about half past four. From the public gardens opposite."

"O dio mio."

"Outside I noticed all the blinds and windows are open. I was wondering whether perhaps anybody here might've seen something."

"How old?"

"About six. She is my goddaughter."

The large woman was shaking her head. "We live in an evil age, Commissario, in an evil age. You know, the young, they say many bad things about Mussolini. And there were bad things—like when they made Andrea Pozzon drink castor oil and he was only a poor half-wit and wouldn't have hurt a lizard. But I don't think Mussolini knew about these things—there were so many things they hid from him. The Duce was a good man and in those days— you can remember—in those days you could leave your door open and nobody would take anything. There were no crimes then."

"Not among the poor people."

"We are Italians, we are poor people. With the Duce, there was none of this crime. The robbery, the violence, the kidnapping." She made a clicking noise with her false teeth. "Look at poor Moro, look what they do to him and he is a good man. A pious man, a wise man and close to the Church. May God help him"—she crossed herself, the chapped hands lightly touching her pendulous chest—"because the politicians won't. What we need is another Duce, Commissario."

"Perhaps."

They stood for a few seconds, looking at each other in silence. Then the woman sighed. "The poor little baby girl. And her mother?"

"Her mother is dead."

"In this world and in this life, there are some people who suffer always." And she screwed up her eyes. "While there are others who never suffer, who live only too well. They do no work and they always have money." She filled her glass with pinot. "Another Duce, Commissario, we need another Duce." She emptied the contents of the glass.

She put the two glasses in a shallow sink. "Talk with Dottor Clerice. He lives upstairs on the second floor—on the street side. He is normally in during the afternoon. A nice young man." With her hand, she pushed Trotti gently aside and looked at the bank of name plates and electronic buttons, all in stainless steel and out of keeping with the drabness of the kitchen. A single red light was on, opposite a large number 37. "Dr. Clerice is in his room now. Why not go up and speak with him?"

"A good idea."

She led him out of the kitchen. "The third floor." She pointed towards a flight of steps at the further end of the hall. Her outstretched arm was laced with the pale lines of veins.

He thanked her, crossed the hall and went up the stairs. A green carpet, thick with pile, covered the cold marble of the stairs. The walls had been plastered. He went up three flights of stairs and found himself on a landing.

"Over here, Commissario."

A man beckoned to him; he was standing by the wooden balustrade. He was not very tall and rather stocky. Dark hair fell across the forehead. Black eyebrows, long dark lashes and a hint of expensive eau de cologne. A fresh face of a young man just out of adolescence.

"Dottor Clerice." He held out his hand.

Taking it—the grip was firm, friendly—Trotti enquired, "How do you know my name?"

"Your name?" Clerice's face opened into a smile. "Because the concierge told me."

"Told you?"

"Over the internal telephone." He directed Trotti through an open door and pointed to a telephone attached to the wall. "That connects with the concierge's office."

The room was small, tidy, with the same thick carpet of the stairway. The fittings were of dark mahogany. A bed with a spotless counterpane and above it, on the wall, a wooden crucifix. A reading lamp, standing on the desk, threw its circle of light on to an opened text book. Human anatomy; Trotti caught sight of a couple of flesh-colored photographs.

"This is where I study and sleep."

"And pray?"

Several devotional paintings, somber and in the style of the nineteenth century, hung from the far wall. And on the desk, another crucifix. The bare steel cross glinted in the light of the reading lamp.

Clerice was wearing a beige, sleeveless sweater over his open-necked shirt. "I am a Communist, Commissario. Certain compromises are necessary—indeed, they can be very sensible. This is a postgraduate college for Catholic gentlemen. And rooms for Catholic gentlemen are a lot cheaper than any private lodging I can find in town. The beds are made, the rooms are swept and we can eat for a very reasonable cost in the refectory of the undergraduate section of Sant'Antonio." He raised his shoulders, still smiling. "If Paris was worth a Mass . . ."

Trotti frowned.

"Can I offer you something to drink? Some tea, perhaps? I have some Earl Grey that my mother brought back from London."

"I have already drunk too much. The lady downstairs has some interesting homemade wine."

"She is a good woman." Clerice's lips were thick and of a dark red. "She works hard."

Trotti nodded.

"How can I help you then, Commissario?" He gestured towards a couple of straight-backed armchairs. "Please be seated."

Trotti lowered himself onto the side of the bed and let his hands hang slightly between his legs. His head felt like putty. "Perhaps coffee if you've got some."

There was a little kitchen built into the corner of the room. Clerice spent the next few minutes screwing and unscrewing a tiny espresso machine. He poured in water from a sink and added several heaped spoonfuls of coffee.

The window was open but not much daylight entered the room. The lace curtain fluttered outwards into the air.

"Sugar?"

"No thanks." The coffee was good; black, strong and slightly bitter. Trotti placed the cup on the carpet and offered a sweet to Clerice, who shook his head. "I prefer to keep the taste of coffee in my mouth."

They smiled at each other. The doctor—he was twenty-four, twenty-five—was young enough to be Trotti's son. It was the smile that Trotti liked.

"I find that good coffee is necessary after a night in the emergency ward."

"You are working nights at the moment?"

"You could say that, I suppose. More like standing in. As an observer. I haven't got enough confidence in my skills yet. I don't trust myself with a scalpel."

"You've been trained?"

"I spent seven years at university—if that's what you mean—but I wouldn't say that I've been trained. Oh, I know about the circulation of the blood and the basics. But this is Italy, Commissario. Big classes at the university—sometimes four hundred students in an amphitheater built for fifty. And if there are four hundred students present, that means there are a thousand doing the course. University lecturers who haven't got the time—or the inclination—to dedicate much time to teaching. You see, the best people want to be at the university because that's good for their brass nameplates. Then—they can ask more for private consultation. Private practice, Commissario—that's where the real money is."

"And what's your specialty?"

"Surgeon."

"And you had no practical training in seven years?" Trotti was puzzled. "On night duty—who does your work?"

"What work?"

"The cutting and the sawing and the sewing."

"Oh, that!" There was something sad about his smile. "The nurses."

"They're not qualified."

"As I said, this is Italy. Do you want the casualties to die? Because that's what'd happen if I got my hands on them. For the time being, at least. You see, I'm getting my first practical training now. And I'm one of the lucky ones—the professor seemed to like me and he managed to get me a place in the hospital. All students want to get into the hospital to get a real training. About one student in twenty is accepted. There just aren't the places."

"I'll make a point of not coming to the hospital for treatment."

"You're better off at our Policlinico than in most Italian hospitals. In most places you can go in with a broken arm and come out with glandular fever." He shrugged modestly. "And I'm not all that bad. I've done a few things—a few childbirths, even a caesarean. And . . ." He opened a bedside drawer and fumbled around. "I can't find it but there should be an appendix around somewhere. All my own work."

"Congratulations."

"I'm sure I left it here. Perhaps Tania took it."

"Tania?"

"A friend."

"She has strange tastes."

"She wasn't going to eat it. She likes to tidy up."

They looked at each other without speaking. The corner of Clerice's mouth twitched as though he wanted to laugh. "Commissario, how can I help you?" He paused. "Don't tell me it's about somebody I've slaughtered. The old lady with cystitis? Or the Neapolitan with piles? Terminal hemorrhoids."

"I'm looking into the disappearance of a child." He produced the photograph and while the young doctor looked at the picture, Trotti moved past him and went to the window. It looked down onto the intersection of via Darsena and vicolo Lotario. The three boys were still in the public gardens; the two older ones were striking the trunk of a tree. The small boy stood slightly apart, his head bowed. "Yesterday afternoon," Trotti said, "at about this time, the girl you're looking at disappeared from the gardens opposite. Were you at home?"

"Yes."

"What were you doing?" Trotti turned round, his hand still holding the billowing edge of the curtain.

"Sleeping. Or at least, I think so. I normally get back at about one. Then by the time I've eaten, I feel tired. I need to sleep." He scratched at the side of his head where the dark hair met his cheek. "At this time yesterday I was sleeping."

"You're not sleeping now and the bed is still made up."

"I'm waiting for you to go, Commissario."

The atmosphere had changed. It had suddenly grown a lot colder and Trotti knew it was his fault. A young man—an innocent, law-abiding doctor—and he was treating him like a criminal. He could hear the professional disbelief in his own voice, the flat, untrusting monotonous questions of a questurino.

"You didn't get up at any time to go to the window? You didn't look out onto the public gardens?"

"I don't think so."

"You didn't notice anything suspicious?"

"I was asleep, Commissario." The smile had lost its friendliness, the corner of the red lips remained still. "And with your permission, I'd like to sleep now." Even as he spoke Clerice pulled back the bed sheets and started closing the blinds.

"I shall go then," Trotti said emptily.

They shook hands. No smile. As the door closed behind him, Trotti heard the key turning in the lock.

He went down the stairs slowly. In the main hall, the door to the concierge's apartment was open but she was nowhere to be seen. The smell of boiled vegetables was strong.

Trotti was about to leave when he noticed the telephone call box in a shallow alcove. He took a token from his wallet, dialed. The phone was picked up immediately.

"Gino?"

"Questura."

"It's Trotti."

Gino laughed. "Where are you?"

"Never you mind."

"The Avvocato Romano phoned again for you."

"Is Magagna back?"

"No."

"Well, who is there?"

"Pisanelli. He came back half an hour ago."

"Okay." Trotti clicked his tongue. "Tell him I want him. Tell him to take the yellow folder from my desk and to come in a car. I'll be at the gypsy camp in twenty minutes and I don't want him to be late. Understood?"

"Understood."

Trotti hung up.

He found another token in his hip pocket. He dialed and as the phone was picked up at the other end of the line, the token clattered noisily within the machine.

"*Pronto.*"

Pioppi.

"Papa here. Is mother back yet?"

"Where are you calling from, Papa? Are you coming home for supper?"

"If I'm late, eat by yourself. Take something from the freezer."

Pioppi's voice was lower. "Mother's not here." There was a note of reproach and Trotti did not know who it was directed at. "Please hurry back, Papa. You know I don't like being alone."

"Do your homework. And if you want, you can watch television."

"I'm lonely."

"I'll be back later, Pioppi. Ciao, ciao."

He lowered the telephone gently and moved out of the alcove.

"Commissario!"

With heavy splayed movements of her legs, the concierge was coming towards him. She brushed the hair from out of her eyes. She was smiling and in her hand she held a bulging plastic bag. "For you, Commissario."

"What?"

She handed him the bag. "Freshly cut from the garden. Giovanni's best—no insecticides and no fertilizers."

He looked into the bag; it was full of green lettuce.

"It is for your wife. I'm sure she must be very beautiful, being married to a nice man like you. And a good man. Get her to make you a nice salad—with fresh eggs and olive oil."

Trotti took the bag, thanked her and left the college.

10

THE WOMEN OF Borgo Genovese wore black dresses and they used to come down to the river to wash their dirty linen. Now everybody had a washing machine and the women had disappeared. However, there were still the old photographs. They stood, their backs to the camera, beating the sheets against the pebbles of the Po; in the background, the city rising up from the river and on the horizon, the majestic dome of the cathedral. Now an enterprising baker used one of the ancient photographs as decoration on his packages. He had a smart shop in Strada Nuova and around Easter time, his sponge cakes—liberally dusted with icing sugar—could be bought in boxes and on the lid, a sepia tinted reproduction of the old women.

Trotti could remember seeing them before the war.

On leaving the college, he cycled along the Lungo Po. The road was flat, there was a slight wind behind him and the white tires hissed on the surface of the road. It was nearly half past five. The air was warmer, the threatening grey clouds had disappeared. The sky was cloudless. Tomorrow it would be hot.

On the far side of the bridge, he stopped outside a tobacconist's and leaned his bicycle against a lamppost. He went into the shop. A bell rang above his head as he was greeted by the dusty smell of black tobacco and licorice. The man behind the counter had a round head and hair the color of straw. He was out of sweets, he said without looking up. "And I can't give you any change."

"I don't want change." Trotti placed a five hundred lire note on the dish which advertised—incongruously, he thought—fodder for cattle and fowl. "I want five packets of sweets."

The man looked up and was apologetic. "They come in here, you see, and they all want change. They think I've got change because I've got a public telephone. But believe me, coins are hard to come by and I can't keep running backwards and forwards to the banks. And anyway, the banks won't give you coins any more. They've all been taken, the fifty lire pieces and the hundred lire pieces. Gone to Japan to make watches." From under the counter he produced a carton of pineapple-flavored sweets. "In France and Germany they've got change. It's only us, the Italians, who have to put up with this absurdity. The tourists laugh at us, you know. 'No small change?' they say. '*Nix gut.*'"

"I don't really like pineapple."

"I can't give you any change," the man said unhelpfully as he shook his head.

"Give me two packets." Trotti moved towards a rack of postcards. "And I'll take a couple of these." He took two views of the Sforzesco castle.

The man put the sweets in a bag—which advertised the same brand of animal fodder. "Four hundred and fifty lire. But I haven't got cash. Another packet perhaps."

"Keep the change." Trotti left, the doorbell ringing after him.

The people of Borgo Genovese had the reputation of being tight-fisted.

Trotti put a sweet in his mouth and, taking his bicycle, he went along the path that led down between the shops to the river's edge. The wheels slipped on the fresh mud of the incline. The rims were too wet for the brakes to function well. Trotti got off and, holding his bicycle by the saddle, he let it run down to the flat. Occasionally, the front wheel jumped as it hit a large pebble.

In the last two years, the banks of the river—and the river itself—had been made a natural park. It was the mayor's idea.

All building projects had been halted and now waste water and sewage from the city went through purifiers before being recycled into the grey water of the Po.

He followed the edge of the river; from time to time he lifted the bicycle to step over the rails that ran from several boathouses down to the water's edge. There were a few floating jetties, too, their grey wood bleached by the sun. As Trotti walked, a swarm of kayaks nosing upstream moved past him, the faint sound of people calling to each other.

The gypsy camp was partially hidden by a copse; the path moved away from the river towards the trees. Beneath Trotti's shoes, the ground squelched and the bicycle left deep, overlapping tracks. For twenty meters the trees cut out much of the afternoon light; then he stepped out onto the grass field and into the sunshine.

There were a few caravans. Forming a loose square, they stood alone, deserted by the vehicles that once pulled them. The triangular trailer attachments rested against the grass.

It was a large, open field with trees on two sides and to the south, the high embankment of the Milan-Genoa motorway. The ceaseless hum of traffic was partly drowned by a cassette recorder; it stood on the top of a pile of tires and emitted a strange, harmonic music. Two young girls in dark red dresses that came down to their bare feet were dancing. They stopped suddenly when they saw Trotti. They stood as though petrified, their dark eyes following him distrustfully.

On up-ended boxes seven men were sitting round an open fire. Sparks jumped upwards towards the sky; the men sat forward, their forearms resting on their thighs. Several of them held glasses; they stopped talking and turned to watch Trotti approach.

Their clothes were worn. Shabby jackets that came no lower than the waist, felt hats pushed back on the head and boots without laces. Grey trousers, black trousers—they were shiny with wear and mud-stained where the edges rubbed against the boots.

Two Mercedes Benz Saloons stood apart. Gleaming, spotless, with their gunmetal finish, they looked like an advertisement against the damp grass. They had oval German registration plates.

As though pulled by hidden strings, the two girls suddenly came alive again; they darted into a caravan, closing the battered door behind them. Trotti noticed the edge of a curtain move behind the caravan's misted window.

Here and there across the grass there were bits of paper, car tools, a few plastic utensils and a broken doll.

He leaned his bicycle against a tree. "Dimitri."

A man stood up. He had a narrow, worn face—a curve of thin wrinkles formed an arch above his mouth. He wore a felt hat; beneath the battered brim, the man's hair was quite white and it hung in loose lanks down to the shoulders of his jacket.

They stood facing each other, a couple of meters apart.

"We had an agreement," Trotti said.

The man opened a mouth full of gold teeth; he did not speak.

"I don't want any of you going into the town, stealing from the shops."

"They know." He moved a pace closer. Trotti could smell his odor of wood smoke and old dirt. "They are young."

"Don't steal and you can stay—as long as you like. That was the agreement. You must keep your young people under control."

The eyes were the same color as the band around the hat; they now sparkled. "We harm nobody."

"In a half hour I can have you cleared out."

"The young ones want"—he shrugged—"some pocket money."

"They could work for it," Trotti said. "All of you could work. You could settle down, buy houses—not cars."

The man seemed amused. "That is not our way of life."

"It is the way of other people."

"We travel," he said simply. "We know no other way." He turned and nodded towards the caravans. "We are together, we are happy."

"Other people have to work."

"We work." He folded his arms.

The cassette player wailed. No one was listening.

Trotti took the photograph from his pocket. "This girl—do you know her?"

With his arm stretched out as far as possible, Dimitri took the photograph. The hands were slightly greasy and he smeared it with his shapeless fingers. "Your daughter?"

"My goddaughter."

The man nodded; a small bridge of compassion.

"I need information."

Dimitri did not appear to understand. He moved back to his companions and, speaking in the strange language, handed them the photograph. The men stood round, some rising to their feet, each turning his neck. They spoke excitedly, they pointed. They shook their heads.

"They haven't seen her."

"If you see her, you must tell me."

A woman appeared from beyond the caravans. She wore a satin floral bodice and a dark turquoise skirt down to her feet. High upon her chest, she held a child; dark hair, dark inquisitive eyes and tearstains down his sunburned face. The woman ran nimbly across the grass towards Trotti and began shouting at him. Her voice was harsh, her tongue grating against the palate. She gestured with her free hand towards the child she held; then she prodded at Trotti. Her dark finger touched his shirt.

"What does she want?"

Dimitri clicked his tongue and moved away.

"Tell her to be quiet."

The woman continued shouting.

"Tell her to be quiet. What's wrong with her, what does she want?"

A crowd of children was forming. They appeared from out of nowhere; smiling faces, dark lustrous hair, they were enjoying the entertainment. They held their hands against the sun and watched Trotti and the screaming woman.

"Tell her to go away. It was you that I wanted to speak to." Trotti raised his voice. The men were watching him without any apparent emotion. He became aware of his own vulnerability.

In the distance the kayaks had now reached the bend in the river, the paddles hitting the water's surface in silent unison.

"She wants her husband," Dimitri said; he had now rejoined his companions. He put the stub of an old cigar in his mouth and took a cigarette lighter—Dupont or a very good imitation—from his pocket.

The girl was still prodding.

"I haven't got her husband."

Perhaps she understood Italian. She raised her voice yet louder and, hitching the child higher on her chest, she began to scream, "*Sotsul meu, sotsul meu.*" Her mouth was large with several teeth missing. She had a kind of prettiness but she was prematurely old.

The children clapped their hands in delight; the men, sitting round the campfire, stared with blank faces. They had rounded features and skin of a soft, oily texture.

"Her husband has done nothing wrong."

"I know nothing about her husband." Trotti was beginning to feel angry. And absurd, and perhaps even slightly ill at ease. He could not fend off the jabbing dark hand for fear of hurting the woman. The cars hummed past on the motorway; it was another world. He was alone, he was among strange people. He could have been in a foreign country.

"*Sotsul meu.*"

A foolish dog barked angrily from the end of its short chain.

Dimitri spoke with the woman, who answered him in the same high scream.

"She says your friend took him."

"Which friend?"

Dimitri asked the woman and then translated, "The man with the car. He came an hour ago; over there." He pointed towards Borgo Genovese.

"I know absolutely nothing. Why didn't you tell me?"

Dimitri shrugged.

"In uniform?"

Again Dimitri translated, "Yes."

The woman was now wailing; a keening cry of lamentation.

The children ceased to smile. She fell slowly to her knees, still holding the little boy.

The other men stood up. They moved towards Trotti. Their arms hung loose at their sides. One—he had a cold face and a drooping nose—wore a corduroy jacket. The men looked at Trotti. Blank faces, dark eyes and a cold, concealed anger. The woman was screaming on a single, high-pitched note. Trotti looked about. The kayaks had moved out of sight. The traffic continued to rumble with distant indifference.

It was then that Pisanelli arrived.

He came in an Alfetta and skidded on the muddy track that ran down from the road. He parked the car alongside the two Mercedes and got out. He smiled sheepishly and raised his hand in a vague salute towards Trotti.

11

LATER THEY SAT in the car while over the radio the woman's voice scratched unnecessarily. From time to time, Pisanelli picked up the microphone and spoke softly, almost apologetically, into the black wire mesh.

"He's a fool," Trotti said.

"Who?"

"Spadano. He's a fool."

Pisanelli was wearing an expensive hide jacket over a blue shirt. Well dressed; dark blue trousers and polished shoes. But his shoulders sloped and his long hair needed combing. It was generally believed that Pisanelli had once studied to become a doctor. The hands which now held the steering wheel were certainly long; and the fingers were delicate. A bright young man and—this was Trotti's opinion—someone who would go far once he made up his mind that he wanted to be a policeman. Pisanelli had the reputation of being intelligent—but also of being absent-minded, of being a dreamer.

The sun was sinking to the west beyond the river and the row of gaunt cypress trees on the far bank. The sky was quite clear and of an unreal blue.

Trotti was staring at the caravans. "We can't afford to arrest anybody. Spadano knows that."

"The Carabinieri see things differently." There was a light powder of dandruff his shoulders.

"The Carabinieri think that brute honesty and the book of rules are a substitute for common sense." Trotti bit his lip. Through the windscreen he watched the two girls who had come out of the caravan and now stood hand in hand looking at the police car.

"Is that what you wanted me for?"

Trotti turned sharply.

"About the gypsies, I mean," Pisanelli said and smiled feebly. He had a small chin and a half-hearted mustache the color of twigs. "I brought the file."

"And you didn't look at it?"

"I wasn't told to." He took the file from the back seat and handed it to Trotti. Trotti untied the string and opened the beige cardboard cover. He held out the photographs.

"You know them?"

Pisanelli shook his head and behind him, against the sky, a sheet of metal on the dome of the cathedral caught a ray of the sun's light. The distant square shone brightly, like a dazzling headlamp. Trotti blinked. "Because you soon will. I want you to do a twenty-four hour surveillance. You and di Bono."

"Who are they?"

"The Red Brigades."

Pisanelli smiled foolishly. "And who have they assassinated?"

"No one."

"What have they done wrong?"

"That doesn't concern you." Trotti was terse and immediately he regretted it. "In my opinion, they have done nothing."

Pisanelli coughed politely. "I see."

"You don't see anything—and neither do I. This is all Leonardelli's idea. He wants no scandal that could possibly harm the smooth running of the city."

Pisanelli was leaning back, looking at the padded roof of the car. "Or his personal prestige." He spoke quite flatly.

"Keep them under surveillance round the clock. And you must be quite invisible. Apparently the NP are on to them, and I don't want the NP watching you, too—and then complaining to the Prefetto about the deliberate lack of coordination between

PS and Carabinieri. And they'd be justified, too, because we shouldn't be wasting our time with political surveillance."

"Then why bother?"

Trotti couldn't stop himself from smiling. "You ask too many questions."

"Where do they live? This Guerra—is she really pretty? Or did she pose for the photo?"

"The girl is a student in one of the university colleges but she lives with him. Somewhere behind the Cairoli barracks." Trotti tapped the file. "You'll find all the details here."

"When do I start?"

"Now."

Pisanelli appeared shocked. "I haven't eaten."

"You wanted to become a policeman. If you wanted five meals a day, you should have stuck to medicine." Trotti opened the door of the car and put a shoe on the wet grass. "Any more news about Moro?"

Pisanelli shrugged. "No. Just that the Socialists are still trying to make a deal with the Red Brigades."

Trotti grunted and got out. "I had better see that the gypsies haven't stolen my bicycle." He closed the door and spoke through the window. "Keep in contact with Gino. And you have my home number if anything important comes up." With the palm of his hand Trotti banged the roof of the car. "Good luck."

Slithering slightly and throwing up mud and grass, the Alfetta drew away.

Trotti walked back to the camp.

12

IT WAS NEARLY eight by the time Trotti got home. He went up the stairs and rang the bell while he fumbled with his keys. He was tired, his eyes ached. The door opened before he could find the right key.

"Papa."

Pioppi stood on tiptoe to kiss him. She was wearing yellow slacks and a loose v-neck sweater three sizes too big. She ran her hand through his hair. "You're just in time for supper." Her smile dropped. "You're wearing that awful suit."

"It's comfortable, Pioppi. I like it."

"But it makes you look like an old man."

"I am an old man. Now, what's for supper?"

She turned round and headed back to the kitchen. "Risotto with saffron." She was nearly sixteen and with each passing day she seemed to be changing. She was leaving her childhood; her body was filling out, her waist was growing narrower. She gave him a smile over her shoulder. "Your favorite."

He made an Italian gesture of approval, tapping his cheek. "But give me five minutes to wash."

He threw his jacket over the back of a chair and went into the bathroom. He showered noisily, letting the water splash against the plastic curtain and fall onto the bathroom floor.

"Anybody phone?" he called out.

"A man." Pioppi's voice was muffled by the sound of clattering utensils.

"What did he want?"

"He didn't say. He just waited and so I hung up."

"And your mother?"

Pioppi said something that he did not hear. He turned off the hot-water tap and let the cold water run through his hair and into his eyes. He then stepped out of the shower and looked at himself the mirror. "Look like an old man," he muttered. He dried his hair on a clean towel, then put on a T-shirt.

"No news from your mother?" Water was still running down his legs and was forming tiny pools on the tiles. Trotti had wrapped the towel around his waist.

Pioppi was standing before the stove. She shook her head. On the table were the dark husks of peeled onions. In the pan, hot olive oil bubbled quietly. "I phoned the nonna."

"You shouldn't have done."

"Mama's been away for three days now."

"It's happened before."

"I want to know where Mama is. I am worried about her."

"There's no reason to worry your grandmother."

Pioppi let her hair fall forward, hiding her young face. Sitting down at the table, Trotti placed his hands on the plastic surface. The parish newssheet had been tucked behind the alarm clock on top of the refrigerator. The clock ticked softly.

"Where is she, Papa?"

"How do you expect me to know?"

"Why's she gone? Why does she do it?" His daughter sniffed and although she had her back to him, he knew that she was crying. He felt angry.

Her eyes were red when she turned round. She tried to smile. "I'm sorry. It's the onions."

"I could do with something to drink."

Pioppi bent over and opened the cupboard door. "There's nothing left," she said, holding up an empty bottle of aperitivo.

"In the cellar, there's a bottle of Martini. And bring a bottle of wine, too. I'll keep an eye on the rice."

She was wiping at a tear with the back of her hand as she went out of the kitchen and he felt a sudden sense of remorse. "Pioppi."

"Papa?" She stopped.

"Smile," he said and though her face was flushed and her eyelids slightly swollen, she tried to grin. She turned and went out of the corridor down to the cellar.

Trotti was lost in his own thoughts, his eyes fixed on the parish newssheet, while next door in the sitting room, the television continued to flicker.

"Signori, signore, buona sera."

The voice sounded lugubrious after the light, cheerful music. Trotti stood up and went into the sitting room.

"Three more acts of terrorism by the Red Brigades."

On the small screen, there was the serious familiar face of the newsreader. The bags beneath his eyes seemed larger and darker than usual.

"Forty-nine days after the kidnapping of the Onorevole Aldo Moro, the Red Brigades continue in their acts of political terrorism. In Genoa and Milan today, two men were treacherously attacked and shot in the legs."

At first, Trotti had difficulty understanding the newsreel picture. Then he saw a Carabiniere, plump in his uniform, with a machine gun across his chest. He was wearing a bullet-proof jacket. Several men in raincoats were standing in front of a large iron gate; two were taking measurements on the ground that was marked with dark stains.

"Signor Alfredo Lamberti, personnel manager of Italsider in Genoa, was attacked by two men as he came to work this morning."

"Papa, Papa. I couldn't find any red wine."

"Be quiet."

Pioppi came into the sitting room, her eyes now bright in the reflection of the television. "What's happened?" She put a hand to her mouth.

"The Red Brigades."

A different piece of film, showing the flat hinterland of Milan. A crowd of men in overalls stood with their hands in their pockets.

"At the same time to the minute, Signor Umberto degli Innocenti was stopped on his way to work at Sip Siemans in Milan and seven bullets hit him in the legs. He is now in the hospital. Neither he nor Signor Lamberti is in a critical state."

The camera swung round to the group of men. Several were smoking; they appeared worried. The reporter held out his microphone to a man in dungarees; a woolen blanket had been placed across his shoulders. "I was coming off the night shift."

The journalist wore sunglasses and had a beak-like nose. He held the microphone to the man's mouth.

"Then what happened?"

"They were in a car. Two men and a girl. They got out and they approached him. I didn't know it was Signor degli Innocenti. I thought they were friends but then they pulled out their guns."

"Did they say anything?"

The man faltered.

"Did you hear the terrorists say anything?"

"The girl. She shouted . . . it wasn't very clear, as they were getting back into the car. Something about the justice of the proletariat."

In the kitchen the frying onions had begun to splutter angrily and Pioppi hurried away while Trotti sat in his T-shirt and the towel in front of the television. Slowly he shook his head as though trying to clear it of strange, incomprehensible ideas.

"The risotto is ready, Papa."

The image on the screen returned to the Rome studio. "The Red Brigades have also claimed responsibility for the destruction by fire of the car belonging to Signor Gianfranco Bucciarelli. Signor Bucciarelli is a director at Alfa Romeo."

"Papa."

Trotti stood up and switched off the set. He went into the kitchen. On the table, Pioppi had placed two plates of yellow-tinted risotto and a bottle of white wine.

"I'm not hungry."

"You must eat, Papa."

They sat down opposite each other and Trotti opened the bottle.

From outside came the muted sound of the traffic in via Milano. Pioppi watched her father.

He lifted a forkful of rice to his mouth and ate.

"Buon appetito."

For a while they did not speak, then Pioppi remarked, "There is no red wine left. We must go and see the nonna soon. It would be a nice change. And we could do with some fresh vegetables."

"I have some salad, some lettuce. Damn, I must have left it with Pisanelli. Unless it's on the back of my bike."

"I'll go."

Pioppi dropped her fork and went out. When she came back a couple of minutes later, the white plastic bag in her hand, she saw that her father was lost in thought.

The clock ticked discreetly.

"There's some garlic. I'll make a salad dressing."

"It's wrong," her father said. He lowered his fork and propped it against the side of the dish. "It is all wrong. We never wanted this."

"Wanted what?"

"You heard on the news. Fifteen murders and a hundred wounded by the Red Brigades. And then there are the other groups, the Fascists and the anti-Fascists." He shook his head. "The war was bad, of course it was bad. And it was Mussolini's fault because he should never have made an alliance with the Germans. He should never have dragged us into a war that the Italian people did not want. And when the war was over and Mussolini dead—they strung him up like a pig in Milan—we all thought that the violence was behind us. We'd had twenty-three years of Fascism. I was still young—I was your age, Pioppi—and I had seen things that you could never imagine. Dead bodies—they killed your uncle. People shot, people burnt to death. Italian, German and American bodies—when they're burnt to a cinder, they're all the same. It was . . ." He sat back. "It was hell and we wanted a change. We were determined to make a better world." The lines on his cheek were drawn. "So what do they want? What can they possibly want?"

"Who, Papa?"

"The Red Brigades, the terrorists—all of them. What do they want? They have got everything. Cars, television, houses. When we were young, we were hungry. Life was hard and you had to be careful what you said. But we were satisfied. We didn't kill people, we didn't shoot them in the legs."

"Papa, eat your food."

"We made sacrifices. The years after the war were lean. They were hard for everybody—even for those who had money. They were the years of reconstruction and we believed that things would get better. And they have. Of course they have. We eat meat regularly, the children have got shoes to wear, there are schools for everybody—even in the south. Nobody goes hungry." Again he shook his head. "What do they want, these young terrorists?"

"I don't know, Papa," Pioppi said. She squeezed his hand. "Now eat your food."

13

TROTTI TRIED TO push the hammering away and rolled over onto his side; but the banging continued and he opened an eye, squinted at his watch—a present from Agnese. Ten to four. "The inconsiderate bitch."

He threw back the bed sheets. There was still no noise from the road beyond the closed blinds, but somewhere a cock was crowing.

More angry knocking at the door.

He could not find his slippers and the stone floor was cold. He pulled on his dressing gown—another present from Agnese. A further burst of knocking and the doorbell was ringing with unbroken insistence.

"I'm coming," Trotti shouted irritably. "I'm coming." She had probably forgotten her keys—or left them at a friend's and that was her justification for waking up Pioppi.

The door trembled beneath the banging. He turned on the hall light and pulled back the heavy iron bolt. He opened the door. The morning air was fresh, cool. To the east, through the row of plane trees and beyond the flat open fields, the sky was already tinted with the light of a new day.

Ermagni.

He stood there, one hand pushing against the bell, the other raised in a closed fist. A dark line ran across his forehead and down the side of his nose.

"You bastard."

Above Trotti's head, the electric bell was still ringing.

In the large, closed fist, Ermagni held a gun—a police issue Beretta. He lowered his hand and the black hole of the muzzle looked at Trotti with reptilian indifference. The hand was unsteady. Ermagni was trembling and the gun began to move up and down, searching for its own target.

"You're a bastard, Trotti."

The ringing stopped and suddenly it was quiet; the other hand came away from the bell and grasped the wrist of his hand. Ermagni had not forgotten his training. He tried to stand straight, the large legs slightly apart.

Trotti said softly, "Give me that," and held out his hand.

Ermagni moved back and almost toppled. But the gun in his hand was steady. "You're a bastard and I'm going to kill you."

"I'm not worth it." Trotti smiled and as Ermagni swayed slowly, his face came out of the shadow and the light from the hall fell on his crumpled features. He had been weeping; the heavy lids bulged from tears and lack of sleep.

"I"ll make some coffee," Trotti said. "Come in."

"Stand where you are or I'll blow your brains out." The gun jerked upwards and pointed towards his head.

Trotti took the gun from Ermagni.

"My God!"

There was a pot of cyclamens by the balustrade. Ermagni knocked it over as he tumbled to the floor. The flowerpot fell into the courtyard below and Ermagni banged his large head against the concrete doorstep. His mouth fell open and grey saliva hung from the wet lips. He began to sob like a child and the line of blood ran across his chin, forming black drops that fell onto the concrete slowly.

"Who is it, Papa?"

Pioppi stood in the hall wearing nothing but a nightgown; concern had tautened the sleepy features of her face. "Is it Mama?"

"A friend," Trotti replied, hiding the gun behind his back. He put an arm around her shoulder and steered her away from the front door. "It's just a friend from work." He kissed her cool forehead and directed her towards her room, where the bed sheets lay drawn back and where the bear stared at him astygmatically. "Go back to bed, Pioppi." He closed the door behind her and went into the kitchen, put on the coffee and then removed the magazine from the gun. Caliber 9 Beretta. It smelled of oil, a military smell that brought back memories, but soon the smell was smothered by the odor of coffee as the small machine bubbled on the gas ring. Through the kitchen blinds, the day was growing brighter.

He placed the gun inside the washing machine.

The coffee was ready. He poured two cups and added a lot of sugar. Ermagni was still sprawled across the doorway, his head on his arm and his feet pointing over the edge of the outside staircase. The body heaved spasmodically. Trotti set the two cups on the floor and tried to pull him into a sitting position. The head lolled like a puppet's.

"Her godfather," he mumbled through bruised lips. "I trusted you, damn you."

"Drink your coffee."

"A policeman like all the rest." A red angry eye squinted up at Trotti. "I thought you were my friend."

Trotti squatted and pushed the cup into Ermagni's large hand; within the cup, the coffee formed a heavy swell of dark sea. Yet he managed to drink it in one gulp without spilling a drop.

"Now tell me why I deserve to die."

Ermagni moved and managed to prop his back against the jamb of the door. "A bastard of the worst kind. A sbirro."

Trotti shrugged.

"It was a secret. Between you and me—for her sake. You promised."

"I promised nothing. I simply said I'd help you."

"Help me? You're a bastard." He laughed, a cold grating in the thick throat. "You couldn't care whether my child lives—it's all the same to you. And to think that I trusted you—trusted you because you were her godfather, because I thought you cared. My daughter, Anna." He began to sob again, tears forming at the corners of his eyes. Then he let his head fall against the doorpost.

And as he cried, he took the newspaper from his pocket and let it fall onto his crumpled trousers.

Trotti read the headline:

LOCAL GIRL (SIX YEARS) KIDNAPPED IN THE CITY.

TROTTI TOOK THE car.

There was an old packet of chewing gum—yogurt flavor—in the glove compartment. Perhaps Pioppi had left it there. He unwrapped a stick and chewed at it mechanically. He should have eaten something before leaving the house. He could feel the coffee lying on the emptiness of his stomach.

He saw Angela, the transvestite who stood beneath the arc of neon light by the railway station, touting for one last customer. But the streets were empty. When Trotti reached the viale Libertà, a large bus trundled past him in the opposite direction, brightly lit inside, taking a couple of workers to the sewing machine factory and the early-morning shift.

At the lights—they were against him and there was no other traffic—he lowered the window. The air was cold but it did not stop a bird from singing noisily. It was somewhere in the lime trees along the pavement and he envied the cheerfulness of its monotony.

He drove the car into the pedestrian area—a specially printed windscreen sticker had been supplied by the town hall to public officers and doctors—and parked in Corso Cavour. The lamps, suspended from wires above the old cobbled street, swayed gently in the first breeze of the morning, their electric glow paling against the dawn light.

He crossed the road, the sound of his shoes echoing against the wall and went into the offices of the *Provincia Padana*. The iron grilles that protected the windows were still down and the lights had been turned off, but the glass door was open. He could hear a faint murmur of talking. He stepped past empty desks towards the light at the far end of the office. On one desk, a telephone console blinked into the unheeding gloom.

"Who's in charge here?"

A couple of men—ruffled hair and fingers black with ink—turned round to look at Trotti. "Who are you?" They wore unbuttoned overalls and one of them held a pornographic magazine in his hand.

"Pubblica Sicurezza."

They returned to their conversation, turning their backs to him. One, speaking over his shoulder, said, "The deputy editor is in the office," and gestured towards a clutter of printing presses.

Trotti thanked him.

The deputy editor was a fat man and he had not shaved for some time. But there was a kind of elegance to his scruffiness, as though he deliberately chose to appear worn out and crumpled—an unbuttoned shirt collar, a greasy tie, a bulging dark waistcoat. He was smoking and leaning back in a functional metal armchair; his small feet placed on the edge of the desk, he watched the blue rings of smoke rising towards the single electric light. An old-fashioned upright typewriter stood on the desk, pushed backwards with a sheet of unsullied paper in the carriage.

"Ciao," he said, without taking his eyes off the wisps of smoke. "Ciao, ciao, ciao."

"Buongiorno."

Close-set eyes turned towards Trotti. "Already?" The head and thick neck remained motionless.

"I am a police officer."

"We all have our cross to bear."

The cage was a cluttered cubicle with windows on three sides that gave onto the indistinct shadows of printing machines. On the fourth wall there was a large map of the province. Superimposed upon that, a pin-up calendar. Drawing pins had been pushed into the nipples of the girl of the month.

"You wrote this article?" Trotti threw the paper onto the desk.

"Don't shout." The eyes had returned to the scrutiny of the tobacco smoke; with a slow gesture, he moved the cigarette to the corner of his mouth. His lips were red like a woman's.

"A child's life may be in danger."

The editor shrugged.

"Did you write it?"

"It is rather well-written. Simple, precise and to the point."

"Where did you get your information from?"

The eyes returned to Trotti. "In ten minutes' time—after a last cigarette—I'm going to remove my feet from the table, I'm going to spit into the waste-paper basket and I'm going to go home."

"In ten minutes you may find yourself in the basement of the Questura."

"You frighten me, Commissario Trotti." Very slightly the head had moved backwards. The clouds of smoke jostled round the lamp bulb and the single flex covered with dead flies.

"I see you know my name."

"I know most things about this town."

"Then you can tell me who told you about Anna Ermagni."

"She's not your daughter, Commissario." The tone was ironic. "She's the daughter of a friend."

The feet came off the desk with a clutter. The deputy editor was a small man and very fat. He had to push with his plump arms against the sides of the chair to stand up. He faced Trotti, only a few centimeters away, looking up. The cigarette was now no more than a smoldering stub in the corner of his red lips. "You're not a very stupid man, Commissario, and you have the reputation for being honest. But . . ." He pointed with his thumb towards Trotti's chest. "I am afraid you are a cop—and that is a terminal disease."

"You wrote this article?"

The small man shook his head slowly; his eyes remaining fixed upon Trotti as though upon a well-loved animal that was in pain and would soon die.

"But you checked it?"

"I read it."

"But you didn't check?"

"Commissario, if I had to check the work of all my colleagues, I wouldn't be a journalist. I'd be a cop."

"Who wrote it?"

He sighed theatrically. Then he said, "Stefano Angellini."

"Where is he?"

"If he's got any sense, he's at home in bed." He added, "Via Lugano, seventeen."

Trotti turned and walked out of the cubicle.

Mockingly, the man called after him, "Ciao, ciao, ciao."

14

TROTTI LEFT HIS car outside the offices of the *Provincia Padana*. Via Lugano was one of the narrow streets at the back of the town hall.

Although the air was already warming—there was a slight mist, but above it, the sky was blue and cloudless—the ground was still damp with dew. Trotti walked along one of the lines of parallel stone slabs of via Petrarca. The slabs had been placed there three hundred years previously by the local aristocracy so that their carriages should run smoothly between the cobbles. These quiet, leafy streets had once been privately owned; the high walls hid ornate baroque palaces. Every inch of brickwork seemed to be caught in the grasp of ivy and climbing plants. There was a smell of spring flowers and of fresh-baked bread.

An old woman was sitting outside a café. She was wearing a black dress and above her head there was the yellow enamel sign advertising a public telephone. A broad ray of early sunshine came from between two neighboring roofs and lay across the metal table where she was slicing runner beans.

"Buondì," she said and Trotti, who was lost in his own thoughts, looked up and smiled.

"Buongiorno," he said.

To get to via Lugano, he went under a small, private bridge between two houses. Flowerpots at every window with bright red flowers and green damp leaves. Already the fretful lizards were darting between the crevices.

There was no gate to number 17. Trotti went through a porch into a courtyard that smelled of drains; a rusting bicycle, deprived of the rear wheel, leaned against the wall and a serried double rack of zinc letterboxes had been nailed into the plaster-work of the entrance.

"Can I help you?" An old man appeared from the shadow; he spoke in strange sibilants because he had no teeth.

"Angellini."

The man appeared both upset and surprised. He stepped backwards and then came forwards and, taking Trotti by the arm, almost whispered, "Over there."

Trotti thanked him and walked across the open courtyard; washing hung from a couple of rope clotheslines. White sheets, bleached overalls and the intimate garments of an outsized woman. Beyond the lines, a stairway ran upwards to a wooden door. A cat was weaving between the bars of the rusting iron banisters; it darted away at the sound of Trotti's shoes on the stairway.

Trotti looked back. The old man was staring after him. He stood in the middle of the courtyard, his old legs slightly apart and bent at the knees. He wore a loose black jacket and woolen striped trousers that had once been elegant. He nodded emphatically and with his gnarled hand made a knocking movement in the air. Then he pointed at the door.

Trotti knocked and waited; the cat returned and sniffed diffidently at his shoes.

"Yes?" A thin woman stood before him. Her hair was grey with pink tinting that matched the color of her skin. She looked at Trotti, hesitating between indignation and fear. Her eyes were a dirty grey and her face was wrinkled with the wrinkles of a life that was clearly fast approaching its end. The cheeks were hollow and the bones of her shoulders pushed through the thin cotton of her dress.

"Pubblica Sicurezza. I wish to speak with Stefano Angellini."

"He's asleep," she replied in a shrill voice and tried to close the door.

"Please wake him."

Trotti had placed his foot in the door. She looked down fearfully as though it were some beast that could do her irreparable damage. "He's tired," she said. "I suggest you come back later."

Trotti pushed the door open and went past her. She did not resist but merely uttered a strange squeak.

Trotti went down a dark corridor; the carpet, once oriental, was now worn thin and the wallpaper had darkened with age. There were one or two photographs with the gloomy, unsmiling faces of relatives long dead.

The woman trotted after him. "Stefano's asleep. You mustn't disturb him." A claw-like hand grasped his sleeve but he pushed it away. "My nephew's not well."

"You had better make him some breakfast, signora."

"Signorina," she corrected him and straightened her back beneath the insult. She turned away.

Trotti went into the bedroom.

The bottom of the door scratched against the floor as he opened it. It was of ground glass with an ornate engraving of cherubim and the coat of arms of the house of Savoy. The air was stale and Trotti was met by the unpleasant odor of human sweat and unwashed bed linen. A few strokes of light filtered through the closed blinds. Trotti went to the window, opened it and unlatched the wooden shutters.

The old man was still out in the courtyard. He was staring up as though he had expected Trotti to come to the window. His curved arms hung at his side and he nodded. "Ecco, ecco," he said in his toothless voice and smiled with satisfaction.

Trotti turned around; a small table cluttered with a typewriter, a large angular lamp stand and a lot of books, many of them left open and piled up. The walls were lined with oak bookcases. *The Cambridge History of the World*, *The Complete Works of Gramsci*. And a lot of books about the Mafia. A deckchair, low beside the table, sagged with the weight of a portable television. The set had not been turned off and the screen trembled with the bright image of the test card. Swiss television.

Stefano Angellini was snoring. White plump shoulders

appeared from beneath a grubby sheet. Trotti approached the bed and prodded at the body with the tip of his shoe.

"Wake up."

"It's early."

"Not early enough." Trotti grasped the shoulder—it was warm and damp with sweat—and shook it. "Pubblica Sicurezza."

The eyes came open. "I want to sleep."

"Later."

Trotti switched off the television set and put it on the floor beside a pile of books. *The Honored Society, The Mafia Republic*, and several collections of poetry—Leopardi and Montale. Trotti sat down in the deep lap of the chair and set a cushion behind his head. He placed his feet on the edge of the bed. "We had better talk."

"It's about the car license?" Angellini was like a stirring leviathan. He lifted his head, propped himself up with his elbows and pulled himself into a lopsided sitting position. His two white feet touched the floor. He pushed the sheet away and was quite naked. He was large and he had the breasts of a woman; a few dark hairs ran down the central ridge of his chest and joined the bushier region of his groin. The outer side of his thigh was scarred.

"Put something on."

He grunted and wiped the sleep from his eyes. Then looking about him as though he had no idea of where he was, he screwed up his eyes. He found a dressing gown—a moth-eaten kimono—where it had slipped off the edge of the bed.

"I don't get in until late. Christ, what's the time?"

Trotti could smell his body; there was an acrid note to the odor of sweat. He was grateful for the smell—perfume by comparison—that came from the kitchen. Coffee and warm bread.

"Who told you about Anna Ermagni?"

Angellini yawned—a wide ugly yawn that showed yellowing-grey teeth.

"You could cover your mouth."

Angellini looked up sharply. "Who invited you?"

Trotti kicked the side of the bed angrily with his heel. "Tell me about Anna Ermagni."

"There's nothing I want to say."

"There should be. Your article—your scoop on the front page of the *Provincia*. Where did you get your information from, Angellini?"

He pulled the kimono closer about him and shivered. He then scratched at an armpit. "What time did you say it was?"

"You'll get time to sleep."

The flat face blinked at Trotti. "My glasses. Pass them to me. They're on the typewriter."

Trotti handed over the glasses. Angellini put them on and the eyes came into focus behind the thick lenses.

"What the hell do you want?"

"How did you find out about Anna Ermagni?"

A light of understanding came into the eyes.

"Well?"

"I checked."

"You checked? Who did you speak to?"

"I phoned her home. I spoke with her mother."

"Her mother is dead."

He shrugged, it was not important. "Her grandmother. I phoned and she sounded quite distraught. I think she thought I was one of the kidnappers."

"How did you know the child had been kidnapped?"

There was a discreet tap on the door and the aunt came in carrying a large tray that she placed on the floor beside Angellini's feet. A jug of coffee and two chipped cups; a basket of bread, some butter, some jam. She gave her nephew a wan smile. She ignored Trotti and left, quietly closing the door behind her.

"One of the last real pleasures in life," Angellini rubbed his hands. "I'm lucky to have an aunt who dotes on me."

"Where did you get your information from?"

Angellini was in the process of opening a bread roll. He stopped and looked up at Trotti. He was a lot younger than Trotti had at first thought. Twenty-five—if that, Trotti thought. What aged him physically was the prematurely high forehead.

"A phone call."

"Where?" Trotti leaned forward in the deckchair.

"I was on duty at the *Provincia Padana*—in the main office."

"When was this?"

Angellini returned to his roll and was lowering the knife into the butter dish when Trotti knocked roll and knife out of his hand. "When was this, damn you?"

"I don't know," he answered petulantly. "About half past nine, I suppose. About two hours before deadline. It's a local paper, the *Provincia*, and we like to get it printed early."

"Who phoned?"

Angellini ignored the question. "A kidnapping—it's not the sort of thing that happens often around here. I didn't have much time to cross-check." He stopped, looked at Trotti. "Oh, shit."

"What?"

"I forgot. I've got to have my prod—if you'll excuse me." He stood up and moved towards a bookcase. There was a leather box on the floor.

"Who did you speak with on the phone?"

"A man." He took something from the box and held it up to the light. "And I didn't talk with him, he talked with me." He screwed a small container into the syringe and slowly squeezed the plunger. A few drops, like dog urine, arched in the air and fell onto the floor. A few minute splashes, tiny bubbles of liquid.

"Who was this man? What did he say?"

"That he had the girl."

"That's all?"

"I'm afraid this isn't very pretty—but you weren't invited." He pulled back the skirt of his kimono and lifted a foot onto the edge of the bed. The skin of his thigh was pocked with red marks, like a rotting orange. He dabbed at the skin with a piece of cotton wool. "Drink your coffee, Commissario."

"What's wrong with you?"

"Cancer and being woken up by uninvited visitors."

A sharp jab—Trotti winced—and then Angellini pressed on the plunger and the yellow liquid was pushed through the needle into the deformed skin. "He even put the kid on the line," Angellini said in a matter-of-fact tone.

"You spoke with Anna?"

"She seemed to be enjoying herself. Well, perhaps not quite, but she certainly didn't sound very subdued." He unscrewed the needle and threw the empty cartridge into a shoebox. "But I don't see why you're asking me all these questions."

"The child's life is in danger."

"You know her?"

Trotti nodded. "I know the father."

"A taxi driver."

"He used to work for me—a long time ago."

Angellini put the medical paraphernalia away and, crouching down beside the tray, the kimono scarcely covering his body, poured coffee into the two cups. He handed one to Trotti.

"What was the man's voice like?"

"Don't ask me, for heaven's sake. It's all monitored."

"What do you mean, monitored?"

"On the tapes."

"What tapes?"

Angellini picked up the knife and the roll. Speaking casually while he spread butter with the knife, he said, "All incoming calls are recorded. Standard practice in most newspapers since Moro's kidnapping. You never know when the Red Brigades are going to give you a ring."

Trotti stood up. "Why the hell didn't you tell me?" He moved towards the door and opened it; it screeched against the floor. "Don't go away too far—and thanks for the coffee."

He ran down the dark corridor.

15

THE WORKMEN WORE loose blue dungarees and hats made of folded brown paper. There was the sound of hammering and a low whine of feedback. A fingernail, scraping against a microphone, was amplified and the jarring sound echoed across Piazza Vittoria.

Trotti crossed the square. His head ached—four hours in the smoke-filled laboratory of the Polizia Scientifica—and he needed the fresh air. He also needed to be alone.

He stepped over the electric cables that lay on the cobbles of Piazza Vittoria.

"Commissario, we don't see much of you."

He sat down just inside the Bar Duomo and the proprietress brought him an analcolico and a saucer of pitted olives.

"I'll take a sandwich, too," he said, looking up at her.

She was a widow—her husband had died in an air crash while visiting Sicily—and for the last ten years she had run the bar single-handed. She had two daughters; when Trotti had left for Bari, they were little girls with blonde ringlets. Now they were in their early teens, a bit younger than Pioppi, and were rather plump. They were not as pretty as their mother, who had somehow managed to keep the figure of her youth. If anything, she had grown prettier with the passing years.

A friendly, happy smile and beautiful dark eyes. Signora Allegra; of course her clients called her "the merry widow."

He sipped at the aperitivo while Signora Allegra prepared his sandwich behind the zinc bar. "They drive me mad with this noise."

"Noise?"

"The hammering and banging and those wretched loud-speakers." She laughed. "Yet another political rally tonight." She nodded towards the piazza while her hands busied themselves with the operation of slicing salami. "The Socialists this time. And they are pulling out all the stops, they've even got the First Secretary speaking. He's come up specially from Rome. Obviously they place a lot of importance upon our local elections. Down in Rome the Communists and the Socialists are at each other's necks—with the Communists saying that a deal with the Red Brigades is out of the question while the Socialists maintain that Moro's life is more important than political ideals. But up here, in our little provincial backwater, the PCI and the PSI are good bedmates." She laughed again and Trotti smiled. "Our Communist mayor knows that he needs the support of the Socialists; and thanks to the Communists the local Socialists have a share in the power. So they can afford to overlook their national differences. A gherkin, Commissario?"

"Yes please."

She brought him the sandwich wrapped in a paper serviette and placed it on the tablecloth.

Trotti looked out into the piazza and said softly, "These meetings remind me of the rallies when we were little."

"I don't remember." Her eyes flashed.

A long time ago he had phoned up the transport department and checked on her driving license. She was the same age as him. "Of course not, signora."

Like a surfacing whale, the coffee machine began to spout. Steam poured from the thin metal tap. She took no notice. She was standing by his table and he could smell her gentle perfume.

"And your wife, Commissario? I no longer see you with her in town."

"Lately I have been very busy."

"Women need affection, Commissario."

For a few moments their eyes met; then he turned away and caught sight of himself in the tinted mirror behind the bar. His face looked back at him—a thin face, a narrow nose and closely set eyes. His dark hair oiled and no longer as thick as it once was. Thin creases running down his cheeks.

Like an old man, he thought, and he bit angrily at the sandwich.

Then he took another sip at his drink.

Signora Allegra had moved away and she was now wiping glasses with a stiff cotton cloth. Another whine of feedback came through the door.

"I'm an old man," Trotti said softly.

She laughed lightly. "Commissario, I think you are fishing for compliments." Her laugh was light like the sound of the glasses that she neatly arranged along the shelf.

The memory of her laughter accompanied him back to the Questura.

16

GINO WAS SITTING back in his chair, his hands folded across the plumpness of his belly. He looked benign, like a favorite uncle. It was the effect of the thick lenses that magnified his sightless eyes.

Principessa dozed beneath the desk.

"They're waiting for you." Gino jerked a thumb towards the small antechamber where visitors could sit and thumb old magazines—*Famiglia Cristiana*, *il Carabiniere*—while waiting for the law and its officers to take their ponderous, inexorable course.

"You can send them through in a minute—but first, get me Spadano on the phone."

Trotti went into his office and started to tidy. He opened the windows, letting the enclosed air escape into the mid-morning. Outside it was hot and it was getting hotter; on the roof, the pigeons cooed languidly. Trotti's eyes ached. For no apparent reason, the radiator started to vibrate with distant banging. He put several folders into a pile and tidied up the newspapers. He stopped to look at the headlines on the morning's *Corriere della Sera*. A photograph of one of the directors shot in the leg, and the continuing debate on Moro. "Reasons of State cannot outweigh humanitarian reasons," the Socialist First Secretary said. "We must save Moro at all costs."

Trotti snorted.

"Spadano's on the line." Gino banged against the wooden hatch panel. "Number six."

Trotti picked up the telephone and pressed the blinking rectangle.

"Hello, Spadano?"

"Capitano Spadano. Who am I speaking to?"

"Commissario Trotti. Good morning."

"Ah, you, Trotti." The voice was less aggrieved but more cautious. "How can I help you? You realize I am busy. I imagine you've heard the news."

"What news?"

"There's just been a communiqué from the Red Brigades—in Rome, Genoa, Turin and Milan. It looks genuine—at least at first sight."

"What do they say?"

"Communiqué Number Nine states that Aldo Moro has been executed. And at the same time," Spadano went on in a brisk, military tone, "Signora Moro has received a farewell note from her husband."

Trotti turned to look out of the window. The neighboring roofs were dazzling beneath the high sun.

Spadano was still talking: "And I quote, 'Dear Norina, they have told me that they are going to kill me in a few minutes. I kiss you one last time. Kiss the children,' signed Aldo."

"So it's certain?"

"Nothing is certain until we find his corpse. However, the Red Brigades have been silent for eleven days. Moro's assassination now would certainly fit in with the logic of their strategy."

The pigeons continued to coo.

"So you can understand, Trotti, that I am busy."

"I am busy, too, Capitano Spadano."

"Of course. How can I help you?"

Trotti breathed deeply. "It's about the gypsies—the camp on the far side of the river. I believe that one of your men arrested a gypsy yesterday in Borgo Genovese."

"Yes?"

"Can you confirm?"

Spadano sounded irritated. "I have more important things to do at the moment. It's quite possible—really, Trotti, I don't know."

"Please check. It is important, Capitano. I had come to an agreement with their chief—and now it looks as though I can't keep to my side of the agreement. I can't expect them to understand the difference between Carabinieri and Pubblica Sicurezza."

"A pity," Spadano replied drily. "I'll ring you back—but please understand it's not easy. I've got other—"

"When?" Trotti interrupted.

"Within the hour," and without another word, the captain of Carabinieri hung up.

Trotti put the receiver down slowly and then took a packet of sweets—aniseed—from the top drawer. Perhaps he was being stupid. One of the most powerful men of the country had probably been executed—and he was worrying about a handful of nomads. He sat in silence for a few minutes while he thought and while he sucked noisily at the pale lozenge of boiled sugar.

"Okay, Gino, you can send them in."

Signor Rossi wore a tweed jacket that was too large for him; it had a large check pattern, the color of boiled rutabaga and parsnips. It stood away from the collar of his poplin shirt. But the material, Trotti noticed, was smooth and of good quality.

"Please come in."

He entered the office, steering his wife by the arm. She was broad but a lot shorter than her husband. She was dressed completely in black. Her strong legs were scarred with protuberant veins.

"Kindly be seated, signora." Trotti helped her to a chair. "It is kind of you to come in like this. I am most grateful and I am sure that there are some points we can clear up." He smiled as he returned to his desk. "Points of mutual interest."

"We didn't need any help." Rossi's tone was belligerent. He had lowered his large frame into one of the canvas armchairs; he looked both angry and apprehensive, like a man being sent

unjustly to his death. He had a large face and large, flat cheeks.
A thin nose and a few strands across an almost bald head. His
hair was the same color as his jacket.

"Are you sure?"

"I could have paid."

"That is not the way to deal with kidnappers." Trotti added,
"And I'm afraid it's illegal."

"That's our problem. Anna's our girl—all that we've got left."

Trotti sat back in his chair and let the tension slowly ease from
the room. Again he smiled at Signora Rossi. She cast her eyes
downward and looked at her old hands. Her only concession to
fashion was a simple silver necklace.

"You'd care for a drink perhaps?"

Rossi said, "No."

His wife looked up. "Commissario, we own a bar. We didn't
come here for a drink. We're here because you asked us to come—
and because we are worried about our granddaughter."

"You have seen the article in the *Provincia Padana*?

"Of course."

"The kidnappers have contacted you?"

The old woman looked down at her hand. Rossi answered,
"Nothing at all."

"Strange they should contact the newspaper without first
contacting you."

The large man moved forward in his chair. "What exactly
did they say? Have they got her? She's alive, isn't she? Isn't
she? . . . Because if they've touched so much as a hair . . ."
His voice was throttled by the prospect of his own rage. His
wife calmed him, softly tapping the shapeless, clenched fist.

Trotti said, "She is quite well."

He raised his head. "I don't believe you."

"She was in perfect health last night—you can hear for yourself." Trotti opened the hatch. "Gino, is Magagna around?"

"Yes."

"Get him to bring a recorder—and a tape of the message."

They sat for a few awkward minutes waiting for Magagna to
bring proof of the child's continuing existence. When Magagna

arrived he placed the recorder on the desk, plugged it in and inserted the tape.

"It now looks as though it's a hoax," he whispered to Trotti. Rossi glared. "What?"

"The communiqué from the Red Brigades. It's not in their jargon and it's been written out with a different typewriter."

"You can hurry up," Rossi said.

Magagna saluted. "I'm down the corridor," he said and left.

Trotti pushed the button on the cassette recorder and the small reels began to turn behind their perspex barrier. Rossi and his wife leaned forward, staring at the machine as though it were a newborn baby, somehow both reassuring and—by implication—terrifying. The threat of responsibility.

Silence until the tape scratched with the beginning of its recording.

"The *Provincia*?" A man's voice, slightly muffled.

"City desk. Angellini."

"We've got the child—she's with us and safe."

"What child?"

"Ermagni's daughter."

"Who's Ermagni? What child?"

"Anna Ermagni. We have her—the daughter of the taxi driver."

"Who is she? Why have you kidnapped her?"

"Twenty million lire and she will be home with her parents tomorrow. She is quite safe. Twenty million in used notes by tomorrow morning. We will contact you again. Tell the parents. Tell the parents that if they want to see their daughter alive and well—if they want to see her again—they must pay. Twenty million."

There was a short pause and then Angellini asked, "How do they know that she's alive? How do they know that you haven't killed her?"

"I am a man of honor."

"Men of honor don't kidnap children."

"She is well." A suspicion of irritation.

"I must speak with the child. How old is she? I must hear from her."

"That is impossible."

"The parents will not pay."

Another pause, the muffled sound of hands about the mouth-piece. "Wait." It sounded as though he was speaking through a stuffed cloth and that the cloth had slipped. The voice was clearer. "Here she is."

"Hello."

Again a long pause accompanied by the sound of movement.

"Hello." A girl's voice.

"Ciao." Angellini sounded falsely cheerful.

"Ciao."

"Anna?"

"Yes. Is that you, Grandpapa?"

"I am a friend of your father's, Anna."

An intake of breath. "I don't like my papa."

"You don't like him? And your mama?"

"I like the nonna and I like my grandpapa. I miss them but I am very well. I want to . . ."

The voice was stopped as though against its will.

"Tell them to prepare the money." The man again, with the loudness of false conviction. "Twenty million."

Click and the hum of the phone died; the reels continued to turn but now in silence. Trotti stopped the machine.

"At least she is alive."

"A bastard." Rossi, now quite pale and his lips drawn. "A murderous, southern bastard."

"Southern?"

"You can hear the accent." He was almost shouting. "You can hear as well as I can, Commissario. A Calabrian—one of my own people."

"Where are you from?" Trotti asked while at the same time taking a notebook from the drawer. He started to take notes, writing with a fifty lire ballpoint pen.

"Calabria—yes, I'm from Calabria. But I work, Commissario, I have worked all my life." And he held up his hands as an objective proof. They were large and ugly, shapeless. "With these I have worked. We are not all criminals or bandits. I left school when I was eleven and for twenty years I worked on the pylons. The electricity men came and I helped them. Mussolini said that in the twentieth century every Italian should have electricity in his house. We used to work with donkeys, we used to climb the hills and there were days when I'd travel twenty miles to work on a breakfast of dry bread and goat's milk. It was hard work—but I have never been afraid of hard work."

"Then you came here?"

Rossi's face flared into a short-lived rage. "You ask me questions. Why aren't you looking for Anna? Why do you waste your time?"

"She may have been taken in an attempt to harm you." Trotti added softly, "I must know everything if I am to find her. When did you come here?"

The anger disappeared as quickly as it had come. "I wanted a better job and I was too old to climb the hills—even if the money was a lot better on the whole after the end of the war. I had a brother—God rest his soul—who was working in the textile factory—he died of lung cancer. I worked with him for five years. Then in 1952, I had put enough aside—with the help of Graziella, who worked in the factory too—I had enough for the bar." He shrugged slightly and the collar of his jacket moved away from the shirt. "We've done well for ourselves but nobody has helped us. And we haven't stolen. What we have got we have earned by our own efforts." He leaned forward to tap at the tape recorder. "And I will lose it all—lose it happily—just so that we can have our Anna back. She is all we have—now that our daughter is gone. The rest—the house, the bar, the villa near Rimini, I'll sell it all. I want Anna."

Beside him, his wife nodded; she held a pale blue handkerchief to her mouth. "We will pay, Dottore," she said softly.

Trotti wrote something on the paper, then looking up, gave a pale smile. "I understand. However, I have given orders to your bank. There can be no further transfer of money without my permission. You must understand that it is better this way. Give them money and they will want more—you know that.

They've made no agreement with you and there is no reason for them to respect your good faith. They are kidnappers—there's no reason why they shouldn't be thieves and murderers. We must protect Anna."

"I will pay. I want to pay." He moved clumsily out of the armchair.

"Sit down, Signor Rossi," Trotti ordered calmly. "Sit down, please."

Rossi sat down slowly; he glared at Trotti.

"Do you have any enemies?"

The question surprised Rossi and in his surprise he turned to look at his wife. Her face remained expressionless.

Trotti repeated the question.

"No, I don't think so. There are people who don't like me—and who I probably don't like either. But enemies, no. When you own a bar, you can't afford to have enemies."

Trotti decided that Rossi was not lying—at least, not deliberately. But he had the impression he had put an idea into his head—an idea that had not occurred to him before.

"Listen again," Trotti said and he rewound the tape. "Tell me what you hear."

They listened to the recorded conversation; this time the static of the telephone was amplified and the tape scratched noisily. "You hear?"

"Hear what?"

Trotti stopped the machine, pressed the rewind button and they listened to the same section. "There."

"What?" Rossi frowned with frustration.

"There are bells."

"I can hear nothing."

His wife said, "Please play it again." And then, "Yes, I can hear them."

"The Gabinetto Scientifico can't identify anything for the moment. But they think they're church bells. So I've had a copy sent to Milan and maybe the specialists there will come up with something more precise."

Rossi's excitement had drained away. "And perhaps they

won't and all the time, Anna is alone in the hands of dangerous criminals."

"You must have faith in us, Signor Rossi."

"Faith, faith, faith." He snorted angrily. "Faith in the police force when you allowed Moro to be gunned down in the street like a cheap gangster and his five bodyguards killed, without even the time to use their weapons. Faith! In the Pubblica Sicurezza and the Carabinieri and the Finanza when with all your money and all your equipment, your guns and your helicopters, you can't protect the public. I want the child back, Commissario Trotti. I want her back alive." He screwed up his lashless eyes. "Faith, how do you expect me to have faith in you?"

"Because you have no choice. No payment will be made to the kidnappers—now or later. That is out of the question."

"Her blood will be on your hands."

Trotti could feel that he was losing control of his temper. Intellectually he understood the man's anger, yet at the same time, his bovine stubbornness was irritating to the point where Trotti felt that only physical violence would silence him. "I don't have to remind you, Rossi, that Signor Ermagni is the father. All decisions about Anna must come from him."

"A queer! An incompetent, lazy bastard. I never wanted her to marry him. And now look what's happened. It's his fault isn't it? He left her alone, he went out into the street."

"I know Ermagni—he used to work for me. He has his problems but then we all do. You have no right to criticize him. He is hard working, and he loves his daughter. Has it occurred to you that it's because you have turned his child against him that she decides to go with strangers? Because that is what happened. Anna did not leave the gardens in via Darsena under duress."

"He killed my daughter."

"Absurd. I knew your daughter, Signor Rossi—you may not remember but I was at their wedding. She loved her husband and he loved her. Anna is the child of their union and you have no right—either moral or legal—to come between Ermagni and Anna."

"I hate him."

His wife caught her breath. "You mustn't say those things."

Trotti put the cap on his pen. "Listen carefully, Signor Rossi, if you don't want to get into trouble. Go home and stay there. You don't do anything, you don't open the bar. You just sit by the phone and you wait. And you don't get any clever ideas and you don't consult any lawyer. You just sit quietly and you trust us to get—"

A knock on the door and without waiting, Magagna came in. He was not wearing his sunglasses and his eyes were slightly red.

"Go away," Trotti said and gestured towards the couple. "You see I'm busy."

Magagna remained motionless; he held a large envelope in his hand.

With thumb and fingers, Trotti made an Italian gesture of anger and incomprehension. "What do you want?"

"Another leg," he said as he held out the envelope. "They've found another leg in the river."

17

Two old men sat in the sun on a painted bench; they wore loose coats over their striped pajamas and they both smoked, sharing the same stub of a cigarette. A thin trail of blue cloud hovered over their heads.

It was late afternoon and Trotti shivered.

He moved away from the window. It was cold in the morgue and the sweat on his body had dried. He buttoned the collar of his shirt and straightened his tie. His jacket he had left in the car.

"The same woman."

Bottone looked like a priest, despite the white tunic and the stethoscope hanging from his neck. There was a pallor about his skin and he had pushed his steel glasses back onto his forehead while the long hands probed the dead flesh.

Magagna watched in silence, his mouth pursed beneath his mustache. He had not taken off his sunglasses even though the light was artificial in the long chamber.

"Without a doubt," Doctor Bottone said without looking at either policeman. "And she was cut up some time after death. You see, there's little sign of bleeding."

Magagna remarked, "The left leg was found further upstream."

"Probably got caught against something. A partly submerged root or a sandbank."

Magagna turned to Trotti. "The disposal bags are identical. Nothing particularly interesting about them—they can be bought in any Standa or UPIM throughout the country."

There were two steel trays and a limb lay on each—mauve-blue flesh with a jagged tear where the severing had taken place.

"Not a very neat job," Bottone said, running a finger along the mutilated thigh. "They probably used—the people or persons who did the cutting—a professional instrument. But without skill. There are definite signs of hacking. You see?" A hurried glance in Trotti's direction.

"Could it be a woman?"

"Of course it's a woman," Bottone replied peevishly. "You can see by the depth of the thigh, the size of the feet. Varicose veins—probably in her late thirties, early forties—but not very well-preserved. The legs have been shaved—but need shaving again. Bristly."

"Of course," Trotti said humbly. "I meant something different."

"Different?"

"Could a woman have done the cutting—the butchering?"

The smell of formaldehyde in the morgue was overpowering. One wall was covered with a cabinet of large lockers. Trotti wondered how many corpses were concealed by the antiseptic steel doors.

"A woman?" Bottone looked up and with his sharp nod, the glasses slipped from his forehead onto the bridge of his nose. He looked at Trotti with the disapproval that a scientist feels for the profane. "A woman?" He turned to see what Magagna thought. Magagna was taking notes in a small leather booklet. "Yes, I suppose it's possible but rather unlikely. I can't be certain. A lot depends on the instrument. And the woman. You must give me time, Commissario. Time. And then it would still be little more than conjecture." He screwed up the pale eyes. "Why a woman?"

"Why not?"

Bottone raised his voice slightly and spoke in a querulous tone: "Is it likely? A whore—she," he gesticulated with the stethoscope towards the lifeless legs, "she was a whore and women don't normally kill whores. Not normally."

"What makes you think that she—that these legs once belonged to a prostitute?"

A knowing smile. He pushed the glasses back onto his forehead and turned to scrutinize the flesh again. "Look, look. Skin lesions—and here, you see, there are ulcers. The signs of tertiary syphilis."

"Is that proof?"

"Proof, no. But for me, experience is proof. But here, the texture of the skin. Sure signs of a poor diet, poor in fruit and vegetables. A sign that she was fairly far down the socioeconomic ladder. The shape of her ankles," he ran his nail against the instep, "here it bulges. Deformed by bad shoes, by high heels. Traces of dark red varnish on the nails. It all points to somebody who wanted to appear attractive, glamorous. It was her meal ticket."

Trotti thanked Bottone without shaking hands.

"My pleasure."

"And I'd be grateful if you could do any further research."

"As you wish—but you'll find I am right, Commissario. The woman's a whore."

Trotti nodded and with Magagna left the morgue, letting the rubber barriers beneath the door swish silently behind them. Outside, in the hospital corridor, with its well-scrubbed wooden floor, the air was hot again. It hit Trotti like a damp flannel across the face. But he shivered.

Magagna took an MS from a packet and lit it as they went down the stairs. "Ah," he said. "The real world." He turned and made a gesture with his first and smallest finger towards the morgue.

"I didn't know you were superstitious."

"I hedge my bets."

They went out into the sunshine. The two old men had disappeared; a couple of nurses went past. One was telling a joke in dialect. The other opened her mouth to laugh and then caught sight of Trotti. She moved on hurriedly.

"Check out the whorehouses. Not just in the city but also out near the barracks. You never know, it could be a frustrated kid doing military service. Ask the girls, check out with all our informants. Check even with the transvestite who hangs out near the station—he might know something. But it's possible she's not local so check again with the Carabinieri. But specify that you're looking for a prostitute."

"Nothing so far on missing persons. Neither from Milan nor from the Central computer. Pronto Intervento are deliberately cagey."

"Spadano wouldn't give you the time of day without a directive in triplicate from Rome."

"But I don't have the impression they've got anything to hide."

"Keep at it. I don't want the Carabinieri interfering—you know what they're like." He put a hand to his forehead; he was now perspiring freely. "Christ, it all happens at once. We've got sawn legs being fished out of the river and a kidnapping. And yesterday Leonardelli was on to me."

"What does he want?"

"Just that we drop everything and keep an eye on a couple of spoiled kids. A round-the-clock job and I haven't got a man to spare."

"So?"

"I've given it to Pisanelli."

Magagna laughed, a spluttering laugh that came through his nose and blew at the strands of his mustache.

"It's not funny."

"It's very funny. I like Pisanelli, he's all right. But he's not exactly the smartest man in the Squadra. He should have been a doctor or a teacher."

"He's not stupid."

Magagna looked at Trotti in silence. Then, blowing out cigarette smoke, asked, "Why all the fuss, anyway?"

"Leonardelli wants no scandal at election time."

"He's not a Communist, is he?"

"He's a survivor."

Trotti took Magagna's arm and together they crossed the hospital courtyard to where the car was parked. Magagna climbed in.

"I've got things to do," said Trotti, leaning through the open window. "And later this evening, I'd better see how he's doing, our Pisanelli. Take the car and I'll see you tomorrow."

Magagna switched on the ignition.

"One other thing. Look, until the elections—unless I tell you otherwise—I'd rather you didn't wear uniform."

Magagna looked disappointed. "Just when I've got her to iron it. You haven't noticed? The sharp creases?"

"Who irons it?"

Magagna lowered the glasses on his nose and looking at Trotti, smiled and gave him an exaggerated wink. Then the car pulled away. It took a large swing and leaving a thin, blue vapor, went through the hospital gates.

Trotti went out of the hospital; the fat porter sitting at the main gate, *L'Intrepido* on his knee, gave him a friendly wave and a large smile.

He crossed the main road and went to a tilted parasol and a large, deep, red refrigerator where a man was selling soft drinks. In scratched script across the front of the refrigerator COCA-COLA had been painted. Trotti bought a bottle.

The man placed two straws in the neck.

"Give me a paper cup."

"Paper cups cost money."

"And the bubbles make me belch."

With a closed face, the man handed him a cup; Trotti poured the dark liquid and drank. It was sweet and there was a thin rainbow of oil beneath the bursting bubbles. And a slight smell of wax.

Trotti moved away and beneath a large oak tree sat down on a concrete slab. It probably came from the nearby building site where luxury apartments were being constructed. A crane swiveled slowly against the sky.

Trotti watched the passing traffic—yellow buses, cars and the occasional ambulance, snub-nosed Fiats, turning into the main gates of the hospital. On the other side of the road, a woman was selling flowers; from time to time she sluiced down the pavement with a bucket of water.

The cup was cold in his hands.

"Commissario?"

Trotti turned. At first sight, he did not recognize the man. He looked thinner in the well-pressed white lab coat and the dark hair was hidden by a nurse's cap. He was smiling.

"I caught sight of you purely by chance. I've got to go back but I saw you coming out of the morgue. Visiting friends?"

"Dottor Clerice." Trotti stood up and they shook hands. Behind the smell of hospital antiseptic, there was still the hint of expensive eau de cologne.

"You recognize me in my disguise?" He laughed.

"You should be sleeping." Trotti looked at his watch. "Nearly four o'clock. You ought to be resting after a hard night watching the nurses work."

The young face was pale. "I haven't stopped since one o'clock this morning."

"A good day for appendices?"

"An articulated truck came off the main Milan-Genoa road; it swung right around and four cars went straight into it. It was carrying toxic gas but fortunately it didn't explode. Five major casualties—and three have died already."

Trotti could feel the chill of the morgue again. "I shouldn't have said that. I'm sorry."

Clerice shrugged. "These things happen. I imagine in your line of business you must come across a lot of gruesome sights."

Trotti had the impression that Clerice was waiting for a reaction.

The traffic hummed by; another ambulance pulled slowly through the hospital gates. And slowly the shadow of the large oak moved across the pavement, exposing the toe of his shoe to the afternoon sun.

"Can I buy you a drink?"

"Thanks." Clerice's face lightened. "Yes, thanks. I'll get it," and he went over to the refrigerator. Trotti watched him. Slightly over-weight but a good-looking young man, with an intelligent face.

"Mind if I sit beside you?"

He was not wearing any socks and Trotti noticed that the

pale ankles peeked from between the bottom of his trousers and his thick leather moccasins. He sat on the concrete slab beside Trotti. He drank through two straws.

"Commissario," he said as he placed the bottle between his feet on the asphalt pavement. "You must excuse me."

"For what?"

"May I see your identity?"

Trotti took the wallet from his jacket pocket and opened it. Clerice nodded towards the perspex and the narrow stripes of red and green.

"I'm sorry," he smiled, "but I had to be sure. I was rather rude towards you yesterday but . . ." He shrugged with one shoulder. "Well, I didn't know if could trust you."

"You can trust me."

"I hope so."

There was a pause; the two men looked at each other, Clerice's plump face in a lopsided smile.

"Collegio Sant'Antonio di Padova is a Catholic establishment," Clerice said, "and we are supposed to live in the odor of sanctity."

"Difficult."

"And I am not married." He blushed very slightly.

"Tania?"

"How did you know?" He frowned his incomprehension and then laughed. "We intend to get married. Once I've got a decent qualification and I can be sure of a job in a hospital—even in some fly-blown place in the Mezzogiorno. Tania and I are in love."

"And you share your afternoon siestas with her?"

Clerice lowered his eyes. "The concierge knows—but we have an agreement. I can get her special treatment at Gynecology." He lifted the bottle and sucked briefly at the striped straws. "You see, the Dean mustn't know. He's an old priest and he has old-fashioned ideas. If he finds out, I'll lose my place in the college. And I could never afford lodgings in the city. I must stay."

"With all the crucifixes?"

"With all the crucifixes." Clerice's cheeks were dark, he

needed a shave. He looked up. "You see, Tania did notice something the other day—something a bit strange."

"What?"

"When she was with me. I couldn't tell you that, but apparently she noticed something. I had no idea about it until I mentioned your visit to her. I saw her for a few minutes this morning—she works in obstetrics."

"What did she see?"

"A Citroën. She was looking out of the window—it must've been the day before yesterday—and she saw this car in via Darsena. It's not the sort of back street where you expect to see a large, expensive French car. An ID or a DS. And there's another thing."

"What?"

"It had a Milan license plate."

18

A SOFT SUMMER evening; the street lamps swung gently and cast their moving circles of light onto the stone slabs of Strada Nuova. A few taxis went past and some new buses, brightly lit, headed along the corso towards the edge of the city and the flat suburban fields.

Trotti had eaten at home with Pioppi; she had been quiet during the meal and then had gone through to watch an old film on television.

There were times when she and her father were close friends, and other times when she went, like this evening, into her own universe and Trotti knew that the best thing was to leave her alone.

Yet he felt depressed as he left his car outside the Questura.

The university stood out against the failing evening light. The old walls, pitted with bullet marks and the memorial to dead patriots—Abyssinia, Caporetto, the partisan war—was lit up by floodlights. A student went past on his bicycle and the lights caught him like an insect, casting his grotesque shadow onto the pitted ocher plasterwork. The Italian flag hung from its staff and moved with the evening breeze.

As he walked towards the Piazza Vittoria, Trotti's ears were assailed by the metallic noise of amplified voices. The sky had taken on the silver glow of artificial lighting.

Trotti recognized immediately the First Secretary of the Italian Socialist party. He was wearing half-frame glasses and leaned forward to speak into the microphones, placed like a bunch of flowers on the desk before him. The piazza was crowded. Serried ranks of wooden chairs, laid out in even rows upon the medieval cobbles. The faces were lit by the reflected light of the incandescent beams. There were old men with wrinkled skin and eyes that glinted ferociously. Some wore berets and one man had the deep red scarf of the old partisan tied loosely at the neck. The women stood, often in small groups, at the back of the crowd. With them, their well-fed children and grandchildren. More people watched from the long arcades that ran along the two sides of the piazza.

"Which is one more criminal act in the spiral of tension, another attack upon the basic liberties of each Italian, man, woman and child, as defined by our constitution!"

The delivery was hesitant; the First Secretary gesticulated with a closed fist while reading his note.

The applause was thunderous.

Among the audience there were young people in short-sleeved shirts and open-necked sweaters. The boys wore jeans, the girls billowing summer frocks. Several wore the red scarf.

"The Socialist party of Italy repudiates violence as a means to an end, it repudiates the tactics of tension, it repudiates all form of terrorism, whether from the Left or from the Right."

More applause. Caught in the converging circles of white light, the speaker scarcely looked at his audience while his voice boomed from a dozen well-placed speakers.

"Here, in this city, the Socialists, by giving their support to the Communists and to the mayor, Signor Mariani, have shown that the Italian people are capable of discipline, good government and social justice. Capable of throwing off the secular blackmail of the ruling classes."

There were several bars around the edge of the piazza and people were sitting on the terraces in the cool air, listening to the First Secretary or talking quietly among themselves. Heedless of the affairs of State, waiters darted to and fro, carrying their trays high above their heads or fishing for small change in their black waistcoat pockets.

Trotti looked for familiar faces; he recognized a few shop-keepers who owned premises around the piazza.

"Let us defend the Republic, let us defend its institutions with the same power of democracy that has made this city a model and an example. We shall not allow this country to be ensnared in the murderous plots of the terrorists—or in the evil machinations of the hidden interests that support them."

Trotti pushed his way through the crowd. Despite the oratory, despite the news of Communiqué Number Nine and the possibility that Moro was dead, there was an almost festive air about the public meeting.

One or two policemen stood around and there were several groups of Carabinieri. Hands behind their backs, they tapped nervously at the old-fashioned leather pouches of their belts. They watched the crowd and from time to time, looked up at the people sitting at the balconies of private houses. He recognized a civetta and, at the far end of the piazza, another unmarked dark blue Alfa Romeo with two expressionless passengers. A whipcord pointed upwards from the gleaming, dark roof. Only official cars were allowed onto the piazza.

He reached the far colonnades and walked down the lit arcade towards the Bar Duomo. A few children, taking no notice of the political speech and excited by the freedom of being up so late, zigzagged their tricycles along the paving. A little boy almost went straight into Trotti but braked in time and looked up at him with surprised, wide eyes.

Trotti went into the bar.

"Commissario!"

He turned, and looked at the tables in front of the café.

"Commissario Trotti."

The woman stood up. She had been seated at a small table and on the clean cloth in front of her there was a teapot and three cups.

"Signorina Belloni," Trotti said, smiling, and shook her cool hand. "A pleasant surprise."

She introduced him to a small, old woman who sat staring straight ahead of her, gnarled hands resting on a walking stick. "My mother."

"Pleased to meet you, signora."

The woman did not react. "I am afraid my mother is quite deaf. She is eighty-six years old."

The other person at the table was a plump, middle-aged woman with unnaturally red hair. Several gold rings were embedded in the soft flesh of her fingers. Her lipstick matched her hair and when she smiled, she revealed teeth stained with the glossy lipstick. "Signora Quaranta," she said rising with difficulty. The sides of the chair caught at her large hips. "I write poetry."

Trotti smiled.

The headmistress tapped at her bun. "Perhaps you could join us for a few minutes."

"I'm afraid I'm meeting somebody."

She placed a hand on his arm. "Please sit down—just for a few minutes. Something has happened."

He took a chair from a neighboring table and placed it between Signorina Belloni and her mother. The old lady smelled faintly of lavender water.

There was more applause from the audience and the First Secretary looked up from his notes and gave a slightly embarrassed smile, as though he did not realize that so many people had been listening to him.

"More an intellectual than a politician. Would you care for something to drink, Commissario? Some tea, perhaps?"

"Thank you, I can't stay."

The poetess smiled at him and then with an unexpectedly sharp movement, slapped her own, firm arm. "Mosquitoes."

Attached to a column there was an electric apparatus that gave off a bluish glow; mosquitoes, attracted by the light, were incinerated noisily on the electric grille.

Other mosquitoes stung his ankles.

"They breed in the rice fields," the fat lady said, "and then they come into the city to suck our blood."

Her red teeth reminded him of Dracula.

Again Signorina Belloni touched his arm. "I just wanted to tell you, Commissario, that Ermagni was at the school today. He was very noisy and he insisted upon seeing Signora Perbene. I told him that if he wanted to see her, it would have to be out of school hours." She lowered her voice. "I think he had been drinking."

"What time was this?"

"About eleven o'clock. He said some very strange things. He seems to think that it is all a plot—that his daughter has been kidnapped to spite him. And he obviously feels very guilty." She paused, "I saw the article in the paper. I must admit I was rather surprised. You had said . . ."

"I knew nothing about the article. The kidnapper telephoned the *Provincia* and then Ermagni came round in the middle of the night and woke me up."

"Strange that Anna should be so unlike her father. She is quiet and very shy whereas I am afraid he is rather excitable."

"It is a difficult time for him."

"He is a strange man—but I like him. There is about him . . ." She paused, moving her head slightly. The bright lights from the piazza were caught in her neat, white hair. "There is warmth. And I feel that he needs affection." Her hand went to her bun. "Is there any news about Anna?"

"Just that we think she is alive."

The poetess slapped at another mosquito and in doing so, nudged the table. Cold tea slopped into the saucers.

Trotti stood up. "Thank you, headmistress." He nodded towards the other two women. The poetess held out her hand, the old lady continued to stare. "And if anything else happens—anything strange—please contact me."

Signorina Belloni held his hand. "Of course, Commissario, of course."

He left her and went into the Bar Duomo.

"Buona sera, Commissario."

The widow was talking to some men; they were retired shopkeepers and local businessmen who wore neat, lightweight suits, cotton shirts and tasteful ties. They looked at Trotti as he entered and some nodded. They could not afford to be on bad terms with an officer of the PS, but Trotti knew that they did not like him. Or trust him.

The widow came towards him, placing her hand—it was slightly moist from washing the glasses—on his wrist.

"Buona sera, signora. Is there anybody in the back room?"

The customers sat on plastic chairs or along the leather bench and they talked softly. The buzz of their voices dulled the noise of the microphones in the piazza. They were playing scopone and occasionally raised their voices as they placed the brightly colored cards on the tablecloth. They were men who had no time for the Socialists and even less for the Communists who now ran the city. Thirty-five years earlier—when they were still fairly young men—they had been Fascists. They had believed in the New Roman Empire and in Mussolini's promises. Now they sat playing cards or talking about football or reading the evening paper. They had worked hard and they had made their money. Now, in the last years of their lives, they ignored the doctor's orders and drank coffee or grappa or bitter digestivi and remembered the good days that were gone forever.

"The room is free."

"Thank you. Bring me some herb tea please."

He was greeted by the image of the television reflected in the mirror—an old American film with Tyrone Power. The television set was perched on a shelf high on the wall. He stretched up and turned it off; the image dwindled into a bright, disappearing spot.

He sat down and waited.

Several minutes later, the widow brought him a pot of chamomile. Without asking, she poured the amber liquid into a cup.

"Thank you."

"You know her, don't you?"

Trotti looked up. The woman's regular features were troubled; the corners of her lips had edged downwards, revealing a genuine concern.

"Know who?"

"The child—the one they kidnapped. Her father used to work for you—before you left."

"You've got a good memory."

"What else have I got to do?"

"He is a taxi driver now. Do you ever see him?"

The widow bit her lip. "Once or twice. Sometimes he takes

tourists from the station to the fur shop." With a gesture, she indicated the far side of the piazza. "Then he comes in here. But he never talks to me. He just takes his drink and then goes. I think he is shy."

"Not necessarily."

"Is there any news of the child?" She held her hands to her body and for some reason that Trotti could not explain, he found her concern moving.

"We know that she's alive."

"I hope so. He can't be very rich, the father. The paper spoke of a ransom."

"If all goes well, he won't have anything to pay. We'll have found the kidnappers."

"The poor man."

She shook her head slowly and then left to return to her clients. Five minutes later, while Trotti was sipping at the bitter chamomile, di Bono arrived. He came through the side door.

"You're late," Trotti said.

Di Bono did not reply but sat down on the chair opposite him. He had blond, curly hair that he had allowed to grow. He wore a T-shirt beneath a windbreaker advertising American cigarettes; the logo of a camel on the breast, beside the white plastic zip. A gold St. Christopher and chain about the neck.

"Pisanelli's outside with a crowd of kids."

Kids, Trotti thought with irritation. Di Bono was a kid himself, scarcely into his twenties.

"Gracchi and Guerra are with a group of students—Left-Wing extremists, long hair, dirty. Some of them have been heckling, but so far nothing from our two friends."

"Is Pisanelli watching them?"

"Yes—unless he's fallen asleep." He paused and with his finger—he wore a steel identity bracelet about his wrist—di Bono wrote invisible letters on the table. "He thinks other people are watching Gracchi."

"Other people?"

Di Bono shrugged. "The Nucleo Politico."

"It's possible. Whatever happens, I don't want them realizing you're there. I don't think two of you are enough. I'll see if I can get help from the Squadra."

"Good. It's tiresome." Di Bono smiled and Trotti could not help thinking that he looked more like a criminal—a petty criminal, a thief of old women's handbags, or a shoplifter—than a policeman. He had the narrow face of an animal, cunning and stupid at the same time.

Di Bono pulled out a notebook. "Here's a rundown on Gracchi for today. He spent most of the morning at the university. In the main courtyard, there's a flight of steps up to the main library. He was sitting there, talking. Some friends put up a long, handwritten poster, signed Autonomia Studentesca."

"What was it about?"

"University exams or something. Then in the afternoon, he was at his place—with Guerra."

"Doing what?"

"I can guess." Di Bono gave a vulpine grin. "Pisanelli quite fancies her—in his own way. He's got a soft spot for intellectuals." He added, "Especially when they've got big tits."

"What's her background?"

"Guerra? According to the dossier, she's been involved with quite a lot of political movements—on the left, of course. Once was a card-carrying Communist. More recently has moved further left—Lotta Continua, Prima Linea and a few specifically local things. Mainly feminists. There was a time when she claimed to be a lesbian." He laughed, the young face breaking into easy wrinkles. "She's obviously grown out of that."

"You had better be getting back. Phone in at midnight—I'll have fixed up a replacement for both of you. Check back tomorrow morning. And you can tell Pisanelli . . ."

The side door came open and Pisanelli appeared. "Thank God you're there." He was wearing his suede jacket but had put a red partisan scarf about his neck. "Just got a message through on the radio." He was slightly out of breath and his stooping shoulders heaved as he spoke. "The Ermagni child . . ."

"What about her?" Trotti rose to his feet.

"They've found her—at the bus station."

19

ONLY A FEW electric lights had been left on and they illumi-
nated the silent forms of the stationary buses. The air was warm
and heavy with the smell of oil. The man pulled the sliding door
shut—it folded like a concertina—and Trotti approached the
small crowd.

Anna was hidden by a group of people standing in a pool of
light. A man was crouching; a woman held a glass of water in
her hand.

The man stood up. "Commissario." It was Magagna; he
looked tired but gave a thin smile.

"I thought you were at home."

"I was sleeping," he said and shrugged. He looked strange
out of uniform. "So they phone me." He took Trotti's arm and
directed him towards Anna. The crowd—employees of the bus
company—men in blue shirts and matching trousers—drew
aside.

Anna was sitting on a chair. Her head lolled forward and her
eyes were hidden by the fringe of dark hair; her feet only just
touched the concrete floor.

"She came in on the bus from Genoa."

A large woman detached herself from the crowd; while speaking with Trotti, she tried to force the glass of water into Anna's
hand. "On the nine o'clock bus."

"When did she arrive here?"

The woman looked surprised. "At nine o'clock."

"It's almost midnight, signora."

Her voice was truculent. "The poor child was sleeping."

"You should've woken her."

"We tried to, of course we tried to." She turned about, looking for support from the men. "Giovanni, we tried to wake her, didn't we?"

Giovanni was a narrow man with drooping shoulders and a drooping mustache. He wore neatly pressed trousers and there were large damp patches at the armpits of his shirt. He held a leather satchel.

"Yes," he said. "We tried to wake her but she was sleeping."

"You called a doctor?"

"Not at first." The woman raised her broad shoulders. "We thought she was tired so we let her sleep. There are a couple of beds in the office. There was no harm in that." Her hair had been dyed an unnatural golden yellow; the roots were black.

"We let her sleep," Giovanni nodded.

"So when did she wake up?"

"Half an hour ago. We've called for the doctor—but I managed to wake her." She glanced at her hand and its grey, dirty fingers. "I slapped her, you understand. Just enough to bring her round. But it was getting late and it's high time that I went home. My husband doesn't like me home late." She looked at Trotti. "Beppo recognized her."

"Beppo?"

"That's me." Another driver, small and wiry, with a friendly face, humorous wrinkles at the eyes. "I came in on the Piacenza run. I saw the girl sleeping and I recognized her. I used to know Ermagni." The corner of his mouth implied that Ermagni was not a happy memory. He shook his head. "Poor little girl."

Trotti crouched in front of the child. Her eyelids were heavy and there was no flicker of recognition. She was still half-asleep. Her body was slumped forward and she had difficulty in keeping her head upright.

"Get an ambulance—quickly."

Magagna was standing beside him. "It's coming."

For a while, nobody moved, nobody said anything. Trotti stared into the young, drugged eyes and he was aware of the smell of spilled gasoline. Then in the distance he heard the wail of the ambulance.

He stood up.

20

"No."

Trotti was driving, one hand on the steering wheel the other holding the door. His elbow leaned through the open window and caught the breeze. Saturday morning, seven o'clock; the streets were empty as he drove through the city center. A vigile urbano stepped into Strada Nuova; he wore a pudding bowl crash helmet and his large motorcycle was parked diagonally across the road. He was about to flag Trotti to a halt and then he caught sight of the sticker fixed to the windscreen. He saluted; he was wearing lace-up leather boots that went almost to his knees.

The bars and shops were beginning to open.

"I looked for you but you weren't at home and nobody knew where you were."

Ermagni sat on the back seat. His eyes were bloodshot and he had not shaved. But there was hope in his eyes. He raised his body from the dirty upholstery. "I was asleep. At home. I had been drinking." He added lamely, "Too much, perhaps."

"I thought you were on nights."

"Not always." He clicked his teeth. "Are you sure she's all right?"

"She's still suffering from the sleeping pills—but otherwise she's okay."

"Sleeping pills?"

Trotti looked at the man's eyes in the car mirror. It was

difficult to believe that this was the man whose wedding he had been to only a few years earlier. His face was drawn and the skin had taken on an unhealthy pallor. The uncombed hair revealed a fast receding hair line. "She's sleeping them off."

Ermagni hesitated. "Did they—have they . . . ? Is she, well . . . ?"

Their eyes met in the mirror. "You must ask the doctors."

They pulled over the railway bridge just as the Milan train came into the station; Trotti caught sight of the station master with his blue peaked cap and red baton.

The hospital porter recognized Trotti as they pulled into the courtyard and he nimbly saluted. The flowerbeds were still damp with the morning dew.

Trotti parked the car and they went into the main hospital building, up a flight of stairs and along an endless green corridor. Trotti's legs ached; he had slept for just over four hours. One of the doctors—a young man with stainless steel glasses and a matching stethoscope—had unlocked a whitewashed room and he had slept on the high bed that smelled of chlorine until Magagna had come to wake him at six.

"This way."

They went up some more stairs and then through two pivoting doors, along a dark corridor until they came to a door where a policeman sat. He was staring at his shoes—they were spotlessly clean—and Trotti had to shake him by the shoulder before he came awake. He jumped to his feet and saluted clumsily.

"The girl?"

"She is sleeping."

"Lucky girl."

The policeman took a key from his hip pocket and was about to unlock the door.

"Wait."

"I want to see my daughter," Ermagni said.

"The doctor will be along at seven thirty."

"I must see her. Let me touch her. She's my daughter."

"I know and that is why we haven't notified the grandparents yet. I wanted to speak with you first."

"Let me see her."

"In a minute. Sit down."

He pushed a wooden chair towards Ermagni and the large man allowed himself to fall onto the imitation leather seat. Tears had formed at the corner of his eyes. Without looking at Trotti he asked, "Is she safe?"

"Don't be stupid, of course she is safe." He placed a comforting arm on Ermagni's sleeve. "Now tell me, has anybody been in touch with you? Has anybody contacted you?"

Ermagni shook his head.

"No messages? Nobody's approached you?"

"No."

"You're sure."

"I was asleep. Last night I went to bed early and I didn't wake up until you arrived." He continued to shake his large head. Strands of spiky dark hair stood up on the back of his scalp.

"Do you have any friends in the area of Alessandria?"

A look of surprise. "Alessandria? I've never been there."

"In the vicinity? Do you ever go that way? Friends, acquaintances? Do you ever take your taxi out that far?"

"Why should I?"

"Answer my question."

"I've told you—I never go there."

"Anna was on the Genoa-Milan bus and she got on it yesterday at about seven o'clock. At Albana—which, as you know, is just into the Province of Alessandria. The driver says that she was waiting at the bus stop with a man. A well-dressed man, with mustache and glasses. He paid for Anna's fare and then got off."

"Albana's off the main road."

"That's right. The bus makes a short detour to drop off passengers."

Ermagni shrugged. "I've been to Genoa often enough—I sometimes get customers who can't be bothered to wait for the train—it's usually in the afternoon when there are no trains for a couple of hours. But I don't think I've ever stopped in Albana."

"Or in the immediate area?"

He ran his hand across his forehead. "When Anna was little,

when she was very little, we used to go up into the hills on Sundays. For a picnic and a day out." He brushed a tear from the corner of his eye. "Further to the east. But coming back, rather than take the slow roads, I'd sometimes head for the autostrada. We'd get on it at the Albana intersection." He paused. "In those days, the autostrada wasn't expensive."

"Where'd you go for your picnics?"

"Anywhere—nowhere in particular." He was about to say something, but there was the sound of shoes on the corridor floor and he looked up. The doctor appeared from around a corner. He was bald and wore white shoes.

"Can I see my daughter?" Ermagni had stood up.

The doctor smiled. "But of course," and he stretched out his arm towards Ermagni's large, stooping back.

"Is she all right?" Trotti asked.

"No problem," he said breezily, nodding towards Trotti. "No problem at all. She has not been touched, I can assure you. All the tests are negative—we had to check of course, even though there was no sign of blood or bruising. No problem." He gave Ermagni a large, professional smile. "She'll be a bit comatose for the next twelve hours or so. She's still under the effect of the sleeping drugs. What I don't understand is how she managed to get on the bus unaided."

"The bus driver says that a man helped her; she was unsteady on her feet."

The doctor looked at Trotti with interest. Then to Ermagni, "But her system'll soon clean itself out. Have faith in the human body." He nodded to the uniformed policeman, who, after a quick glance for approval from Trotti, unlocked the green door.

Ermagni pushed his way past and in a strange, ambling run, headed towards the bed.

A vase of bright roses had been placed by the bedside and the red and yellow petals were lit up by a shaft of morning sunlight.

21

THE QUESTURA SEEMED almost empty.

They ate breakfast in silence. Magagna had phoned the bar opposite, and ten minutes later, the thin-shouldered boy, his white waiter's jacket mysteriously dirty even this early in the morning, had brought over the tray; a pot of coffee and a pot of milk. It was not yet nine o'clock; another hot day. The pigeons were already cooing among themselves.

Wisps of steam rose from the coffee pot. Magagna, who was sitting in the canvas chair that he had positioned close to the desk, dipped the end of a croissant into his bowl of coffee and then, like a juggler with a cricked neck, brought the food to his mouth. He ate noisily; coffee dribbled on his chin.

Trotti felt feverish and his eyes ached; but the food, croissants, rolls and butter, made him feel better. While eating he looked at the papers, *Corriere della Sera* and *Provincia Padana*. In neither was there any mention of Anna. The *Corriere* published a photograph of the Red Brigades' Communiqué Number Nine. He read the political jargon and snorted.

There was a portrait of the Socialist First Secretary on the front page of the *Provincia*. He was reading a speech and looked like an absent-minded professor with his half-frame glasses. In the circle of light cast by the photographer's flash, there were several local dignitaries, including the mayor, Gaetano Mariani.

Magagna leaned forward and poured more coffee into his

bowl. "It doesn't make sense." He nudged at the thin-framed sunglasses. He needed a shave; his civilian clothes were grimy and crumpled after a night at the hospital. "Kidnapped and then returned safe and sound two days later . . . without a ransom."

Trotti did not reply immediately; he stared at his left hand that lay motionless on the front page of the *Corriere*. He frowned, trying to concentrate, trying to getting his mind to work. His vision was slightly blurred. He drank some more coffee.

There was dampness at the end of Magagna's mustache. "If they wanted money—if that's why they kidnapped her—there was no reason to release her."

Trotti looked up. "You remember Martini in Naples. A case of mistaken identity. It's happened before." He shrugged, drank more coffee. "Ermagni's not rich. Anna was perhaps mistaken for another child. Another girl whose parents are a lot richer."

Magagna clicked his tongue. "Via Darsena's not the sort of place where rich kids go. And anyway," he said, looking over the rim of the bowl, "that wouldn't explain why Anna went with a man, apparently of her own accord, when we know that she's a shy kid. And when they kidnapped her and they phoned the *Provincia*—it's on the tape—the man knew her name. He knew all about her."

"He could have got information from Anna herself." He paused. "It's possible that Ermagni's richer than he admits—but I don't think so. Where would he have got his money from? More likely that the kidnappers wanted to put pressure on the grandparents. They're not poor and since the mayor closed the city to traffic, there has been a boom in the bars and restaurants. More shoppers coming from out of town. And the San Siro has the added advantage of being right on the edge of the pedestrian zone."

"You think somebody is trying to pressure Rossi, perhaps? Pressure him into selling?"

"It's a possibility."

"But it doesn't explain why they telephoned the *Provincia*. Whether they wanted money or simply to put pressure on Rossi, they would have wanted to observe a certain amount of secrecy." Magagna went on, "And twenty million, by today's standards, is nothing. Peanuts. Even Paul Getty would have paid that."

"Telephoning the newspaper certainly doesn't make sense."

"None of it makes sense." Magagna heaved another dripping horn of a croissant into his mouth and, speaking through a mouthful of wet dough, added, "No sense at all."

Trotti rubbed his hands against his face. His voice muffled, he asked, "What did Anna say?"

"You were there. You heard."

"Later, when the doctor put her to bed. Did she say any more?"

The younger man shook his head. "You heard everything, both last night and this morning. She couldn't remember much, poor kid. A woman who was nice to her and a man who was gruff."

"It was with him that she left the gardens?"

"She couldn't remember the gardens. Nothing at all. But she remembered that it was the same man who took her to the bus stop at Albana. He gave her sweets, she said—probably sleeping pills. And she never saw the woman because they put a bandage round her head and she couldn't see a thing. They kept her in bed and most of the time she slept. The doctors reckon they must have pumped her full of sleeping pills and it was when she was in a semi-comatose state that the man took her to the bus."

"Why did she leave the gardens?"

"You heard her; she couldn't remember anything. The only memory she has—apart from sleeping—is the angels. But the doctors say that this is quite normal—an illusory effect of mild drugs, probably due to a ringing in the ears. Something to do with blood pressure."

Trotti said, "It could have been a radio. Or perhaps somebody singing. Angels, and on the tape there was the sound of bells."

"She could've been kidnapped by her recording angel and taken to the pearly gates of heaven. Perhaps Saint Peter put her on the bus at Albana."

The phone rang.

Trotti picked up the receiver.

"Papa?"

He smiled. "Pioppi. You've just woken up."

"You didn't come home last night and I'd prepared some gnocchi."

"We've found the child."

"Congratulations." Her voice was distant. "It's Saturday, Papa, and you did promise me—you remember—that you'd come with me to church tonight. I am singing in the choir."

"I'll try—I promise you I'll try; but I am busy."

"It's a long time since we've been to church together, Papa, you're always busy. But without you, I'm lonely here. Alone in the house, without you and without Mama."

"No news?" he asked, almost against his will and trying to keep his voice normal, matter of fact. "Nobody's phoned?"

"No, Papa."

An awkward silence.

"Please come, Papa. It's tonight at six o'clock. And you've never been to Our Lady of Guadalupe—not since they've rebuilt it."

"I'll try," he said. "But I am very busy."

"I want you to come, Papa."

In the ensuing silence, Trotti placed his hand over the mouthpiece and told Magagna to get a roadmap. "Of this province," he whispered, "and the neighboring provinces, too."

"Are you there, Papa?"

"I am busy, Pioppi my love. Something has come up. But you know I love you. I'll try to be home at six."

"Earlier. You will have to change, you will have to get ready."

"I'll be on time."

"You promise?"

"I promise."

Softly his daughter said, "All right, Papa," and she hung up before he could say anything else.

"Have you got those maps, Magagna? Look over there, in the filing cabinet—it's not locked."

The light on the telephone began to flicker and again the bell rang.

It was Gino.

"Spadano phoned twice yesterday, Commissario. He says he wants to see you, that it's important. He wanted to know whether you were conducting enquiries into the disappearance of the Ermagni girl."

"What did you tell him?"

"That I know nothing about what you are doing. That it is not my job."

"Good."

"And," Gino resumed (and Trotti could hear his real voice, not the metallic reproduction of the telephone, coming through the sliding panel of wood that separated Trotti from the reception desk), "he said that Pronto Intervento know nothing about the gypsy."

Trotti was surprised. Slowly he said, "I see."

"He insists on seeing you, Commissario. He said something about collaboration."

Trotti gave a dry laugh. "Thanks," he said. "Thanks, Gino," and he hung up.

Magagna had pushed aside the tray and the newspapers and had opened a road map on the desk.

"Albana's here—on the edge of the Province, just in Alessandria. A man and a girl at the bus stop—it's not much of a lead."

Trotti no longer felt tired. He poured himself a bowl of black coffee—it was now almost cold—and drank quickly. He felt well, almost excited.

"Angels and bells, Magagna." He smiled. "Singing and a bell tower. Let's go into the hills and see if we can find a church and a choir."

22

TROTTI DROVE.

Along the city streets he noticed the new posters: VOTE FOR GAETANO MARIANI—YOUR MAYOR. The photograph, repeated along the walls and billboard in a grainy black and white, flattered the mayor. He looked younger and healthier, Trotti thought, and a lot thinner. The smile was reassuring, the eyes intelligent and wise, the face kind. On some of the posters, the red hammer and sickle had been overprinted and the accompanying letters, PCI.

"The Communists must have paid a lot for that," Trotti said over his shoulder as they reached the traffic lights in viale Cremona. There was no reply. Magagna was already asleep; his unshaven chin had sunk to his chest and he looked, with his dark sunglasses, like a crumpled locust.

Trotti could have taken the autostrada but he was afraid that, like Magagna, he might fall asleep on the fast highway. It was Saturday morning: there would be the normal convoy of articulated trucks, panting on the uphill sections and lethal as they came downhill, carried forward by the momentum of the Apennines.

He took the small, provincial road and headed south. There was hardly any traffic. A few fishermen, returning on their motorcycles from an early morning at the river; they held their rods like aerials and their legs appeared deformed by the protruding wader boots.

They came to the Po and the Alfetta shook as the front wheels hit the planks of the wooden bridge. An old Bailey bridge, built by the Americans in 1945, it had never been replaced. The planks rattled angrily and then the car was back on the soft tarmac. It was a clear, hot day and already the hills could be seen standing out against the mist of the horizon. The distant patchwork of vineyards and then, above them, the dark mantle of pine forest. Trotti whistled softly; a tune that he could not place. Donizetti, perhaps.

It was another half hour before they started to climb, winding between the vineyards, green and neatly terraced. Perhaps because of the fresh air coming through the open window or perhaps because of a feeling that he was returning to his home territory, Trotti felt less tired. His eyes no longer ached.

The cherry trees were still in blossom, as though they had been caught in a freak snow storm. Forgotten smells that brought back his childhood came through the window and Trotti felt an uncharacteristic sense of nostalgia. Over thirty years earlier he had left these hills and, as he drove, he told himself that one day he would return forever. He would keep bees, he would make his own wine, perhaps keep a few chickens and some cattle. Pioppi would be married by then; she would come at the weekends, bringing the grandchildren.

Pioppi. Her real name was Lucia and neither he nor Agnese could remember where she got her nickname from. Somehow it seemed to suit her; when she was seven years old and plump and she wore ribbons in her hair. But now she was growing up. She did not have any boyfriends—or so Trotti believed—but he knew that quite soon the time would come when she would leave him. Trotti had always wanted children; but after Pioppi, Agnese had said no. She criticized him, she said that he was a man and that he did not know how a woman suffered in childbirth. She even refused his suggestion of adopting a child. "I have my career to think about."

Trotti would have liked a son.

His ears were beginning to pop as the car came to the top of the pass and beneath him, to his left, stretching away from the smooth black ribbon of the road, there was a pine forest. A flat, red-brick building was the university research center. To his right, just perceptible on the misty horizon, nearly ninety kilometers away, he saw the grey glitter of the Mediterranean. The wind whistled against the car and he turned, following the green signs indicating the autostrada. The smell of pine was sharp and clean.

Twenty minutes later he was back in the valley on the outskirts of Albana. He went under the cement bridge of the motorway with its graffiti in praise of Juventus or some local team. When he was a boy, Albana had been a village—a few houses along either side of the main road, stables, some dusty shops and a busy market every Tuesday.

Sometimes he used to come with his mother in the brown train; that was before the war, before the Germans blew up the line. There was no longer any train, only a blue bus for those who did not have their own car. Now the old church was hidden by new blocks of apartments, painted red and pastel green. The narrow, dusty streets were cluttered with cars and, in the early afternoon, teenagers were scurrying backwards and forwards, deliberately skidding on their Vespas and "Ciao" mopeds.

The mountain river had dried up; along the stony bed, with on one side the open countryside and on the other the squalid backs of the old, stone houses, the water trickled in a silvery snake. Everywhere there was the litter of old prams and rusting, upturned cars. A few young children were playing cowboys and Indians.

Magagna yawned noisily.

"Where are we?"

Without answering, Trotti took the map from the glove compartment and got out of the car. He crossed the dusty square. Earth and stones rasped at his shoes. The wreaths at the foot of the war memorial had withered. The air was still and hot.

At the corner of the square, there was a petrol station; two pumps stood like forgotten aliens beneath a stout pillar and a yellow and black sign; the six-legged, fire breathing animal advertised AGIP PETROL. In a uniform of the same yellow and black, sitting at a distance from his pumps, a peaked cap pushed back on his head and a comic between his hands, was a young man.

"A good restaurant?"

The man had been watching Trotti since the dark blue Alfetta had parked on the edge of the square. Now he just sat with his mouth open.

"Is there a good restaurant in Albana?"

The young man's mouth continued to gape. He raised an oil-smeared hand from the comic and pointed down the street, his own eyes following the indicated direction with interest, as though the pointing hand belonged to someone else.

"Thanks."

The dull staring eyes followed Trotti until he was lost to sight round the corner of a house.

Magagna caught up with Trotti. "Lively place."

Together they walked along the main street.

A dog barked somewhere and the sound of a radio being played came from behind closed wooden blinds. A car went past—a dilapidated Fiat 600, gnawed by rust and followed by an eddy of dust.

"We"ll have something to eat first."

Magagna said, "We've only just had breakfast."

"Time flies when you're sleeping."

The restaurant, La Campagnola, was at the next corner.

They went in. It was cool inside after the dusty heat of the street. The air was heavy with the smell of rancid wine and yesterday's cigarettes. Two young men were playing billiards at a large table in the middle of the room. They watched the new-comers while chalking their cues. One placed a cigarette in an ashtray and returned to the game with frowning concentration.

In the corner, beneath a tank filled with a stuffed fish, a bulbous jukebox glowed with orange and mauve lights; the glass was smeared and the titles hardly visible beneath the surface.

Trotti and Magagna sat down at a table and the Commissario opened the map out on the green baize. He stared at the map without speaking. Magagna sat opposite him and yawned, revealing his tongue and gold fillings. He then lit a cigarette and inhaled, letting the blue-grey smoke curl from his nostrils. He stroked his mustache.

Not looking up, Trotti said, "You could give up smoking."

A girl approached the table. Her hands behind her back, she said, "Signori?"

"We would like some ham—local ham. Some olives, some cheese and some wine—all local."

The girl nodded.

"Red wine, that is."

She nodded again, her face expressionless and walked away.

Magagna's eyes followed her and the gentle movement of her hips.

"Very young—and no ankles. But a nice little body."

Trotti took no notice. He was using a small pencil to make rings on the map.

"Of course we can't be sure of the radius. It's quite likely that they brought Anna here deliberately to confuse us. But it is something to go on. It doesn't make sense. According to Clerice they've got a car. Why should they want to run the risk of being recognized by putting Anna on the bus here? They could just as well have dropped her off somewhere in the city. During the night, nobody would've seen them."

"Exactly," Magagna said, his eyes now watching the girl as she returned from the kitchen. She walked in small, rapid steps, her rubber sandals flip-flopping on the floor. She set a large sheet of paper over the green baize and placed a knife and fork in front of each man.

"The raw material is there but it could do with dressing up."

Trotti said, "She can't be much older than seventeen."

"A good age. It's then that they start getting interested in the good things of life."

The girl returned with a large dish of prosciutto, which she set on the table. The bottle of wine she put between her legs and with a gleaming steel bottle opener expertly removed the cork. She did not smile; her face was motionless. Her features were pale but regular; her mousy hair was parted in the middle and pulled into two plastic clips.

"Thank you," Trotti said.

He no longer felt tired. He ate hungrily while Magagna prodded at the small plate of olives. The wine was sweet and dark; there was something reassuring about the full red color. Trotti filled the glasses to the brim.

"Good ham."

Magagna did not agree. "One day, Commissario, I will take you to a little restaurant in the Abruzzi, not far from l'Aquila, and there you will eat ham . . ." He did not finish the sentence; instead he kissed his fingers in appreciation.

Trotti smiled and helped himself to a slice of cheese.

Around the walls, interspersed between calendars and posters advertising films that were to be—or had been—shown at the town's cinema, there were several fish. Stuffed trophies in waterless green tanks.

Magagna followed Trotti's glance. "And I'll take you to a stream—I used to go there as a boy—where you can catch trout. This long." With his hands, he made an exaggerated claim.

"Only of course," Magagna went on, "there's no fish there now. Ten years ago they built a fertilizer factory upstream and now all the fish are dead."

"I hope she's all right."

"Who?" Magagna asked, his fork poised in mid-air.

"Anna Ermagni."

"Of course she's all right." He placed an olive in his mouth and chewed. "They didn't touch her."

"But her relationship with her father is strange. On the tape, it's quite clear she doesn't like her father. It's not normal."

"Her age." Magagna rubbed his mustache, put down his fork and took his cigarette from a battered ashtray that had once advertised *Fernet Branca Liquore*. "A difficult age—and her mother's just died. But she'll grow out of it."

Trotti laughed. "What do you know about children? You're not even married."

"Don't have to be married to have children."

Trotti raised an eyebrow.

"Seven brothers and sisters. You forget that I grew up in

Pescara. Seven brothers and sisters and probably as many more that my father wouldn't admit to." A vaguely obscene gesture. "We have hot blood where I come from." He turned away and as though to prove his point, he stared at the girl who now stood idle behind the counter, propping herself on the zinc bar and staring in front of her.

"The same age as Pioppi," Trotti remarked.

"I haven't seen her for some time. How is she?"

Trotti smiled. "Still too young for you." But there was a glint of hardness in his eye. "I must get back in time to take her to church."

"And your wife? How is she?"

"Agnese?" He made an open gesture with the hand that held his fork. "When we were here ten years ago, she wanted to get away. She found everything so provincial. When I was transferred to Bari she was over the moon; but within six months she hated the place. I didn't like it much either, but I had my job. She was out most of the day, playing bridge or going to the yacht club. She had friends, she was never lonely but she hated it. Wanted to come back."

"The Mezzogiorno is special. They're different, they're unreliable, the southerners."

"Pescara is not the South?"

Behind his sunglasses, Magagna seemed genuinely offended. "Pescara is Central Italy. We were never invaded by the Arabs or the Spanish. We are European."

"Now my wife is fed up here. She wants to go to Bologna, she says. Somewhere more exciting and less provincial."

"She's right. The city is provincial."

"And Pescara?"

"It's a city, a real city. They've spoilt it with the long esplanades of skyscrapers like something in America. But beautiful even so. The sea, the long, sandy beach. And girls—there is no one who can beat Pescarese girls."

"Of course."

"Commissario. Your wife is right. I'd rather live in my own city, with its sprawling new suburbs and its streets snarled with traffic, its whores that line the road at nights and all the poor peasants who have come from the countryside to look for a job—I prefer all that to this provincial, stuck-up city. Arrogant. A town of shopkeepers and lawyers. A town that pretends to be proud of its theater and its university and its historic churches, but in fact all it cares about is making money. A town of money-makers who go to bed early. It votes Communist but in its stony little heart—and in its wallet—it is grasping and indifferent. A town without a soul, Commissario, a hardworking, provincial little city. Give me Pescara any day. Far from the foggy plain of Lombardy; pine trees, sandy beaches and the smell of the Adriatic."

When they had finished the ham and the cheese and when they had emptied the dark bottle of wine, the girl came over and placed a scrawled bill on the table. Trotti paid. "One other thing," he said, placing his hand on her arm—she had dark black hairs that ran in neat parallels across the pale flesh. "We're looking for a church."

"A church?" She looked unhappy. "You'd better ask the manager."

"This place is full of cretins," Magagna whispered as the girl hurried off, her shoes flapping on the ground, towards the kitchens. "Perhaps there's something in the water."

She came back a few minutes later accompanied by a large man in a dark suit and brown shoes. She led him to the table like a road accident victim leading a policeman to the scene of the crash.

"Signori?" A glint of gold teeth.

Trotti showed his identification.

The man visibly paled. Brusquely he turned to the girl and made a motion of dismissal. She returned to her place behind the bar where she stared intently into the air.

"The ham was excellent."

The man gave an ingratiating smile while his hands wiped nervously at his trousers. "You are very kind." He nodded sideways and sat down slowly on a wooden chair beside Trotti. He had a large belly that swelled out beneath the dark fabric of his trousers; the leather belt unsuccessfully attempted to keep the swelling back, but it pushed from either side of the narrow strip of crocodile leather. He sat with his legs apart and his hands on his knees.

"How can I help you?" His forehead was damp with perspiration.

"We're looking for a choir."

The man puffed his cheeks and looked about him with offended dignity. "This is a restaurant, signori."

Magagna gave Trotti a worried glance.

"We're trying to locate a choir because if we can find it, it might be of use in our enquiries." He added, more softly, "A case of kidnapping."

"What sort of choir? I know nothing about choirs." The dark eyes looked intently at Trotti.

"A church choir in this area that probably practices during the week."

Magagna added, "And somewhere where there are bells. Church bells."

"Ah," said the man and he sat back in his chair. "Strange." He scratched his ear. He was probably about fifty years old and was almost bald. His nose had the same shining, greasy texture as his dark suit. "There used to be a church here with a choir. But now they use records. Young people—they don't go to church any more. A shame. Not that I'm devout, of course. But it's wrong. The young people today, they've got everything but they are not grateful. They've got no time for church." He scratched his ear again. "A choir that practices during the week. Bells." He looked at Magagna, then back at Trotti. "In one of the villages, perhaps."

"Or in the hills?"

"In the villages. You need young boys for a choir. All the young people have left the villages. They go to Milan or Genoa for work. The villages are dying, they are full of old people. Who wants to spend his life working in the fields when you can earn twice as much in the factories—and when you've got independence? The hills are empty. Bells, you say?"

"Bells," Magagna repeated and very slowly, like a worried doctor, he removed his sunglasses.

"Not in the hills. There are no choirs there. The young have all left. Independence, they want independence. They go to the big cities"—he threw a hurried look at the girl—"where nobody knows who you are, where you can do what you like. I don't know. Bells?"

"And a choir."

"Well, I don't know. Unless . . ."

"Unless what?" Magagna was leaning forward in his chair, his glasses dangling in one hand, his young face only a few centimeters from the man's flabby face, "Unless what?"

"It's only a guess."

"What?"

"Well, if you take the road on the left as you head south— left, mind, not right or you'll land up on the autostrada—if you take that road and follow it as it winds upwards, following the signposts—the yellow ones, they were put there by the Ufficio Provinciale del Turismo, a real waste of money . . ."

"Well?"

"You follow the road for twenty-five kilometers and you come to Tarzi."

Trotti nodded.

"Just before you get to Tarzi, on your right, there's a convent."

"Of course," Trotti said, standing up. "Of course, Santa Roberta."

The fat man nodded and smiled hesitantly.

"Why didn't I think of it before?" Trotti slapped his forehead with the palm of his hand. Then picking up the map, he thanked the proprietor, placing a hand on the shoulder of his shiny suit.

"And the ham was excellent."

Trotti left, followed by Magagna, who replaced his sunglasses before stepping out into the street.

The billiard players and the fat man watched them leave; the girl continued to stare at some private horizon.

23

UNLIKE ALBANA, TARZI had hardly changed since Trotti's childhood.

It was as he remembered it. It nestled, a small, forgotten town, between the Apennine slopes. The church tower rose and like a grey finger pointed out the cloudless sky.

"When I was ten," Trotti said, leaning forward to turn off the radio, "I came here with my cousin Anna Maria. I cycled on a bicycle lent to me by her brother Sandro—he's an important doctor now at the hospital in Brescia. In those days—it was just at the outbreak of war—the roads weren't surfaced and you had to be careful of getting a puncture."

Magagna drove, an arm resting against the door frame. Without taking the cigarette from his mouth, he said, "These hills—I wouldn't like to climb up them on an old bike. A strong girl, your cousin."

"To own a bike of my own." Trotti shook his head. "That was my dream. The freedom to be able to escape." He paused. "Later, after the war, I bought a Vespa. I had it for ten years and it was with it that I courted my wife—she was a student at the university. She used to ride side-saddle—all the girls did in those days. Then later, as the money came in we bought a car—a little Fiat. Then a bigger one when Pioppi was born." He shook his head again. "My first love. You know, I don't need a car and I could get by without one. Ugly, expensive and dangerous. But a bicycle. Nobody can build bicycles like the Italians. It was an old Legnano—I can remember it—with slightly buckled wheels. I had to stand on the pedals to get up any hill. And sometimes like Anna Maria I had to get off and push it. Then when my cousin went off to war he left the bike with me. Perhaps that was the happiest day of my life."

"And Anna Maria?"

"My cousin? She went to university and there she met a foreigner and got married. A Dutchman. She lives in Amsterdam now."

"Anything to get away from the hills." Magagna grinned and threw his cigarette out of the window. "And this convent?"

"A couple of kilometers south of Tarzi. There." Trotti pointed. "You can see the roof from here. Along the ridge where the two hills appear to meet."

They went through Tarzi and followed the winding black road that went uphill between the small fields towards the convent.

The convent had once been completely isolated, cut off from the rest of the world and looking down upon it with disapproval. It was here—or so the tradition went—that Dante had spent a night in his flight from Florence. Now modernity had begun to encroach upon the convent's independence. There was a hotel and a couple of hundred meters down the road a few shops selling souvenirs and Kodak film. Newly built villas stood in various clearings of the wooded slopes, their flat roofs and painted blinds out of keeping with the local architecture.

"The Milanese," Trotti said. "They leave the countryside to make their money in the city and then they come back to the hills bringing the ugliness of Sesto San Giovanni or Rho. They buy the land cheap from the peasants and then they put up their monstrosities. Look." He pointed at a house, built in Spanish American style, with a patio and white plastered colonnades. The red earth at its foundations was a wound in the slope above the convent. "Of course the mayor lets them build—even if there is no water or drainage or electricity. The village mayor and the local inhabitants are only too happy for the work that building these villas brings. And anyway, the local people hate their own land. They don't care about the way these villas spoil the country. They want to get away, too, get away from the soil that has kept them prisoner for centuries. They want to go to the city to get rich."

"Like you."

"I had no choice. When I was young, there was not enough food to eat. There was a war on and there was no mechanization. At harvest time, we couldn't go to school; we had to help our parents in the fields. Things have changed. When my father was young, he worked for a kilo of bread a day. Now there's a decent wage for a man's work."

"You heard what the man in the restaurant said. The young leave as soon as they can. They can't stand the life."

"Because they don't know what the life is like in the factories."

The car came to the top of the hill.

The convent Santa Roberta was in a clearing, its tiles of red and pink partially hidden by a row of high cypress trees, whose tops moved with the wind. Opposite there was the hotel, its name in sculpted yellow letters. One or two cars—local registrations—were parked in the shade of a couple of trees.

Magagna parked the car and switched off the engine; the sound of the wind seemed loud; the mountain air was fresh and whipped at their ears. There was the sound of crickets, their monotonous and interrupted song competing with the wind.

"I think we've come to the right place," Magagna said and Trotti smiled briefly. "We've found our angels." There was a distinct sound of women singing.

A few people were sitting on the hotel terrace. Although the sun was shining, the air was cool because of the wind. One woman, her horse-like teeth caught in an ice cream, wore a heavy cardigan. A child in a sailor's hat and white short trousers was playing with a colored ball.

Somewhere on the far side of the valley a bird began to sing, and in reply, another bird, much closer, gave an answering song.

They entered the hotel; the smell of boiled milk and bleach. A man was sitting behind the long bar; he was reading a newspaper balanced on his knee.

"Commissario Trotti, Pubblica Sicurezza."

He lowered the paper. "Yes?" he said uncertainly. He was young and his dark hair fell into his eyes. Green eyes.

"Two cups of coffee."

While the man busied himself before the Gaggia machine, Trotti said, "We're looking for a car. Perhaps you might be able to help us."

"I have a car of my own." His voice was highly pitched, almost effeminate.

Magagna looked at Trotti. In a flat voice, Trotti said, "We're not making any accusations. We just want your help."

"What sort of car?" He placed two cups on the counter and then set a couple of envelopes of sugar in each saucer.

"A French car—a Citroën."

The man seemed genuinely surprised. "A red Citroën—one of those long things that have special suspension?"

"Yes."

"Of course I know it."

"Here in the village?"

He nodded and his hair fell into the green eyes.

"Who does it belong to?"

"The mayor."

"You have a mayor here?"

"This is part of Tarzi, administratively at least; although they make such a fuss of coming up here to empty our dustbins."

There was disappointment in Trotti's voice. "And the mayor of Tarzi has a red Citroën?"

"Of course not." With a movement of his hand, he made a gesture of frustration at Trotti's stupidity. "Your mayor—the mayor of your city. He's got a villa on the hill. Gaetano Mariani."

24

IT WAS LATE afternoon when they returned. Magagna drove while Trotti stared ahead in silence. For some time they had been able to see the city lying before them in the Po valley. Trotti was reminded of the old lithographs he had seen; the city looked like the medieval fortress it had once been. Sharing the horizon with the dome of the cathedral were several high brick towers. In the eleventh and twelfth century, private citizens had built them as a sign of personal wealth. Once there had been a hundred; now there were only seven, caught against the blue of the summer sky.

Trotti spoke. "There was no sign of movement; the ground hadn't been disturbed near the front or back of the house." He offered a sweet to Magagna, who shook his head.

"Use dogs."

"Probably the only solution. But it's by no means certain Leonardelli will give me permission—particularly now. A warrant to search the mayor's private villa—just before elections. You know Leonardelli, he'll refuse."

They crossed the river, running sluggishly between the pebbly shores and the raised fishing huts, standing on their wooden stilts.

Then they were in the city and Magagna took the northbound road out to via Milano.

It was just after six when Trotti got home. Pioppi was waiting for him impatiently. She stood on the front balcony, wearing a blue skirt and a white blouse open at the neck. She was visibly relieved at the sight of her father.

Magagna pulled into the curb and Trotti got out.

"Tomorrow morning in the Questura."

"Ciao."

"Ciao."

Magagna did a three-point turn and drove back into the city.

"Papa, you are late," Pioppi said as he came up the stairs.

He smiled. "A breakthrough. I was up in the hills and something unexpected came up."

"It could have waited."

He looked up and the effect was almost uncanny. The evening sun caught her black hair and she stood with one hand on her hip; an aggressive stance. Her voice was querulous. Unwittingly, she imitated her mother.

"Five minutes to get washed," he said lightly, stepping past her.

"And put on a suit, Papa."

He showered quickly and shaved; then he slapped aftershave onto his wet cheeks.

"We're in a hurry."

He went into the bedroom—leaving a trail of wet footmarks on the hall floor—and took a shirt from the wardrobe. In theory, he shared the wardrobe with his wife, but gradually her collection of clothes had built up, leaving him little more than thirty centimeters for his suits and jackets. The floor of the wardrobe was cluttered with ill-assorted women's shoes. Agnese often promised that she would tidy up; more promises that she never kept.

His best suit, neatly pressed and still under the cellophane wraps from the dry cleaners, smelled slightly of cleaning fluid. He put on a white shirt, a dark tie and later, a pair of brown shoes.

Pioppi was waiting for him downstairs. He bolted the door, placed the key under a flowerpot and ran down the stairs. Pioppi held the garden gate open for him.

"Now take me to church." He passed his arm through hers. "My daughter."

After a hot day in the windless Po valley, the air was

beginning to cool with the approach of evening and from beyond the road, where the new blocks of flats petered out into open fields and ditches, there came the gentle cacophony of croaking frogs. Early Saturday evening and still little traffic along via Milano. One or two cars parked outside the brick walls of the new pizzeria—the neon sign had been turned on—and a few cars heading towards the city. A bus went past, almost empty and the driver smoking. Then a motorbike; and then an old Guzzi van, its engine beating with the slow rhythm of its single ageing piston.

Pioppi walked fast and it was with surprise that Trotti noticed she was wearing high heels.

"Did you have a nice day?" he asked.

"Yes," she replied without looking at him. It was probably the effect of her shoes that made her appear taller, more mature.

"What did you do?"

"Nothing much." Her lips formed a pout; then, sensing the abruptness of her reply, she relaxed her face. "I studied in the morning and then Angela came over and we watched television. There was a film on Monte Carlo."

"Your mother didn't phone?"

Again the face hardened. "No."

"I'm sorry I was late in getting back—but it could be something important."

"You could've tried to get back just a bit earlier."

Trotti did not reply; he did not want to irritate her further. As a child, she was able to sulk for days on end. It was strange, Trotti mused, that although Pioppi was much closer to him than to Agnese, she had nonetheless many of her mother's characteristics. He could now feel Pioppi's mood as he walked beside her.

They turned into viale Caporetto. Five years earlier, there had been only fields here—and an occasional, red-brick farmhouse, with the familiar smells of animals and the earth. Now there were low villas, slightly back from the road and hidden by trees and fences of cascading poinsettia.

At the traffic lights they had to stop; then they crossed the road to the new fountain. The air carried the gentle smell of the tree blossoms and the odor of roasting coffee.

Our Lady of Guadalupe was once a village church; by accident it had been bombed during the war as the Germans were in retreat. Then for thirty years it had been left unused and forgotten. It was the new priest who had organized the rebuilding program. The church was virtually new, built of red brick and a steeple of square cement. At the top, there stood a gaunt iron cross, silhouetted against the sky.

People stood on the stairs leading up to the main porch.

"You see," Trotti said cheerfully. "We're not late." Then holding her arm tightly, he added, "You look very pretty in your shoes. A young lady."

She tried to smile but then looked down at the concrete steps; particles of glass-like sand glinted in the sun's glow.

"Pioppi," he said softly.

She stopped and looked up at him; around them, several young people, well-dressed and in dark clothes, made their way towards the church entrance. The lines about Pioppi's mouth were firm—again he recognized her mother—and he knew that she was both angry and embarrassed.

"Papa, you know that I love you."

"I love you, Pioppi."

She sighed. "Then why do you do it, Papa?"

Trotti smiled. "Do what?"

"Why do you wear that suit?"

"My suit?" He looked down in amazement. A good suit, well cut and of a light brown color. "What's wrong with my suit?"

"It's terrible." She screwed up her eyes. "It's absolutely terrible. I want to be proud of you, Papa—but you dress like a scarecrow. It's old-fashioned, it's too short for you and it's tight at the waist like a sack of potatoes. And your shoes are the wrong color, Papa." She shook her head. "You really don't understand, do you? For you, it's not important. But . . ." She blushed slightly. "You look like a peasant. A peasant, Papa—someone who's never been to the city before."

The bells of the grey, concrete tower began to peal.

25

SUNDAY MORNING. ALREADY the sun was hot in the narrow streets. Half past eight; Trotti stepped past the fast-drying damp patches where the shopkeepers had sluiced down the pavements, and he could smell the tang of ammonia.

The streets were empty. There used to be cars about the town hall; parked on the broad marble slabs, along the pavement and even at the top of the stairway. Now there was just a small sign indicating that the town hall was a historic building. If it had not been for the oil stains, black on the veined marble, Trotti would have found it hard to believe his own memory. Not a car in sight. A few bicycles leaned against the plastered walls of the town hall and two porters, hands behind their backs, stood talking. They were both looking up at the cloudless morning sky.

Without ending his own conversation, one of the porters stepped in front of Trotti, barring his entrance.

"I have an appointment."

The man nodded to his companion; then he turned to face Trotti. The smile on his face disappeared.

"An appointment with the mayor." Trotti showed his card. "Now."

The smile returned, but less sincere, more ingratiating. "This way, Commissario."

The city was Roman in origin, with the two ancient roads, Strada Nuova and the Corso that crossed at right angles and the bridge over the river to Borgo Genovese. But the churches, the private houses with their shaded courtyards and the winding cobbled streets were all medieval, the signs of a new, affluent class of burghers.

The town hall was out of keeping with the city, out of keeping with the medieval architecture and the later Habsburg expansion. The town hall was baroque.

The grandeur of the building still impressed him. The facade with its bulging balconies and its ornate, intricate decoration; the smooth marble pillars and on the inside, the winding staircases and the red—admittedly threadbare—carpet, the dark paintings of forgotten notables that hung from the high walls, themselves in need of a fresh coat of paint. Trotti was impressed and perhaps even intimidated. A sense of tradition, of both bourgeois frivolity and purpose filled the somber halls with an almost tangible quality. The city as a republic, as a responsible, self-governing entity. It was an atmosphere that he had rarely felt in Italian public buildings and certainly never in a Questura. But then, most Questuras had been built at the time of Mussolini in an age of national bombast. The curving brick facades, the granite faced statues of purposeful, muscular men and women with firm, molded breasts, marching towards the new era of the Fascist, corporate state—they were buildings that were too old to be modern but not old enough to have character.

The town hall had character.

The sound of the street, the rest of the city—it was a world away; here there was silence and the continuing tradition of civic responsibility.

The air smelled of damp carpets and furniture wax.

Trotti followed the porter up two flights of curving stairs and they came to a wooden door opposite a painting—very large, it took up an entire wall—of St. George, his escutcheon the same as the city's, slaying a grotesque dragon. Lit up by spectacular rays of sunshine on an otherwise gloomy horizon, the familiar silhouette of the city, its cathedral and its towers.

A man was sitting at a desk before the door. He was reading a book, a yellow-bound paperback edition of Agatha Christie.

Evidently the literature was too engrossing for him to look up. The porter bent down and whispered something, his lips almost touching the man's ear.

The sitting man did not raise his glance but continued to stare at the print of his book; nervously, the fingers of one hand played a tattoo on the scrubbed desktop.

Then he looked up; a younger face than Trotti expected, narrow shoulders in a well-pressed serge uniform. The eyes were hidden by a pair of sunglasses, similar to those of Magagna, but with lenses tinted a pale, almost bilious yellow.

"Yes?" Behind the glasses, the eyes looked at Trotti.

"I have an appointment with the mayor."

Carefully a strip of paper was placed between the pages, the book was closed and relegated to a corner of the desk. The porter stood up. He was a midget.

His small legs—the trousers well-creased and without a speck of dust—took him to the door where he tapped reverentially before opening and allowing his small frame to slip into the mayor's office. The door was closed quietly behind him.

Trotti and the other man waited a couple of minutes, without either of them looking at the other. The door opened again, very slightly, and the midget emerged backwards, his small body bent in a bow. Like a priest retreating from the Holy of Holies.

"The mayor informs me that he is busy. But as the appointment has been made . . ." A sigh of vicarious responsibility, weighing heavy on the narrow shoulders. "Please." He pushed the door open. Trotti squeezed past the man and through the narrowness of the aperture.

The mayor's office had been completely redecorated and the style—Italianate nordic, harsh lines, pine wood and pale, angular furniture—had little in common with the rest of the building. A low lampshade, pale pink like an anaemic toadstool, hung from the ceiling at the end of a long white flex; the carpet was of a pale grey. Beside the window, a varnished tabletop of pine, supported by trestles.

The morning sun lit up the room; a black cat nestled on the carpet.

The door closed behind Trotti.

He crossed the carpet. "It is very good of you to allow me an interview at such short notice. This must be, I realize, a busy time for you."

The mayor raised his shoulders in acquiescence.

"I see that the forces of order are equally caught up in the events of our contemporary history." Sitting behind his desk, the mayor tapped at the open newspaper.

Since his return to the city, Trotti had seen the mayor on several occasions; official functions or political meetings, once or twice even in the street, accompanied by an entourage of well-dressed men, like him wearing a dark green loden overcoat. And of course, Trotti had seen the electoral posters that had appeared a couple of days previously.

Trotti was surprised that the mayor looked like the posters; he had imagined him older and unhealthier. Mariani was sturdy without being fat. Large, heavy jaws that even this early in the morning appeared dark with stubble.

The cold, grey eyes drew away from the newspaper and looked up at Trotti.

"Yes, I am busy." The mayor rose to his feet and held out a hand which Trotti shook. "But I am always willing to help. Please be seated."

There was a pale varnished chair against a wall that Trotti carried and placed before the desk. He sat down. "I had to phone you because I needed to speak with you as soon as possible. In the course of an enquiry."

The eyes returned distractedly to the newspaper. "And you are . . ."

"Commissario Trotti, Pubblica Sicurezza. We haven't met but . . ." Trotti shrugged. "I have of course often seen you."

"Your name is not familiar to me."

"I returned here less than a year ago. I was in the Mezzo-giorno—in Bari."

"But you are not from the South?"

"From the hills, Signor Sindaco. I studied at the university here, as did my wife."

"Signora Trotti? Do I know her?"

"She is a doctor. But she no longer works; occasionally she works as an agent for certain Milanese pharmacy companies."

"She is a colleague, then?"

The mayor's smile was bland. "As you know, I too am a doctor. But with my responsibilities here," he looked around at the office, inviting Trotti to do likewise, "I no longer have the time to practice. I am a pediatrician by training and I still give a few lectures at the university hospital." The mayor gave a rapid smile. "In the last four years, I've had to give up any private work. Perhaps one day I shall be able to return to medicine. Who knows?" The dark hands brushed the cover of the *Corriere* with a smoothing movement. "Now, Commissario, how can I help you?"

"I am investigating the disappearance of a child."

"Anna Ermagni?"

"You read the newspapers."

"Part of my job, Commissario. As a politician, I have to know what the Press is saying; and I have to read all the newspapers, Left and Right. And of course, I have to read the *Provincia.*" Another smile. "At the moment, we are in favor. The result of the pedestrian precinct, I imagine."

"Perhaps."

"Like everybody else, the journalists were up in arms about a pedestrian zone. The Fascism of the Left, that's what they accused us of. But now they're only too glad not to have trucks running past their offices in the Corso. But to return to the child, I see in the newspaper that she has been found."

"That is correct. But we do not know why she was kidnapped."

"Kidnapped?"

"The people who took her—a couple, we think—asked for a ransom of twenty million lire. A small sum by modern standards. Then they returned the child before having made contact with the grandparents."

"The girl is safe now?"

Trotti nodded.

"Then, Commissario, I don't really see why you need worry.

The matter is over; no money was paid and the child is home safe. I imagine you have other problems on your hands—like political terrorism." Very slightly he raised the shoulders of his suit; it was then that Trotti noticed, against the soft weave of the wool lapel, a small enamel badge. Red enamel with a yellow decoration—the hammer and sickle. "I know that I have many other problems."

"A crime has been committed, Signor Sindaco," Trotti said and he was aware of the foolishness in his own voice. "A crime has been committed and those responsible must be brought to justice."

"A moralist, Commissario. I see that you are a moralist."

"A police officer," Trotti replied quickly. "And I don't believe that moral indignation is the prerogative of the Italian Communist Party."

Faint amusement flickered across Mariani's face at the prospect of a battle of ideas. "There is much for us to be indignant about, I think you"ll agree. Thirty years of a republic, Commissario, and we still have an Italian Fascist party. Thirty years of so-called democracy and the real power in this country is still in the hands of the same people. People and interests actively defended by the Carabinieri and the Pubblica Sicurezza." His eyes glinted with amused hardness.

"It is my duty," Trotti replied slowly, "to find out who kidnapped Anna Ermagni."

Mariani's dark eyes stared at Trotti. Disappointed, perhaps, that Trotti had not risen to the bait. The wrinkles moved towards the eyes. Forty-seven, forty-eight, the mayor was younger than Trotti; but the eyes were underlined by dark rings from overwork and lack of sleep.

"You know, of course, Commissario, that I am a relative."

"Relative?"

"Of the child. A very distant one—but for us, family ties are still important. Her grandfather—he owns a bar, the San Siro, on Corso Garibaldi. I suppose that it's about that you want to talk to me. Michele Rossi—he's a distant cousin."

"I didn't know."

Again the smile, slightly patronizing. "You know at least that I am from Calabria. I came here to study at the university and I decided to stay. No need to tell you that the local people still see me as a meddling outsider—except when I do things that will bring money into their pockets. Rossi, too, is from Calabria—Lago Negro. We're related by marriage." He paused while he stared at his fingers. "There are several of us here—all of us more or less related. We've been coming north since the end of the war. To get work. In the sewing machine factory or in the textile factory. I was lucky; my father had a shop and he could afford to pay my fees. He wanted the best education for me and it was decided to send me here, where I could stay with an aunt." A downward movement of his mouth. "I haven't seen Rossi for a long time."

"You know Anna?"

"I know who she is; I knew that she was Michele Rossi's grand-daughter and I went to her baptism. But that was before . . ." He raised his hands from the desk and gestured towards the room. "Before I became mayor."

"I, too, was at the baptism."

The mayor raised an eyebrow.

"I am Anna's godfather," Trotti said simply.

"Which explains your interest in the affair."

"I am also a friend of Ermagni's."

"Ermagni—I scarcely know him. A taxi driver. Over these last four years, I really haven't been able to keep up with family affairs. For us, the family is still very important, but because of my work, I have become like a northerner. However . . ."

"Yes?"

"I should perhaps tell you that as soon as I read about Anna's disappearance, I phoned Michele. It was the least I could do. I told him that I was willing to help him as much as I could. But within the framework of the law." A brief flicker of amusement and again the wrinkles tightened at the corner of the eyes. "But what could I do? Money, I suppose I could give him money—and I suggested it. But he assured me that he had enough and any-way, he said that you," the hand pointed vaguely towards Trotti, "had forbidden any payment. Not that that would have made any difference. I know Michele and no law would prevent him from caring for his granddaughter. He loves that child—more perhaps than he loved his own daughter—and he would go to any lengths for her."

The desk was almost bare; a few newspapers, a telephone and a framed photograph. A small, silver frame. Trotti imagined that it contained a family portrait but as he leaned forward, resting his arms, he recognized the features and the round spectacles of a young Antonio Gramsci, founder of the Italian Communist Party.

"There was nothing I could do. I am a politician but that does not mean that I have power over criminals—although, I don't have to tell you, many politicians are little better than criminals—and you don't have to go all the way to Rome to find them."

He brushed at dust, probably imaginary, on his lapel. "I was upset, of course. Kidnapping—if indeed that is what it was—is not something we expect in this town. This is a quiet city—thanks largely to the deliberate policy that we have observed since we have been in power. A small city with a human dimension. Of course, I was also upset as a relative. But," he shrugged, "what could I do?"

"There is nothing that the individual citizen can do in a similar situation. It is for the police to deal with these matters."

"A criticism of the Socialists, Commissario? You don't perhaps approve of their overtures towards the Red Brigades?"

"I am a police officer. I simply wished to point out that in the case of Anna Ermagni, there was little that her grandfather could do."

"There is a difference, then, between Anna Ermagni and Aldo Moro?"

"That is not for me to decide."

The mayor stood up. From somewhere downstairs there came the soft hammering of a typewriter; regular hammering, a small tinkle and then the metallic slide of the carriage returning to a new margin.

Sunday morning and people at work in the town hall.

"There is nothing else, Commissario . . . ?"

Trotti did not move.

"There are pressing matters . . ."

"It is about a car, Signor Sindaco." Trotti crossed his legs and took a notebook from his pocket. "A Citroën."

"What about it?"

"I believe," Trotti said, looking at the bare sheet of paper of his notebook, "I believe that you own a Citroën. A DS." He looked up and the mayor returned to his seat. The face had a look of puzzlement. Trotti could not decide whether he was genuinely puzzled or merely acting.

"I own a Mirafiori. A Fiat. Very humdrum."

"You don't own a red Citroën DS?"

"No." He shook his head. "And even my own car I scarcely use. In town I prefer to use a bicycle—now that it is safe to use it. And when it's absolutely necessary, I use an official car and chauffeur."

"You've never owned a Citroën at any time? A Citroën with Milanese registration."

"I used to, yes." There was no change in the mayor's voice. "I used to—but that was some time ago."

"You got rid of it?" Trotti's voice was matter-of-fact.

"I sold it." The mayor hesitated slightly. "Or rather, I gave it to my son, Sandro."

"Your son?"

"That is correct, Commissario."

"And he still owns it?"

"I don't know." A slight movement of his hands which now lay on top of the newspaper. "I scarcely have time to see my family. I am here seven days a week. Today it is Sunday and I have work to do; my family life, I'm afraid, has to take second place. But to answer your question, no. I don't think he still has it."

"You know the registration number?"

"No." His mouth closed sharply. "But wait." He took a small diary from his jacket pocket and flipped through the pages. "Perhaps it is here. No." He went through the pages several times; then he picked up the phone. "Carla," he said, "get me my home number." He put the phone down; then looking at Trotti, he went on: "It was a Milan number. I was working at the Policlinico in Milan several years ago and a colleague had the car to sell. I had done him a favor and at the time it seemed a bargain. But that was before the price of petrol started rocketing."

"The reason I need to know . . ." Trotti began.

The mayor held out his hand as the phone rang and he picked up the receiver. His face softened and he smiled. To Trotti, he mouthed, "My wife."

When he put the receiver back in its cradle, he was smiling. A genuine smile and he looked younger. "MI 74220. My wife is marvelous; a memory like a computer."

Trotti jotted the number down on the page of his notebook. "And when did you hand the car over to your son?"

"A year ago—perhaps more." Mariani smiled and for some reason—perhaps the eyes, perhaps the mouth—Trotti felt for the first time that the mayor was ill at ease.

"May I ask, Commissario, the reason for all these questions?"

"You own a villa in the hills?"

"Yes. There's nothing wrong with that, I hope." The mayor's voice was sharp. "Nothing illegal."

"And you go there regularly?"

"I used to. I get a lot less time nowadays."

"Of course." Trotti doodled on the notebook; a series of parallel arrows. "You haven't been there recently?"

Mariani answered promptly, "No."

"You are quite sure?"

The dark eyes stared at Trotti. "I don't see why I should answer these questions. Are you trying to accuse me of something?"

"I make no accusations. I merely ask for information." He drew three more arrows before continuing. "Can you tell me in whose name the car insurance was taken out?"

"I handed everything over to Sandro. It was an expensive car to run and I hadn't used it for a couple of years. Nice to look at but a beast to run and not the sort of vehicle adapted to the

narrow, cobbled streets of this city. I gave it to him as a gradu-
ation present."

"You can prove this?"

"Prove? You are accusing me of something, Commissario? I
don't enjoy being treated like a criminal."

Trotti replied softly, "Forgive me, Signor Sindaco." He smiled
broadly, showing his teeth. "It's just that we have evidence—
circumstantial and probably unfounded—that the people who
kidnapped Anna Ermagni used a red Citroën."

The mayor held his glance. "Commissario Trotti, I am not a
kidnapper. Nor is my son."

"Of course not. I merely . . ."

The mayor brushed Trotti's remark aside. "It does not mean
because I come from Calabria, because I am a southerner, that
I am a bandit. I can assure you that I have no need to kidnap
children—and certainly not the children of my own relatives."

Trotti replied blandly, "I apologize. You understand, I am
sure, that all evidence, however circumstantial, must be followed up."

"Then everything is quite clear." The mayor stood up and held
out his hand. "The matter is over. You have the registration of
the car. As I said, I am not certain whether Sandro still has it.
But of course, you can check with him."

Trotti took his hand. "What does he do, your son?"

As if by magic, the door opened and the midget porter came
into the room.

"Like his father, he is a doctor."

"At the university?"

"In Naples. He is doing his military service."

26

TROTTI CAME OUT of the town hall into the sunlight. He stood for an instant at the top of the stairs and watched the soldiers. There were five of them, walking arm in arm along the Corso; their dark khaki shirts were pressed and their uniform trousers just a bit short for their long legs. They were Alpini; on their young, blond heads they wore the round felt hat of their regiment and the long feather.

Trotti came down the steps as they went past. They did not notice him for they were listening intently, their mouths open in anticipation of laughter, to a joke being told by one of the soldiers in the harsh gutturals of the Bergamasque dialect. Trotti smiled and turned to watch them as they disappeared into a dark café.

He walked back to the office.

A lot of activity for a Sunday morning. On the door, an appuntato saluted him and along the cool corridors, men in shirtsleeves were hurrying purposefully. One or two acknowledged him—hastily, a brief smile and without stopping to talk.

Inside the lift—with its permanent smell of old smoke and the hammer and sickle scraped into the aluminum paint—he pressed the button for the third floor. The lift moved slowly.

Principessa was slumbering beneath the desk, her paws extended on the cold floor.

"On Sunday?" Trotti said with surprise.

Gino raised his head; like the dog, he had been dozing. A

smile flickered behind the thick glasses. "Leonardelli called me in." A cup of cold coffee stood on the desk, pushed aside and forgotten. "Something has come up."

"What?"

"I just answer the phone. You mustn't ask me these questions." He tutted. "A blind old man."

Trotti placed a hand on his shoulder; Gino was wearing a blue cardigan over a white shirt, cloth slippers on his feet. "Did anybody call for me?"

"Your friend Avvocato Romano."

"An old bore." Trotti laughed. "He doesn't seem to realize that other people have their own lives to live—and that we have a job to do. A dog and playing scopone with his cronies in the Bar Duomo—that's all he's got to do and he thinks everybody else has as much free time as himself."

"He said it was important."

"It always is." Gino sneezed, suddenly and noisily, taking Trotti by surprise.

Principessa rose to her feet, walked to the other side of the desk and sat down. Gino extracted a handkerchief from his pocket.

"A woman phoned, too." He blew his nose.

"Who?"

"She didn't say."

"My wife?" Trotti immediately regretted the hint of hope he had allowed into his voice; but behind the glasses, Gino's eyes did not move. He snuffled at the large handkerchief. "It didn't sound like her. Agnese knows me, she would have chatted. This woman hung up."

"I see," Trotti said, his voice normal—or so he believed. Still with his hand on Gino's shoulder, he stood in thought. Then, "And Pisanelli?"

"Gone to bed." Gino laughed. "He spent most of the night near the Cairoli barracks—surveillance of some sort. Now dell'Orto and di Bono have taken over. Don't know where they are now but they called in an hour ago from down by the river."

"What the hell is di Bono doing down there?"

"Commissario Trotti, you mustn't ask me these questions."

"You know nothing." Trotti laughed. "Is that right?"

"I do my job—I don't ask any questions. I'm too old to understand any of the answers." From where he was standing, Trotti could see the eyes blinking; the white lashes almost touched the lenses.

"One other thing," Gino said as Trotti moved away.

"Yes?"

"Capitano Spadano. And he said to phone him."

"Of course." Trotti went towards his office. "Thanks, Gino."

Magagna was smoking, a packet of Marlboro and his feet upon the desk. He was reading the paper but as Trotti entered, the large feet came off the desk and fell heavily to the floor, narrowly missing a pile of folders. Magagna got to his feet.

"What the hell are you doing?"

"You told me to come in this morning."

"I didn't tell you to treat this place like a pigsty. This isn't Pescara."

"I was looking at the newspaper." Magagna looked mildly foolish. He raised the *Corriere*.

"I can see you were looking at the newspaper."

"Have you seen?"

"Seen what?" Trotti asked as he moved to his desk. He took a crumpled piece of paper from the waste paper bin and carefully rubbed the spot where Magagna's feet had been.

"They've got some of the Red Brigades." He prodded at the front page; the photograph of a young man, handcuffs at his wrists and his crossed arms raised to hide his face from the photographer.

"You believe that?" He sat down. "Give me the paper."

A vast police operation, concentrating on the capital; several suspects arrested and the discovery of an important cache of arms including Czech machine guns. Satisfaction among the Carabinieri. "You really believe all this?"

Magagna sat down in another armchair and took a cigarette from his pocket. "They are members of the Red Brigades."

Trotti laughed. "Terrorists. It's not like that—a swoop on

Rome like a swoop on a gambling den—that we're going to find Moro." He clicked his tongue. "Don't tire your brain. Do something useful; run down and get some coffee. And some doughnuts—I haven't had breakfast. Do something constructive."

As soon as Magagna left the office, Trotti picked up the phone and asked Gino to put him through to vehicle registration.

"Pronto."

Trotti gave the number of the Citroën and the voice of a woman told him to wait ten minutes. Smiling, Trotti put down the phone; then carefully moving a pile of dossiers, marked with black writing 73/8, he opened the sliding drawer to his desk and took out a bottle of grappa. He then sat staring out of the window.

A few birds darted through the air; the street below was quiet and, seen from the rooftops, the city appeared peaceful. From the roof of the Questura, there came the ceaseless cooing of pigeons.

Another hot day. 9:15, seventh of May, 1978.

"At last."

Magagna set the tray on the desk—two vacuum cups of coffee and two sugary doughnuts, each loosely held in soft tissue paper.

"Grappa?"

Magagna shook his head; his sunglasses were now back in place on his nose. He threw the smoldering filter out of the window and lit another cigarette.

"You ought to give up smoking," Trotti said as he unscrewed the top of his coffee.

"And get diabetes from your hard-boiled sweets?" He lowered himself into the armchair; he winced slightly as he sipped his coffee.

"Good."

Trotti ate his doughnut; crumbs fell to his shirtfront.

"You're not impressed by the Carabinieri's work yesterday?"

"It's not that I'm not impressed, I'm cynical." He sat back in his chair and brushed at the particles of sugar. "I've just seen the mayor—and I discover that he is a relative of Rossi's."

"You think he's paid the money?"

"It's possible—just as it's possible that the blackmail wasn't directed at Ermagni or Rossi at all. Perhaps—it's an idea, only an idea—it wasn't Ermagni at all who was being blackmailed. The blackmailers, whoever they may be, were possibly trying to get to Mariani."

"Why?"

Trotti sighed. "You ask stupid questions." His two hands on the desk moved apart. "I don't know why but I can think of a thousand possible reasons. The same as Moro. Mariani's a politician, his is the world of the palazzo with its intrigues and its uncertain alliances. He has got where he has got through favors and support. Perhaps somebody wanted to remind him—indirectly but efficiently—of a favor he has failed to return. He's a Communist but that doesn't mean that the path to power is less . . ."

The phone rang.

"Piero, is that you?" No sooner had he pressed the blinking light and put the receiver to his ear than he recognized her voice. More than anything else—joy, anger and all the other emotions she had caused him to feel—it was relief that flooded through him.

"Agnese?"

"Where have you been? Of course it's me. I've already phoned goodness knows how many times. You're never there."

"I've been busy." He made a clumsy, hurried gesture to Magagna, indicating the door.

Magagna got to his feet. "Don't disappear." Trotti said, while holding his hand over the mouthpiece. Magagna closed the door quietly.

"Where are you, Agnese? I'm on a case."

"You always are."

"Where have you been? I was worried about you. How are you? Pioppi was worried about you."

"You were both worried, of course you were." There was no hint of mockery in her voice but he could imagine her face, with the harsh lines at the corner of her mouth and the unflinching eyes. "I hope at least you haven't forgotten about tonight. It is Sunday."

"I know it's Sunday," he replied.

She paused for a silent sigh. "The opera. Or perhaps you don't remember. All you can remember is your work; then let me remind you. A month or so ago you booked a couple of tickets for the opera at the Teatro Civico." Her voice was cold. "*Aida*. Verdi."

Trotti had forgotten.

"I"ll expect you here at six, Piero. I hope you've got something decent to wear," Agnese said and hung up.

He put the receiver down slowly and noticed with a strange sense of detachment that his hand was trembling. His entire body was trembling. He smiled to himself—a wry, private smile like that of a child proud of his own naughtiness. Twenty years of marriage and she still was able to make him feel inadequate—a fumbling, gauche adolescent. Even when she left him, when she went away for days on end—even then he could not bring himself to hate her. The lover and the loved; she knew that he was weak and she played upon his weakness. If it hadn't been for Pioppi, he might have left her—no, he would never leave her. He needed her—like a house needed firm foundations.

Only the foundations were not firm—and the ground, unstable and unreliable, did not need the house. He was still smiling with the bitter aftertaste of grappa, coffee and a rhubarb sweet on his tongue when the phone rang again. He started slightly and thought it must be Agnese. But the flashing light told him it was an internal call.

Gino banged on the wooden partition, "Line number three."

"Trotti."

"Commissario, this is vehicle registration. You made an enquiry."

"That's right."

"A Milan number—that's why we've been a bit long. But we've got it." The woman's voice paused and Trotti could imagine her inhaling on a cigarette. "MI 74220?"

"Yes."

"A Citroën DS, year of first registration 1972, now belonging to one Signor Angellini, Stefano, resident in Milan, viale Buenos Aires, number three."

Trotti smiled. "And his profession?"

"It is given as journalist."

27

THE SAME OLD man in the dark suit, his legs bowed, stood in the gateway, staring possessively at the rusting bicycle, a wheel missing, that leaned against the zinc letter boxes. His pale eyes glanced vaguely at Trotti without recognition.

Trotti went into the courtyard. More overalls and large pieces of women's underwear hung from the parallel clothesline. The cat bounded towards him and then, surprised by its own exuberance, backed off and tried to hide behind the grilles of the balustrade. Trotti knocked at the door.

"Stefano Angellini."

The woman's dirty grey eyes looked at him with a mixture of disapproval and fear. She pulled at the nylon dressing gown that hung from her narrow shoulders.

"He's not here."

Trotti blocked the door with his foot before she could close it. "Let me in, if you don't want the place surrounded by police."

"Why don't you leave him alone?"

Trotti pushed past her and entered the dark hall, along the worn carpet. He went into the small room. The desk lamp threw its feeble light over a pile of books—it was nearly twelve o'clock—and there was the familiar odor of old sweat and bed sheets. The bed had been made and the room was empty.

The woman pushed past him and switched off the light.

"Where is he?" Trotti asked. A syringe lay on the table.

The woman stood beside an old painting that hung from the wall; a fisherman's boat drawn up on a beach, the darkening waters of a lake and in the background, alpine snow on the mountains. The frame was a dusty gold.

She shook her head vigorously.

"Where is he?"

"You have no right to come in here. Leave me alone." Her face, a weathered, pale face, marked with the lines of a hard life, was bitter. Disappointed. She added, more softly, "He is a good boy."

"Who kidnaps little girls." Trotti spoke tersely and the woman's pale face grew paler. She began to sway, the narrow shoulders scraping against the dirty wallpaper.

Trotti moved forward to catch her before she fell; with a brusque movement, she regained control and brushed his hand away.

"Anna Ermagni?" A soft whisper.

Trotti nodded. She slumped down into a wooden chair, placed beneath a plaster cast of the Virgin Mary, a dusty infant in her blue arms. "My God."

"Where is he?"

She wrung her thin hands together, her head bowed.

"Where is he?"

She shook her head.

"Where?"

"The library," she mumbled.

"What library?"

"Sant'Antonio." She paused. "Sant'Antonio di Padova."

28

THE PIAZZA BETWEEN the psychiatric hospital and the main part of the college had not been closed to traffic; the parked cars—mainly small Fiats, belonging to the students, no doubt, to judge from the rusty state of their bodywork and the rainbows of adhesive advertisements applied to every available centimeter of window—crowded against the scaffolding. Workmen had been cleaning the front of the college; the gaunt carcass of tubing and planks clung to the crumbling, high walls.

Trotti went up the steps and through the small wooden door in the large gate. He found himself in a small room. A man looked up from a desk, half hidden by a grey telephone exchange.

"The library?"

"Who are you?" the man asked, his eyes running with disapproval over Trotti.

"Pubblica Sicurezza." He flashed the card.

"Up the stairs."

Trotti went into the shaded courtyard of the college, past the smooth rounded pillars—they stood in pairs—and the walls of painted ochre. Large patches of damp had caused the plaster to fall away; little piles of powder ran along the edge of the wall. A few students went past, including a girl. She was wearing a blue skirt and looked at him smiling, before returning to her conversation with a young man, his hair neatly brushed and highly polished shoes at the bottom of tight jeans. Together they looked well-dressed and healthy—only a few years older than Pioppi. They were talking about Montale.

He went up the broad stairway; there were several alcoves with the once-white busts of notables staring sightlessly into the gloom of the stairwell; light came from the cloisters and high in the wall, several narrow windows. Badly cracked marble stairs.

The cloisters on the first floor were identical but protected by a low wall. He walked the length of the cloisters, his feet echoing hollowly on the worn tiling; on the other side of the quadrangle, there was a man in black—a priest, no doubt—walking with his hands behind his back and a look of concentration on his thin, pale face.

BIBLIOTECA SANT'AGOSTINO, the plastic sign read. Trotti turned the heavy handle, the door opened and he went into the creaking silence of the library. A rubberized linoleum floor of a dark, scored green. High ceiling, the plaster now tawdry and rows of high, glass-plated bookcases, withholding old books.

A man sat at the door; he was reading *Topolino* but the humor of the comic seemed to be lost on him; he wore a green sweater and an unsmiling mouth. He looked up at Trotti and then his eyes traveled to the large crucifix on the far wall.

Angellini was there.

Trotti recognized him at once. He was hidden behind a pile of books, many open and stacked haphazardly on the leather surface of the long desk. He was writing—he was left-handed and his arm was held in a clumsy curve. His pink tongue peeped from between his teeth. His glasses lay upside down on the desk-top. A wise but fragile bird, balding and in a world of his own.

As Trotti approached he could see several titles; books about the Mafia.

"I want to speak to you."

Trotti whispered softly. He stood beside Angellini. Angellini did not appear to hear. The clumsy hand, holding a large, promotional plastic pen, continued its scrawled journey across the paper.

"I want to speak to you."

There were other people in the library. All men, all with the same healthy look that he had seen on the couple downstairs. Trotti had raised his voice and they now looked up, disturbed and displeased by the interruption. Angellini continued his writing.

"Go away."

Trotti caught his arm and twisted it backwards, pulling Angellini to his feet. The body was a lot heavier than Trotti had imagined.

The myopic eyes turned to look at Trotti. "Can't you see I'm working?" He tottered slightly and the chair tipped over backwards onto the floor.

Trotti pulled Angellini towards the library door; the young man's large shoes dragged on the green linoleum. "I want to talk with you and you will reply civilly."

The body was unresisting but it was heavy as though there were weights in the large shoes. Trotti was soon out of breath. Then Angellini stiffened and broke away from the hold.

"My glasses, let me get my glasses."

The other students were now watching, intrigued and embarrassed. The porter had put down his magazine and was staring at Trotti with an open, gaping mouth.

Angellini put on the glasses and his eyes came into focus.

"Hurry up," Trotti said, without even bothering to whisper. "Hurry up." He caught Angellini's arm and put it into a sharp half-nelson. "Let's have a quiet talk, you and me." The ease of the movement came back to him from the years of training.

The porter was undecided; he sat at his desk, *Topolino* now forgotten and his hands spread out as though in preparation for a sudden movement. But there was fear in his eyes; worry pulled at the skin of his cheeks.

Trotti had little time for introspection; but as he pushed Angellini towards the door he realized that he was allowing himself to indulge in anger. It was unprofessional—and something he managed to avoid normally without too much difficulty.

The porter got to his feet but Trotti whispered "PS" hoarsely and the man moved away with the speed of a scalded cat. Trotti pulled Angellini out into the cloisters and the mid-morning sunshine.

He pushed Angellini against a pillar. The man's lethargy, the strangely mocking face behind the glasses, his weight, his glistening forehead—everything irritated Trotti and an irrational loathing swelled within him. He wanted to hurt Angellini, to knock sense into him.

"You're in trouble."

His hand held the shirt—a loose-weave cotton—but Angellini pushed it away and Trotti stepped backwards. Angellini shrugged his shirt back into place—a button fastening the collar had broken away and the box pleat had been ripped.

"So you'd better tell me the truth."

Angellini nudged at his glasses. "You've got no right."

The blow struck the side of Angellini's dull cheek and there was a soft bump as the head, driven backwards, hit the smooth surface of the marble pillar. There was more force in the blow than Trotti had intended; he had allowed his anger to escape from his control. He was like a spring that was suddenly released and flew with unexpected violence.

Angellini staggered and put a hand behind him, seeking the support of the pillar.

"You've been lying," Trotti said.

The eyes had seemed to lose their focus.

"Where were you last Thursday? Damn you, you've been lying." He breathed in. "I want the truth."

Angellini looked up at him with foolish innocence from behind the glasses; already the red weal was beginning to form at the side of his unhealthy face—four thin red lines pointing towards the wet, loose mouth.

He blinked. "Last Thursday?"

"Last Thursday when Anna Ermagni was kidnapped from via Darsena and your car—" Trotti prodded at the soft chest beneath the cotton shirt. He could smell the man's sweat of fear. "Your car was there—at the gardens. A red Citroën. You were there, you were seen."

The eyes blinked. "I work in via Darsena."

"Don't lie, damn you." Trotti pulled his arm back. It was as though his hand had a mind of its own and wanted to hit the fat man. Angellini was fat, and even in his pain he had a kind of complacency that was enervating. The hand wanted to hit him, to wake him up, to shake him violently. But Trotti controlled himself and suddenly, without warning, his anger seeped away. It was an almost physical sensation; his hand seemed to lose its autonomy.

"Where do you work?" Trotti let his arm drop.

"Via Darsena, of course."

"You're a journalist with the *Provincia*, aren't you?"

"The main printing press is in via Darsena."

Trotti turned away and it was then that he noticed the priest. He was still standing on the far side of the cloister, a frown on his face. He was staring at Trotti.

Trotti turned back to Angellini. "You're a journalist, not a printer."

"I sometimes read the proofs." He was now truculent. "You don't object?"

Of course he had been stupid. Trotti was angry with himself; he had jumped to conclusions. He had let himself be influenced by a coincidence. But now he was caught in his own trap and he knew he could not back down.

"Your car is registered in Milan." Trotti's voice was hard, impersonal. "You don't live there."

"I've always lived in Milan, with my parents. My father is the city surveyor." He raised his shoulders. "I prefer to stay here with my aunt. I was an undergraduate here at Sant'Antonio, this is where my friends are, this is where I work. But my residence is in Milan."

"If you're permanently resident here, you should have changed the plates."

"I've told you, I'm not permanently resident here. I live in Milan and anyway, they were Milan plates when I bought the car."

"When was that?"

"When was what?"

Trotti could not be sure whether Angellini was deliberately trying to annoy him; his manner was becoming increasingly truculent.

"When did you buy the Citroën?"

"I can't remember. About a year . . ." The rounded features paled; Angellini seemed to sway slightly. "About a year ago—perhaps a bit more. You can check. I bought it from Sandro Mariani—the mayor's son."

"A friend of yours?"

The heavy lids blinked. "We were in college here together." He smiled slightly, recalling perhaps happier times spent in Sant'Antonio. He swayed again and the hands against the pillar blenched with effort. Angellini swallowed. "We used to be friends."

"Used to be?"

Without intonation, Angellini replied, "I haven't seen him for some time."

"Can you prove that you were at the printing works on Thursday?"

Angellini laughed. "Ask the printers. Unless of course you don't trust them, either." He nodded. "Perhaps they helped me kidnap the little girl."

"Don't worry, I"ll check," Trotti replied coldly and then Angellini fell, collapsing like a paper bag that lost its air. The large body fell slowly, sliding against the marble surface of the column until the legs—the blue cotton trousers riding up to reveal white, hairless ankles—stretched across the pitted tiles. The eyes rolled, showing the bloodshot whites; then the head rolled forward, and was blocked by the chin caught against the heaving chest.

"Christ."

The priest had disappeared; nobody was in sight. Trotti bent down and slapped at the loose, hanging flesh of the cheeks. Without any effect; behind the thick glasses, now propped at an improbable angle on Angellini's nose, the eyes were sightless. A slight trickle of viscous saliva formed at the corner of the large lips.

Holding Angellini by the collar of his shirt, Trotti slapped him again, forward and backhand until the skin of his palm began to sting.

The eyelids fluttered.

Trotti struck him again. The lips began to move like the mouth of a fish.

"My jacket—quickly."

Trotti let the body fall back against the pillar and ran back to the library. A look of surprise from the students who watched him as he went to where the chair had tipped over—an unreal corpse in a strange rigor mortis. He pulled the jacket—lightweight, linen—from the chair and hurried back to where Angellini lay.

The porter followed him.

A hoarse whisper, "In the pocket." A whisper that Trotti could remember from his childhood, a whisper he associated with death. He found the small tube in the pocket, wrapped up in a handkerchief. He unscrewed the top and several pills, like pink insects, tumbled into his hand.

"How many?"

The slow arm lifted and Angellini fumbled, taking the pills that Trotti gave him and putting them in quick succession into his mouth. The lips moved, the jaws moved and then a few seconds later, the porter was kneeling beside them and putting a glass—a bulging glass with Coca-Cola in flowing white script—to the salivating lips. Angellini opened his mouth—the glimpse of a yellowish tongue—and the water disappeared. Several large drops hurried down the grey chin.

The effect was immediate.

Angellini began to recover and took on a more natural color. He propped himself, shifting his weight onto his backside. He then sat up and wiped his mouth; Trotti handed him the handkerchief.

"I'm sorry," Angellini said while the porter placed a reassuring hand on his shoulder. "I'm sorry." The eyes, now in focus and the glasses squarely sitting on his nose. "I'm very sorry. All my fault." He looked at Trotti, then at the porter and a small crowd of students who had gathered in the doorway.

"Go away," Trotti told them; then to Angellini, "How do

you feel?" His voice was soft. "Are you all right? Shall I call an ambulance?"

Angellini nodded and tried to smile. A small, foolish smile. "I"ll walk home."

Trotti felt suddenly very relieved.

29

ANGELLINI'S LARGE HAND still trembled as he unlocked the door and as they stepped into the dark corridor, the old woman appeared, wringing her hands.

"A man was looking for . . ." She stopped, looked at Trotti with disapproval, her eyes glinting coldly, and returned to the kitchen.

Trotti recognized the smell—pasta, potatoes and olive oil—of cooking gnocchi.

"A good woman." Angellini's smile was pale. "My mother's sister. She never married," he whispered, "so that she could look after her father. He owned an ironmonger's shop here. And now he's dead, she looks after me." He smiled. "She likes cooking— but hardly ever eats."

He pushed open the ground glass door and they went into the small bedroom.

"Sit down."

Trotti moved a pile of books from the deckchair and let himself slump into the low-slung canvas. His feet ached. He took the packet of sweets from his pocket and offered them to Angellini. Angellini shook his head. "I must control my sugar intake."

Speaking slowly, while unwrapping the sticky cellophane, Trotti said, "I'm sorry about what happened. I had no right . . ."

Angellini shrugged as he lowered himself onto the edge of the bed. "You've got your job to do—even on a Sunday."

"I allowed myself to get angry." He put the sweet into his mouth and then stared at the rusting nails of the deckchair where they had been hammered into the canvas. "Not very professional, I'm afraid. Ermagni is a friend. I've got involved."

"My fault." Angellini grinned. "I should have taken my tablets earlier." He laughed, a wet gurgle in the throat and his Adam's apple bobbing up and down, while his eyes continued to look at Trotti. "It really doesn't matter."

"It's serious?"

"What?"

Trotti did not answer.

"My disease, you mean?"

Trotti nodded.

Angellini turned away and looked through the gap between the wooden blinds. The sun was hot on the cobbled courtyard and the double line of washing. "I've got another six months," he said softly, "give or take six months. A year at most."

"I didn't know."

"Few people do." Angellini continued to look out of the window. "I can do without sympathy."

"There's nothing you can do?"

"The magic cure?" He laughed. "I'd rather not bother. The end comes sometime." He turned to face Trotti. "It's a bit like the Olympic games. Most people think they're running the ten thousand meters—they've got time to catch up. I'm lucky. I know that my race is the eight hundred meters. I've got to pace myself if I'm going to give a good performance." He shrugged. "That's all I ask for."

There was an awkward silence while from beyond the closed door there came the metallic rattle of pans on a stove.

"You understand," Trotti said, "that there are still a few things I want you to explain?"

"You don't have to whisper." He grinned. "I'm not dead yet."

Outside in the hall, a telephone bell rang.

"Ask your questions, Commissario."

Trotti moved forward in the chair and propped his elbows against the narrow wooden rests; he let his hands hang, the thumbs touching. "I want to know what connection there is between you and the mayor."

"Connection?"

"You know him."

"Only indirectly." Behind the glasses, the eyes blinked.

"How do you know him?"

"Through Sandro."

"His son?"

"That's right. We shared a room in our first year at Sant'Antonio."

"He didn't live with his parents?"

"We both had scholarships."

"I thought it was a Catholic establishment. The son of the mayor—a Communist—with a scholarship to an old church foundation? A bit strange, isn't it?"

Angellini laughed solemnly. "This is Italy, Commissario—the land of compromise."

Trotti frowned.

"Commissario, for the last ten years, Italian universities have been open to virtually everyone; the number of students has increased tenfold while the number of lecturers has remained the same. Inevitably, the standard has fallen. Our universities have become open to the blackmail of everyday life in Italy. Mark a student down, give him a poor mark and he will accuse you of Fascism. Worse still, he may even take physical revenge upon you. No wonder that the lecturers opt for the famous sei politico, the political six out of ten. Better to give a student a mark to scrape by on than risk a bullet in the knee." He paused. "But of course, don't think that the universities were any better before the reform. It was probably exactly the same thing, but in those days, the students came from well-bred, bourgeois families. The modus agendi was probably much the same thing—just more discreet. But the government, faced with increasing numbers of young unemployed, decided to give itself a four-year respite by opening up the universities. Which now explains why we've got graduate street cleaners and dustmen." He smiled. "Excuse me if I'm a snob—an intellectual snob—but I believe in academic excellence. And I believe that against the background of our pauperized universities, the massive number of students and the baronial, all-powerful professors, a place like Sant'Antonio has a useful role to play. A place for academic excellence. Of course it is Catholic—it has been Catholic, violently Catholic since the Counter-Reformation. But it has integrity, it has no time for academic compromise, and it seeks students from all social classes. Sandro Mariani and I were lucky—we were accepted by a private college where we could study in peace, away from the student demonstrations and the provincial demagogies." He grinned. "For four years, it is not all that hard to pretend to be a good, practicing Catholic."

"And you studied languages?" Trotti asked flatly.

"History, Commissario." Angellini looked around him and made a gesture towards the books scattered on the floor, desk and bed. "I still study. I'm preparing a doctorate."

"On what?"

"The Prefetto Mori."

"The policeman?"

"That's right," Angellini replied, "the policeman. The man that Mussolini sent to wipe out the Mafia—and who no doubt would have done it, if he hadn't been working for another kind of mafia. And the time came, Commissario, when Mussolini realized he needed the Mafia more than he needed Mori."

"You'd be better off studying in Sicily. Why do you remain here?"

"A hobby, Commissario. This is my adopted home and this is where I work. If I prepare a doctorate, it is to give myself a sense of continuity. I know I won't ever finish it—I'll never have the time." He tapped one of the books. "Eight hundred meters—but I want to be running at full speed as I go through the tape."

Trotti frowned again, but before he could ask his next question, Angellini said, "To get back to Sandro Mariani—that is what you were asking me about—I can tell you that he sold the car to me about a year ago. When he graduated. I finished before him because he was studying medicine. Seven years. This last year, he's been in the South somewhere doing his military service."

"You are still friends?"

Angellini hesitated. "Yes. Yes, we are still friends—but as you grow up, you begin to see things differently. Friends, yes—but not as before."

"Things such as what?"

There was a light tap on the door and Angellini heaved himself off the bed; he opened the door and Trotti heard him whisper hoarsely with his aunt.

Trotti looked at the books.

"The telephone, Commissario," Angellini said, coming back into the room. "You're wanted on the telephone."

The telephone was in a small cubbyhole; an old plastic machine, the mouthpiece encrusted with damp dirt, screwed into the wall. The wallpaper had been scratched and worn by the movement of hands picking up the receiver.

The aunt watched him from the kitchen door. She wiped her hands slowly on a floral apron. Her eyes glinted.

Trotti turned his back on her and put the phone to his ear. He stared at the wall.

30

TROTTI HAD DRIVEN past the Casa sul Fiume a thousand times, but he had not been through the gates, thick with ivy, for fifteen years.

It was here that he first met his wife. In those days there used to be a wooden dance hall, a creaking, pitted wooden floor that the young people used to dance on. Young men in baggy trousers and v-necked cardigans with colorful patterns; the girls in billowing cotton skirts. And he remembered how the band, four short, bald men with a wheezing accordion, managed to keep the same glazed smile throughout the evening as they bounced their instruments rhythmically to the music.

In the winter, the young people danced; Saturday nights they came to dance to the new rhythms from America, the translated songs of Edith Piaf and the timeless, lilting waltzes. In the summer, they came to bathe. On the verandah, a man would sell ice creams from his trolley, a bright red cart with two chromium lids. Gelati Motta—there was an advertisement on the side of the trolley, a blonde girl with blue eyes and short, waving, Germanic hair. She held an ice cream in her hand. Trotti remembered the advertisement and he remembered the taste of the pistachio ice cream.

Agnese had been eating an ice cream. A hot day in June, 1952, and she was already in her first year of medicine at the university; he kissed her. Against the broad elm tree. It was unexpected and then, suddenly, so easy. For some time he had been intimidated by her, by the way she belonged to a different group, smarter and richer than he was and quite out of his reach. She was twenty years old and very sophisticated.

But when he kissed her, she did not resist; she held his head in her hands and her small tongue touched his lips. A milky coolness to her breath.

He remembered the rippling reflection of the river dancing against the bark of the tree. That was twenty-five years ago. The wooden hall had long ago been pulled down and in its place a long, low concrete building had been erected. It stood squatly on the hard earth.

On the new verandah, tables, dark table cloths and para-sols advertising Italian liqueurs; a discreet juke box beside a refrigerator, this time white, but still advertising Gelati Motta; the Wagnerian girl had gone—just a blue and white logo. Waiters moved gracefully between the tables, leaning from the waist, and taking the lunchtime orders with profes-sional detachment. Many of the tables were empty, plates of food still untouched.

The elm tree was still there, nor had the river changed. It continued to flow as it always would, slowly in summer, fast in the spring and autumn when the snow melted in the Alps, just visible beyond the far pine trees.

Magagna was leaning against the elm; he stood with one leg against the bark. He was stroking his mustache while he held a notebook before his sunglasses. His face was pale. He did not see Trotti until he was beside him.

"Ciao."

Trotti said, "I haven't eaten yet."

"And you won't want to."

Trotti followed Magagna. They went across the hard earth, cut across the edge of the verandah, down four concrete steps and onto the stretch of sand beside the river. There was a crowd of people, many in swimming costumes—Trotti noticed a couple of lithe bikinis and softly tanned backs, blond hair running the length of the spine—that jostled forward against the rope. Magagna pushed through the crowd and a policeman in uniform lowered the rope to let them past.

The smell of the river brought back forgotten memories. A clean smell that caught at the nostrils, reminiscent of washed clothes. It was a smell of the summer.

Dr. Bottone was wearing a dark suit and the steel of his stethoscope appeared from the corner of his jacket pocket. He was kneeling. His highly polished shoes were now dusty, a grey patina covering the thin black leather.

The body, too, smelled.

A woman's body. Two breasts that tilted sideways, over the side of the ribs. A patchy triangle of pubic hair. No arms and no legs. The body had been decapitated.

"In another black bag," Magagna was saying with laudable matter-of-factness. "Washed up upon the beach here and some swimmers"—he nodded towards the crowd—"noticed the smell."

The skin was a yellowish blue and had been attacked by fish; a series of irregular, mauve pockmarks.

"Badly bruised before death," Bottone said, then looking up, he saw Trotti. His thin face smiled behind the steel glasses. "We're gradually piecing it all together, Commissario."

Another man whom Trotti did not recognize nodded. He was smoking a cigar, which he held between his teeth. Rings glittered on his fingers. The odor of the cigar and the sight of the pale, inert flesh, the red circles and the ragged edges where the limbs had been severed—Trotti remembered the corpses of his childhood. He turned away and, moving through the crowd, hurried to a bush. An empty Limonsoda can and a water rat that darted away beneath the dead leaves. Trotti kneeled and retched.

Five minutes later, when he came back, Trotti found Magagna talking with Bottone. Bottone spoke without looking up; the delicate plastic gloves ran over the flesh. "We've just got the arms and head to find."

Magagna nudged his sunglasses. "It won't change the identification. We know who she is."

Bottone continued to caress the lifeless torso. "Probably

beaten to death with a blunt instrument." There were several converging lines and a damp, black gash beneath the right breast. "Or several instruments. A stick or a spade, perhaps."

Trotti's mouth tasted of yellow bile but he felt better. To Magagna, he said, "Give us a cigarette." He took an MS from the box and snapped off the cork filter; then he lit the cigarette and inhaled. A familiar taste that soon washed at the bitterness in his mouth, at the side of his tongue. He let the shortened cigarette smolder in the corner of his mouth. There was silent surprise behind Magagna's sunglasses.

"Who would want to beat her up?" Trotti kneeled down beside Bottone, who kept about him the antiseptic odor of the morgue.

"That's your job, Commissario." He spoke evenly; and in the same, detached tone, he added, "I need to get her on the table and have a good look at her. Should be interesting." The eyes glinted behind the steel spectacles.

Trotti stood up. "You know who she is?" he asked Magagna.

"The name is Irina Pirvic. Yugoslav—about forty-eight years old, with no fixed address. She has no work permit." He corrected, looking up from his notebook, "or rather, she didn't have. She won't be needing it now."

"She works here?"

"She'd been here for the last six months. Probably came down from Milan where the competition is stiff and where a woman of her age would be outclassed. Younger, prettier girls from South America or even the Mezzogiorno, with better protection. Probably edged her out of a job. Or perhaps she was looking for a better class of clientele—she'd had enough of standing by a roadside fire, keeping warm through the night in the dreary suburbs."

"How did you find this out?"

"She was reported missing this morning by Signora Cucina, who runs the hotel."

"Hotel?"

"Albergo Belsole—a whorehouse in the center of the town, near the fish market. Dirty place. It should have been closed down a long time ago. But apparently Signora Cucina has friends in high places."

"Who make use of her services?"

Magagna smiled wryly. "Unlikely. It's the old Albergo Zuavo; it's changed names but it still caters for out-of-town workers or soldiers doing their military service who can't afford anything better—who need to satisfy their needs and who aren't too demanding. Not very salubrious. The sort of place you're likely to get more than you paid for." He grinned and ran a finger along his mustache. "Gonorrhea, *papillon d'amour*."

"The Cucina woman—she's taken nearly a week to inform us."

Magagna shrugged. "She claims that the woman had been talking of going back to Milan—for the weekend, to see some friends." Magagna took a cigarette from his packet and lit it. "Not very convincing, I'm afraid."

Some men in white overalls were pushing through the crowd. They carried a rolled stretcher; through the trees, where the cars were parked, Trotti saw the blue flashing light of the ambulance.

The police photographer wore a loose, seersucker jacket and jeans; dark black hair fell into his eyes. Without taking any notice of Trotti or Bottone, he had moved about the corpse, taking photographs. Now the large camera hung in his hand and like a child who had lost interest in a game, he stood staring, his back towards the dead body, at the far side of the river where young people were splashing in the water.

A kayak went past.

The ambulance men wore soft shoes and as they lowered the stretcher beside the severed remains of the body, Trotti had the unpleasant impression that he had been here before. The sun was strong on the back of his head. The ambulance men unwrapped a colorless plastic sheet. The sand was white and the reflected glare hurt Trotti's eyes. Somebody was talking to him. His mouth was dry with the taste of cigarette smoke.

He threw the cigarette into the river and as he watched, the charred paper began to disintegrate and the specks of tobacco were carried away by the eddies of the current.

"Signor Guerra."

The man with the cigar now stood with his hands behind his back. He was addressing Trotti while his eyes followed the deft movement of the ambulance men. The crowd drew apart and the odd bulk of the stretcher—they had placed a grey woollen blanket over everything—was carried away to the impatient ambulance.

"You must be Commissario Trotti." He had removed the cigar from his mouth and was smiling. He held out his hand.

Trotti tried to concentrate; very slightly, he shook his head. "Yes."

They shook hands. "Guerra." He wore a well-cut suit with thin lapels and a white shirt without a tie. Almost apologetically, he went on, "I own the restaurant. And I believe I have the honor of knowing your wife."

The sleepy sensation of living through the events for the second time disappeared suddenly. Trotti looked at the man. Guerra. Bright eyes, his grey hair neatly combed, quiet elegance. A curved nose.

"My wife?"

"Signora Trotti." He nodded. "She sometimes comes here to eat. On several occasions I have asked her to bring you. But you are a busy man."

Dr. Bottone and the photographer were walking away; the camera banged loosely against the photographer's thigh.

"She used to be a doctor," Trotti said, without knowing why. It was a foolish remark; Guerra simply nodded.

"She told me that. I must compliment you, Commissario. A truly beautiful woman." The glance he gave Trotti suggested both admiration and surprise. "Perhaps you'd care for a drink." His voice was persuasive. "You and your friend. A strong drink after this unpleasant experience."

Trotti called Magagna, who was writing something in his notebook. Magagna threw his cigarette away.

Together, with Signor Guerra holding Trotti's arm, they went through the crowd and up the concrete steps, out of the afternoon sun into the cool, conditioned air of the Casa sul Fiume.

31

WITHOUT SMILING, MAGAGNA told a couple of jokes about the Carabinieri and Trotti laughed, noisily and unexpectedly. They had drunk too much, both of them. It had been a normal reaction to the ghastliness of death; and l'architetto Guerra had been generous with his whisky. But now, as they rode the lift up to the third floor of the Questura, Trotti had difficulty in controlling his laughter. He giggled while his fingers ran across the hammer and sickle engraved in the metallic paint. The enclosed space was thick with the alcohol of their breath.

When the lift stopped and the doors slid open, Trotti was looking in the mirror. His own image appeared blurred. He did not look at his face but at the reflection of Magagna's head and his thick black hair. It seemed squashed.

She was back, thank God.

Magagna directed him, taking him by the arm, through the open doors onto the polished marble. Principessa did not move; only her sad eyes followed the unsteady movement of the Commissario Trotti and Brigadiere Magagna.

"Trotti."

Not a question; with his developed sixth sense, Gino recognized him. The eyes moved languidly behind the distorting glasses; the mouth was hard set. "You're wanted immediately." He put out a hand looking for Trotti's arm; finding it, he pulled

Trotti towards him. Magagna watched, his thumbs caught in the webbing trouser belt.

"The boss." Gino whispered, the garlic competing with the rancid wine of his breath. "He's in a bad mood. He came in half an hour ago, and he was angry when I had to tell him you were out." The short-lived euphoria drained from Trotti's body like rainwater. "He wants you."

Somewhere along the corridor, a door opened noisily and Gino pushed Trotti away and let his unshaven old chin fall to his chest as though suddenly overcome by sleep. Principessa emitted a muted growl.

Trotti returned to his dingy office while his shoes squealed unpleasantly on the marble floor.

"Ah, Commissario Trotti."

Leonardelli was walking briskly, an arm raised, along the intermittent light of the corridor, past the toilet and past the Faema coffee machine. A few paper envelopes that had once contained sugar had overflowed from the ashtray and now lay like large confetti on the marble floor.

"I really must talk with you." He was slightly out of breath as he reached the two men and he adjusted his tie. He was as neatly dressed—double-breasted suit and a different pair of English shoes, the color of oxblood—as on a weekday. "And then I think you'll have work to do." The smile he gave Magagna was cold, brief and dismissive. "It is with you, Commissario, that I must clear up some points."

Magagna nodded and went into Trotti's office.

"I am not sure, either, that I like my men to wear civilian clothes."

"My orders, Questore," Trotti replied.

"Of course, of course. This way please."

"And furthermore, today is Brigadiere Magagna's rest day; his helping me like this is a personal favor."

"We're not Turin metalworkers, Trotti, and we are available at all times if our duty so requires."

His mouth closed sharply and without another word he walked down the corridor to his office. He went through the

door without the normal courtesy of holding it open for Trotti.
Nor did he ask Trotti to sit down.

"I am far from satisfied, Commissario."

Trotti stood still in front of the desk; the dying taste of the
whisky lingered like a bad idea on his tongue. He held his hands
behind his back and looked at Leonardelli's cold, symmetrical
face. The features were sharply contrasted by the strong sunlight
coming through the blinds, throwing zebra stripes on the desk
and the white pile of the carpet.

Leonardelli's fingers had intertwined above the empty desktop; the thumbs collided rhythmically. "You are not doing your
job, Trotti."

The sight of the mutilated corpse on the beach darted through
his mind and for a second he thought he was going to be sick
again.

"You are behaving like a fool, Trotti."

Trotti looked at the nervous movement of the thumbs.

"If I didn't know you well, I would certainly be tempted to
ask for your resignation."

Trotti waited; he felt a strange sense of indifference. Outside
there was the muted sound of Sunday in the city. A child laughing. Through the blinds, he could see the Italian flag hanging
from the monument to the dead. The red, white and green stripes
were limp, unmoved by any breeze. Unimportant.

"You are a good policeman." Leonardelli raised his shoulders
to underline his own magnanimity. "A good policeman with a
rare sense of devotion. I am not a fool, Trotti; every day, I must
praise the devotion and self-denial of our officers, but do not
think I am my own dupe. This is Italy and I know Italy. Where
nothing works and where the state, the army, the forces of order
are just names. Self-denial and devotion—they don't exist. Most
policemen do a job they hate for purely economic reasons—the
pay packet on the twenty-seventh of each month. But you are
different. You love your job and you bring to it an almost Germanic conviction. In a way, you are not Italian, you don't allow
yourself to be pushed away with appearances—because if you
did, you would have got a lot further. Instead you have done

your job—and made enemies." He raised his shoulders again. "Not least, I imagine, your wife, who would have preferred a husband with an important position in the Pubblica Sicurezza."

"There is no need to talk about my wife."

Leonardelli paused. "Please," he said. "Please sit down." He smiled and Trotti pulled up the low, white leather armchair. Leaning back in his seat, Leonardelli took a cigarette from his silver case. "A good officer and a devoted policeman. That is why I wanted you back from Bari. Oh, I know, you think I am a political animal—and perhaps you are not wrong. But above all, I want a quiet, peaceful town. No headlines, no scandal, just the quiet day-to-day routine of a small Italian city getting on with its business while the rest of the country"—he took the cigarette from his mouth and pointed towards the blinds—"lives through its hell of violence, armed robbery and kidnapping. A quiet city at all costs, Trotti, that's what I want. And it is why I am having second thoughts about your usefulness here."

"Why?"

Leonardelli inhaled again while his eyes looked at Trotti, looking for insolence behind the brusqueness of the question. Trotti's face was devoid of emotion. He answered Leonardelli's glance.

"You are not objective, Trotti. You are allowing yourself to get caught up because you are working among people you know and who are close to you. In short, you are not acting professionally."

"Professionally?"

"This child—the Ermagni girl—she's your goddaughter. The father is a friend of yours—goodness knows why, from what I've heard of him—and you are clearly allowing yourself to be blackmailed into helping. When it is no longer necessary. The child is back, she is safe and sound, there is nothing wrong with her." With the cigarette between his two fingers, he pointed towards his desk. "I have the medical report. Nothing. No physical damage."

"She was kidnapped."

Leonardelli smiled understandingly. "You say that because

you are her godfather." He then lowered his voice and continued, speaking more confidentially, "You are being emotive, Trotti, and I am surprised. It is the last thing any officer should indulge in and you more than anyone else should know that."

"She was kidnapped," Trotti repeated.

"Of course we have good reasons to believe in a criminal act. Anonima Sequestri—the Mafia organization that specialises in kidnapping. There's no reason for their not working here as they work everywhere else in Italy—and believe me, if I thought that there was a real chance of this girl having being kidnapped by the Mafia, I would give you carte blanche and I'd tell you to go out and get them. A quiet city—I want a quiet city. This is a quiet place and I do everything to keep it so, but objectively speaking, we have our percentage of wealthy industrialists and manufacturers. People who don't pay taxes and who are ready to sacrifice anything for the few people they genuinely care about. But Trotti," the thumbs had returned to their nervous tapping, "kidnap the daughter of a taxi driver? I don't think it's really very likely."

"It could be a mistake."

"The Mafia doesn't make mistakes, Trotti." A brief, patronizing laugh. "Be reasonable, Trotti, be reasonable. The child—how old is she? Five, six? She's not important to the Mafia—or to anybody other than her family. She probably went off with somebody—perhaps even a relative. I say perhaps—it doesn't matter anyway."

"It matters to her father."

"A drunk, neurotic retired policeman."

"My friend," Trotti said softly. Outside, the flag had suddenly snapped into movement, caught by a breeze along Strada Nuova. Leonardelli brought his hand hard down onto the desktop.

"Damn it, Trotti, it doesn't matter."

"It matters to me."

Leonardelli stubbed out the cigarette. "Then I will have no choice but to ask for your transfer." He was trying to control himself but his voice trembled slightly. He took another cigarette from his case. "You're causing me a lot of trouble."

"I am doing my job."

"There are times when it is your job to do nothing." He lit the cigarette and stood up; the back of his hand flicked at imagined dust on his jacket. Then he pointed at Trotti. "It is not your job to pester the mayor."

Trotti felt tired; again the sense of déjà vu. His head ached and because of the whisky, he was now finding it difficult to concentrate. What Leonardelli was saying was important, very important. His career—his future—was in this man's hands. Like the smoldering cigarette, Trotti could be dispensed with prematurely. Trotti breathed deeply, tried to concentrate.

"Something's happening to you, Trotti. You are overreacting and you don't seem to be concerned by anything other than your immediate—and mistaken—goals. This is Italy, Trotti, this is Italy. Nothing is simple and you know that. There are elections—or perhaps you haven't seen the billboards and the soldiers in the street with the strange feathers in their hats. The meetings? The First Secretary of the Socialist Party? The papers? Or perhaps you don't read them? Perhaps you're too busy with your private vendetta to see these things?"

Trotti did not reply.

"Or the fact that Aldo Moro has been kidnapped? That this country is living through the worst crisis in thirty years? Then let me tell you. While you play your little games, the freedom and the democracy that we have built up, the freedom that has transformed Italy from a backward, third-world country into one of the major industrial nations, is being threatened. And you don't care. You don't give a damn. Or you are above such things."

"Anna Ermagni was kidnapped. I have been trying to identify her kidnappers."

Leonardelli sat down; he nodded with ironic sympathy. "Of course, of course. And that entitles you to take police procedure into your own hands? It entitles you to go and see the mayor on a Sunday and to ask him foolish and offensive questions. You have that divine right. It doesn't matter if you make him angry, if you call into question the probity of this city's first citizen." He pointed at the phone. "I have to do the mopping up. I have to come into the Questura on a Sunday. I have to apologize and explain to Mariani that you are a good policeman and a good officer." He tapped his chest and ash tumbled from the cigarette without his noticing, "I have to carry the can."

"I was acting in accordance with what I considered to be my duty."

"It is neither your duty nor your right to take the law into your hands and to act unilaterally, without the spoken or tacit agreement of your superiors. You have never been officially charged with the Ermagni affair. You took it upon yourself—simply because Ermagni once used to drive your car. You had no right." A long pause. "And now you must let the matter drop." His voice softened. "Trotti, let us be reasonable. We are all overworked." He looked down and caught sight of the ash; he frowned and brushed at it. "Let us be reasonable. Kidnapped or not kidnapped, the girl is back with her father, alive and well. The matter is over."

Trotti looked at Leonardelli.

"I want you to get on with your job. Gracchi and the Guerra girl—I told you expressly that I wanted you to keep an eye on them and I discover that you're wasting your time over an affair that is finished."

"Pisanelli and di Bono are doing a good job."

"Where are they?"

"By the river—at least, that's where they were earlier. They haven't been in touch because they've moved away from the car."

"I want to know what's happening. I've got to know and I don't want the Carabinieri moving in. Not now, not with elections a week away. I want you on the job, Trotti, and I want you reporting back to me every four or so hours." A brief smile. "I don't think you understand politics—no doubt because you don't think that politics are important. You are wrong, I am afraid. In Italy, politics is everything, because politics is where the power is. That's the system and there's nothing that you or I can do to change it. We have to play by the rules the politicians impose because if we don't, we go under. I have got where I have got by being careful, by respecting all the little prides and *amour propre* of the politicians." A cloud of smoke. "I won't have you destroying everything."

Trotti stood up. "May I go?"

Leonardelli looked up and scrutinized Trotti's face. "You are not a fool. And in a different context, I would have a lot of admiration for you and for your honesty." He shrugged. "But this is Italy—and you are expendable. If you cause me any more problems, I shall ask for your reappointment elsewhere."

Another world. Trotti could not persuade himself that what was being said concerned him—or that it was important.

"I'll have you sent back to Bari. To the South. The Mezzo-giorno, Trotti. And although it doesn't appear to matter to you, I am sure your wife will be far from happy. And I know you care about your wife, Trotti."

Trotti turned and went silently to the door.

"Forget the child, forget Ermagni," Leonardelli said softly to his back.

32

A SENSE OF depression came over him. Depression and fatigue. Twice he picked up the phone and then put it down again. He knew he should be making enquiries about the gypsies—he had a promise to keep—but he could not be bothered. His head hurt; the effect, he knew, of drinking too much on an empty stomach. He now wished he had not accepted Guerra's Chivas Regal.

Above, the pigeons continued their cooing and in the cloudless sky, the sun moved slowly westward; the shadow of the window frame crept across the dusty floor. He stood up and went to the door. "Magagna."

Magagna did not come and when, ten minutes later, Trotti left his office to go to the reception desk, he was surprised to see that Gino and the Principessa had left. The soft cloth slippers lay neatly beneath the desk and the dark spectacle case was placed beside the telephone. A red button glowed, unheeded; a small padlock had been set through a hole in the dial.

Trotti went back to his desk, sat down and opened the bottom drawer. He lifted the bottle onto his desk, unscrewed the top and poured colorless grappa into the lid. He drank. The slightly serrated edge of the lid cut at his lips. Two lidfuls. He shuddered, ran a hand through his hair and returned the bottle to the bottom drawer. He sat then for five minutes, staring out of the window over the terracotta rooftops while the alcohol burned its way down to his stomach.

"Magagna."

There was no sound in the corridors; just the pigeons, who did not know that it was Sunday.

He's gone home, the lazy bastard, Trotti thought and, picking up the telephone, managed, after a long wait—seventeen rings—to get through to Central Operations. The woman spoke in a soft voice with a marked Milanese accent. He wondered whether he had ever seen her.

"About Pisanelli and di Bono."

"Which extension, please?"

"This is fifty-seven. Trotti of Squadra Mobile."

"Ah, you, Commissario." She laughed.

"Can you tell me where they are?"

The line went dead while the woman made her enquiries; when she came back, her voice seemed distant. "Last report was at eleven o'clock."

"Where from?"

The woman paused. "They were together. On the Piacenza road, at the riverside."

"Nothing since?"

This time the phone squealed as she put her hand over the mouthpiece. Her voice was muffled; yet Trotti heard her mention the name Pisanelli.

There was a forgotten packet of sweets in one of the drawers. Tutti frutti; bright greens, reds and oranges and on the side of the packet, a couple of darkly printed lines, stating the artificial colorings. E 110, E 133.

"No further information, Commissario. Do you want me to contact you?"

"That would be very kind. Thank you."

Then the woman said, "We don't often see you these days, Commissario. You no longer eat here."

"Things have been busy lately." He felt embarrassed.

"A good-looking man like you." She laughed.

He thanked her and hung up; he could feel that he had blushed slightly. Then he stared out of the window while sucking on a succession of sweets.

It was another half-hour before Magagna tapped on the door and then put his head into the room.

"Where the hell have you been?"

He grinned, the hairs of his mustache stretching along the upper lip. His teeth were bright.

"Well?"

Magagna shrugged, still grinning. "Someone here for you."

"On a Sunday?"

Magagna stepped back and the woman came into the office; smaller than Trotti remembered her and had it not been for the hair pulled back from the high, pale forehead, he might not have recognized her immediately.

"So I was right?" The corner of her lips gave the very slightest hint of a smile.

"Right about what?"

"When you came to the school, you told me you were a social worker but I can sm—I can recognize a policeman."

While Magagna closed the door behind her and then hurried past her to usher the woman to an armchair, she looked at Trotti with her unblinking eyes. Unblinking and cold.

"Kindly be seated, signora."

She sat down without looking at either Magagna or the chair. She was wearing corduroy jeans and she crossed her feet at the ankles and looped her arms about her knees, pulling them up towards her chin.

"You see." Trotti gave her a brief smile and pointed at the piled folders, the dusty radiator, the scratched desktop, the various, fading wall maps, the threadbare armchairs. "This is where I work. A policeman—and I spend my weekends here."

The grey eyes looked at him; they were devoid of expression.

"You have already met Brigadiere Magagna."

Magagna said, "I met her at the main entrance. She was looking for you."

Again Trotti smiled. "So you remember my name, signora?"

"It has been in the papers."

"Ah."

Magagna had pulled up an armchair beside her; now he was leaning forward, his hands hanging between his knees and his face towards the young girl. He was frowning slightly.

Trotti took a sheet of paper from one of the drawers and unscrewed a ballpoint pen. "How can I help you?"

She sounded surprised. "Help me?"

"A young married woman like you—I imagine you can think of better ways of spending your free afternoons than in the gloom of the Questura. You have better things to do. I know that I have."

She pulled her knees closer to her chin. "It's about Anna."

"Then I think I should perhaps tell you that the affair is over."

"Over?" Her head to one side.

"The child is back with her father."

"You've found the kidnappers? You've got them?"

"I didn't say that. No—we have arrested nobody. But because of the political situation, I am afraid we have more pressing things to do." He watched her face carefully, looking for her reaction. "Anna is safe with her father—that is what matters most."

"It's precisely why I've come to see you." She was wearing a loose checked woolen shirt, several sizes too big for her, with a worn collar. She took a packet of cigarettes—American, without filters—from the breast pocket and with a casual, strangely masculine movement, she flicked at the bottom of the packet. A cigarette jumped upwards and she set it in the corner of her mouth.

Immediately, Magagna had a flickering cigarette lighter in his hand. He held it to the end of the cigarette; the tobacco smoldered and came alight. She inhaled and thanked him perfunctorily. Her eyes remained on Trotti.

"Ermagni phoned me," she said.

"What did he want?"

"Twice. He phoned me twice to make accusations. To tell me that I was responsible for the disappearance of his daughter."

"He said that you kidnapped her?"

She shook her head. "No—but he said it was all my fault."

"Your fault?"

She breathed on her cigarette and watched with worried disapproval as the two streams of smoke poured from her nostrils. "He phoned me last night. It must've been late and I was alone and about to go to bed. At first I didn't know who it was—at first I thought it was my husband playing a joke. The sort of thing he does. The funny, gabbling voice and the strange accusations; it was only when I caught Anna's name that I realized it was Ermagni." She put a hand to her large, pale forehead. "My God, he's quite mad. Neurotic, paranoid. He is quite convinced that everything that happens is directed against him—a universal plot and everybody is ganging up on him. Me, his father-in-law and you—he seems to think we have all mounted a fiendish plan together to take his daughter away from him. She hates him, he says, and it is our fault. We've all told her that he murdered his wife. His daughter is scared of him, it is our fault."

Trotti was frowning. "Anna's back with him. What more does he want?"

"It doesn't seem to have stopped his drinking. He was offensive. He started calling me names and I hung up. He rang back and started to make threats."

"What sort of threats?"

"He didn't say—he just said that I'd be well advised to be careful—careful in the way I teach his child." She ran a hand along her hair, following the straight, combed lines. "He feels guilty, of course."

"In what way?" It was Magagna who asked the question. He looked from the girl to Trotti.

"About his wife." She shrugged. "Perhaps he feels that he really did kill her; he's trying to punish himself."

"You don't kidnap your own daughter to punish yourself."

"No—but perhaps that's how he interprets things. Divine retribution."

"That's all very well," Trotti said, playing with the pen, "but it doesn't explain why the girl was taken."

"She was kidnapped," Magagna said.

"Ermagni has not got any money."

"Several million lire—a fling on totocalcio, a nice little holiday in Pescara, the best restaurants. I could do with several million."

Trotti asked Signora Perbene, "He mentioned his wife?"

She nodded. "He always does." More smoke from her nose. "He says that I look like her."

Again Magagna spoke. "You think he killed her then?"

"She died of leukemia. You can't drop leukemia pills in your wife's cappuccino." The hurried glance the young woman gave Magagna was far from flattering.

"You said," Trotti went on, very slightly embarrassed, "that he made advances. Sexual advances, when his wife was in the hospital."

The girl nodded.

Trotti tapped with the pen on the desk; for a few seconds he looked out of the window. The roofs were beginning to be ridged with the lengthening shadows of their own tiles. The pigeons continued their ceaseless cooing. "There is something in what you say. He couldn't have killed his wife—that's obvious. And anyway, he's not a killer. A few days ago, he came round to my house and he had a gun that he pointed at me." A dry laugh. "I knew he wouldn't do anything. Too gentle. He was too gentle for his job in the police force. But it is possible—as you say—that he is trying to punish himself. Unwittingly. Or perhaps . . ." He stopped and put the pen to his lips.

"Yes?"

"Who took the child? Somebody must've done it. But so far, there is no motive. It was not for money. If we could find the reason for her disappearance, then we'd know where to look for the culprit."

"You said the matter was over." Signora Perbene's eyes were sharp.

Trotti smiled. He continued. "Perhaps somebody wanted to put pressure on him. Why? I don't know. A taxi driver, an ex-policeman, it is not as though he were in a position of importance or power. But it is possible that he told somebody how he felt—about his wife and how she had died. Somebody who was close to him and somebody whom he thought he could confide in."

"I don't understand." Magagna was still frowning.

"The way to blackmail was then clear. Blackmail him for what—I don't know. But the way to do it was there. Ermagni believes that he was responsible for his wife's death; by taking the girl, the kidnappers knew they could blackmail his conscience." Trotti stopped; then brusquely, he threw the pen down onto the desk. "That's where we'll have to leave things for the time being."

"You mean you have no wish to search for the kidnappers?"

"I'm afraid, signora, that I have to obey my orders. There are other more pressing occupations for this office."

"And the threats to my life? Make no mistake, Commissario . . ."

"There are no threats to your life, Signora Perbene. Believe me."

She unclasped her hands and let her legs down onto the floor. "It doesn't matter, then, that this man can make threats, that he can make my life a misery. I'm just a woman—a silly, hysterical woman. That's it, isn't it?"

"Signora, you are not silly and you are not hysterical."

"Then what do I do, Commissario Trotti?"

Trotti stood up. He picked up the pen and screwed the top on tightly. "You go home."

"And if Ermagni phones again?"

"If he pesters you, you tell him the truth. You tell him that you have been to the Questura and that you have spoken with me."

Her eyes flashed angrily. "You are his friend."

"Perhaps—but I am a policeman." Trotti shook his head. "No, signora, you have nothing to be afraid of. I will do my duty." He moved round the desk and approached her; she remained seated.

A knock on the door.

"However, I must repeat that the Anna Ermagni affair is over, for the time being at least."

An appuntato who worked in Communications, a Sicilian. He put his head through the door; his face was pale.

"Commissario Trotti?"

"Yes?"

"Ah." He seemed relieved. "I've been trying to get you on the phone. Your extension doesn't seem to be working."

"What is it?"

He pulled at his tie. "Somebody on the phone for you. Can you come down to take the call?"

"Who?"

He clicked his tongue, his head went backwards slightly. "A journalist. He said it was very important—something about the kidnappers having contacted him."

33

TROTTI GOT HOME at six and though his head felt hollow—three very strong cups of coffee at the offices of the *Provincia Padana*—he was nonetheless cheerful. Agnese's small car was parked outside the garage and as he came up the stairs, he heard the noise of the television.

"Ciao, Papa." Pioppi was sitting cross-legged before the flickering image, its light reflecting on her features. She smiled and as he bent over to kiss her, she whispered softly, "Mama is here."

Agnese was in the kitchen.

She sat at the small table with her arm outstretched across the plastic top. In her hand, she held a glass that was almost empty. Small cubes of ice, the edges rounded, jostled against the moist sides. The liquid was red. A bottle of Campari stood in the middle of the table; a wasp worried at the open mouth and the spots of crystallized sugar. Propped against the bottle, the parish news-sheet that Agnese appeared to be reading.

He noticed the ticking of the clock.

She was wearing a velvet dress that sloped down from one shoulder, revealing the brown softness of her skin and the gentle divide of her breasts. Her dark hair glistened; across the back of the kitchen chair, she had placed a stole.

He approached his wife and kissed her on the cheek.

Her hair smelled as it had always smelled and the memory of the elm tree by the river flashed through his mind.

"Buona sera," he whispered.

She did not move. The motionless green eyes stared at the piece of paper; one hand was on her lap. He looked at her long, thin fingers.

"I've put a suit out for you." Her voice was cold. "A suit that isn't too shabby. And a shirt and tie. And I'd be very grateful if you'd polish your shoes—the black ones, of course. And you had better shower. You smell of the Questura." She turned her head and at last the green eyes looked at him. "By the way, what do you want me to do with the pistol you left in the washing machine?" Before he could answer, she went on, "And for God's sake, shampoo your hair. Don't put on that wretched hair oil. It makes you look like a village gigolo."

THEY HAD THE best seats and Trotti felt like a child awaiting Christmas.

The lights dimmed. The plush red curtain was silently drawn back and the spotlight caught the two singers, neatly delineated on the stage. The soprano was a large woman but she had fine features and Trotti soon found himself being caught up in the unreal world of Verdi.

The dismembered corpse, the gypsies, Leonardelli—he forgot about them all. His wife, too, seemed happy. She let him hold her hand and her green eyes followed the movement on the stage. From time to time, along with the appreciative audience, she clapped and on two separate occasions, she turned towards her husband and smiled.

"I like your tie," she whispered. The thin fingers ran along the silk while her eyes sparkled.

There was a long interval and people—friends of Agnese's—came to speak with them in the opulent bar. The chandelier appeared to hold flickering candles, the carpet was deep red and the barmen wore mauve epaulettes to their white jackets. Agnese laughed often.

"La Scala of Milan," a woman said to Trotti. "The best." She raised her plucked eyebrows and took a large sip from her drink. "And this is the first time they have ever come here since the end of the war." She lowered her glass. "And who are you?"

"Commissario Trotti."

"Ah, you have a beautiful wife." She had green eye shadow and her white hair formed blue-tinted profiteroles. "The Scala—we have to thank the mayor."

"Of course."

Agnese was nearby, talking to two tall men; from where he was, Trotti could not see their faces. They wore elegant dark suits, had broad shoulders and neatly cut hair that was greying at the nape of the neck.

"Not that I have any time for Communists." The old woman fiddled at a silver crucifix hanging in the wrinkled pleats of her powdered throat. "Horrible people. I remember that awful man, Togliatti, and look what they've done to Aldo Moro—a good man, even though he is from the south." Her fingernails were deep red; her knuckles grey. "Communist or not, this Mariani has saved our theater." She looked at Trotti with the bright, inquisitive eye of a bird. "The other people wanted to pull it down."

He heard the light laugh of his wife.

"Close it down. Friends of mine, friends for fifty years, respectable people from the best families—they wanted to pull down this wonderful building." A gesture towards the bar, the rows of bottles faithfully reflected in the mirror, the serious-faced waiters and the old brass water heater. "They wanted to knock it down and put a supermarket in its place."

"Terrible."

"He's a southerner, you know. The mayor—he's not one of us." The lines running from her thin nose to her lips were lengthened with disapproval. "But at least he has kept it alive. I suppose we will have to pay for everything on our taxes—but as my dear husband used to say, we are the people who have to pay for everything." They were standing near a staircase and her claw-like hand touched the gilded, baroque rail.

"Communist or not, he has kept it alive. La Scala? In our city? It is a great honor—the last time was in '37 when they were collecting money for our poor soldiers in Spain."

The bell rang and excusing himself—"A nice man," he heard

her say as he moved away—he approached his wife. She was still talking with the men. They gave him tight, small smiles. He slipped his arm through hers and he sensed the tension in her body.

"Time to take our seats."

Later, as they were walking along the carpeted corridor and he could feel her body beside him—he looked at the movement of her silver slippers on the dark carpet—he asked her, "Who were those men?"

She stopped, shrugging off his arm; the distant reflection of a chandelier was caught in her green eyes. She looked at him and Trotti did not know whether it was pity or anger that hardened her face.

"You are a policeman." She spoke in harsh sibilants. "A policeman and even at the opera, with your own wife, you can't stop asking your stupid, prying, flatfoot questions."

They returned to their seats in silence.

Trotti did not enjoy the music. He was angry with himself and felt that with his stupid question he had ruined the relaxed atmosphere of the evening. In recent years, it was rare that they went out for an evening together. Agnese had her own friends and her own interests.

Trotti felt wretched, then halfway through the last act, at the end of a rather moving aria, his wife had whispered to him, "Let's go," and he had felt her soft breath on his cheek.

The taxis were already waiting outside in the street. Yellow Fiats, their drivers smoking quietly in the gloom of the front seat, while overhead, the street lights swayed gently. The evening air was warm. They got into a taxi and Agnese held his hand in the back seat. They reached via Milano; the road was dark. The last customers were coming out of the pizzeria and from the fields came the sound of the crickets' night chorus. Trotti paid the driver while Agnese let herself into the house. He then went up the stairs and as he entered the house, he saw her bent over Pioppi, who lay asleep. Agnese's hand brushed at their daughter's dark hair and Trotti recalled the same silhouette and the same motherly gesture when Pioppi was still a little girl.

More than fifteen years earlier.

They went into the bedroom.

"Your tie," she murmured, smiling, and undid the knot. She unbuttoned his shirt and pulled at the long shirttails. He had no time to undress. She began pulling at his clothes and threw them hurriedly to the floor. Then she clung to him. She raised her thigh, rubbed it against his body and her mouth kissed his face.

Agnese's skin was soft and silky and her slender body was reassuringly familiar beneath his hands. She whispered words that he did not understand.

34

THERE WERE POPPIES, Trotti noticed, that formed a bright red line along the edge of the cornfield. Magagna turned off the Piacenza road; in the distance, the contours of the Apennines were clearly visible like ridges seen beneath a microscope. He took the track following the line of poppies towards the trees.

Then Magagna turned off the engine and the car rolled a few more meters with just the sound of the rubble beneath the tires. It came to a halt, having lost all momentum. Through the high corn—there was a slight breeze causing ripples along the green surface—they could see a couple of tiled roofs. Old farmhouses. A chicken cackled and then another; the air had the pungent yet pleasant smell of manure. A smell that almost hid the synthetic odor of the textile plant. The two brick stacks, like long black fingers, belched their grey translucent smoke into the sky.

Beyond the smoke stacks, dull and almost insignificant, partially hidden by the trees of a thicket, the dome of the cathedral.

Trotti looked again at his watch; not yet midday.

"They're over there." Magagna had opened the door. He ran a finger along his mustache and pointed towards the trees where a reflection of sunlight sparkled through the narrow trunks.

Magagna lit a cigarette.

"Put that out." Trotti's whisper was angry. "He'll smell the smoke." He held out a packet of sweets. "Take one of these. Aniseed."

Magagna stubbed the cigarette into the dashboard ashtray, but unlike Trotti, he did not take a sweet. "Thanks."

They got out of the car. Magagna closed the doors silently and they set off towards the trees. They followed the grass verge between the blazing white of the rubble track and the cool of the ditch. A frog jumped away in surprise and with an indiscreet plop fell into the stagnant water.

Pisanelli waved. He was lying on his belly. He lay on the river bank and his feet dangled out beyond the hard red earth and only a meter beneath his shoes, the Po hurried by. The shoes, Trotti noticed, were well polished and without a hint of dust. Beneath them, the river followed its own swirling logic.

They clambered down beside him. In the shade, the air was much cooler. Trotti lowered his head onto his arm and he had to resist the temptation of closing his eyes. He had slept little that night.

"Di Bono?" Trotti lifted his head.

Pisanelli's voice was hoarse. He tried to smile. "He'll be back later. He's gone to get something to eat." There was sleep in Pisanelli's eyes. His young face was haggard. "The bike's over there."

In one hand, Pisanelli held the small two-way radio. In the other hand there was a pair of battered binoculars, which he handed to Trotti.

"We brought you a sandwich."

Magagna now had an unlit cigarette in his mouth; he was chewing at the filter as he gave the small plastic bag to Pisanelli. Pisanelli took it and propped it among the roots of an oak tree.

The motorcycle was a Laverda. It had a deep petrol tank and handlebars that sloped downwards like the ears of a cow. 1000 cc and powerful, sloping lines, glinting disc brakes. It leaned heavily to one side, pushing against the stand; the earth was creased with the flattened tracks of heavy-duty tires.

Still smiling, Pisanelli whispered, "And on the other side of the river there's a fisherman. With a long rod. He's been there since early morning and he hasn't yet cast a line."

"Perhaps he prefers to buy fish fingers," Magagna said.

Trotti did not turn to look. His eyes went from the dappled light dancing on the exhaust pipe to the hut. Overlapping slats of creosoted wood that formed the dark walls. No windows and the door appeared padlocked from the outside. A roof of corrugated iron.

Nothing stirred other than the tall weeds and the yellow dandelions, rubbing against the harsh planking. Bees, flies, insects droning through the air and the sound of grasshoppers. And the soft hiss of the river.

"I'm not hungry," Pisanelli said. He was still wearing his leather jacket but the suede elbows were now scuffed. He had not shaved; the growing stubble was pale and gave his face a haggard look. "But I could do with some sleep."

The dredger floated almost motionless on the water, pulling at the rusting hawser. The river formed minute swirling pools along the bulwarks. Rusting scoops, tilting downwards, hung from the overhead conveyor belt. They moved with the breeze. There was a small, natural beach where the white sand glistened, unrelieved by any shadow. Sloping pyramids of sand, higher than two men, that had been bitten into by the dredger. Now that the scoops had stopped, the piles looked like half-eaten apples.

Pisanelli pointed. "It's where they get the sand for cement; they pick it up along the river and stockpile it here. Or they did until the mayor put a stop to it. When this"—a nod indicating the river and its banks—"became a natural park, they had to stop. Of course, they're taking the mayor to court—as you can imagine, the local building trade and their architects are no friends of the mayor. They'll probably lose their case—and a lot of money, too."

"What's in the hut?"

"Dynamite." Pisanelli smiled and then the small radio—a woman's voice—emitted scratching sounds; a voice that Trotti recognized. Pisanelli answered softly, "He's with me now. Yes." A pause. "Am ceasing contact," and he switched off the radio, closing the aerial with a snap.

Magagna was sitting on the riverbank, staring across the water. "You're right. He doesn't seem to be very interested in his fishing." He moved the unlit cigarette across his mouth. "He's got a pair of binoculars."

"Maybe they're small fish."

"Long time since I've done any fishing," Magagna mused. "Long time since I've had a holiday." He pushed at the rim of his glasses.

"He's an NP man," Trotti said simply, without taking his eyes off the hut. "We'll have to act fast before they move in."

Pisanelli was wearing a gun beneath his jacket; he undid the two buttons and the yellow leather holster was visible against his shirt. Large damp patches at the armpit. "We flush him out?" The gun, like Pisanelli's grin, was unmenacing.

Magagna turned round. "What if he's armed? You say there's dynamite. We can't afford to play at cowboys and Indians."

It was Trotti who noticed the door open; immediately he recognized Gracchi from the photographs—but he was taller than he had imagined. He carried a bag under his arm and he looked around carefully before stepping out onto the hard earth. There was a keyring attached to his belt—he was wearing long blue jeans and a yellow tennis shirt—and he turned to close the padlock.

Trotti had to make a decision.

Adidas running shoes and scruffy long hair. There was a helmet on the saddle of the motorbike; he attached the bag—made of plastic and advertising a boutique in the city center—to the saddle and put on the helmet. Then he lifted his leg and sat easily on the machine.

Magagna had drawn his gun.

Pisanelli glanced at him but before he could undo the holster catch Trotti said, "Pick him up."

The two policemen scrambled up the riverbank and immediately Trotti knew that he had not been thinking; he was tired and he was allowing Leonardelli's obsessions to get the better of him. He had no right to risk their young lives—young men whom he liked and for whom he felt responsibility.

The engine of the motorbike coughed and came alive; blue exhaust erupted from the chrome pipes.

Magagna was running and Pisanelli was behind him, both shouting. Magagna held the gun, Pisanelli fumbled at his shoulder. Trotti came up after them.

Perhaps it was the noise of the engine or the muffling effect of his helmet—he looked like a medieval knight—that had prevented Gracchi from hearing them immediately. For that, Trotti knew he should be grateful; a question of a fraction of a second and Gracchi could have drawn a gun.

He did—but slowly. A P38. Trotti shouted to his two men, but of course, they had seen. Trotti watched—it was like a film, the individual frames moving slowly before him and yet he was confused.

Trotti was about twenty meters behind them.

Magagna veered to the left and moved in front of the Laverda. He stopped, facing the rider. Gracchi was clumsily trying to kick away the side prop; he had let the gun fall.

Magagna stood, his legs bent at the knee and the gun pointing towards the rider.

"Dynamite! Be careful!"

Gracchi released the clutch, the side prop had come up against the body of the cycle but the earth was churned up on the powdery ground and formed a neat arc of grit and billowing petrol fumes in the air behind the machine.

Too late.

By now Pisanelli, running slower, his jacket flapping, had reached Gracchi and with the palm of his hand, he slammed against the helmet. The Laverda kicked up more dust but the front wheel was askew, pointing towards the hut. The motorbike started to topple sideways and then it fell. Gracchi was caught against the side of the hut. Angrily the rear wheel started to spin faster and faster, unchecked by friction. Pisanelli was sprawled over the bike and he was screaming.

A deafening whine, more clouds coming from the exhaust. Gracchi was on the ground, his head at a strange angle, like a broken puppet, his body caught beneath the weight of the revving motorcycle and Pisanelli. Magagna had not moved, his gun still held at arm's length. Slowly he straightened his body.

The plastic bag lay on the white dust near the spinning rear wheel.

The engine roared like an angry, wounded animal.

35

GRACCHI DID NOT look up.

The policeman unlocked the door—a dark grey sheet of thick steel with welded rivets—and Trotti entered the cell.

The smell of old vomit, disinfectant and desolation. They had given him some coffee and a couple of doughnuts; he ate greedily. Trotti nodded to the uniformed man who took the tray and left.

The clang of the closing bolt.

Trotti sat down.

"My father is an important man," Gracchi looked up at Trotti's face, "with important connections in Rome. There's nothing you can do to me."

"I can do what I want."

"And lose your job." He folded his arms.

"You run to your father now you need him—despite your differences of opinion."

"I don't have to justify my political allegiances to you."

"You'll have to justify them in court. Why kidnap her?"

"Kidnap who?"

"The little girl."

"What little girl?"

"You don't even read the newspapers?" Trotti laughed drily.

"Fascist rags."

Trotti moved behind him. The yellow shirt smelled of sweat and fear. "Why did you take her?"

"I don't know what you're talking about."

"Anna Ermagni."

"I don't know what you mean."

"You don't know. And the letter? 'A target chosen at random. The first attack against the so-called Communist Mariani and his lackeys?'" Trotti pushed the photocopied letter before his face.

"It means nothing to me."

"Surprising." Trotti now faced him. "You wrote it and you signed it. The Proletarian Army of Liberation."

He sat with his hairy arms resting on his thighs; the blue jeans were scuffed and patched with white dust. Large adhesive bandages on his forehead and temples. "Fairy tales."

"Fairy tales—but you write them. And, my friend, they will send you to jail. Ten years, perhaps, if you behave yourself. In Sicily or Sardinia; you'll have plenty of time to write fairy tales."

"I don't know what you're talking about. If you are trying to find a culprit, I'm afraid you're not going to have any luck. I know nothing about the child. Nothing." His voice trembled. "You can keep your fairy tales for your friends in the Questura."

Trotti waited. "Just one problem, Gracchi."

"No problem at all."

"This . . ."—he ran his finger along the typewritten lines of the photocopy—"was written with your typewriter. With the little Olivetti you keep in your dirty apartment—and which we've confiscated."

"There's nothing you can prove."

Trotti laughed again. "And the dynamite?"

"I'll have the best lawyers. They will make fools of you; they will make fools of the Questura and they will make you, Commissario, the laughing stock of the city."

"Why did you kidnap her?"

Gracchi raised his head and shoulders; he clicked his tongue.

"You and your friends, you took her. You needed money, perhaps to buy dynamite or to buy your P38s to put bullets into people's legs. But something went wrong and you chickened out. You were scared. Something in the paper—or something the child said. Perhaps you realized you had made a mistake, that she didn't come from a rich family, but you went ahead. After all, you're terrorists."

"I don't kidnap children."

"You handed her back just at a time when the grandfather was collecting the money together. You could've waited for the payoff. Good money. Why go to the effort of snatching the girl, terrifying her, making the life of her father and her grandparents a misery just to put her back on a bus?"

"I tell you, I don't kidnap children."

"We've picked Guerra up."

There was no reaction.

"We'll see what she says."

"She'll say nothing because like me, she won't know what you're talking about."

"We'll see."

Gracchi crossed one leg over the other. "I never touched the child and your clumsy attempt to frame me will get you nowhere. My lawyers will see to that."

"But you blow people up? You admit to that?"

The eyes looked up and again he showed his regular, white teeth. "If it's necessary."

"And it is necessary?"

"A bomb can be a clinical instrument. With fools, Commissario, there can be no dialogue."

"Why did you kidnap her?"

He sighed. "I don't know what you're talking about." He turned away. The sweat on his body had an unpleasant, rancid smell. "Look, I want to speak with my father. And I want a lawyer."

"There'll be time for all that later."

"I know my rights. I insist upon speaking with a lawyer—with my father's lawyer."

"Why did you take her into the hills?"

"You're a fool."

"Why did you take her into the hills?" Trotti repeated the question flatly; a droning intonation.

Gracchi was about to reply angrily but he then let his anger escape like the air he expelled from his lungs. "Be careful, Commissario, be careful."

For about thirty seconds the two men stared at each other.

Trotti knew he was overreacting; he was allowing himself to get emotional, and it was not necessary. The child was safe. There was no need to get angry. It was like a clever card trick; insignificant but puzzling. He wanted the truth—that was all.

"You kidnapped her," Trotti spoke very softly.

"I don't kidnap little children. Unlike you, Commissario, I have my values. I am not a criminal."

"When you use bombs, you kill. Indiscriminately. Men, women and children. Yes, children. Dynamite is no respecter of persons. So don't give me your moral cant. You have the scruples of an animal. You don't give a shit."

"The scruples of a soldier fighting a just war."

"A just war?" Trotti was genuinely amazed. "A just war—you must be mad."

"You're mad if you can't see the truth. This is Argentina. We're living in South America, a banana republic. Only we're not going to allow a Pinochet here. When the forces of reaction—your friends, Commissario—with the help of the American imperialists, the CIA and the multinationals—decide to topple this tottering, corrupt regime, then we'll be ready. Ready and waiting. There will be no Colonels here. They've been working at it for ten years, slowly building up an atmosphere of tension with their provocation. Provocation—that's what they want; push aside the old hag of a syphilitic republic and get the power. Do away with the myth of democracy. They want power to set up their dictatorship. Your Fascist dictatorship."

"That's why you kidnap?"

"Frighten the middle class and soften them up—nothing the bourgeoisie will not do to protect its creature comforts, its country villas and its vested interests—for the totalitarian coup."

"And the Communists?"

"Ha ha." He wiped the mocking smile from his mouth. "Traitors. They've sold out—just to lick the arses of the powerful and the corrupt. There was a time when they were Communists, when they stood for something, when they had genuine goals. And when they had morality."

"You alone have morals?"

"The Communists are like all the others—constitutional and corrupt, fighting for their little piece of the cake of power. Corrupt and insidious and duping the working classes. But the working classes won't be fooled, just as we won't be fooled by the Fascists. We'll be waiting for them. We'll answer their repression with blood. With blood and with violence and with the knowledge that we are right. And out of the heroic struggle, from the blood of our companions killed in the war of resistance, we will set up a new Socialist State. For the workers, for the productive classes. A free society. Not a puppet of America. Not a lackey State—but a People's Democratic and Socialist State. A society based upon freedom."

His eyes had begun to sparkle. He raised his voice but he did not gesticulate and now he looked at Trotti. There was silence.

"You belong to the Red Brigades?"

Gracchi clicked his tongue.

"You use the same slogans," Trotti said.

"We can see the same, glaring truth. Since '69, they've been preparing—you've been preparing the coup, making your plans. Because the Italian miracle scared you. The working class and the Italian peasants, who for centuries had accepted the exploitation and the blackmail meted out to them, started to rebel. And that scares you. The autumn of '69 when the workers in Milan and Turin demanded better treatment—less medieval treatment. The unionization in the factories, the new political awareness. And all you could do was answer by transforming the police and the Carabinieri into forces of repression; and you started your strategy of tension. Piazza Fontana you remember? In Milan? For years public opinion believed it was Leftist extremists who placed the bomb that killed innocent men and women. But it was you. It was the reactionary police who wanted more power, who wanted to get greater, more repressive powers. And it worked. New laws, more power, new men, new guns, more repression."

He shook his head. "We learned our lesson. You won't catch us out a second time."

"You say we."

"No, Commissario—I am not a brigatista. I do not believe in the indiscriminate use of violence. Lotta Continua, yes, but not the Red Brigades."

"And the dynamite?"

Gracchi ignored the question. "Violence is a trap—a trap set by you and the forces of repression, the anti-democratic forces. We fall into it and we are playing your game. The excuse to clamp down, a justification for more repression. A further excuse to exploit the working masses of this country. No, we will not be provoked; we will not make the mistake of the Red Brigades who by their action have unleashed the Fascist forces of the totalitarian State."

"Then why the gun—the P38?"

"We must be ready."

"That's why you kidnap?"

"You are a fool, Commissario. A fool, a dangerous fool. You don't understand, you can't see what's going on." He smiled; a well-fed, unshaven, middle-class revolutionary. "I called you a Fascist. You must forgive me. I was crediting you with a political understanding that you don't have. Fascism—you don't even know what it means. You are a fool, an idiot—and because of that you are the worst kind of Fascist." He snorted. "You can't even see that you're being exploited, that you are being used by the agents of international Capitalism to uphold a creaking system that exploits you, that alienates you from your class, that enslaves you and denies you your self-respect and your human dignity."

"And the child?"

"Damn you," he shouted, suddenly angry and standing up, "damn you, you flatfoot, Fascist pig. The child's alive. She's alive, isn't she? What more do you want? She's alive. Consider yourself lucky."

36

CARS WERE PARKED carelessly, their front wheels almost beneath the arcade. The air smelled of cheese and sawdust. The morning's fish market was already over and apart from a few empty wooden cases, standing against the scarred brick wall of the cathedral, and apart from a few glistening fish scales, drying in the sun, there was no sign of the bustle that had animated the small square. They had gone, the eager fishmongers and the fat housewives prodding at the silvery goods.

It was nearly four o'clock and the shops were opening after the long lunch.

"She was in his apartment, waiting for him. Di Bono picked her up; she spat in his face, but apart from that she didn't put up any struggle." He stroked his mustache. "A pretty girl. Shame that she should be a terrorist." Magagna nodded wisely.

"We can't hold them without a charge."

The sound of their feet echoed along the arcade.

"Even if the parents don't complain, the NP will want to know what's happened to them. They saw us pick up Gracchi." Trotti popped a sweet into his mouth. "It's as though Leonardelli doesn't want to admit to these things. He's like an ostrich; he hides his head and thinks the problems will go away. Only it's not his neck that he sticks out—it is mine."

Near the urinals, daubed with graffiti, a water tap ran ceaselessly, its overflow staining the cobbles. A couple of boys, their neat shirts and short trousers now damp, splashed and kicked water at each other and screamed with unrestrained joy.

"He's a politician," Magagna said simply.

This was one of the oldest quarters of the city. The shops jostled together, forming a protective ring around the walls of the cathedral. They walked along the arcade and turned into the narrow street that ran down to the river.

Trotti knew the brothel; once, many years ago, when he was still a student at the technical institute, he had come here with some classmates. Together they had found some money—goodness knows where.

In those days, the place had not acquired its tired appearance, its atmosphere of pervasive seediness. If Buonarese—the nephew of a priest in Cremona, a tall boy with short hair and outrageously large ears—had not told him it was a whorehouse, Trotti would never have guessed it. From the outside—the faintly glimpsed wicker chairs and the opaline lights—it looked like rather distinguished tearooms.

They went inside.

The brothel was called Albergo Belsole and behind the chipped ormolu reception desk, between the rows of hanging keys, there was a trusty plaster statue of a north African soldier in his loose baggy trousers, a kepi pushed back from his forehead and his tunicked arm leaning on an upright musket. A woman—blonde, with bright lipstick that made her lips look like colored rubber bands—emerged from behind a curtain of hanging plastic ribbons.

"Signora Cucina?" Magagna asked peremptorily.

She nodded.

"Pubblica Sicurezza. We received your call. Where is he?" Magagna did not even show his card. Trotti could sense that he was ill at ease and he wondered why.

"At last," the woman said in a low, masculine voice. The short hairs along the upper lip were dark. She made a prodding movement with a finger; a rough finger hardened by work and a fingernail with dark varnish. "Over there, on the third floor."

She watched them leave and cross the narrow road.

Somebody, somewhere, was singing an aria from Tosca. From an open door, further down the road, there was the sound of a hammer regularly striking hard metal. They went into a small courtyard and up an outside stairway.

"It was the woman who phoned," Magagna said, slightly out of breath.

Beneath their feet the stairs were thin slabs of flint; the flint had begun to splinter and beneath the slabs, nothing but the emptiness of the stairwell.

They stopped at the landing of the third floor.

The dirty brown door was not closed; they pushed against the fissured wood and entered the apartment.

A smell of encrusted dirt, old wine, garlic and blocked drains. A single flyblown lightbulb hung from the ceiling. The window giving onto the street was open and there was a bed along the wall. Shafts of sunlight formed parallels on the grime of the floor, across the tiles that had once been black and white but were now crossed and creased with dirt and dried mud. A radio, an old-fashioned box of walnut with warped inlay, and cloaked in dust, blinked hopefully, the amber dial glowing. The sound of Tosca filled the room, echoing off the soiled plaster of the empty walls.

The old man was listening to the music. He was slumped in a broken armchair. His head lolled forward, his chin propped by the swelling of a goiter. His eyes were open, bloodshot. He looked up slowly at his two visitors. Trotti turned off the radio.

"I killed her," the old man said.

His feet were propped against a stool; he lowered the naked feet onto the floor. The toes were ill-formed and grimy; the pale flesh of the instep lined with protruding blue veins.

"Pubblica Sicurezza."

"I was expecting you." He had not shaved for several days and white bristles had sprouted from the leather of his deformed jaw. "She deserved it, the stupid whore."

"Who?"

"A stupid old cow." He spat onto the floor and then wiped the damp lips with the back of his hand.

"That's no reason to kill her."

"And you're a fool." The bloodshot eyes looked at Magagna. "You don't know what you're talking about." He leaned in the chair and an outstretched hand tapped the floor. There was a dark green bottle and beside it an empty, crumpled packet of Calipso cigarettes. The hand found the packet and the old man uncrumpled it like a banker smoothing a valuable banknote. "Christ." He looked at his visitors and attempted a smile.

Several teeth were missing; those that remained were badly stained. "A cigarette?"

Magagna produced his packet and held out a single cigarette. The man took it, looked at it, sniffed it and snorted. Then he snapped off the filter tip and stuck the end of crumbling Virginia tobacco in his old mouth. His eyes remained on his visitors.

Magagna held out a light.

"Christ." He breathed in deeply. "Christ, that's better."

"Why did you kill her?" Trotti had moved towards the wall near the window to be near the fresh air; it was hot in the room.

"I didn't say I killed anybody."

Magagna and Trotti gave each other a glance. Magagna raised an eyebrow.

"Signor Gerevini, we know you killed her."

A silence while the old man smoked; then he started to laugh. "Who told you, then?" He laughed again.

"You lived with her, didn't you?" Trotti replied.

The smile vanished fast. "The worst mistake of my rotten life." Again he spat, the spittle landing in the same place. "She was a pain in the arse. She spent all her money on herself and she was a lazy, dirty old cow." He shook his head. He held the cigarette in the corner of his mouth and the twirling smoke caused his eyes to water.

"Her money."

"She earned it. We were married, weren't we?" The old voice squealed with outrage.

Trotti was amazed. "Married?" He moved away from the wall and approached the man.

"Of course. We were living together, her and me. We were together."

"Except when she was working."

He now looked at Magagna with hatred in his watery, red eyes. "You think I can work? What am I supposed to do? A pension that the government refuses to give me. What do you want? To beg." He pointed a finger at the goiter. "With this? It's all right for you—you're young and you've got your health. But me, what am I supposed to do?"

Trotti asked, "You loved her?"

A pause while the man still stared angrily at Magagna; then he shrugged. "She was useful, wasn't she?" He lowered his voice. "And there were times when she needed me. Just like in any marriage."

Magagna spoke softly, "You shared the same bed."

"Of course," Gerevini replied without looking at him. "You think I'm a cripple? But more recently . . . she was busier and when she came back, she was tired."

"Wasn't she getting a bit old for the game?"

The laugh was cold. Cold and humorless. "Old—of course she was old, but that's what they all want. They're perverts, aren't they? Vicious and depraved; the older the flesh, the more flabby it is, the more they like it. Perverts." He stopped to stub out the cigarette on the dirty floor; it continued to smolder, the smoke curling towards the open window. "She thought it was love, the silly cow."

"Love?"

"She was like a child; still believed in all that fairy tale shit. She fell for him. The silly old hag, she was old enough to be his mother—and certainly stupid enough." He gave a rasping laugh. "Could have been his grandmother but she believed him."

He then rose to his feet; he was unsteady and he tottered slightly; his naked, runnelled feet on the cold floor. He moved towards a large refrigerator that had once been white. He pulled open the battered door and took a can of Peroni beer from the unlit inside. He returned to his seat, ripped the can open and threw the steel ring out of the window. "A soldier, a kid from Reggio Calabria," he said, after taking a swig at the can of beer. "She thought he loved her. She was going to leave with him.

When his military service was over. You realize"—he threw
up a hand; a movement of frustration and poorly assimilated
amazement—"they were going to live in the south. Work the
land and be together. Grow artichokes."

"Who was this man?"

"You think I know? You think I met him? I would have
killed him, the lying, fornicating southern bastard." He looked
at Magagna; there was no hostility in his eyes. "A cigarette?"

Magagna gave him another and again he snapped off the
filter. He breathed in the smoke gratefully. "She knew I'd kill
him. I told her so."

"So you killed her instead?"

"She was mad." He shrugged, the shoulder touched the growth
on his neck. "I was doing her a favor. A big favor." More beer, a
drag on the cigarette. "In love. She told me she was in love. She
didn't understand that all he wanted was to get it free. Love her?
Of course he didn't love her. She was a fat, ugly old fool. But she
was easy pickings for a southern peasant." Saliva and beer and
smoke caught in his throat and he started to cough. Slowly at first
and then the cough, like a fire, caught at his body and the thin
frame within the dirty pajamas and stained T-shirt began to shake.
Magagna found a plastic mug—it was lying under the bed—and
filled it with water. The old man pushed away the proffered cup
and continued to cough for several minutes. When he ceased,
there were more tears in his eyes and beer-tinted saliva dribbled
down the stubbly old chin in two lines, like snail tracks.

"When did you murder her?"

"Murder?" The word hovered, filling the dirty room.

"You killed her, didn't you?" Magagna asked brusquely.

"It wasn't murder." He appeared offended, the running
eyes glaring at Magagna. "I didn't mean to kill her. It was a
mistake, an accident. You see, she made me angry. She did it on
purpose. Taunting me; she called me an old man, an old wreck.
She—nearly fifteen years younger than me and breasts down to
here?" The old hands tapped at his skinny belly. "And she called
me an old man. Not up to it, she said. Past it, time I was put
out to grass." He snorted, his eyes angry, and made an obscene

gesture with his forearm. "Like steel. An old man but I can get it up with the best of them. Sixty years old and then some but I can get it up all right." He glared at both of them. "Probably harder and longer than you—the younger generation, they're all queers. Tempered steel." He tapped at his groin and the stained pajama. "Tempered steel."

"How did you kill her?" Trotti was unsmiling.

"An accident. She killed herself." The eyes were now cunning. "She fell."

"Where?"

"On the stairs. She was drunk, like the slut that she was; and she was late. She'd been with him, hadn't she, and he had got her drunk and screwed her senseless. But I was waiting for her." He now stared at the floor. "I didn't mean to harm her. The old fool. Just a lesson, that's all I wanted to give her. I hit her." He shrugged. "I'd hit her before, she was used to it, but this time she fell. Must've cracked her head. Fell down two flights." He repeated, "Two flights."

"What time was this?"

"Six in the morning," he answered hurriedly as though irritated by the interruption. "And when I picked her up—I'm not a young man, I can't move fast—when I picked her up, she was dead. I've seen dead people often enough and I knew she was dead. There was blood in her mouth and her eyes were staring. The silly bitch, it was all her own fault."

"So what did you do?"

"She was dead—what could I do? It wasn't my fault, was it? Was it? But nobody had seen me and I thought—well, when I was in prison, I used to work in the kitchen and I had learned a little about butchering."

He grinned. "I carried her back upstairs. Not easy, but I didn't make much noise. And the next day—she was lying on the bed, there, Commissario, but with her head in a funny position and her neck was bloated. The next day I bought a couple of knives. A large one, a chopper, and a smaller one." He pulled again at the cigarette and drank some more beer. Then he slowly got down onto his knees. He began to cough again, spitting light flecks of spittle onto the floor. This time the coughing bout was short and once he had regained control over his trembling body, he pulled a cardboard suitcase from under the bed. He opened it; a few paper clippings, a photograph of the Pope and almost hidden by brown wrapping paper, the glinting steel edge of a knife.

"I cut her up, Commissario." He gave Trotti a smile—a craftsman pleased with his work. "I cut her up here on the floor."

37

TROTTI WAS DEPRESSED.

While Magagna had been interviewing the Guerra girl—Trotti had not felt up to it, he knew he could not face the young arrogance and self-righteousness of the revolutionary—he had spent two hours in a stuffy room, thick with smoke, listening to the old man's confession while a uniformed policeman banged away at an old typewriter. The sporadic rhythm of the machine, the bittersweet tobacco smoke, the smell of the old man's unwashed body—they were like burning spikes in his brain. He wanted to go home. He had had enough of other people's suffering.

Trotti recognized the tall clumsy figure coming up the steps. He turned away.

"Commissario!"

Ermagni lurched towards him and Trotti, realizing there was no escape, gave a weary smile.

"I should be working," Ermagni said as they shook hands. The large cow-eyes were now red and were underlined by black half-circles. "I had to see you." A quick, appeasing smile.

"I'm busy, I'm afraid." Hearing the harshness of his reply, Trotti added, "My wife is waiting for me."

"They won't let me see her."

They were standing at the top of the stairs outside the Questura. It was evening and after a long day, the air was beginning to cool. A few passers-by in Strada Nuova, some eating ice creams. There was a smell of honeysuckle blossom and fumes from the buses.

"Come." He pulled at Trotti's arm. The yellow taxi, its plastic signal already switched on, was parked on the pavement by the typewriter shop. "Come—it won't take long."

"I've got to go home." Trotti tried to shrug off the large, hairy hand on his arm. "My wife's waiting for me."

"They won't let me see her." Ermagni did not let go but instead, pulling Trotti, led him towards the taxi. "They say that I'm not reliable. They've told her that I killed her mother." He opened the car door. "That I killed my wife."

"Look." Trotti resisted the hand that was pushing him into the front seat. "I can't come. You understand? I can't come. I'm busy, I've got to go home."

"But you must." His eyes were strangely innocent; and though his breath was heavy with alcohol, he was not drunk. "I'm asking you for Anna's sake."

"I've done enough for Anna. She's alive, isn't she? Alive and well. What more do you want?"

The large eyes looked at him; large, bloodshot eyes that failed to understand the reluctance in Trotti. "You're her godfather. A policeman. They'll listen to you." He tapped his chest; he was wearing a yellow sweater. "They despise me because I'm a taxi driver. Not good enough for them or for their daughter."

"There's nothing I can do. My wife is waiting for me." He pushed the hand away and at the same time placed a hand on the shoulder of Ermagni's jacket. "I've had a busy day. Understand me. I'm sorry."

He then turned and walked towards the Questura parking lot.

"I'm not a good father." A voice that trembled on the edge of self-doubt. "That's why they don't want Anna to see me. A drunkard, a dangerous man." He was now imploring. "But you can tell them. Tell them that I love her. They will listen to you."

Trotti unpadlocked the bicycle. "Tell them tomorrow. I'll come tomorrow."

"My daughter—I must see her tonight." Ermagni had stood with his feet apart and his mouth open as he watched Trotti walk away. Now in his top-heavy amble, he came towards the bicycle. Trotti pulled the front wheel from the concrete slab and swung his leg over the crossbar.

"You're my friend, Commissario."

"My wife's waiting for me."

"And I've got to go to work. It'll only take a few minutes. A few minutes of your time. She's your goddaughter, Commissario, don't forget."

"Tomorrow." He released the brake and pushed on the pedal. The bike moved forward and Ermagni began to walk faster.

"Please," he said.

"Tomorrow," Trotti called and he pulled out into the middle of Strada Nuova, cutting in behind a large bus. Then later, before reaching the traffic lights, he turned round. Ermagni was still there, standing by the roadside, his large hands hanging emptily at his sides.

A large, clumsy man. A sad man.

38

PIOPPI WAS SITTING cross-legged in front of the television; a few school books were scattered on the floor beside her. She was writing, one eye on the thick green pen and the notepad, one eye on the television. A simple, repetitive jingle and then a famous footballer advertising chocolate.

"Where's Agnese?"

She jumped up and kissed her father. She smelled of fresh clothes and soap; a clean, reassuring smell after the smoke and the old man in the Questura. "Ciao, Papa." She gave him a hug and lifted one of her feet.

A clean, youthful smell; it gave him a twinge of envy and of nostalgia.

"Your mother?"

"She waited for you as long as she could. But I'm cooking."

"Where's she gone?"

Pioppi's smile faded. "She had to go out. She waited for you but you're late." Pioppi was wearing a loose sweater that hid her young body. She looked like a boy. "There was a phone call and then a man came. About half an hour ago."

"Who?"

The television was now advertising a brand of floor tiles; a fat baby, unsteady on his podgy legs and a flower in his hand, was walking across a polished floor. Naked except for a spotless diaper.

"Who?" He looked into her eyes, still holding her; then he looked away.

"I don't know, Papa. He had a car. Mama said it was important and that she had to go—but that she'd be back early. And she said not to wait up for her." She leaned forward and kissed him again, her hair brushing against his skin. "She'll be back soon." She took his hands in hers. "Now, tell me what you want for supper. There are some anchovies in the cupboard and I feel like making a pizza. And we could open a bottle of wine."

She was trying to cheer him up.

He undid his tie and threw his jacket onto the settee.

In the event, they watched the news on television and then went over the road to the pizzeria.

Quattro stagioni for Pioppi and a Coca-Cola. Trotti had a pizza pugliese and a can of Nastro Azzurro beer.

Pioppi talked cheerfully. Trotti was silent; he had been overworking, he told himself, and he needed to sleep.

No news of Moro on the radio before he went to bed.

Trotti slept for a couple of hours and then woke up, the weight of the pizza and the onions heavy on his stomach. He lay in bed looking at the patterns of lights on the ceiling as cars drove past along via Milano.

He could not get back to sleep and at half past two he got up and put on a dressing gown. He went into the kitchen, heated some water and made a cup of chamomile tea. He did not feel well; his eyes ached and from time to time, he belched. A bitter, bilious taste at the edges of his tongue.

He poured honey into the tea and sipped slowly while his eyes scanned the parish magazine. The clock ticked noisily. Pioppi's bedroom door was open; he could hear the soft sound of her breathing and he envied her restful sleep.

From time to time a car went past in via Milano; no car stopped.

The phone woke him. He must have dozed off, his head lolling forward. He sat up with a jerk and looked at the clock. Four o'clock. The chamomile was cold.

The telephone continued to ring.

"Commissario Trotti?"

"Yes—I was sleeping."

"You'd better get dressed."

"Who's speaking?"

"Get dressed quickly, Commissario." Something familiar about the voice, a man's voice. "Get dressed and go down to the Bixio barracks."

"The Carabinieri?"

"As quickly as you can."

"Who's speaking?"

The line was cut. Trotti replaced the receiver and stared at it. Then he shrugged. "A practical joker," he said. He went into the kitchen and made some coffee. Then he got dressed.

Caserma Bixio stood at the far end of via Bixio.

The air was chill as Trotti got out of the car; he parked outside the derelict church and walked across the road, across the circles of white light from the street lamps.

There were no cars in front of the barracks.

A Cabiniere came out of the darkness of his box and asked Trotti in a southern, uninterested voice what he wanted.

"Commissario Trotti, Pubblica Sicurezza."

The Carabiniere shrugged; his face was pale in the street light; pale and with grotesque shadows deforming his nose and the dark sockets of his eyes.

"I want to speak with Capitano Spadano."

The Carabiniere must have pressed a button, hidden somewhere in the recesses of the box; a door opened in the large gate and he nodded to Trotti. Trotti stepped out of the street into the courtyard of the barracks.

It was brightly lit, like a football stadium for a late game. Incandescent beams shone down onto the cobbled courtyard. Several jeeps, a few motorcycles and a couple of cars. Men were sitting in the two cars; several whiplash aerials pointing at the dark sky. There was the sound of distorted voices over metallic radios. There was also the sound of music.

Trotti looked up and saw, blinking against the sky, a red light. It went on and off with a slow, pulsing rhythm.

Two potted plants on the far side of the courtyard. A jeep

started up, the headlights were turned on and caught the stalking silhouette of a cat. It scampered into hiding.

Trotti crossed the courtyard, breathing in the mixture of cold pre-dawn air and petrol fumes. He went through a small wooden doorway and entered a long hall. Newly painted walls—grey paint and matching, narrow bars against the high windows. A colorless carpet running along the tiled floor. A few posters along the wall.

Everything was neat; again, Trotti found himself admiring the organization of the Carabinieri. A purposefulness that he had never met in any Questura; a purposefulness that was impressive and slightly frightening.

A man in black uniform went past. His face was familiar; he nodded imperceptibly and disappeared into a room off the corridor.

Trotti went up a staircase, along another corridor, identical in its color and cleanliness to the other one, until he reached a door marked NUCLEO INVESTIGATIVO printed in the ground glass. He raised his hand to knock but the door opened before his knuckles fell against the glass.

"Ah, thank goodness."

The room smelled of smoke and stale cigars.

The man stepped back. "Come in, Trotti, come on in."

Trotti entered.

"I just phoned your place. A young woman answered. She sounded very sleepy."

"Most people prefer to sleep at this time of night."

"A friend of yours?"

"My daughter." Neither man smiled as they shook hands.

Physically Spadano was small. He was wearing a khaki uniform shirt, dark patches of sweat at the armpits. The sleeves were rolled up. The eyes were grey and his black hair was cut very short and brushed backwards.

"I'm glad you're here, anyway."

"What's happened?"

He glanced at Trotti and frowned, as though he were surprised by the question.

Moths battered noisily against the desk lamp.

Trotti repeated the question. "What's happened?"

"Perhaps it would be best if you came with me." Spadano held out his arm and moved towards the door. Trotti followed.

They went to a lift and while they waited, neither man spoke. Spadano frowned, staring at the ground; then when the lift arrived, he politely stepped back to let Trotti enter first.

Three floors; they stepped out into another corridor, this time slightly cooler. They were beneath ground level; there were no windows. The air was damp.

"This way please."

Although Spadano had lived in the north for most of his life, he had not lost his accent. Palermo. Trotti followed him, a step behind the small, muscular back and the thick neck. Hair that showed no sign of thinning. For a man well into his fifties, Spadano had aged well.

"Here."

Spadano hammered at the grey door, the sound feeble against the thick, riveted steel. A scraping noise of a bolt being pulled back. The door opened outwards, and following Spadano, Trotti entered into a flood of blinding neon light.

It must have been in the first two years of marriage that Trotti had bought the stole. Agnese was only just starting out on her medical studies and they were still relatively poor. Her family, disapproving of the marriage, had made little effort to help them. Trotti could not afford a summer holiday—at least nothing more than a run into the hills or a day by the sea near La Spezia—and then, with the autumn, Trotti remembered, he had received a pay raise. Fifteen thousand lire—chickenfeed by today's standards but then, in the early 1950s, the strangely large banknotes were hard to come by. Autumn, the first fogs along the Po; and so, to celebrate, he had decided to buy her the stole. Once, walking along Strada Nuova, she had pointed it out in Vanizza's. It was real fur—but of what kind, he could never remember. Vanizza himself had sold it to Trotti; Vanizza who was himself heading out on a career that was to make him one of the richest men in Italy, a household name, the ambassador of fashion to New York and Moscow—a career that was to put his name on the advertising billboards around every professional football pitch in the peninsula. A career so successful that he now had to send his grandchildren to school in Switzerland, beyond the grasp of potential kidnappers.

Agnese had loved it. She who had had everything, who had never gone hungry during the war, who had scarcely known about the shortages—she loved the humble present. She threw her arms about Trotti's neck and kissed him while he smiled, his reflection caught in the bedroom mirror.

"You are an angel," she said, and for several years, there was not an occasion when she did not wear the black stole.

Then the fur started to wear thin and, after a while, she seemed to wear it less. She was approaching the end of her studies. It was about the time that she qualified as a doctor that she gave up wearing it completely.

Trotti assumed that she had thrown it away. She had occasionally a fit of clearing up and then everything that she did not like or that she considered too old was relegated to the dustbin. It was something he had never really understood; he had grown up in the hills where a shirt would be mended several times before it was handed down to the younger brother who would wear it for as many years again. Nothing was thrown away.

Then they had gone down to Bari. Pioppi was still a little girl and Agnese had managed to get a good job with the American pharmaceutical company. She earned enough money to be elegant at all times, she no longer had to wait for Trotti's meager monthly salary. Trotti saw nothing wrong in Agnese's spending money on clothes; the latest dresses from Paris fashion houses, shoes from Florence and several fur coats—scarcely necessary in the mild Adriatic climate—including a mink coat that she wore only a couple of times.

He entered the cell.

The stole was part of the past, a happy past, with its memories of sacrifice and optimism. It now lay like a docile animal on her white shoulders.

The dress she wore was simple and from where he stood, Trotti could have sworn she was still the young student he had married.

She turned to look at him. The eyes were red—she had been crying—and the illusion of youth vanished. She whispered in a hoarse voice, "Go away."

Trotti stepped towards her and hesitantly placed a hand upon her shoulder. The skin was cool. She shrugged his hand away and he stood with arms hanging loosely at his side.

"Agnese."

She turned her back to him. "Go away, go away, go away." She put her hands to her face.

Perhaps her body shook slightly; perhaps she was sobbing. Trotti stared down at the curve of her neck and at the regular lustrous spheres of a pearl necklace he had never seen before. He wanted to help her—of course he wanted to help her but he knew there was nothing that he could do. She did not need him. Spadano coughed.

"Agnese," Trotti said, addressing himself to the back of her head—there were the first white strands nestling in her black hair. "Agnese."

He did not know what to say. Tell her that he loved her? It would have sounded foolish, here in the clinical harsh light of the cell.

Elsewhere somebody was shouting and banging a utensil against the bars of a cell; the muffled sound came through the brick wall; it was followed by a brisk shout of command. Then silence.

She knew he loved her—perhaps that was why she despised him.

"Agnese."

"Go away." She did not move; her voice was unclear as though she was talking to herself. "Go back home. Pioppi needs you."

Spadano took his arm softly. "Come," he said and he led Trotti out of the cell. They went back to his office. Neither man spoke in the lift. Trotti stood with his hands in his pockets and his shoulders hunched.

In the office, Spadano pointed Trotti to a chair—in a lot better condition than the canvas ones in the Questura. Spadano went to his desk and took a packet of Toscani cigars from his shirt pocket. He lit one. A pungent cloud of smoke, pierced by his dark eyes. Trotti sat silently. He was staring at his hands, his eyes unblinking.

Spadano coughed to clear his throat. "We got a phone call at about eleven o'clock. Somebody—an anonymous caller—saying that there had been a knife fight at the San Siro."

Trotti raised his head. "The San Siro in Corso Garibaldi?"

Spadano nodded. "That's right. Old man Rossi—grandfather of the little girl."

Trotti's face had drained of all color. "A knife fight?"

"A couple of men went down to check—it's standard procedure." Spadano did not take his eyes off Trotti. "The place was closed. Blinds down, the tables on the terrace had been cleared—which was strange because it was early for the San Siro to close. It would normally stay open until the end of the last performance at the Arti cinema. Then one of the men noticed light coming from the ventilation bars just above the level of the pavement—and the sound of people laughing. They got suspicious and called for reinforcements."

"Gambling?"

"Roulette. About thirty people there—well dressed and well heeled. Quite a surprise because the San Siro is not a very sophisticated place—jukebox and a billiard table in the back room. Not the sort of place that you associate with the city's wealthiest and most beautiful people. But that's what they were. Men in evening dress and bow ties, women in gowns and jewelry. The cream of the local citizenry, Commissario." Spadano allowed himself a small smile. "Including your wife."

Trotti was frowning. "She's in a cell by herself."

"The least I could do for a fellow policeman." A hint of irony in his voice. He breathed at the stubby cigar. "For the others it doesn't really matter. You know these people as well as I do, Commissario—they are always safe. Doctors, architects, professional people with money. They can look after themselves—they've got the money and they've got the contacts." He paused. "But Signora Trotti is the wife of a policeman."

Trotti remained silent. He looked at Spadano—regular features, tanned skin and hard eyes behind the rising cloud of smoke.

"It puts you in a difficult position, Trotti. A very difficult and embarrassing position. People know that she was there. She's your wife and you're responsible for her—you who are a policeman and who should be above suspicion." He paused. "I imagine you have powerful friends."

"You are going to press charges?"

"Of course not. We wouldn't even have taken her into custody if we had known who she was. But she said nothing."

Trotti looked at Spadano and then looked down at the floor. "I'll have to resign."

"Resign?" Spadano laughed. "I don't think that the Pubblica Sicurezza is that demanding."

"She never tells me where she goes. I had no idea." He raised his shoulders. "I'll get another job."

"And lose your pension." Spadano took the cigar from his mouth. "Let's not exaggerate, Commissario. Certainly your wife is an embarrassment. She allowed herself to get caught in an illegal gaming parlor—goodness knows where the wife of a policeman can get that kind of money from. She could have informed us straight away of her identity rather than forcing us to bring her here—with the consequent humiliation for both her and you. The law must take its course—but there'll be nothing more than a fine; and perhaps the embarrassment of publicity." He replaced the cigar. "But for you to resign, Commissario—that won't be necessary. You have friends—friends who want to help you and who want you to stay where you are. Perhaps you have friends who owe you a few favors."

"I don't ask for any favors."

"The problem," Spadano said simply, "is bad publicity."

Their eyes met. "The *Provincia* was there?"

Spadano nodded. "I think so." He tapped ash into a tray. "A young chap, fairly large. He was there when my men broke in."

"Angellini."

"You know him?"

"Yes. How did he know what was happening? Why was he there? Who tipped him off?"

Spadano shrugged. "Could have been him who phoned us with the bogus story of a fight. He knew what was going on and wanted to be in on our arrival. A nice front page story—and you know how the *Provincia* hates the local *nouveaux riches*. The paper would have collapsed years ago if the editor hadn't been pumping into it his own considerable wealth. The shopkeepers all hate him and refuse to advertise. And the editor hates them. That's why he's always supported the mayor—even though the mayor's a Communist and the editor is an old Fascist." Spadano laughed—a genuine, warm laugh. "An illicit casino in the basement of a bar. Thirty arrests—including the wife of a prominent policeman. Just the thing for an ambitious journalist—especially before the municipal elections." He looked at his watch. "The paper should've come off the presses. We'll see just how much political advantage the *Provincia* hopes to get out of all this."

Trotti bit his lip. There was a long silence.

"She didn't need money," he said.

"Perhaps she was looking for something else." Spadano raised the wet end of his cigar. "Excitement. Adventure. Perhaps she wanted to run the risk of being arrested. Perhaps she wanted to embarrass you."

"If that's what she wanted, she's succeeded."

"Trotti," Spadano said softly, "I don't owe you or the Pubblica Sicurezza any favors. There are a lot of people in this place who would like to get even with you—your professional behavior, you and the Questura, is not a source of joy for us. You moved in on Gracchi at a time when we had him under surveillance."

"He kidnapped the girl."

Spadano laughed; then he picked at strands of tobacco caught on the tip of his tongue. "I think you must be dreaming."

"The type on the kidnap note corresponds with his typewriter."

"Absurd. We had him under surveillance. That's why we asked you not to touch him."

"Asked me? Nobody asked me anything."

"The PS was informed—and from what I heard, Trotti, you personally were informed."

"I received no request from the Carabinieri."

"I'd like to believe you." He stubbed out the cigar.

There was a short pause. "He is guilty. He took the child—the typewriter proves it."

"Gracchi may have typed the note—it's possible but not very likely. But he certainly did not take the child." Again Spadano laughed. "He's been under surveillance the last two weeks—perhaps you think that stupid, southern Carabinieri wouldn't notice the minor detail of a kidnapping?" A short coughing laugh. "We can supply Gracchi's alibi."

Trotti remained silent, embarrassed.

"They were watching him. They were watching him and perhaps he could have led to more important arrests. And so you move in—the Pubblica Sicurezza moves in and blows everything—at a time when we should be collaborating. It's not my concern, of course—I leave that to the specialists. But it looks strange, Trotti. It looks suspiciously like protection."

Trotti shook his head.

"A cover-up."

"No," Trotti replied emphatically but Spadano held up his hand.

"It doesn't concern me, Trotti. But let me say this: I personally have no desire to see you destroyed. I suspect that you are being used. I don't have much respect for the Pubblica Sicurezza and I know about Leonardelli. There are people in Strada Nuova I would rather see eliminated than you." He lowered his voice. "But there are people who would like to see you go. Take my advice." He was now sitting, his arms flat against the top of the desk and his eyes glinting. "Be careful—before you're out of your depth."

A knock on the door.

"Avanti!"

"The *Provincia*, signore." A uniformed officer entered and placed a neatly folded copy on the scratched varnish of the desk. Spadano stood up. He ran a finger over the columns of the front page. Then he turned to the inside pages.

"Thanks."

The uniformed man left.

Spadano took another cigar from the packet and held the end between his white teeth while he lit it. He pushed the paper towards Trotti.

A picture of San Siro, caught in the pale light of the photographer's flash.

"Looks as though you're in luck, Commissario Trotti."

39

Via Lugano.

Trotti did not wait for the aunt to answer. He knocked at the door, while at his feet the cat moved sensuously, its green eyes staring at him. He tried the handle; the door was unlocked. He pushed it open and entered the dark hallway.

A smell of breakfast, warm bread and coffee. The woman's grey face appeared from the kitchen.

"Pubblica Sicurezza."

The haggard face disappeared and the kitchen door closed.

Trotti went to the bedroom and opened the ground glass door with its cherubim, seraphim and its coat of arms.

Stefano Angellini was asleep. There was an empty whisky bottle on the floor and the radio was emitting cheerful chatter for those who had to get up early and go to work.

"No news from Rome, no communications from the Red Brigades." The voice was deliberately optimistic, as though speaking of the washing powers of a new detergent.

The air was stuffy, with its familiar odor of sweat and unwashed clothes; over the floor, books and dirty washing. Several unwashed glasses.

Angellini snored, his white, fleshy body, only partially concealed by a sheet, rising and falling gently with the slow rhythm of his breathing. Air rasped at the open throat.

Trotti went to the window, almost falling over the typewriter.

He unlatched the blinds and threw them open. The sun had already risen; its early rays caught a far window of the courtyard. The soft, damp smells of early morning; another day.

Trotti looked at his watch. 6:30.

"What do you want now, Commissario?"

Trotti turned round. Angellini had opened one eye; he then closed it; the large head nuzzled into the pillow. Trotti went to the sink—a disposable razor, French shaving cream and the minute traces of yesterday's beard against the grubby porcelain. He ran water into his cupped hands and crossing the room, threw it—it curved, like a silvery cat raising its back—into the pale face.

"Wake up."

"Shit." Angellini sat up. Water trickled down his face and chin onto the sheet; two blotches slowly formed. "What do you want?"

"The truth."

"Go away—let me sleep." He wiped the back of his hand against his face.

"Get up."

"It's early—let me sleep. Go away, leave me alone."

Before Angellini could fall back onto the pillow, Trotti caught the edge of the sheet. Angellini tried to grasp it but Trotti was stronger. He pulled it off the bed and threw it into a corner. Angellini was naked. His hands went to his groin.

"Now get up."

"You've got no right."

Trotti scooped up the kimono from where it was lying on the floor and threw it at Angellini's head.

"Christ."

"How did you know about San Siro?"

Angellini put his large feet on the floor and wrapped the kimono about his flabby shoulders. "San Siro?"

"Be careful, Angellini, be careful. Don't play with me." Trotti pointed a finger at the younger man; very slightly, his hand was trembling. "Tell me about the San Siro and don't get clever. You knew, didn't you?"

"That it was a gambling den?" He laughed. "Of course I

knew." He wiped his face again. "Pass me my trousers, will you?"

"For how long? When did you find out?"

"Come on, Trotti. The San Siro is common knowledge—it's been there for years, everybody knows about it. Where else do you think the rich can go for their fun? Gambling is illegal outside San Remo or Venice. Your rich friends have got to spend their money somewhere."

"You didn't tell me."

"You didn't ask, Trotti. You didn't ask." He laughed.

Trotti's face was drawn. He looked at Angellini without blinking. "My wife is in jail."

Angellini shrugged.

"My own career is in jeopardy."

"Scarcely." Angellini went over to the dark oak wardrobe and from the pile of discarded clothes, pulled out a pair of jeans. They were of faded denim; he put the jeans on. They were tight and he had to pull in his belly in order to close the zip. From the same pile he took a loose cotton shirt. In his eyes, there were still traces of sleep. He ran his hand through his hair. "Zia," he shouted, turning his head towards the door. "You can bring some coffee."

A muffled grunt from the kitchen.

"You have friends, Trotti—an influential and respected man like you. Politically you are safe."

"Let me decide that—I can do without your opinions and I can do without your trying to justify your behavior. You informed the Carabinieri. Why?"

Angellini laughed. "Trotti, I informed no one."

"Don't lie. You were there when the Carabinieri arrived." Again he pointed. "You'd do anything to get onto the front page of the *Provincia*."

Angellini put his hands in his pockets; he leaned against the wardrobe, his bare feet peeping from beneath the faded jeans. "If this is your way of thanking me, Trotti, I think I prefer toothache. Your wife was conspicuous among the people arrested. I was there. I saw her being put into the van. We took photographs, I could have put that in my article."

"You want to blackmail me."

"You're a fool, Trotti. It wouldn't have done me any harm to put the photographs in the paper—and it wouldn't have done the paper any harm, either. But I didn't, did I? Why not? To blackmail you? You come here, you wake me, you throw water in my face and pull me out of bed. Some way to thank me." He snorted. "Perhaps I should blackmail you."

"You invented a story about a fight and you phoned the Carabinieri. You engineered everything."

"You're a fool, Trotti—but I thought at least you were an honest fool. I now see you're dangerous—a Fascist. You treat people as you please. You don't care. You're dangerous."

Trotti raised his hand. He was about to strike Angellini when the door opened and the aunt, her face grey and marked with more lines of suffering, entered carrying a tray. A steaming coffee pot.

"I didn't inform the Carabinieri."

"A coincidence, then."

The woman set the tray on the desk and, making room, pushed aside several books—about the Mafia, in bright dust-jackets. One of the books toppled, and falling, it knocked a small photograph in a glass frame.

"Ah," she said, a hand going to her mouth.

Splinters of glass on the cold floor.

Trotti picked up the photograph. A photograph of Angellini, taken several years previously, when the hair was lower on his forehead. He looked healthier. He wore the long, peaked cap of Italian students. On one arm, he held a girl; the other arm went over the shoulder of a young man. All three were smiling into the camera.

Trotti set the photograph back on the desk.

He had seen the girl somewhere.

Angellini took the photograph and put it away in the wardrobe. "Zia, get a broom." To Trotti, "Coffee?"

"Who informed you, Angellini?"

Angellini poured black coffee into the two cups. "Sugar?"

"Who informed you—if it wasn't you who set everything up, tell me who told you."

The aunt had returned with a broom and now she brushed at the broken glass with quick jabs; she looked at neither Trotti nor her nephew. She bent over, swept the glass into a yellow pan and left silently, her dark stockings, rolled about her ankles, scraping softly as she walked.

Angellini sipped some coffee. "You forget that I am a journalist." He paused, looked at Trotti. "The son-in-law."

"Who?"

"Rossi's son-in-law, Ermagni. I suppose it was him—I don't know him personally, but if it was somebody else, he was a good actor."

"What did he say?" Trotti held a cup of coffee in his hand but he did not drink.

"They were trying to take his daughter from him."

"Anna?"

"Yes." Angellini nodded. "That's why she was kidnapped. The old man wanted to discredit him. Discredit him as a father."

"And he phoned you?"

"Yes."

"Where did he get your phone number from?"

Angellini shrugged, drank some more coffee. "He said that he had seen you and that you had let him down. You couldn't be bothered with him. So he phoned me. Of course, I told him he was crazy. And he was."

"What did he say?"

"That you didn't care, that you were just like the rest of them—whoever they may be. He seemed to think there was a plan to take Anna from him. Rossi had gotten some students to come into the gardens and take her. The real reason was to show that he couldn't look after his own daughter, not even in public gardens, and that she'd be safer with her grandparents." Another sip of coffee. "A lot of what he was saying was close to gibberish. He was speaking fast and I had difficulty following."

"I saw him last night. I didn't realize that he had worked out his own theory." Trotti looked at Angellini. "He's mad."

"He said you used to be his friend." Again he laughed. "He called you a questurino."

Trotti raised his voice. "I almost lost my job over his daughter—
and now I probably have lost it. He told you about the San Siro?"

"He told me that he had contacted the police."

"You could have stopped him."

"Why should I?"

"And my wife?"

"How was I to know that she was there? And even when the
Carabinieri came, I didn't recognize her. I've only seen her a
couple of times. And anyway, she appeared to be with a man;
why should I think it was your wife? It was my photographer
who recognized her. And as soon as he told me I phoned you."

"Thanks," Trotti said, almost mechanically. And then to
himself, "With another man."

Angellini nodded.

Trotti placed the cup back on the tray. He had not touched
the coffee. He now stood up and went to the window. The sun
had moved, but its blinding reflection was still caught on a windowpane opposite.

The old man in black had returned. He was sitting on an
upright stone, part of the ancient doorway, and was staring at
the carcass of the wheelless bicycle. He propped his hands and
chin on an old stick that he held between his legs. He seemed to
be nodding, as though in conversation with himself.

A chicken crossed the courtyard, followed by four adventur-
ous chicks, walking in a line.

An early bee buzzed against the windowpane.

"I knew she had men friends—I knew that. But I thought she
went dancing—or to restaurants. But gambling—I had no idea.
Where did she get the money from?"

"She didn't necessarily play for money. Perhaps she just watched."

Trotti turned round and faced Angellini. "You realize what
this means?"

Angellini did not reply and Trotti turned again to look out
of the window. The old man caught sight of him and raised the
stick in a wave. A toothless smile.

Trotti said, "You're right, of course." He smiled. "I'm a fool."

Noisily, Angellini finished his coffee.

40

TROTTI CROSSED THE piazza and entered the Bar Duomo. It was early and Signora Allegra, standing behind the long, spotless counter, was shouting at a couple of men. They wore blue singlets and baggy cotton overalls. Their snub-nosed truck was parked in the empty piazza alongside the potted plants that formed a barrier to the open terrace. They were ferrying crates—yellow plastic containing Coca-Cola and Birra Peroni—from the truck to the cellar of the bar.

She smiled, a large, spontaneous smile. "Commissario—how nice to see you." She approached him and placed a hand on his sleeve. "You look tired, Commissario. You must have something to eat."

Even this early, she was well-groomed; her lipstick was perfect, she wore a beige cardigan and a scarf of red, white and green—Italian colors. Her eyes sparkled as she spoke. "Please sit down." She moved a table away from the long, leather bench. She brushed at imaginary crumbs on the spotless blue table-cloth—and from the next table, she took an ashtray. "Coffee, Commissario?"

Trotti nodded.

She went behind the bar, scooped a couple of spoonfuls of coffee—a reassuring, familiar odor—into the steel receptacle and then inserted it into the hissing Gaggia machine. She pulled at the black handle. A jet of steam escaped into the air.

Two papers lay on the table, the *Corriere* and the *Provincia*. He looked at the *Corriere*. The front page spoke of Moro, there was a photograph of his wife, and there were long black columns of print reporting on the political debate. A conflict of values; the integrity of the state versus the physical integrity of a destroyed man.

No real news of Moro; no communiqué from the Red Brigades. But as Trotti read, trying to concentrate on the dancing lines of print, he was aware of a sense of disaster. Inevitable disaster.

"Ecco, Dottore."

She brought him the coffee and a glass of grappa. She set the tray on the table then, stepping back, placed a hand on her hip. She wore a blue skirt with a box pleat running down the front. "You haven't slept, have you?" She scolded him like a loving mother with a wayward son.

Trotti shook his head.

"You look a wreck. And with your permission." She bent over and straightened his tie. She placed a hand on his lapel; it brushed lightly against his chin. A soft hand. "That's better." She moved backwards, her head to one side, appreciating the improvement.

The muscles in his cheek were stiff. Trotti tried to smile. He poured the grappa into the coffee. The small cup advertised the local coffee roasters: CAFFÉ MESSICANO and a little man in an outsize sombrero.

The two men emerged from the cellar, each whistling a different tune. They returned to the truck; one of them laughed.

"I can see you've been up all night, Commissario. I can make you something to eat, if you want. Some eggs? I have some fresh eggs from the country. And some ham?"

Trotti shook his head. "Just a brioche."

Signora Allegra took the large jar from the counter and placed it before Trotti; inside, the sugary doughnuts were deformed by the walls of bulging glass. She handed him a paper serviette.

"There is no news?"

He tapped the *Provincia*. "The Carabinieri have discovered a gambling den."

"But they can't find Moro." She shook her head. "You'd think that at this moment they'd have more important things to do than go looking for gamblers."

He could feel the grappa warming the lining of his stomach. "No," he said, "they haven't found Moro."

TROTTI CAUGHT A bus.

It was full of early morning commuters. Girls in pretty dresses and no brassieres; dark hair, dark eyes and smooth, olive complexions. Businessmen, their narrow shoes well polished and their hair carefully groomed. They carried attaché cases as tangible proof of their social standing and success. And one or two housewives, holding empty shopping bags to their ample bodies.

The bus trundled through the old city center. Pedestrians along the Corso Mazzini edged towards the pavement as the bus went past and then swelled back into the middle of the road like waves in the wake of a ship.

Trotti stood on the back platform of the bus, staring through the window.

Outside the Casa di Risparmio delle Provincie Settentrionali, a blue Fiat was parked on the mosaic of the portico. And beside it, in front of the door of the bank, stood the Security Officer. He looked like a New York policeman; his belly bulged over a leather belt and his peaked cap had the sharp edges of a polygon. His left hand on his hip; the right hand fiddled with the wooden butt of his hand pistol.

Teenagers stood outside the cinema pointing at the new posters of a film with Laura Antonelli. Her flesh, painted a hyperrealist pink, strained against a tight bodice.

There was a newsstand and from the cover of the displayed magazines Moro's tragic features stared mournfully. Behind his grey head, the star of the Red Brigades.

Trotti felt less tired; the coffee and the warm grappa had revived him. And less worried. There was a solution, he told himself. The *Provincia* had been deliberately discreet. And at this time, there were other things more important to worry over than the peccadilloes of the wife of a policeman. An insignificant, provincial policeman . . . There was a crisis, a crisis of identity. The worst crisis in the thirty years of scandal and corruption of the Italian Republic.

A gambling den at San Siro. Not important. Common knowledge; a secret of Pulcinella.

The headmistress was engaged and for five minutes Trotti had to wait. He sat on a plastic chair and stared at the green paint of the wall in the waiting room. There was only one window, high in the wall. The air was heavy and Trotti had the impression that soon the good weather would break and there would be rain. He loosened his tie and undid the top button of his shirt.

"Ah, Commissario."

Signorina Belloni opened the door. He had to turn round; he stood up and shook the cool white hand. Her smile was warm and friendly.

"I'm sorry to keep you waiting. A phone call—another—from the town hall." She smiled while her hand smoothed the newspaper on the desk before her. "They still can't make up their minds when they want to disinfect." She paused. "And on Sunday we vote."

"Administrative problems." He smiled. "I know them well."

Signorina Belloni moved back in her chair. She folded her arms; the blue cardigan about her shoulders was unbuttoned. "The last time you came"—she frowned slightly, as though recalling the event with difficulty—"it was raining." She turned to look at the sky; beyond the rooftops, clouds were forming. "It is going to rain again."

"I can assure you that it is not my fault." Trotti smiled.

"Cause and effect, Commissario." She did not return his smile. "That is perhaps our problem in Italy. We know that something is wrong but find the cause, that is the problem." She seemed to have aged since he had last seen her. The cheeks seemed greyer and more hollow. The eyes stared at Trotti without blinking. Dye the hair, Trotti thought, and she would appear a younger, healthier woman.

"Anna came back yesterday. Quite unaffected, it would seem, by her ordeal. Signora Perbene assures me that she has fitted into the classroom routine as though she had never been away. We are all very proud of her."

"It's about Anna that I'm here."

The face stiffened; the wrinkles about the eyes grew deeper as she narrowed the lids. "Yes?"

"I wish to speak with her."

She smiled before saying, "The child has already lost enough time. I'm afraid—you understand, I'm sure—I'm afraid I can't let you speak with her during class hours." There was a day-to-day calendar on her desk. May 8. "In a couple of days we'll have to close the school for the elections. I only hope that they'll send those awful disinfectant men in time." She shuddered slightly. "With their vile language and their dirty fingernails. The last referendum—abortion or divorce? I can't remember—one of them made a highly unpleasant remark. Yes—abortion. The remark was tasteless and offensive." She ran a finger through the pages of the diary. "These elections are giving me ulcers." A tight smile. "Having too much responsibility in a country where responsibility is a bad word has turned my hair grey prematurely."

"Your hair suits you."

"You flatter me, Commissario." She smiled again, this time unguardedly. "But no." She shook her head. "I'm afraid I can't let you speak with the child. I'm sure you understand." She sighed. "These children lose so much time." Her hands went over the newspaper again. "Too much politics and not enough teaching. I'm afraid you find me in a bad mood. Angry, frustrated with their incompetence at the town hall, and in a bad mood. I have to put up with it all. Elections, strikes—a week doesn't go by without the children losing a day of work. And when they do come, I often wonder what they can possibly learn." Again the tight smile. "You know, sometimes I am surprised that they ever learn to read and write." She stood up and went to the window and looked out towards the rising bank of clouds. She lowered her glance towards the courtyard. "Fascism was an evil thing. It did a lot of harm and in the end, it brought about the downfall of this country." A pleasant memory pulled at the corner of her lips. "You remember the American soldiers that used to give us sweets? And for four years our parents had scarcely found enough polenta to keep us alive. Suddenly those young men produced Christmas from out of their khaki bags. We had starved—and for years the Fascists had told us it was necessary—the hardships, the sacrifices—if we were to win the fight against the foreign invader." She ran the back of her hand across her flat belly, as though recalling the hunger of thirty-three years before. "I have reason to hate Fascism, Commissario. The man—the only man—I have ever loved was killed. I was just a girl but I knew I was going to marry him when he returned from Albania. I wrote to him every day." She stared at the floor. "He didn't return."

Trotti felt embarrassed.

"Fascism, Commissario, was an evil thing—but at least it was an ideal. Italy, Il Duce, the mother country, the battle for corn—we believed in those things. Empty, false ideals—but we believed in them. Others—the cunning and the dishonest—made use of our gullibility. They became Fascists just as today they become Communists. They look after themselves and they change their ideals just as they change their shirts. But you and me—we believed in those things. We believed that Il Duce was good, that he was infallible, that he kept the lights burning late into the night for our sake. We believed that Italy deserved a place in the sun. You remember how at school they taught us that the Abyssinian had a heart as black as his face? And we believed it all. Because throughout history, the poor and the humble have always believed what they've been told by the rich, the powerful and the church. Because Italians have never had any choice. Stupid, naive and deliberately misled. You remember the uniforms, those fezzes, the guns? But for all its failings, Fascism offered an ideal. What ideal do they have today? My children, what values can they have when they see their teachers who tell them to distrust everything?" She sighed. "I have always wanted my children to learn and to understand. I have always wanted them to be excited by the adventure of life, its possibilities—by the gift that life is. So the Provincial authority sends me teachers who know nothing and who understand even less. They have their university diplomas and degrees but they are ignorant."

She returned to her seat. "You find me in a bitter mood, Commissario, and in my bitterness, I am unfair perhaps. Of course the situation that we all find ourselves in doesn't have much to do with schools or teachers. School is always the reflection of the society it is called upon to serve. Perhaps I, too, have failed. I have always tried to do my job well—but we are all caught up in the corruption and petty dishonesties of our lives. We all carry within us the contradictions of Italy." She sighed. "Yesterday, I was walking down by the river. There is a path that runs along the water's edge. It was a nice day and I wanted to get away from here, from this place with its smell of chalk. I was walking near the boat sheds that belong to the university and I was nearly knocked off my feet. A big motorbike went past. Young men go down there with their big machines, noisy and with poisonous fumes, with their goggles and their helmets. Yesterday, I was knocked off my feet and I hurt myself. I could have broken a leg. And the motorbike didn't even stop."

"You are all right?"

"Yes, thank you, Commissario." She looked at him. "But the strange thing is this. The motorcyclist turned round and I am sure I recognized him. He was one of my pupils—a nice boy with blond hair and lovely eyes. I know his parents. He used to be a very pleasant child and very affectionate. Now he knocks over old ladies."

"It wasn't deliberate."

"That is not the point. The point is, Commissario, that we live in a country that makes monsters out of human beings. A nice child transformed into an egotistical, selfish motorcyclist. But of course, it is quite normal. We live in a state that doesn't really exist—at least, not for the individual. So in order to survive, the individual must look after himself—because if he doesn't, he knows he will go under. Italy is not a nation—it is a land of fifty-five million individuals struggling to keep alive . . . where there is only one law: might is right."

She paused, tapped lightly at her bun. "We've lost a leader. Moro, whether he's been killed or not—his career is over, poor soul. We all have long faces, we think we have lost the one man who could save this country—because we like to believe in the man of providence, the man who is above the melee of corruption." She shook her head, "We've never had leaders. Not even Mussolini. We didn't understand, you and I, we were too young at the time. Mussolini—like Moro—was a puppet. He danced, he strutted, he gave the Roman salute and he led his country to destruction. But he was a puppet—the strings were held in Milan and Turin. You look at France and England. A ruling class— they've always had it. A self-perpetuating ruling class that has always gradually assimilated the emergent bourgeoisie, assimilated it and imposed upon it its own patrician values. We've never had that. Just rich peasants—rich, grasping peasants."

Trotti said nothing.

The headmistress continued, "When I was a child I used to read the novels of Rudyard Kipling . . . and I could never really understand them. The British Empire—it seemed so organized, so civilized. But of course, I now realize that Kipling's India was like England. They went out there, the pink-faced Englishmen, and they imposed their values—the values of a Protestant middle class. They had no right to be there and they were trying to give a moral justification for the depredations they made. The raw materials they sent back to England. But they gave a system, they united India into one country. They created a state and they created in people a respect for that state. We Italians have been invaded and conquered by everybody, but nobody has ever given us a state. And now that we are free, we allow the peasants and the Mafia to govern us, to usurp the true Republic." A sad smile. "It is not India, Commissario, that is the third world; it is Italy. For us, state is a hollow, meaningless word—corrupted by the people who govern us. It means nothing. When a policeman or Carabiniere is shot down by terrorists in the street and his young blood pours into the gutter, our President sends a telegram to the parents. He speaks of the grief of the state. Meaningless. There is no state, our grief is individual. And now as the politicians in Rome squabble over Moro and evoke the reason of state to justify their own immobility, they are talking rubbish. They are trying to dress in the clothes of integrity; they have never had any other consideration than their own self-advancement."

"Perhaps it is our fault, signorina. It is we who vote."

"We had a chance, Commissario. After the war, we all believed things would get better. We were united—we'd all fought against the common enemy of Fascism. Catholic and Communist, we had been united by a common enemy. But we allowed our chance to slip away. The chance of a real Italy—a real Republic. Excuse me." Her eyes were slightly damp. "I lived through those years, I remember our optimism. And still for me, Republic is a beautiful word. But we have let it fall into the grasp of our politicians. In our search for creature comforts, for consumer durables, we have lost sight of our Republic. We have no self-respect. We have been corrupted; the corrupters have made us like them. The Mafia, the men in Rome, the political parties, they have degraded us— and they have assimilated us." She turned to look at him. "At least with Mussolini we had ideals. There was no cynicism. We had false ideals—but we believed in them; many even died for them. Now we have nothing. We have become a godless, value-less nation. We run after our easy luxuries, our daily piece of beefsteak and our motor cars and our fine clothes. The men talk about football and the women read photo-romance magazines. And we pretend not to understand why the young are angry."

More tears appeared at the corner of her eyes.

"I believe in the Republic," Trotti said quietly. Signorina Belloni wiped at her tears. "I believe in the Republic and I try to do my duty."

"Then perhaps, Commissario Trotti, you are like me. You are a fool." A hesitant, friendly smile. "A good man—a very good man—but a fool."

"I must do my duty."

Somewhere a bell rang, muffled behind several doors.

"I must speak with the child."

"I cannot allow that, Commissario."

"It is my duty."

"And it is my duty to protect the child."

"Do not compel me to use the force of the law."

"The law?" She raised an eyebrow; she appeared slightly amused. "The law?"

"I must speak with Anna."

"Commissario, her parents—or rather, her grandparents—told me explicitly that they did not want Anna to be disturbed—not by journalists nor by anyone else. They insisted, Commissario, and I must respect their wishes."

"They are not Anna's guardians."

"The father is incompetent. A good man—I don't doubt it; but not very intelligent and not reliable enough. The child lives with her grandparents—and it was when he should have been looking after her that she was taken from the gardens in via Darsena."

Trotti waited before replying. "I have reason to believe that it was Anna's grandparents who engineered the kidnapping. And they did it precisely with the aim to discredit Ermagni. They want to bring the child up as their own."

"Absurd."

"Absurd or not, signorina, at this moment, Signor Rossi is in a cell of the Caserma Bixio. Under arrest."

She stared at Trotti while a hand went to her throat. She pressed the bell. "You put me in an awkward position." Her voice caught in her throat.

"I am sorry. I, too, find myself in an awkward position." Trotti allowed himself smile. "The truth can be very awkward."

They then sat in silence until Trotti heard the fall of Nino's steps outside. He knocked and put his round face through the door.

"Signorina Direttrice?"

"Bring me Anna Ermagni, please."

He nodded. The door closed silently.

A few minutes later, Trotti said, "I should have looked after her more—I should have taken more interest in her. It is not as though I've got other godchildren. But I was in the South. And since I've been back, I've been busy." He played with the wedding ring on his finger, turning it against the taut skin. "I hope it is not too late."

"She is a shy child," the headmistress replied and then was silent. It was as though she had lost all interest in talking. She sat with her hands on the paper in front of her. Her face was still slightly flushed.

Trotti had the impression that it was rare for her to open her heart and talk freely. He felt flattered and slightly surprised that she should have spoken with him at such length. Once or twice she turned to look at Trotti but when their eyes met, hers turned away.

It started to rain. She rose to close the window and Trotti, looking down, noticed that there was just a trace of blue lines along her calves beneath the dark mesh of her stockings. She wore blue shoes with squat heels.

When he had first seen her, Trotti had found her attractive. She was still attractive but there was something else as well. Something that Trotti had difficulty in defining. A kind of just anger, perhaps. A woman who had her own ideas, her own convictions but who was physically frail. The kind of woman who deserved respect, but who also needed affection. A woman who needed a man to protect her.

She was staring out of the window—the darkening sky threw light onto her profile and she appeared less agitated—when the porter knocked on the door.

He entered, holding Anna by the hand.

The girl was unhappy. She looked at Signorina Belloni and then at Trotti with her large, dark eyes. The fringe of dark hair came down almost to her brow. She hesitated and only reluctantly allowed herself to be prodded, one shoulder before the other, into the center of the room.

"Come, Anna." The headmistress stepped round her desk and brushing past Trotti—the feel of the weave of her dress against his hand—she took the child by the elbow.

"Anna," she said. She bent over, lowering herself to the level of Anna's eyes. She stroked the girl's lustrous black hair. "Don't be afraid." The long fingers were pale against the darkness of Anna's hair.

Anna said nothing. A tentative smile flickered across the small, pale lips and then as quickly as it had come, it vanished. The eyes remained worried.

"This gentleman is Signor Trotti . . ."

"Piero." Trotti smiled. He too crouched and, reaching out, took Anna's right hand. A small hand. Soft, cool, very slightly damp. He remembered the time when Pioppi was that age. "You don't remember me but I knew you when you were very little. Your papa used to work for me."

At the mention of her father, the eyes seemed to darken.

"I am your godfather."

The child nodded.

"Your godfather wants to ask you a few questions, Anna." The headmistress glanced at Trotti. "He is a policeman. You have nothing to worry about."

Again Anna nodded.

"Come," Trotti said. "Give me your other hand." He pulled the child around until she was standing between his knees. She was wearing a white blouse beneath the black overalls and the plastic white collar with its loose red cravat; on her feet, white socks and neat, good quality sandals. Clean nails, well brushed hair and a healthy although slightly pale complexion. A couple of scars on her knees, and beneath the eyes the trace of dark lines. The eyes stared at Trotti while the narrow chest heaved under the dark overalls.

"Don't be afraid, Anna." He gave her a reassuring tug.

Again the flicker of a smile.

"You see, I'm here to help you. It's very important. What happened to you—the way you were taken away—we don't want it happening to other children. You understand?"

Anna nodded; then catching her breath, said, "But I have already answered the questions. In the hospital. I answered them. You were there, I remember. You were with my father."

"You were tired and that was several days ago. Perhaps you can remember more clearly now. Perhaps there are things that you forgot to tell us. It is so easy to forget things." He smiled. "I know I'm always forgetting things."

"I said everything."

"Are you sure, Anna? Absolutely everything?"

She nodded. Her mouth had grown smaller. Firm wrinkles at the edge of her lips.

Trotti looked at her and she lowered her head.

"Are you hiding something?"

"No."

Trotti stroked the back of her hand. "You mustn't be afraid of us," he said gently. "We won't be angry. But you see, we must think about the other children. For their sake you must help us."

"I've said everything."

On the ceiling, the fan blade rotated.

"You don't like your papa, do you, Anna?"

Anna did not move; yet he could feel the hands tensing.

"He is a good man—and a very kind one."

"Anna," Signorina Belloni's voice was kind, motherly. "He loves you a great deal. More than anything else in the world. He often tells me that without you, he has got nothing."

Anna turned to look at the headmistress.

Trotti said, "But you don't like him, do you?"

Anna raised her shoulders and then let them fall. Her head was to one side. She continued to look at her sandals.

Nino was leaning against the door. He held an unlit cigarette between his lips. *La Gazzetta dello Sport* bulged in his pocket. He coughed and, looking up, Signorina Belloni frowned and gestured for him to leave. He went slowly out of the room. Anna's eyes followed him. Then she returned to looking at her shoes.

"Why don't you like your papa?"

There was no reaction from the child.

"Is it because of your grandparents?" Trotti let her hand drop and, with his index finger, he pulled up her chin. Her eyes refused to meet his. "Look at me and tell me the truth. Is it because of your grandfather?"

The eyes came up slowly. They had their own depth. In that moment, she looked a lot older than her age. She moved backwards, pushing Trotti's hand away from her chin. She lowered her head.

"Grandfather tells you that your father is a bad man? That he doesn't love you? You mustn't believe those things, Anna."

The headmistress said, "Your father loves you."

Anna remained silent.

"Your father loves you very much and now that your mama is . . . now that your mama has gone, he needs you to look after him. A man always needs a woman, Anna."

She mumbled inaudibly.

"You know you shouldn't have left him in the garden. It wasn't a kind thing to do. You shouldn't have run away."

She looked up. "I didn't run away."

Trotti gave her a disbelieving smile. "You ran away."

"I didn't. I swear I didn't." She was now looking at him.

"You remember?"

"Yes." Then vehemently she shook her head. "No."

"Where did you go?"

"I don't remember."

"You can tell us, Anna. You mustn't be afraid." Trotti turned to the headmistress. Without any expression, she looked back at him. Between them there was a tacit tie of collusion.

"Would you like something to eat, Anna?" Signorina Belloni asked.

Anna shook her head and, like the skirt of a dancer, her hair rose, lifted by centrifugal force, and then fell against her forehead.

"Your grandfather tells you bad things. You mustn't believe him, Anna. He has never liked your father. He is jealous of him."

By now the sky was dark. The clouds had come over the city, giving a leaden light to the sky. Suddenly the room was brightened by lightning beyond the roofs of the houses. A few seconds later, the rumble of thunder caused the windowpanes to rattle.

Anna shivered.

"Your father loved your mother very much." Signorina Belloni lowered her voice. "She was a very beautiful woman."

Anna looked at the headmistress.

Trotti said, "I was at their wedding." He smiled. "I was the best man. I can remember your mother in her wedding gown. She was like a princess."

The child smiled, then, embarrassed, looked downwards. She mumbled something.

For Trotti, it was a spontaneous movement. He put his hands

to the sides of her head. Her skin was cool against his palms. He pulled her face upwards, bringing her eyes into line with his own. There was something in her features that reminded him of the father. Perhaps a hint of stubbornness.

"What did you say, Anna?"

She tried to shake her head.

"Your mother was very beautiful and he loved her. And she loved your father."

"He killed her."

There was silence. The thunder was moving away, moving north across the Po valley towards Milan. "And he wants to kill me."

41

IT WAS NEARLY eleven o'clock when the taxi dropped Trotti off outside the Questura. The rain was pouring down, the pavement shiny.

An appuntato caught sight of him and came running over to offer the protection of his black umbrella. "Dirty weather, Commissario," he said. Trotti nodded.

He got into the lift and stepped out on the third floor.

Principessa raised her head, sniffed the air, looked through the damp windowpane and then returned to her dreams.

"Magagna?"

"He was here half an hour ago." The blind man added, amused at his own joke, "I haven't seen him since." He took an envelope from where he had tucked it under the large telephone console. "He left you this."

"Thanks." Trotti said, taking the white envelope. "Any messages?"

"Avvocato Romano phoned." The pale eyes screwed up behind the thick glasses.

Trotti went into his office. Rain battered at the window and rattled at the handle. He sat down to look at the envelope.

In scrawled handwriting, Magagna had written, *Milan Central has checked. Voice on tape recording from provincia is not voice of Gracchi.*

Trotti thought for a while; it took him several minutes to

realize that the office was strangely quiet. And it took him several more minutes to realize why. The pigeons had ceased to coo.

Through the runnels of rain on the window, it was difficult to make out the forms of the terracotta roofs. The sky was dark.

The phone rang. It was Gino. "Leonardelli. He wants you. Now."

"Thanks."

Trotti left his office and went along the corridor, past the coffee machine. He was worried; a strange, heavy feeling in his stomach.

He knocked on the door.

"Of course, of course," Leonardelli was on the phone and his smile disappeared as he saw Trotti. With his eyes returning to the telephone, he beckoned to enter. He pointed at a chair; between the fingers of his hand, a cigarette was burning. Leonardelli continued his conversation. "There's not much that I can do at this end."

Trotti heard the scratching voice and Leonardelli nodded emphatically. As though he had been expecting a change in the weather, Leonardelli was wearing a dark suit; and lying across the desk, slightly speckled with rain, a beige raincoat. The inside label was visible.

Burberry.

While he spoke, Leonardelli gestured with his free hand and the glowing tip of the cigarette described short circles in the air.

"D'accordo, d'accordo." Leonardelli nodded, smiling. "Si, grazie. Si. Arrivederci."

He was still smiling as he replaced the receiver.

There followed a long silence. Leonardelli pushed his glasses up onto his forehead and held his long hands to his face, as though lost in prayer.

"Trotti."

"Yes."

The hands came away from the tired eyes that looked at Trotti with evident disapproval. "I'm afraid, Commissario, that you are causing me difficulties."

Trotti nodded. "I was at Caserma Bixio this morning."

"So I hear." The cigarette had now burned down to its filter. The Questore squashed it into the porcelain ashtray that was already full of similar, black-ended filters. Against the background of Leonardelli's eau de cologne, Trotti could smell the bitter ashes.

Leonardelli sat back, his hands together and his thumbs hitting at each other. "A very awkward time, Trotti. A very awkward time indeed."

"The *Provincia* has mentioned nothing."

"I don't see why you had to go to Bixio."

"I received a phone call," Trotti said simply.

"Ah." He frowned. "I'd rather you didn't spend your time with the Carabinieri."

"An anonymous phone call in the early morning telling me to go to Bixio." He shrugged. "So I went."

"It is best if we have as little as possible to do with the Carabinieri. I don't consider them as being able to help us in any way."

"They have my wife," Trotti replied.

"Of course." Leonardelli's smile lacked compassion. "I understand."

Trotti did not speak; he could feel the anger rising within his chest. He stared at the turning movement of Leonardelli's thumbs.

"The trouble is that with the Carabinieri, these things can't be kept quiet. And at this time, we have other things to worry about. Furthermore—and I say this not as a criticism—I don't understand why it is at this hour, Trotti, that you arrive here. I hope you haven't spent your morning drinking coffee with Spadano and smoking his filthy cigars."

"I don't smoke, Signor Questore."

"There's enough work here with Guerra and Gracchi for you to look into." He stopped. "You realize that it's serious."

"What?"

"Outside the recognized casinos in Italy, gambling is illegal. You must know that and certainly your wife does. Also—and it is this I fail to understand—why did you allow her to go to San Siro?"

"I didn't know."

"Come, Trotti. I am not stupid. You did not know, you say. She's your wife—how long have you been married? Twenty years now? And you don't know her tastes. You must have known she frequented these places—because if you really didn't, then what sort of husband are you? Come, Trotti."

"I didn't know."

"I find that very hard to believe." The lashless eyes did not blink behind his glasses. "A commissario of the Pubblica Sicurezza—someone whose job is to see through the petty lies of criminals—who doesn't know what his own wife is doing."

"My wife has always been very independent."

"You realize"—the voice now hardened—"that I can ask for your resignation."

"You can have it." Trotti allowed himself a brief smile.

"But I have to take into consideration other and more pressing points." The Questore chose to overlook Trotti's offer. "There is the crisis the country is going through, the shortage—the drastic shortage of trained manpower. Despite rising unemployment, it is hard to get recruits, young men don't want to join the PS. And there is the fact that I know you, Trotti, and"—a magnanimous shrug—"I know that you are honest and reliable. Perhaps you are too honest, as I've told you before." In a more optimistic tone, "I have friends in the Carabinieri," he added.

"Friends?"

"To help your wife."

"There are no charges. Spadano told me. He said he would keep Agnese—that he would keep my wife until this evening. For her sake, he said. To serve as a lesson."

"You're a good policeman, Trotti, and I don't want to lose you— if it is possible to keep you, that is. The other officers like you, you've got a team that I am satisfied with. You are a valuable element. If I manage to get your wife released, I want a firm undertaking from you that you will keep a tighter control of her. I don't want this kind of thing being repeated. It is embarrassing for me—and it forces me to make use of favors that I have given in the past, favors that I could make much better use of."

"She's not under arrest, Signor Questore. She will be released this evening. Spadano and I came to an agreement."

"It is all very well to tell me she has her independence. If her independence is detrimental to the good name of the force in the city, I'm afraid I will have to get rid of her and you." He smiled, allowing himself to relax. "She'll have to change her ways." He sat back and took the cigarette case from his pocket. He held out the tipped cigarettes to Trotti.

Trotti shook his head.

"I may be able to make an arrangement with Bixio." He put the cigarette in his mouth.

"Spadano said he'd release my wife this evening; there is no need for any arrangement."

Leonardelli laughed, allowing air to escape from his nose and blow at the glowing tip of the cigarette. "I think, Trotti, you are being naive. You don't seem to understand the Carabinieri. They are southerners; Levantines, if you like. They drive a hard bargain." He laughed again. "They certainly don't give any presents. I fear the Greeks, even when they bring gifts."

"I beg your pardon."

A dismissive wave of Leonardelli's hand. "They owe me favors. It is possible I can get them to drop charges. I will look into it. But while I'm doing all this for you, I'd be grateful if you'd get on with your work. Your place is here in the Questura. I don't want you wandering about—not now, not with elections here next Sunday. I want you to get to the bottom of the Guerra affair. Get a confession. And leave politicking with the Carabinieri to me."

Outside in Strada Nuova, the Italian flag, drenched and bedraggled, hung limply from the flagstaff.

42

MAGAGNA WAS WAITING for him in the corridor. He was smoking and he looked worried.

"You're wearing uniform," Trotti remarked, surprised.

Magagna shrugged. "I received orders."

"From him?" With his thumb, Trotti gestured over his shoulder to Leonardelli's office. They went past the Faema machine.

"Indirectly." Magagna pulled at Trotti's sleeve. "But come quickly. There's someone I think you should talk to."

Trotti quickened his step. "You've heard about my wife?"

Again Magagna shrugged. A matter of no importance. "Come," he said.

They went into Trotti's office.

"He's waiting outside with Gino."

Trotti sat down at his desk, opened the bottom drawer and quickly poured a few drops of grappa into the screw-top. He drank and hurriedly put the bottle back in its place. Magagna came back, ushering in the visitor.

"This way, please. Commissario Trotti can now talk to you."

An old man entered. He was well-dressed in a slightly outdated fashion; beneath the open-necked shirt, a white singlet. Over one arm, a raincoat and hanging from his forearm, a black umbrella. Pale cotton trousers, light blue except at the bottoms where the material had been splashed by the rain. White socks and woven leather shoes.

"Avvocato Romano." He held out his hand. In the other hand, he held a leather leash. A small Pekinese dog trotted dutifully behind him.

"I think we've met."

"Yes, I think so." Trotti smiled and they shook hands.

He had a tanned, intelligent face, a high forehead speckled with dark freckles. The eyes, too, were intelligent; cunning even. His thin hair was sandy in color and formed a widow's peak. A thin, peppery mustache—of the type that had been popular before the war in the old telefoni bianchi films—ran along the upper lip.

He gripped Trotti's hand firmly; the hand was dry.

"Please be seated."

The man, seventy years old at least, Trotti decided, carefully attached the dog's lead to one arm of the armchair before sitting down on the dusty canvas. He pulled at the creases of his trousers while Magagna took the raincoat and umbrella.

A smile. "Avvocato Romano, Ettore—now retired."

"A pleasure to meet again. Now how can I help you?"

The lawyer raised a sandy eyebrow. "Help me?" He shook his head. "No, Commissario, I don't need help. I come here as a citizen to do what I consider to be my duty."

"Which is?"

Avvocato Romano seemed taken aback by the abruptness of the question. He glanced at Magagna before answering. "To tell you what I know—or rather, to be more exact, what I saw. I trust it may be of use to you. This young officer here concurs with my opinion."

Magagna smiled.

"Then please tell me everything." Trotti unscrewed the top of his pen expectantly. He took a sweet from his pocket and placed it in his mouth; it clicked against his teeth.

Avvocato Romano sat back in the chair, obviously enjoying the attention now being given to him. He placed his elbows on the armrest and clasped his hands together on the lap of his cotton trousers. The dog lay obediently at his feet.

"I usually take Giuseppina for a walk in the evening."

"Giuseppina?"

"My dog." The pekinese raised its eyes to look at its master. "A good walk does us both good—and well, it helps me to sleep. I'm afraid I've become a bit of an insomniac; since the departure of my good wife, I don't sleep as well as I used to." He leaned forward and on a more intimate note added, "Herbal teas don't help. So a walk around the city—I follow the old Roman walls, you understand, and it normally takes us about an hour. Useful exercise. And then I can sleep."

"I understand," Trotti said and pretended to write a few words on the sheet before him.

"We usually leave at about eleven o'clock in the evening. There are fewer cars for Giuseppina to bark at. Of course, I am very happy about the pedestrian zone; unfortunately, most of the parking places for the cars are now along the old city walls. Earlier in the day you can't walk on the pavement because of the cars. That's where they leave them, the people who come here to work."

"The dog barks at the cars?"

"But she's getting better." A proud smile. "Aren't you, my dear?" He gave a tug at the lead. The dog looked at its master with haggard indifference.

"I follow the Roman walls—as I told you—starting from the river and going round the city. For six years now—ever since the good lady died. And only fifty-four." He placed a hand in his trouser pocket and rummaged, looking for a handkerchief. He pulled it out and wiped his forehead. "Only fifty-four, God rest her soul."

Trotti murmured a few words of sympathy.

Then Avvocato Romano, looking to the window, said, "Humid, isn't it?"

It was still raining outside, the large drops splashing against the window. Through the glass there came the muffled sound of tires running over the wet cobbles in the street below. Trotti, too, felt hot. He pointed to the door and asked Magagna to open it. Magagna got up and opened the door, jamming it with a chair. A timid breeze from the corridor pushed at the dirty curtain. The dog raised its eyes.

"Thank you," the lawyer said. He folded the handkerchief and returned it to his pocket. "I wouldn't have come—I wouldn't be here, wasting your time like this—if it wasn't important. And then when I saw her photograph in the newspaper—and the article—then I knew I had been right." He raised his shoulders. "I don't normally read those articles—the cronaca nera, it's so depressing. Goodness knows how people can enjoy that sort of thing. And yet you know, I had colleagues, other lawyers like myself, who wouldn't touch anything else."

"I'm afraid I don't quite understand."

Avvocato Romano frowned. "I saw her photograph in the paper. The *Provincia*. Most days I go to the bar—Il Senatore in via Cremona—to have a look at the papers, and especially at the obituaries. I like to see who has died. It's nice to know who you've outlived." A little laugh. "A kind of revenge, I suppose. Unfortunately as all my old enemies die off I've got no one left to share the pleasure with. And I've got no one left to hate." He sighed. "Ah! Growing old—it gets very lonely." One hand fell against the other and made a dry sound. "But otherwise, no—I don't read the papers. It's not the same world. So much violence, so much senseless violence. And no real politicians, just rather horrible little men. Now Giolitti—that was a politician."

"What did you see in the paper, Avvocato?"

"Please do not rush me, Commissario." He held up a hand. "I'm an old man now and it takes me time to think. I'll get there, have faith in me—but let me get there under my own steam. At my own speed and in my own way." There was a runnel down his chin—he now ran a finger along it while his eyes were closed in thought. He shook his head. "It was in yesterday's paper. And I saw the photograph quite by chance. It gave me a nasty turn. It was her all right. I recognized her face—and her mouth. She had a nice mouth. You know, those photos, they make everybody look ugly. And in the paper, she looked ugly, poor thing. But she wasn't ugly."

"Who?"

"Oh, I never knew her name. And she probably wouldn't have given it to me if I'd asked. It's strange, isn't it, how there are so many people whose faces are etched into our memory, we see them every day of the week—and yet we haven't got the first idea of what their name is. I used to say hello to her whenever she was there. Sometimes it was almost every evening. Of course, there were occasions when she wasn't there. I was disappointed—I liked to see her—but of course I was being selfish. She was probably with a client, making some money, the poor thing. I would go past at about half past eleven—maybe a bit earlier." He stopped. "Yes, she had a nice mouth."

"You mean Irina Pirvic?"

"That's right. She was Yugoslav, according to the newspaper. She wasn't Italian, I knew that. She had an accent. Sometimes she'd say buona sera and then I would stop and we'd talk about the weather for a few minutes." He stopped, smiling to himself. "One of the consolations of old age, perhaps, is that it teaches you the true value of women. When I was a young man"—he made a rotating gesture—"women, I had as many as I wanted. But it was love not of women but of myself that drove me to conquer more and more. We are so caught up by the need to conquer women that we don't have time to enjoy them. As fellow human beings, with similar passions and this great desire to love—to love unselfishly." Again he gestured. "She was a prostitute probably because she had no choice. I'd like to think that she did that humiliating job because she had another mouth to feed." Quite sharply he pointed at Trotti. "But don't think I blame men for making use of whores. Men are no worse than women; we are all caught up in a system which is much stronger than us. We think it is us, making our own decisions, achieving our own little satisfactions. And of course, we are too self-centered to realize that all that we do, all our petty desires, it's all innate and that we are as much masters of our lives as are puppets masters of their movements. We are puppets—driven on by forces much stronger than us—the force to reproduce and the force to survive."

"She never solicited you?"

"I am old enough to be her father." The avvocato was genuinely shocked. "And I am a respectable man." He turned, looked through the window. "But indeed, there was something engaging about her. Something almost innocent—as though she herself didn't quite understand why she spent her evenings on the pavement, waiting to be picked up by riffraff. It wasn't her real job. She probably had no choice." He smiled. "Or am I imagining these things? No." He shook his head slightly. "No, I don't think so. Her face was gentle—even though she wore the most atrocious wig. A wig of frizzy white hair. And the clothes she wore—mini-skirts and provocative blouses and shoes with strange heels. But despite all that, she didn't look vulgar. A nice mouth—and a nice oval face."

There followed a short silence; then it was Magagna who spoke, removing the cigarette from his mouth. "Avvocato, she was killed by the man she lived with. It was an accident, she fell down the stairs. To get rid of the body, he cut her up."

The avvocato's face darkened. "So I read. I don't normally read those articles, but when I saw her photograph . . . It gave me a shock." He paused. "But in a way, I was expecting something like that. Perhaps not quite so gory—but I knew that something had happened. I suspected something and then when I didn't see her for several days . . . down by the Casa dello Studente, Giuseppina and I would dawdle deliberately—just in case she might turn up. To see her, a nod, a few words—when you reach my age, that can make all the difference. But she didn't come and that only confirmed my worst doubts." He stopped, looked around the office, at the grey filing cabinets, the wall map, the dusty dossiers piled on the floor, the chipped paint of the radiator. He looked at Magagna and then again at Trotti. "That man was lying," he said. "He didn't kill her."

"I beg your pardon?"

"He was lying. The old man in the newspaper. Her lover. He didn't kill her."

"What makes you say that?"

"Because I knew she was dead."

Magagna was now leaning forward in his chair.

Trotti said, "Please explain."

"I was there when she was killed."

"You were there?"

"It was last week. Last Tuesday, I think. Yes, last Tuesday. I was listening to the radio—I can't remember, I think it was Vivaldi—I've always liked Vivaldi."

"And . . ." Trotti prompted.

"And? Oh, yes. I was late. Normally I leave at about eleven but I was listening to the radio. It must have been after midnight." He nodded. "Yes. There were still one or two people about along the Corso—but the gelaterias were all closed. I don't know if you noticed, Commissario, but since this unhappy affair of Aldo Moro, people no longer stay out in the evenings. I've noticed the difference. People are afraid—even here, in our city. Fewer people in the bars, fewer people going to the cinema."

"So what happened, Avvocato?" Trotti unwrapped another sweet.

"Nothing. There was nobody about. So we followed the river, Giuseppina and I. They've spoiled it, of course. The Po—there was a time that you could drink the water. Now it's polluted by all the industry in Milan. And the old bridge that the Germans blew up in their retreat. After the war they put up a modern imitation—and it's another thirty meters downstream. But at night, you know, with the current running fast and the city lights reflected in the water, it's almost as it was before the war. This was a beautiful city once, you know. And sometimes when Giuseppina and I are walking in the evening, it is as though time has stopped. Forty years."

"So you walked along the embankment?"

"That's right. The length of the Lungo Po and then we crossed over the road at the bottom of Strada Nuova—we're in Strada Nuova now, aren't we? But at the bottom, by the bridge. We crossed Strada Nuova at the bottom. On the other side, there are so many truckss parked on the sidewalk. Trucks with their number plates from Messina and Imperia and Naples. Long-distance trucks that are heading up to Turin and Milan and the Swiss frontier. The drivers—I don't know where they sleep—and I don't think I want to know either. They leave their trucks on the sidewalk and it is a disgrace. They disgrace the river, they disgrace our city. But," he sighed, "I suppose it is to somebody's advantage. And I suppose that this is why she—this Yugoslav woman, poor soul . . ."

"Irina Pirvic."

"That's right. That's why she hung around there, it was good business for her."

"Near the Casa dello Studente on the Lungo Po?"

"That's right. It's an old university building that was made out of brick and granite in the Duce's time. It now belongs to the university. I sometimes see young people there, lots of Arabs and Greeks. And sometimes late in the evening, there are young people who go running in their tracksuits and their strange woolen bonnets. It's there that she used to work—if that's the right word." An apologetic smile. "There's an old church—just before the Casa dello Studente and slightly down from the embankment. It's almost hidden and she'd normally wait there—in the shadow."

"I know the place," Trotti said.

"She was there. Last Tuesday. I was pleased to see her. For some reason—it must have been after midnight—there were no trucks. And as I went past—I hadn't seen her—she made a remark about times being hard."

"You stopped?"

"Of course. I wouldn't normally stop—but you understand, I hadn't seen her for several days. And Giuseppina—a good place to have a call of nature—was a good excuse for an old man like me to stop and exchange a few words with a prostitute." His eyes were sad.

Giuseppina was now fast asleep.

"What did the woman say?"

"We talked about the weather—about nothing in particular. I had the impression she was pleased to see me. We chatted for a bit. Then I had to go because she thought she saw a prospective client. I left her. I turned into viale Libertà and headed towards the Corso."

"And that's all?" Trotti was disappointed.

"But no, Commissario. That's why I've been trying to get in touch with you over these last few days. Of course something happened. I wouldn't be wasting your time otherwise."

"What happened?"

"I'm getting there, Commissario. But in my own time. You keep asking me these questions. You confuse me."

"Asking questions is my job."

"Of course, of course." Avvocato Romano was wearing false teeth that clicked on the sibilants. "Beninteso." He sat back and smiled.

"Please go on."

"It must have been ten minutes later. Ten to fifteen minutes later. I was crossing the Corso by the statue of Minerva."

Trotti frowned. "It took you a quarter of an hour to get from the Casa dello Studente to the Corso. Avvocato, that is scarcely more than three hundred meters."

The old man laughed; the teeth shifted slightly. "I stopped to look in the bookshop window. There's a bookshop—I think it must be run by the Communist party, it's full of texts by Gramsci, Neruda and Ceausescu; but nice dust jackets and they change them regularly—where they leave the lights on late into the night. Perhaps they hope to convert an old Giolittiano like me. And of course, I read a lot. What else do I have to do, an old man?"

He was interrupted by the sound of running along the corridor. The heavy regular fall of shoes. Magagna got up and went into the corridor, closing the door behind him.

"Go on, please."

"It was just before I reached the Corso. I heard the sound of brakes and I looked up to see a car. I saw it clearly, Commissario. I have managed to keep my eyesight into the evening of my life. I can see well—even at night." He smiled. "I eat a lot of carrots, you know."

"What sort of car?"

"Oh, I'm afraid I can't tell you that. A sports car—a foreign one, I think, with a convertible roof—and it was going very fast. Very fast and down the wrong side of the Viale. One hundred and thirty or forty kilometers an hour and heading towards the river. I thought it was going for the bridge. I stopped to watch—I knew that something was going to happen, I was frightened.

Then at the last moment the car swung left; it went through the traffic lights and into the Lungo Po. It must've gone up onto the pavement. At least I suppose so—I couldn't see."

"What did you hear?"

"The screech of brakes and then—it wasn't my imagination, I heard a thump. A soft thump like a body being hit."

"A body? A human body?"

"Yes."

"Was there anybody around? Anybody else along the viale?"

"Nobody."

"What did you do?"

"Giuseppina and I, we hurried back to the river." His smile revealed the false teeth. "You may not believe it, Commissario, but I was once an athlete. When I was a student at the university, I ran the two hundred meters in the Olympics. I am still sprightly. We got there in less than four minutes. Yet when I got to the corner of the viale and the Lungo Po, there was nothing."

"Skid marks on the tarmac?"

"It was too dark to see."

More noise came from the corridor; the banging of doors and somebody—it sounded like Pisanelli—shouting.

"And there's something else," the old man said.

The rain continued to splatter against the pane; there was no break in the low grey clouds.

"One other thing," Avvocato Romano repeated. He already had his bony hands against the arms of the chair and was raising himself to an erect position. Giuseppina, now awake, her whiskery muzzle against the cold floor, looked up at her master. "A few seconds after I heard the screech of brakes and the thump," he shuddered, "just after that . . ."

"Yes?"

"And after I was sure that the car had gone up onto the sidewalk."

"What?"

"I started running—well, walking as fast as I could and Giuseppina pulling at her lead—down the viale and I saw a taxi coming off the bridge. And his right light was on—he was preparing to turn into the Lungo Po. But he stopped at the end of the bridge, at the traffic lights. He stopped, the lights changed but he didn't move off."

"You mean the driver could see?"

The old man shrugged. "Perhaps."

"You could see the taxi—but not the car on the sidewalk?"

"That is right."

"A yellow taxi?"

Avvocato Romano nodded. "It was as though the driver was interested—he must have seen the accident, if there was one—but was scared. Because I heard the sound of the tires as the car made a sudden U-turn. The driver turned the car round and went back in the direction he had just come from, back over the bridge."

"Commissario!" The door opened and Magagna put his head through the door. The dog stood up angrily and yapped.

"Commissario, you're wanted." Magagna's face was white.

"A yellow taxi," Trotti said, almost to himself.

"Leonardelli wants you, Commissario." His voice was strained, unnatural. "They've found him—they've found Moro! Murdered—several bullets in his body. Between Piazza Madama and Botteghe Oscure. The BR have killed him!"

Trotti was smiling.

43

RELIEF CAME AS a surprise.

The sense of frustration, the feeling that for five days things had been out of control, now vanished. He felt well. He was in charge. Five days? It seemed longer, so much longer. And Trotti was tired. But it did not matter. Everything was clear.

Along the hall, people were going to and fro, their faces drawn and their eyes revealing a sense of shock. Trotti stood up. "Close the door."

Avvocato Romano was sitting, his mouth slightly open, the tongue visible behind the dentures. He nodded slowly to himself. "The poor man," he muttered.

Later, when the lawyer had gone and Trotti was alone in his office, he sat back in his chair. Outside, through the closed door, there was confusion. Somebody was shouting and from one of the offices there came the sound of sporadic radio static. Trotti unwrapped another sweet and sucked it thoughtfully.

He did not immediately notice the blinking light on the telephone.

He picked up the receiver. "I want you down here, Trotti." Leonardelli. He was out of breath.

"Immediately, Signor Questore." But instead of replacing the receiver, he dialed Gino. It was some time before the blind man answered. "Put me through to the Scuola Elementare Gerolamo Cardano."

Trotti then waited, the telephone to his ear. He pulled a directory that was on his desk towards him.

"I can't get through," Gino said.

"Then give me sixty-seven–twelve–twenty."

"Leonardelli wants everybody in his office."

"Shut up and give me the line."

The distant phone rang several times before a man answered. "City Taxis."

"Commissario Trotti, Pubblica Sicurezza."

"You." Surprise and hostility. "Haven't you got anything more important to do with your time?" The man sounded out of breath as though he had run to answer the phone. "Like capturing terrorists. That's what you're paid for, isn't it?"

"Badly paid."

"Then you're in the wrong job."

"You've got a man working for you," Trotti said, "Ermagni."

"Used to." A short, angry laugh. "He doesn't work here any more, thank goodness. A neurotic. I told him he could go, I don't want to see him again—a drunkard and a maniac." Then more cautiously, "Are you a friend of his?"

"He used to work for me."

"I can believe it." Again he snorted. "Pubblica Sicurezza."

"Last Tuesday." Trotti leaned over his desk to look at an open calendar. "Who was on the night rota?"

"Ermagni, of course."

"Why of course?"

"He's always worked nights. It's something to do with his daughter, something to do with his taking her to school when he came off work." He paused. "A drunkard. He killed his wife. Perhaps if he'd worked different hours and spent the nights with his wife . . ."

"When is the night rota?"

"Midnight to six." He stopped suddenly. "Last Tuesday, you said?"

"Yes."

"Wait, wait."

There was the sound of pages being turned.

"Last week he swapped with Pistone—another alcoholic. That's right. Pistone's gone south and before he went . . . that's right, Pistone was standing in for him most nights last week. They share the same vehicle. Pistone told me about it. But I don't want Ermagni back here, if that's what you're thinking. He's too unreliable and I've got a business to run. He can take his bleeding heart and his self-pity elsewhere. And his boozing." The man hung up angrily.

Trotti laughed.

He kept the line open and asked Gino to put him through to the school. While he waited he stared at the telephone directory. The idea came to him suddenly. He ran through the pages, looking for Tarzi.

And there, at the bottom of the narrow column, he saw the name: Dottor Eduardo Perbene.

44

"HE WAS COVERED in blood. On his hands and down the front of his shirt." Her face was hard, the corner of her lips pulled down. She ran a hand across her hair.

Trotti was standing by the wall, a grey pencil sharpener with a steel handle screwed into the wall at his elbow. "When was this?" he asked.

"Three o'clock, four o'clock." She shrugged, her shoulder rising almost to her ears; she returned the cigarette to her mouth and inhaled, as though hoping to find support in the nicotine. "I was asleep and he woke me. Covered in blood; blood and dirt."

"What did you do?"

She looked at Trotti coldly. "He's my husband, isn't he?" No grievance in her voice; she was stating a fact in the same way that she stated facts to her children in the classroom. "He was like a child. He had been drinking but trying to hack away at the corpse—there were smears of blood on his face, he was pale—had started to sober him up. He was swaying and he had to lean against the door so as not to fall over. A knife in one hand—a damn stupid kitchen knife and tears of frustration and self-pity pouring down his face." She shook her head. "Not a very nice way to be woken up by your husband who's been out with one of his women."

"Tell me what you did."

She breathed again at the cigarette. "Once I got over the

shock, I got up and I got dressed. He needed me—he can't do anything by himself—so I went down to the garage. He hadn't even thought of putting a sheet of plastic down on the ground. The cement was stained, there were several dark puddles. And of course, the body. I knew it was a prostitute; the short mini-skirt with its lurid buttons and the yellow sweater. But she had been badly mangled—even before he'd started his handiwork. The head had been pushed back." She shivered and folded her arms beneath the high breasts. "A human being."

"He'd already cut the body up?"

"One leg. He'd hacked away, splattering everything."

Outside in the hall a bell rang.

"What else could I do? He had killed her. Drunk and out with his woman in his fancy French sports car." She laughed while tobacco smoke poured from her nose. "He was surprised that I knew all about that—his sordid little affair. He wanted to know how I knew." She shook her head. "With his woman and drunk out of his mind, he'd driven the car up on to the sidewalk. He'd killed the poor bitch." Again she shook her head. "And said it wasn't his fault, that she got winged by the bumper and then it was too late for him to stop. So he bundles her into the trunk, takes his girlfriend home and then comes home to me. Perhaps he thought he could get rid of her without my knowing. A kitchen knife—an electric kitchen knife."

Signora Perbene stopped; she walked round the desk, her arms folded while she stared at the floor.

Trotti waited.

Outside it was still raining; above the high windows he glimpsed the grey sky, deformed by the refracting raindrops. He looked at the woman and then at the poster on the wall. The white cathedral in Bari. He smiled to himself; instead of being in this classroom, he should have gone to see Leonardelli. But he had stealthily moved out of the Questura, going down the fire escape.

Trotti looked at the blackboard. The name Aldo Moro had been written in the unsteady hand of a child. Trotti looked at the small desks and at the row of shoe bags hanging from their hooks. The innocent, embroidered names—Antonia, Sandra, Giovanna.

"I told him to make some coffee—at least he could do that—and I then got on with the job he had started. I put a sheet down and I took a kitchen chopper." She smiled. "A wedding present, Commissario." She now stood beside the teacher's desk, a closed hand resting on the dark wood. "You understand, it was too late to go to the police. And anyway, once he had bundled the corpse into the boot—he panicked because he saw the taxi—there was nothing else that I could do. I managed to persuade myself that getting rid of the body was the best solution." She shrugged. "Manslaughter—that is not very serious."

"It was serious for the woman."

"She was dead, wasn't she? There was nothing I could do to save her. I couldn't bring her back to life. She was dead." The face was belligerent; yet the eyes had begun to water. "My father—that's what stopped me from contacting Pronto Intervento. He has got friends among the Carabinieri and the PS—he's a good friend of the Questore—friends who owe him favors. But it couldn't be kept secret. Not now—not just before the elections. He would never have forgiven me. As it is, my relationship with him has been strained enough. I couldn't go to the police—it was out of the question. And I couldn't go to him, either. It would've embarrassed him and he'd never have forgiven me." She attempted a smile, but already a tear had formed at the corner of her eye. "Embarrass him—lose votes, even—no, he would never have forgiven me."

"So you cut the body up?"

"With a small kitchen chopper on a piece of plastic on the garage floor. While Renzo made the coffee." She brushed at her cheek. "The plastic bags were his idea. I wanted to bury the parts—at least they would rot—but he said that we didn't have the time. And anyway, with the current, the bags would go downstream and there could be no reason for associating us with the bits of body." She shivered, pulled her arms tighter together. "No reason for our being associated with a dead whore." She stopped short, her mouth snapped shut as though closed by an internal spring. She turned to look at Trotti. Hostility in her eyes. "She told you."

"She?"

"There is no other way that you could know. She told you—the bitch."

"Nobody told me anything."

"The bitch—a dog on heat—she invites him round to her place, she gets him to drink and then, like the whore she is, she lets him screw her. Afterwards she makes him pay. She told you, didn't she?"

The tears had disappeared. She looked at Trotti with anger and outrage. Her lips were drawn back to reveal her teeth. She trembled, the cigarette burned between her fingers. "The bitch, the fornicating bitch—she'd do anything to come between Renzo and me. She's jealous and she wants to destroy us; and like the idiot he is, he doesn't understand. But I can see through her cheap plans."

"I don't know who you're talking about." He held up his hand, "And I don't want to know. Nobody told me anything." He paused. "Signora Perbene, everybody has lied to me."

The woman took no notice of Trotti's remark. "She wants to take him from me."

"But you told me that marriage was a free union. When I last came here," he gestured towards the rows of small desks and chairs, "you seemed to have a more liberal attitude towards marriage."

"Renzo is my husband," she said. Her eyes were still angry.

"And Angellini?"

"Stefano?" Her face softened.

"I saw the photograph at his place. You and him and someone else."

She nodded. "Sandro—my brother. They used to be friends."

"Angellini helped you?"

"Stefano will always help me."

"And so he helped you take Anna from the gardens?"

"He knew nothing about that." She shook her head. "That was my idea—at least, to talk to Ermagni. When Renzo told me about the taxi and how he had panicked, I knew it was Ermagni. I knew he worked at nights. It had to be him and I had to see him. But then in the gardens, when I caught sight of him—it was difficult. I didn't dare. Not after what had happened between us. I wanted to reason with him, ask him to help me—as a friend—but he is so unpredictable and I realized that he might want to get his revenge." More softly, she added, "I had slapped him in the face, I had told him he was an ignorant peasant. Renzo said that I should talk to him away from school."

She dropped her cigarette onto the floor and stubbed it out with the heel of her moccasin. "Renzo and I went to the gardens in via Darsena. Ermagni was there. He was sitting on a bench, staring at his daughter. He had a strange look in his eye or perhaps I was imagining things—and then there was the sound of a crash in Corso Garibaldi and he immediately got up and came out of the gardens. He went right past me without even noticing me."

"Witnesses in the gardens said that Anna went with a man."

"Renzo was with me. Anna had seen him a couple of times. It was he who called her—she had begun to follow her father and then she saw us. She recognized Renzo and then me." She shook her head. "It was a stupid thing to do. I can see that now; but I let myself be persuaded by Renzo—and his ideas are always wrong. The typical Italian male who thinks he is Vittorio Gassman and Charles Bronson and Alain Delon all rolled into one; and who needs a woman to help him out when he's messed everything up. He told me to get into the car with Anna."

"The red Citroën?"

"Our car—I told you that Stefano had nothing to do with our taking Anna from the gardens."

"Kidnapping."

"She came of her own accord. And we didn't intend to do that, not really. But for the time being, it seemed to be a good way of bringing pressure on Ermagni without having to approach him. Naturally we thought he would understand the reason for her disappearance—he had been the eyewitness to a road accident. The only eyewitness. So we took Anna into the hills."

"Anna is a relative of yours. Your father told me—Rossi is a distant cousin. You could have approached Rossi—he would have helped you."

"Perhaps. But it didn't occur to me. When we went to the gardens, we had no intention of taking Anna. It was done on the spur of the moment. And Ermagni is strange. Renzo said it was better to take Anna with us. Ermagni would know why—but he wouldn't know who. There was no reason for him to suspect Renzo or me."

"No reason at all—as he knew nothing about the death of the whore."

She shrugged. "We didn't know that."

"Why did you feed Anna drugs?"

"Anna wanted to come with us. Anna and I—we've always got on well." She tapped the hard wood of a desk. "She sits here at the front. She's a nice child, serious, kind and helpful. I like her and she likes me. I think she was glad to get away. I don't think life can have been very easy for her since her mother died. She's afraid of her father—but I don't think she's really fond of her grandparents very much either. They use her, you know. As a weapon against Ermagni."

"Then why did you drug her?"

"That was at the end—just before we put her back on the bus. It had to look like a kidnapping. A few sleeping pills—that's all."

"That's when you realized you'd made a mistake?" Trotti took a packet of sweets from his pocket and, looking down, unwrapped the stiff cellophane.

"Mistake?"

"That it wasn't Ermagni who was driving the taxi. It was Pistone who was standing in for Ermagni."

She shrugged. "We would've sent Anna back anyway." She pushed her hands deeper into her pockets; she was wearing trousers made of black corduroy. "We thought that Ermagni would understand immediately why Anna had disappeared. We didn't think that he would go to the police."

"And the article in the *Provincia*? You expected the police to stand by, doing nothing?"

"It was Stefano who suggested that."

"So he was helping you?"

She waited before looking up at Trotti. "He loves me."

"And it was his idea to kidnap Anna?" There was a hint of anger in Trotti's voice. He pushed himself away from the wall.

"No." She shook her head. "No." She took a hand from her pocket and tapped at her chest—the dark rings of her nipples just discernible beneath the white blouse. "I phoned him. When we reached my father-in-law's villa at Tarzi. I phoned Stefano because I needed his help. He laughed when I told him about Anna. He thought it was funny—he said something about Rossi—I don't think Stefano likes him very much. He told me about the gambling at San Siro. It would look like a kidnapping, Stefano said, a professional job. Rossi would think it was for his money; he's rich, he owns several villas and a hotel on Lake Maggiore. But Ermagni would understand the real reason."

"Angellini wanted to get onto the front page of the *Provincia*."

"He wanted to help me. He's always helped me. You don't understand, Commissario. For me Stefano would do anything."

"The phone call." Trotti nodded. "The phone call that he got you to make—he made sure that it came in time for printing."

"So what?" She shrugged. "It doesn't matter."

Trotti was suddenly angry. "It matters to me, Signora Perbene. It matters to me." With a rare gesture of emotion, he tapped at his chest with the side of his hand. "Ermagni is my friend—that may not interest you, but to me it is important. Ermagni is my friend and Anna is my goddaughter. I have a responsibility to both. And your friend Stefano Angellini has deliberately misled me. He has lied to me and he has caused unnecessary suffering. Simply so that he can see his name on the front page of the local newspaper."

She had taken a step backwards. "He was helping us—helping me." Beside her, there was a small chair; she lowered herself on to the polished wood. She looked down at her hands and at the fingers stained with nicotine. "He'd always help me. He always has. He . . ." She hesitated, continuing to stare at her hands; then she turned round, raising her head to look at Trotti. "Stefano and I, we were going to be married, you know. I met him at Sant'Antonio—at an end-of-term ball. He's not handsome, I know—Renzo is seven times more attractive than Stefano. But

Stefano, Commissario . . ." Again she stopped, looking into his eyes, looking for some understanding. "Stefano is good."

Trotti looked away.

"We would have been happy. I would have done everything to make him happy. I didn't care if he was ill—that wasn't important, I would have stood by him. I would have stood by him to the end." She held out her fingers. "I never smoked like this before. When I was with Stefano, I was happy. I didn't smoke, I didn't drink; I didn't feel the need to."

She had started to cry; she now spoke through her hands. "Everybody wanted us to get married. Mama and Papa. And my brother Sandro, who had been his best friend in college. They have never forgiven Stefano for breaking off the engagement. They probably thought he had another woman and I wasn't going to tell them any different. If Stefano didn't want to tell them, I wasn't going to. He didn't even want to tell me. A couple of years—that's what the doctors told him. A couple of years to live." Her body now shook as she wept.

Trotti placed his hand on her shoulder.

"We should have married. We still love each other."

Trotti looked down at the hair pulled back from its center parting, at the bowed shoulders. The arrogant mouth, the cold eyes, the refusal of her own Mediterranean beauty—it was all hidden behind the hands held to her face. Tears ran down the side of her palms. Signora Perbene lowered her head.

The rain was still pattering against the window.

Trotti went to the classroom door and turned around. The shoe bags hanging in neat parallels, the poster of the cathedral in Bari, the rain falling against the high windows, the dusty blackboard; he looked around the classroom.

Signora Perbene, her shoulders hunched, was weeping into her hands. She rocked gently back and forward. Sitting on the low chair, her face hidden, she looked like one of her own pupils. With the cardigan pulled over her shoulders, she looked fragile, vulnerable. A little girl.

Trotti closed the door.

45

THE STREETS WERE empty.

The grey afternoon sunlight was reflected on the damp cobblestones as Trotti walked back into the city center. Even the buses and taxis had disappeared. There were no vehicles and no pedestrians. At several windows, black flags had been placed as a sign of mourning; they flapped damply in the wind. Somewhere a church bell was tolling lugubriously. Trotti looked up but the dome of the cathedral was hidden by a low cloud of drizzle.

All the shops were closed. The blinds had been pulled down and locked. Even the cafés and bars were empty; the chairs and tables stood vacant while raindrops bounced off painted surfaces. A few parasols had been left out and now dripped with rain; water ran down the leaves of the potted plants and along the edges of the cactus.

There were no customers.

In Piazza Vittoria the newspaper kiosk had closed, the metallic blind had been pulled down; only a few posters with Moro's tired face were visible. They flapped in the breeze.

As Trotti approached Strada Nuova, he heard the sound of a motorcycle and then a vigile urbano in knee boots and white helmet appeared on a large Laverda. Behind him, the machine cast up a thin curve of water and dirt. He slowed down to peer at Trotti from behind his smeared goggles and then sped away down towards the river.

Trotti encountered no one else before arriving at the town hall. He went up the broad steps; nobody at the main entrance. The gate was open. The corridor and the stairs were strangely silent.

Trotti was almost surprised to find the porter still outside the mayor's office. He was reading a paperback. He did not appear to notice Trotti's arrival.

"I wish to see the mayor."

The small man closed the book deliberately and pushed it to the side of the desk before looking up. "He is busy."

Trotti went to the door and before the midget could stop him, he turned the handle. The porter had jumped up and with a strong grip pulled at his arm. Unceremoniously, Trotti pushed the man away.

The porter tottered backwards and fell, a look of shocked dignity on his small face.

Trotti entered the mayor's office.

The smile was immediate and appeared sincere. Mariani was speaking softly into the telephone. He looked up and lowered the receiver into its cradle. He stood up.

Trotti closed the door behind him but he did not move; the door handle was cold in his hand. Mariani approached, smiling and holding out his hand.

"So pleased to see you."

Trotti did not take the proffered hand.

"I have come to inform you that I shall be making out a warrant for the arrest of your son-in-law, Renzo Perbene."

The mayor's smile froze; he came closer to Trotti and looked into his eyes, as though not quite certain of Trotti's sincerity. The smile died slowly.

"Arrest?"

Trotti nodded.

The cat was on the sill, curled up and apparently asleep. Beyond the window, Corso Mazzini was wet and empty. "I wanted to see you first."

The mayor turned and went back towards his chair. His shoulders had dropped; from behind he looked old and worn. "Thank you," he said slowly.

"Furthermore," Trotti continued, in the same, even tone, "I will have to inform the Procuratore della Repubblica of your role in the disappearance of Anna Ermagni."

The mayor turned around. "I knew nothing."

"Until I came to tell you about the Citroën car." Trotti nodded. "Until then, you knew nothing. But then you must have contacted your daughter—and from then on, you have done everything in your power to hinder me in my investigations. Everything, Signor Sindaco—including the use of pressure upon the Questura."

The mayor lowered himself into his seat behind the trestle table. He folded his hands on the white surface. The mushroom-like lamp hung over his head.

"I had no choice," he said quietly.

"Interfering with the course of justice." Trotti pulled up a chair; high-backed, of pale Scandinavian wood and with a seat of thickly woven straw.

"At another time," the mayor shrugged, his dark jaw to one side, his eyes looking at Trotti, "I would have done my duty—my civic duty as mayor of this city, as its first magistrate. But now—with all the glaring light of the media turned upon us Communists—and upon the so-called compromesso storico. And with the elections only a week away. I had no choice."

"Your son-in-law killed a woman. Then with the help of your daughter, he deliberately kidnapped Anna Ermagni—a relative of yours."

"They kidnapped the little girl—I had no idea until you came here. When you mentioned the car, I suspected something and I contacted Renzo. It was him I contacted—not my daughter." He stopped, looked down at his hands. He shook his head slowly before continuing, "No, Commissario, I don't approve. And in a different situation, I would have insisted that they go to the police." The dark cheeks formed lines of disapproval. "But then, Renzo has always been like that. Hot-headed, impetuous—and stupid. She shouldn't have married him—that was the real mistake. She shouldn't have married him. Childhood sweethearts—that sort of thing never works. Marriage is more cynical than that. I sometimes think that she married him to spite me." He allowed himself a little laugh. "A doctor, the first magistrate of the city—but not, I'm afraid, a very good father. When perhaps, Commissario, that's what I wanted to be. More than mayor—and even now," he quickly glanced round the office and its pale furnishings, "I would sacrifice it all for my daughter. For Lella. I didn't want her to marry him—but what could I do? When she was a child, she had fallen in love with him on holiday—like us, his parents had a villa at Tarzi. Even at that age, he was stupid; but Lella didn't seem to care. She always said that she was going to marry him. I thought she'd grow out of it—and she did. She went to college and there she met Stefano Angellini. She forgot all about Renzo and believe me, Commissario, her mother and I were pleased. We liked Stefano—I still do. Intelligent, thoughtful—I'm sure he could have made her a good husband. They got engaged—and then almost immediately, she broke the engagement, went back to Renzo and within a couple of months, they were married." He smiled again, sadly. "I don't know if you have children."

"A daughter."

"Then you know how a father feels—the feeling between father and daughter. It is something special, something exciting. But it is also dangerous ground—there are strange and conflicting emotions. Love—but there is also jealousy. Jealousy, sexual jealousy. How old is your daughter, Commissario?"

"Sixteen."

"It is early, perhaps, but you will know the jealousy that a father feels. When your daughter leaves you to live with another man—even the nicest of men—it is not easy. You must pretend to be happy, but you are losing something—seventeen, eighteen years of a shared past—and you lose it all to a complete stranger." He paused. "Perhaps I was too hard on Lella—I couldn't understand why she wanted to leave us—and certainly I couldn't understand why she wanted to go and live with him. Renzo Perbene. Her attitude hurt me in a way that I don't think I've ever been hurt before—and perhaps it was a sense of revenge that made me cruel. I could feel that she began to hate me because

I told her she was making a mistake. She hated me—and I was pleased. Because it is better to be hated than to be ignored—and I couldn't accept the idea that she was leaving me—leaving me for good. If she had gone with Stefano, I think I would have understood. But Renzo? A spoiled, wealthy brat? Wealthy, doting parents and Renzo who has never lifted his finger to help anyone?" He shook his head. "For two years we didn't speak to each other. I went to the wedding but I couldn't bring myself to speak to her. And she ignored me. I never phoned—and neither did she."

He stopped to look at the telephone, hoping, perhaps, that it would ring. "She despised me—everything I stood for—my job, my politics, the ideas that I tried to share with her when she was a little girl." He tapped at the photograph of Gramsci. "Everything, Commissario, I would sacrifice everything for Lella. My daughter. I had carried her in my arms. I used to wash her in the bath. I used to answer all her questions, I used to hold her hand when we walked in the Apennines. And when she cried, it was always to me that she came with her problems." He waited, then added, "A beautiful child."

The two men stared at each other in silence. Then slowly the mayor rose to his feet and went to the window. He raised the cat by its neck and held it in his arms. He stared downwards into the Corso.

"A Communist city. A city that works. A place to live in." He shook his head. "No, it's not just me. I don't run this city alone, a latter-day Mussolini burning the light until late into the night. There is a lot of teamwork, a lot of working together. Behind me, I have a lot of dedicated men and women who sacrifice their time and their family—everything for the sake of this city. Because they know what Italy is like and because they know that here there is a real chance of making things better. Not through demagogy, not with the idle words of the Christian Democrats—but in work, democratically shared and undertaken. Admittedly, ours is a democracy on a very small scale—but then all of us, we live our daily lives on a small scale. Here," he tapped the desk, "in this town hall, in this city, we try to answer the citizen's rightful aspiration to freedom and to democracy. Freedom from the new capitalists and the old mafia, freedom from unemployment, freedom from nepotism, freedom from the network of exchanged favors and silent blackmail. Freedom from the secular blackmail of poverty and unemployment that throughout the centuries have held the Italian people back and have prevented them from living their lives as they would like to live them."

He was now stroking the cat in his arms; the green eyes closed with sensuous pleasure as he scratched at the animal's ears. "I could say that it was for the sake of this city that I decided to help my daughter. It was certainly not for myself—I have held power here for too long to find any pleasure in the responsibilities of being mayor. Believe me, if I could, if it were possible, I would cease being mayor tomorrow." He turned to Trotti as though he expected Trotti not to believe him. "I would earn four times as much as a doctor—with none of the responsibility." The smile died slowly. "I could say it was for this city—but it would not be true. Even this city, Commissario, I would throw it to the wind. I did it for her. For Lella. She didn't want to come to me for help, she didn't ask me for help—when she knew I could give it—and would give it. It was you who made me suspect that she was in trouble—and it wouldn't have been the first time that Renzo had made life difficult for her. You see, I wanted to show her that I cared. She thought that she didn't need me—but I wanted to make her see that I am her father and that I still love her. And that if only she were willing to let me, I could still help her."

"It was you who gave her away."

The hand ceased to scratch at the cat's ear. "I don't understand."

"By finding new culprits. The old man with his false confession, Gracchi and the letters sent to the *Provincia*."

"Gracchi?"

"You don't remember, Signor Sindaco?"

"There's nothing to remember. I wanted to help my daughter. It was wrong—I knew that at the time—but for once I felt she really needed me, even if she was too proud herself to ask for my help. I fully understand that by using the powers vested in me by the city for my own ends I am no better than the Christian Democrats and all the other venal politicians who sit in Rome. I am no better than they, Commissario. Perhaps I am worse— because I, a Communist, I should be above reproach. But Lella, Commissario, is my daughter. I love her."

"I, too, have a daughter, Signor Sindaco," Trotti replied, his voice calm. "But if I were to put her interests—or my love for her—before those of the Republic that I have sworn to serve, then I wouldn't be worthy of the Republic. I wouldn't be worthy of my job."

"You are a hard man, Commissario."

"An honest one."

"And a naive one." The mayor's laugh was cold. He was no longer looking at Trotti. "I am afraid that you are very naive. Perhaps I have betrayed the city—or at least the trust of those citizens who believe me to be above all reproach. But at least my city exists, Commissario. It is no pipe dream, it is no myth. But your Republic . . . I am afraid—for both your sake and mine— that there is no Republic. It doesn't exist. It is a bad joke. There is no Republic—and there is no reason of State. This is Italy, Commissario, and there is only the reason of vested interest. The reason is survival. That is the only reason of fifty-five million corrupt Italians."

Trotti corrected him: "Fifty-five million minus one, Signor Sindaco."

46

"A VIGILE URBANO."

"I beg your pardon."

"A vigile urbano," Magagna repeated, nudging at his sunglasses. He held a small plastic cup between the fingers of the other hand. Instant coffee from the Faema machine in the hall. "The gypsy who was arrested. It wasn't the PS and it wasn't the Carabinieri. He was breaking into a car in Borgo Genovese when a patrol car of vigili urbani saw him. They kept him for the afternoon."

"How did you find out?" Trotti was smiling. The bottle of grappa stood on the desk; Trotti leaned forward and poured more of the colorless liquid into the lid.

"I have friends," Magagna said enigmatically. "You're sure you don't want a cup of coffee?"

Trotti laughed. "Nescafé?" and shook his head. He put the lid filled with grappa to his lips and drank. A few drops trickled from the side of his mouth and ran down his chin. He wiped his mouth with the back of his hand.

"There's no choice," Magagna said apologetically. "All the bars closed down at the news of Moro's death." He quickly glanced at the window; it was still raining. "And everything will remain closed tomorrow. A day of national mourning."

Trotti returned the lid to the top of the bottle and screwed it into place.

The door of the office was open; outside the hall was empty. There was nobody on the third floor of the Questura other than Trotti and Magagna. Leonardelli had disappeared. Gino and the Principessa had disappeared.

Magagna now leaned forward, his arms on the thighs of his blue uniform trousers. "Perbene," he said, shaking his head slightly. "How did you know it was her who took Anna?"

"I didn't."

Magagna frowned, the plastic cup held halfway towards his mouth.

"You guessed?"

"I knew nothing. It was Mariani who gave her away. When I went to see him he was relaxed, arrogant. By the time I left he was worried. He then contacted his son-in-law who must have told him what had happened. The accidental death of Irina Pirvic and the futile kidnapping of the little girl. Mariani was frightened—he wanted to protect his daughter, but he also wanted to protect himself. As a successful Communist mayor, he's in a highly sensitive position. So he tried to cover up." Trotti gave a short laugh. "Unfortunately, there were too many cover-ups. Too many guilty parties."

"Like the old man who claimed he'd murdered the whore? I wonder where the mayor conjured him up from."

This time, Trotti's laugh was cold. "You think Mariani knows where to dig up old men with criminal records who are willing to be a scapegoat? Probably the old man missed the company and the security of a prison cell." He shook his head. "It wasn't Mariani who found him."

"Then who was it?" Magagna took a cigarette from a packet of Marlboro.

"It wasn't the mayor who organized that manoeuvre. He doesn't have the knowledge or the contacts. It was somebody who wanted to help Mariani."

"Leonardelli?"

Trotti nodded.

"Why?"

"Why?" Again the same laugh. "The interest of the city.

'The actual political situation—who is in power and who is in opposition—in this town concerns neither you nor me. Unthinking, flatfooted questurini, we carry out our orders.'" As Trotti quoted Leonardelli, his mouth was narrow with distaste. "Leonardelli helped Mariani for the same reason that he wanted to finger Gracchi and Guerra. Of course, Gracchi sees himself as a café revolutionary—but he never kidnapped Anna. I'm pretty certain that was Leonardelli's idea—and you know," he looked at Magagna, "it wouldn't surprise me to discover that it was di Bono who typed the letter for him. While Pisanelli was elsewhere, it was probably di Bono who got into the apartment and typed out that letter on Gracchi's typewriter. But the letter was too clever, too good, too convincing to be di Bono's idea—or anyone else's. Leonardelli wrote it—of that, I am sure."

"Why?" Magagna had set the paper cup down on the floor beside a pile of dusty newspapers. He lit his cigarette.

"Power."

Magagna shook his head.

"Power," Trotti repeated. "Like the American, Edgar Hoover, who ran the FBI. Of course Leonardelli doesn't want a scandal in this city. He wants to keep his own nose clean. It suits him that there is a Communist mayor and administration running an ideal city. It's all the more glory to him—and it saves him embarrassing work. But it's not because of this marriage of interest that you must think that Leonardelli loves Mariani. If there's a way of the Questore's controlling Mariani without any fuss, then he's interested. But I suspect that there is something that interests Leonardelli more than mere political manipulation." Trotti stopped and shook his head as though even he had difficulty in understanding the truth. "Blackmail—petty blackmail," Trotti said softly. "The Italian disease."

Magagna breathed on his cigarette.

"Power through knowledge—through knowledge that can be incriminating, that can ruin a career—or a life. Power over the mayor, over the parents of Gracchi and Guerra—over anybody who has a skeleton in the cupboard, a piece of murky history that needs to be covered up and overlooked."

Magagna did not speak.

"If you have knowledge, you have power." He smiled. "And Leonardelli would love to have the same power over me. A wife who fools around with other men, who gambles, who gets caught." The smile was bitter, as though the grappa had left an unpleasant taste. "Unfortunately that piece of knowledge is not his copyright. He must share it with Spadano and with the *Provincia Padana*."

It had stopped raining; the raindrops had disappeared from the windowpane.

"Leonardelli can't blackmail me."

"Why would he want to?"

"Because he would blackmail his own mother if he could—if there was something in it for him. With me, he has got good reasons to be afraid; he needs a lever that he can use against me. Because I have knowledge. Knowledge that could be very damaging to him."

"No." Magagna shook his head and stood up. He took the cigarette from his mouth. "No." He went to the window and opened it onto the damp afternoon.

A Vespa went past in the narrow street below; the engine sounded hollow and angry beneath the old brick walls of the Questura. Several birds darted upwards, touched at the gutter of the roof opposite and then flew away.

"No, Commissario, Leonardelli can destroy you. He is more powerful than you are—he has more friends. And he can count on the support of all those people he controls."

Trotti unscrewed the bottle; again he filled the lid.

"He will destroy you, Commissario."

Trotti smiled. "I am already destroyed." He drank.

Magagna snorted and smoke, escaping from his nose, was caught by the breeze from the window. "Scarcely."

"Destroyed. As a policeman, as a father, as a husband—as a human being." He turned to look at Magagna but could not make out the younger man's features, the backlight of the grey sky being too bright. He blinked. "I have nothing to fear, Magagna. I am already destroyed—I have destroyed myself.

The victim of my own myths. Victim of my own naive belief that, in the Republic, there is something more important than individual self-interest. It is my fault. I have allowed myself to be destroyed—with my foolish faith in the Republic. I have destroyed myself. Half an hour ago, I was arguing with the mayor, our good, Communist mayor. He's understood something that I am only beginning to understand—but then, he is from the South, perhaps he has the advantage of an age-old cynicism." Trotti stopped and for a moment stared at the bottle. He reached out to pull it towards him; his hand stopped in mid-air. "I have destroyed myself and I deserve everything that happens to me. I have been equally arrogant. I can see it all now—now that it is too late. My beliefs have been equally selfish. I have believed in the Republic. I have believed against all the evidence of twenty years spent in Questuras, twenty years working among police-men and lawyers, judges and Carabinieri—I have believed in the probity of the State. And for the State, I have sacrificed my own interests. I could have been Questore by now if I had really wanted. All I had to do was behave as they wanted me to behave. A political game, keeping a low profile, saying yes when they asked me to say yes, no when they wanted me to say no. And the rest of the time keeping quiet. Questore in some quiet city, a respected member of the community with a German car and a bespoke suit for every day of the week, a wife and a daughter who would spend their holidays in Baltimore or the Côte d'Azur. Somewhere in the Marche or the Alto Adige. But instead, I have chosen to be proud. For twenty years, I have been proud, believ-ing that I was right, believing that I alone was in possession of justice and morality and fighting my single-handed battle against all the armies of corrupt policemen and administrators."

Trotti pushed the chair away from under him and stood up. He went to the window and stood beside Magagna. He looked out over the roofs, now drying. Before long, they would regain their terracotta glow.

"When I visited her this morning, she had a stole. A stole I gave her nearly a quarter of a century ago. She must've been wearing it and it lay on the floor—mocking me. Reminding me of a time when Agnese didn't care about clothes, about her pearls and her hand-made shoes from Vigevano. In those early days when we were first married she didn't care—oh, she's always liked to be well-dressed, but there was something more important for her. She had given up her life with her parents to live with a young country boy from the hills—an unsophisticated flatfoot. But she knew that I loved her. She knew that I found her beautiful—each morning when I woke up and saw her head asleep on the pillow beside me, I loved her. That was enough for her. And a cheap stole—probably made from the skin of a rat—was more important to her than anything else." He turned away from Magagna. "I have always thought that it was Agnese who'd changed. I couldn't understand. The woman who had once loved me—each day I saw her growing away from me. Growing to dislike me. Despising me. And I didn't know why. At times I thought that she was jealous—jealous of Pioppi and me. But if I began to show more and more affection for Pioppi, it was because Pioppi responded, whereas Agnese no longer seemed to want me." He shook his head. "Agnese didn't want me. She didn't need me."

Magagna stared out of the window. A swallow dropped through the air.

"It wasn't Agnese. It was me. With my arrogance, my professional pride, my private crusade against corruption, dishonesty and incompetence. My obsession. My life." He was now leaning against the cold radiator, his hands folded and his eyes staring at a pile of dossiers on the floor. "I had married my job. I had no time for her, she felt forsaken and betrayed. Because she didn't understand, and not understanding, she felt perhaps that I was deliberately betraying her. This is Italy. Look after yourself or go under. Kick them in the balls before they can stab you in the back. Survival of the fittest, survival of the most cunning. And she couldn't understand me. Instead of furthering our interests—her interests, the interests of Pioppi—instead of keeping my mouth shut and going up the ladder, I tried to do my duty. Or what I considered to be my duty."

Again he stopped. Magagna looked at him.

"I betrayed her," he said simply.

"Then you'll let the matter drop—the entire Ermagni affair, you'll let it drop?"

Trotti laughed. "No."

"Leonardelli will destroy you."

"I am already destroyed—but at least I have twenty years of service. I am entitled to a pension." He glanced at Magagna. "You are still young—perhaps you can't understand—but this has been my life. Dingy offices, empty corridors in Questuras, piles of accumulated, dusty dossiers. Yes, and even coffee dispensing machines." He tapped his chest. "And these have been my values. I have been wrong—but I can't go back on them. The values that they taught us at school along with the guns and the uniform. I can't go back on them. I can't deny them. I have my own self-respect." He went over to the desk and, opening the drawer, pulled out the paper block containing the stamped headed paper. REPUBBLICA ITALIANA. PUBBLICA SICUREZZA. He sat down. "I will inform the Procuratore—and I will arrest Renzo Perbene."

"You can't, Commissario. You are destroying yourself—all that you have stood for. You are destroying it all. It is too dangerous to arrest Perbene. He is the mayor's son-in-law. You will have the mayor against you—and you will have Leonardelli against you."

Trotti picked up his pen, unscrewed the cap. "Ermagni was my friend. Anna is my goddaughter. I owe them something."

"Leonardelli will destroy you. You will have nothing—perhaps not even a pension."

"I have a wife and daughter. It is time that I started looking after them." A ray of unexpected sunlight came through the window, casting a bright square onto the dusty floor.

Trotti smiled. "Perhaps it is not too late to become a good husband and father." He began to write.

The pigeons had started to coo again.

TRAVEL THE WORLD FOR $9.99

PARIS

MURDER IN THE MARAIS
Cara Black
ISBN: 978-1-56947-999-5

FLORENCE

DEATH OF AN ENGLISHMAN
Magdalen Nabb
ISBN: 978-1-61695-299-0

AMSTERDAM

OUTSIDER IN AMSTERDAM
Janwillem van de Wetering
ISBN 978-1-61695-300-3

NANTUCKET

DEATH IN THE OFF-SEASON
Francine Mathews
ISBN: 978-1-61695-726-1

BELFAST

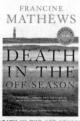

THE GHOSTS OF BELFAST
Stuart Neville
ISBN: 978-1-61695-769-8

SOUTH AFRICA

RANDOM VIOLENCE
Jassy Mackenzie
ISBN 978-1-61695-210-1

CHINATOWN, NYC

CHINATOWN BEAT
Henry Chang
ISBN: 978-1-61695-717-9

SLOVAKIA

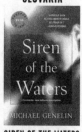

SIREN OF THE WATERS
Michael Genelin
ISBN 978-1-56947-585-0

1970s SEOUL

JADE LADY BURNING
Martin Limón
ISBN: 978-1-61695-090-3

GUADELOUPE

ANOTHER SUN
Timothy Williams
ISBN 978-1-61695-363-8

ALASKA

WHITE SKY, BLACK ICE
Stan Jones
ISBN: 978-1-56947-333-7

The first books in our most popular series in a new low price paperback edition

DENMARK

THE BOY IN THE SUITCASE
Lene Kaaberbøl & Agnete Friis
ISBN: 978-1-61695-491-8

HOLLYWOOD

CRASHED
Timothy Hallinan
ISBN: 978-1-61695-276-1

LONDON

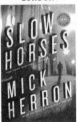

SLOW HORSES
Mick Herron
ISBN: 978-1-61695-416-1

WWII BERLIN

ZOO STATION
David Downing
ISBN: 978-1-61695-348-5

BATH, ENGLAND

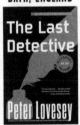

THE LAST DETECTIVE
Peter Lovesey
ISBN: 978-1-61695-530-4

WWII EUROPE

BILLY BOYLE
James R. Benn
ISBN: 978-1-61695-355-3

SWEDEN

DETECTIVE INSPECTOR HUSS
Helene Tursten
ISBN: 978-1-61695-111-5

AUSTRALIA

THE DRAGON MAN
Garry Disher
ISBN: 978-1-61695-448-2

LAOS

THE CORONER'S LUNCH
Colin Cotterill
ISBN: 978-1-61695-649-3

BEIJING

ROCK PAPER TIGER
Lisa Brackmann
ISBN: 978-1-61695-250-7

VICTORIAN ENGLAND

WOBBLE TO DEATH
Peter Lovesey
ISBN: 978-1-61695-659-2

1970s ITALY

CONVERGING PARALLELS
Timothy Williams
ISBN: 978-1-61695-460-4